SPELLCASTING IN SILK

A Witchcraft Mystery

Juliet Blackwell

AN OBSIDIAN MYSTERY

OBSIDIAN
Published by the Penguin Group
Penguin Group (USA) LLC, 375 Hudson Street,
New York, New York 10014

USA | Canada | UK | Ireland | Australia | New Zealand | India | South Africa | China
penguin.com
A Penguin Random House Company

First published by Obsidian, an imprint of New American Library,
a division of Penguin Group (USA) LLC

First Printing, July 2015

ISBN 978-0-451-46578-8

Printed in the United States of America
10 9 8 7 6 5 4 3 2 1

To Kendall Moalem and Susan Baker,
who never fail to remind me of the magic of friendship

Chapter 1

My mother rarely spoke to me. But as I looked out over Aunt Cora's Closet, I could hear her voice in my head, clear as day.

"You're cookin' with fat."

The vintage clothes business was booming. Half a dozen customers were trying on peasant blouses and bell-bottom jeans embroidered with daisies and peace signs. A fortysomething woman rooted through a pile of vintage army jackets, hoping to find one that would accommodate her boyfriend's broad shoulders while he, on the other side of the store, examined frilly, lace-covered negligees for her. A pair of teenagers with Indian-print dresses draped over their arms paused on the way to the dressing room to flick through a rack of pastel 1950s cocktail dresses. Two young men tried on fedoras, checking themselves out in the three-way mirror, calling each other "Frankie baby" and casting surreptitious glances at the young women.

My good friends were staffing the herb stand and the front register; Bronwyn's hearty laugh and Maya's steady smile contributed to Aunt Cora's Closet's atmosphere of warmth and welcome. My unorthodox witch's familiar, Oscar, a miniature Vietnamese potbellied pig, snored softly on his purple silk pillow, tuckered out from the fussing and adoration he received from my customers— and from trying to sneak a peek while they were in the fitting room.

And this evening, a handsome, frustrating, wildly fascinating man named Sailor would be coming for dinner. The ingredients for tonight's feast awaited me upstairs in my apartment's sunny kitchen; the menu featured jambalaya with all the fixings, just like Mama used to make on the all-too-rare occasions when she was pleased with me.

And while there might be a few lingering supernatural issues hanging over my head, at least I wasn't embroiled in a murder investigation.

I smiled to myself and let out a sigh of satisfaction. Yup. *Cookin' with fat.*

Or not.

The back of my neck tingled in premonition. A moment later the bell over the front door rang out, its familiar tinkling sounding sharper, more demanding than usual.

I looked up from the tangle of belts I was sorting to see Inspector Carlos Romero, of the San Francisco Police Department's Homicide Division, stride into Aunt Cora's Closet. He wore his customary black thigh-length leather jacket, white oxford shirt, khakis, and black running shoes. And although he was only about my height, Carlos projected such an air of authority that he gave the impression of being a much larger man. Working the homicide beat in a major city wasn't a job for sissies.

My hand slipped down to stroke the medicine bag on the braided silk rope around my waist. The moment my fingers felt the familiar butter-soft leather studded with the beads I had sewn on as a child, I felt calmer, more grounded.

Maybe he's not here on business, I thought. After all, Carlos and I were sort of friends, and every once in a while he dropped by the shop just to say hello. Or . . . perhaps he was in search of a costume for the upcoming Summer of Love Festival.

But his grim expression and the tingle at the back of my neck suggested this was not one of those times.

Dangitall.

"Lily," Carlos said with a nod. "A moment in private?" His tone was curt, businesslike.

"Of course."

I gestured to Bronwyn and Maya that I was taking a break and led Carlos through the deep red brocade curtain that separated Aunt Cora's Closet's display floor from the work area that doubled as a break room. A jumbo washer and dryer for laundering washable inventory sat to one side, while a galley kitchen with a dorm-sized fridge, a microwave, and an electric teakettle lined the opposite wall. A pile of black Hefty bags and a couple of blue plastic storage boxes held clothing to be sorted, repaired, and washed. In the center of the room was a sixties dinette set, the table topped with jade green Formica. The set was a replica of the one in my childhood home, in the little town of Jarod, West Texas.

Carlos took his usual seat.

"May I get you anything?" I asked, mostly out of habit because Carlos never accepted my offers of refreshments. "How about a cup of tea? Bronwyn has a new blend of carob, orange peel, and rose hips which, I guarantee you, tastes a darn sight better than it sounds. It's all the rage."

"No, thanks," he said with a quick shake of his head.

I sat in the chair opposite him and waited. He said nothing.

"*One* day," I said.

"Beg pardon?"

"I would like one day. Just *one*. When I wasn't thinking about suspicious death."

Carlos gazed at me for another long moment. He wasn't much of a talker under the best of circumstances, and in his line of work the long pauses surely served a purpose. More than a few cagey suspects and reluctant witnesses no doubt had blurted out something incriminating simply to break the oppressive silence. But this time was different; Carlos appeared to be choosing his words with care. And that probably meant he was here because he had come across something he couldn't explain, something that fell far outside the purview of a routine police investigation.

That was where I came in—Lily Ivory, unofficial witchy consultant to the SFPD.

"Today's not that day," he finally replied.

"Yeah, that was sort of my point. I was feeling so happy right before you came in."

One corner of his mouth kicked up in a reluctant smile. "That's me, all right. The bringer of bad tidings. So I ruined your day, huh?"

"Not yet you haven't. But something tells me you're about to—"

"I need to talk to you about a *curandera* shop gone haywire, a suspicious suicide, and a missing kid."

"—Aaaand there it is."

"I'll start at the beginning, shall I?"

I sat back in my chair. "Sure."

"Last week a thirty-seven-year-old woman named Nicky Utley jumped off the Golden Gate Bridge."

"I hear a lot of people jump off the bridge."

"True."

"So, where does a witch come in?"

"Utley was into a bunch of strange stuff—talismans and pentacles, books on everything from Catholic saints to candle magic, medicinal herbs and such. Things more . . . overtly religious than your stuff."

"But how is any of that related to her death?"

"That's what I'm trying to figure out. According to her husband, the woman had been consulting with a woman named Ursula Moreno, who owns a shop called El Pajarito on Mission. What can you tell me about her?"

"Nothing. I've never heard of her."

"I assumed all of your ilk knew each other."

"My *ilk*?"

"You know what I mean."

"I do. But I'm still fairly new in town, remember?"

And though I wasn't going to volunteer this to a member of the SFPD, friend or no, I kept my distance from *curanderas,* a Spanish term for "healers." They were about as mixed a bag as the one I wore at my waist. Many were talented botanical specialists; others wise elders; a rare few were natural-born witches like me. Still others—the vast majority—dabbled in herbs and prayers and rituals, and enjoyed importing and creating talismans and amulets and good luck charms.

But a few were out-and-out charlatans.

In the course of my life I have learned many things, not the least of which is that—witchy intuition aside—I am a wretched judge of character. So I tried to steer clear of such shops and their proprietors. Besides, it was cheaper by far to purchase my supplies at small apothecaries in Chinatown, local farmers' markets, or even the ethnic food aisle of a large grocery store. For the more esoteric witchy items, Maya had introduced me to the wonders of the Internet. A few clicks of the mouse, and a package of freeze-dried bats would appear on my doorstep in just a few days. As if by magic.

"Anyway," Carlos continued. "It looks like the herbs and instructions and whatnot the victim got from the *curandera* may have aggravated an underlying condition that led to her suicide."

"I'm sorry to hear that. As I'm sure you know, *curandera* means 'curer' or 'healer.' The herbs and 'whatnot,' as you call them, are meant to help. But you have to know what you're doing." One of my biggest fears was that those who neither understood magical systems, nor gave them the proper respect, would end up hurting themselves or others. Amateurs experimenting with magic were like toddlers playing with matches—sooner or later someone was bound to get hurt.

Carlos nodded.

"So what happened?" I asked.

"That's what I'm trying to find out. We have a couple of witnesses to the jump, but. . . ."

"But you think there's more to it."

He shrugged. "Possibly. And the mayor's been on a tear lately, going after folks bilking the public with phony love spells, palm readings, fraudulent psychics, that sort of thing. This fits right in with his cleanup campaign."

"I thought fortune-telling was covered by free speech. After all, who's to say they *aren't* seeing the future, or working magic?"

Carlos's lips pressed together. "There's a fine line between spewing predictions and conning people. Most of the time we're looking at charges of grand larceny and fraud, but in the case of Nicky Utley . . . well, her husband's pushing hard to make something stick. The DA is considering filing charges of gross negligence and practicing medicine without a license, in addition to fraud?"

"What was the *curandera's* name, again?"

"Ursula Moreno. Her shop's called El Pajarito. You sure you don't know it?"

I shook my head again. From the other side of the brocade curtain sounds drifted in: the cheerful buzz of customers trying out different personas as they tried on a new style of dress or hat; the chiming of my old-fashioned brass cash register; a young woman cooing over Oscar, who was probably preening, batting his sleepy eyes at her as he stretched lazily on his bed; the bell on the front door tinkling as another shopper arrived; and someone laughing in high, melodic tones.

The sounds were comforting, and I felt a fierce desire to tune out what Carlos was telling me. But I did not have that luxury. There aren't a lot of folks who know enough, or have the requisite skills, to assist the police with supernatural crimes. Carlos was here because he needed my special brand of help. Such, it seemed, was my fate.

"There's more," said Carlos.

"Oh, goodie."

"Something's happened, something odd." His finger traced an invisible pattern on the green Formica table top.

"Odder than occult-inspired suicide?"

"Moreno's store. It's . . . acting up."

"I'm sorry?"

"After Moreno was arrested yesterday, the forensics team went to her shop to gather evidence."

I waited, but he said nothing.

"And?" I prompted.

"The place went haywire. According to the chief forensics tech, stuff was flying off the shelves, the lights kept flickering on and off, a statue flicked a lit cigarette at one of the guys, and a bird skeleton seemed to come alive and appeared to start flying."

"That's unusual behavior for a skeleton. Are you sure someone's not pulling your leg?"

"I know these guys well, Lily. They're pros who deal with serious crime scenes every day. Chief forensic tech's been on the job for years—it takes a lot to throw him off his game. But this time, he and his crew beat it out of the shop in a hurry, and they're refusing to go back. This is . . . unusual."

Indeed. "And you'd like me to take a look."

Carlos nodded. "Shouldn't take too long. See what you see, feel what you feel. Try to figure out what's going on there, and if it's connected in any way to what happened to Nicky Utley."

"All righty."

Carlos gave me a suspicious look and cocked his head in question.

"That's it? You're not going to try to get out of it?"

I shrugged. "You've worn me down, Inspector. Guess I'm the SFPD's go-to witch, right?"

He smiled, and I couldn't help but smile in return. The thing about Carlos was that every smile felt hard-won, and therefore more worth the earning.

"Besides," I continued. "This sounds like a job for an expert. If something untoward really is happening at the shop, somebody's bound to get hurt."

Carlos nodded and started to rise.

"One question, though," I said, and Carlos sat back down. "You're one of homicide's star investigators, aren't you?"

Carlos shrugged.

"So why is the department asking its big gun to work on a case of possible fortune-teller fraud?"

"I requested it."

"May I ask why?"

"First, because of the strange behavior at the store. I believe I've told you I've become the station's woo-woo guy. But, in the interest of full disclosure, it's also true that I knew the deceased, Nicky Utley, and her husband, Gary, though not well."

"Friends of yours?"

"Acquaintances more than friends. They went to my church, St. Olaf's."

"This would be a . . . Catholic church?" I had met many Catholics in my life—including Carlos— and knew they were good people who lived according to a creed of kindness and respect. Still, organized religions made me nervous, what with the witch hunts and the pogroms and the Inquisition and all.

He nodded.

"If Nicky Utley was a practicing Catholic," I said, "why would she turn to a *curandera* for help?"

"You tell me."

"Well, of course the two don't preclude each other," I said, thinking aloud. "Where I'm from, it isn't unusual for churchgoers to turn to my grandmother for herbs and charms. But I haven't run into this sort of overlap here in San Francisco."

Carlos stood. "People are people, Lily. They're not all that different no matter where they live. Listen, I have a quick errand to run. Why don't I pick you up in, say, half an hour?"

"I could meet you at the shop if that's easier."

"That would be better, thanks. El Pajarito, on Mission near Twenty-second." He checked his wristwatch, a sporty model with lots of knobs. "Let's make it an hour, to be on the safe side. And Lily: if you get there first, don't go in without me."

I nodded.

"I'm serious."

"I can tell. I won't go in without you."

He gave me another suspicious look.

"What?" I asked.

"All this easy cooperation is making me nervous. Tell me you're not blowin' smoke up my caboose."

"I'm not even sure how to do such a thing," I laughed. "I told you: I'm resigned to my fate. But I do have one last question."

"What's that?"

"Since I'm the SFPD's official paranormal consultant, do I get dental with that?"

Carlos flashed me a bright white smile. "You're official only in my book. If the department knew I was bringing in a witch to consult on this case . . . Well, let's just say I put up with enough ribbing from my colleagues as it is."

Carlos drew aside the curtain. Folks were milling about, crowding the aisles, inspecting long peasant skirts, faded jeans, and fringed leather vests.

"Quite the hippie convention out here."

"We've been as busy as Grandpa's Sunday tie, as they say."

Carlos looked amused. "*Who* says that?"

I laughed. "I guess we say that back in Texas. Anyway, the Haight Street Summer of Love Festival is this weekend."

The Summer of Love Festival was held annually to commemorate one of the neighborhood's most famous eras. It had been nearly fifty years since hippies sent out the call for "gentle people" to put some flowers in their hair and meet in the Haight-Ashbury to build a new world order of peace, music, and harmony. They hadn't quite achieved their lofty goals, but the neighborhood *had* retained its willingness to accept iconoclasts and freethinkers of all stripes.

Ambitious festivalgoers had been flocking to Aunt Cora's Closet in search of "authentic" hippie clothes for weeks now. Vintage tie-dye and flouncy peasant dresses were flying off the racks; love beads and headbands were in short supply. Bell-bottom jeans, pants in wild colors and embroidered Mexican blouses, most of which I had picked up for a song at flea markets and yard sales, were in great demand.

"Sure, the Summer of Love Festival." He nodded. "I know it well."

"It's my first time; I'm pretty excited. So, do you have a costume?"

"I'm wearing it." Carlos passed a hand over his khaki chinos and black leather jacket.

"Think you look like a hippie, do you?"

"Even better. I'm a narc."

I smiled. "You should at least wear a few love beads around your neck."

"Maybe I'll dig through your treasure chest before I leave."

Recently I had started tossing cheap costume jewelry and plastic items—except for the valuable Bakelite, of course—in an old wooden chest that supposedly came to San Francisco with the pioneers. Now cleansed of cobwebs and its sordid past, it had become my "treasure chest." Everything in it went for under five dollars, and many items were just a quarter. Customers spent a lot of time digging through it with childlike abandon.

Which reminded me . . .

"Carlos, hold on. Didn't you say something about a missing child?"

"Selena Moreno, age fourteen. And we're not positive

she's missing. Weird thing is, we can't get a word out of Ursula. But according to the neighbors, Selena used to live with her grandmother. Hasn't shown up to school, but it looks like her attendance has always been spotty, so it's hard to say what's going on there. Most likely she's staying with relatives, but I'd feel better knowing for sure."

"Do you think something in the shop might point me in her direction?"

"You know me, Lily. I don't think anything in particular."

"But you're suspicious of everything."

He gave me a wink and a smile.

Chapter 2

A tall, dark, and brooding man strode into Aunt Cora's Closet just as Carlos and I emerged from the back room. He wore a scowl, boots, and a black leather jacket, and had a shiny motorcycle helmet tucked under one arm.

My heart beat faster, I smelled roses, and the cacophony of the shop slipped away.

Sailor.

"*There* she is," he said in a quiet, husky voice. There was something about the way he said it . . . as though he had been looking for me all his life. His dark gaze held mine with an intensity that made me blush.

Sailor's eyes shifted and his expression hardened.

"Inspector," he said with a nod.

Carlos returned the nod, but did not speak. For a long moment the two men stared each other down, neither giving an inch, until the inspector turned to me. "Meet me in an hour?"

"I'll be there."

He glanced at Sailor. "Alone."

"Sure thing. See you there."

He gave Sailor another hard look, then left.

"What's up? Another . . . situation?" Sailor asked as the door shut behind the inspector.

"It seems so."

"And you're involved how, exactly?"

"Not involved at all, I am happy—and *relieved*—to report. Carlos needs some help with an out-of-control store—a *curandera* shop—in the Mission."

Sailor raised one eyebrow. "That doesn't sound good."

"I'm just going to give him my take on the situation, no big deal."

"Because that always works out so well. Do you think Rhodes is involved?"

"No, not at all."

He searched my face. "You're sure? I don't want you crossing paths with him until we come up with a plan."

Not so long ago I had gone up against Aidan Rhodes, self-proclaimed "godfather" to the Bay Area's witchy contingent. He was a powerful sorcerer, and not one to be crossed without consequence. Sooner or later I was going to have to face him . . . but I was hoping for later. Much later.

"Carlos will meet me at the store. I'll be fine. So," I said to change the subject, "how are *you* doing?"

"Great, actually. The mentor my aunt suggested is working out well. It seems to be a good fit. I'm already making progress."

"That's great," I said. "Who's the mentor?"

"A cousin, named Patience Blix."

"Well, that seems appropriate." I smiled. "She'll need plenty of patience if she's going to work with the likes of you."

Sailor set his helmet down on the counter, cupped my head in his hands, and brought his lips down on mine.

The world that had dimmed when our eyes met now

disappeared entirely. When Sailor held me in his arms all reason fled and I seemed to escape myself, floating on a rose-scented cloud of sensation and desire, love and hope.

"Lily? *Oops*, pardon me!" said Bronwyn, fluttering behind us. "Oh, by all means, carry on, you two lovebirds!"

"Bronwyn, wait," I said, blushing as I pulled away from Sailor. "Sorry. Did you need something?"

"There's a question for you." Bronwyn gestured with her head to a young woman on the other side of the store.

The customer held up a pale peach, embroidered organza dress with a square pleated neckline and a silver rhinestone brooch accent. The layered frock was considered semiformal in its day—circa 1950—but was a sight more formal than any of the items people were choosing for the Summer of Love Festival.

"Is this silk washable?" asked the young woman.

"No, sorry. It's not." Not at *all*. Maybe I've been in the vintage clothes business too long, but I couldn't imagine thinking a silk antique would be washable. "You can safely assume anything tie-dyed can be tossed in a washer, but almost nothing made before 1960."

"Darn. I don't like to buy anything I have to dry-clean, on account of the environment."

"Lily knows a wonderful green dry cleaner," said Bronwyn. "They're a little pricey, but worth it."

"I still prefer not to buy anything that'll cost me money to clean."

"There are a few washable items on the rack by the dressing rooms. . . ." I suggested, and started over to help her.

"I have to get going, anyway," said Sailor. "Just stopped by for a quick kiss, and to ask what time I should arrive for dinner."

"Seven?"

He gave me another long look, smiled slowly, and whispered, "Wild horses, and all that."

He picked up his helmet, gave me another quick kiss, and left.

My gaze lingered on his broad back. I turned to see Bronwyn watching me, a fond, knowing smile on her face. A blush stained my cheeks.

"*What?* I happen to like the sight of the man in jeans, is all."

"Uh-huh," she said, still smiling. She started to ring up a customer's items, and, in a soft, singsong voice, chanted: "*First comes love. Then comes—*"

"Do *not* sing that next line, Bronwyn Theadora Peters. I'm still dealing with the very idea of having a boyfriend, much less anything beyond that. We're . . . taking it slowly."

"But of course!" she said with a warm, oh so innocent smile. Today Bronwyn had crowned her frizzy brown hair with a garland of wildflowers and wore a gauzy purple tunic decorated with runes over black leggings. She was a chubby, fiftysomething Wiccan who personified the amiable creed of that belief system: "*An' it harm none, do what ye will.*"

I smiled and went to help the customer find a washable dress.

"Oh, by the way—would you mind watching the shop for a while?" I asked Bronwyn twenty minutes later, after ringing up the customer's purchases—she had bought the peach organza after all, a vintage impulse I knew she wouldn't regret. The dress had bright, fun vibrations that would be perfect for her personality. "I have to check out a store called El Pajarito."

"The *botanica* in the Mission?" asked Bronwyn. "It's about time!"

"You know it?"

"Of course I know it. Señora Moreno is my main supplier for *epazote* and juniper berries. I've told you about the place—you refused to go with me, remember? Let's see if Maya can stay late and we'll go together!"

"Maybe another time. Unfortunately, this isn't a shopping trip. Carlos asked me to meet him there, alone."

"Is something wrong?"

"I really don't know. What can you tell me about the owner, Ursula Moreno?"

"Not much. I only know her from our interactions at her shop, and we have a few clients in common—I send people to her if they need something I don't have in stock, and she sends customers to me if they need specialty tea blends."

"What about her granddaughter?"

"Selena? I see her in the shop occasionally."

"What is she like?"

"She's a little. . . ." Bronwyn trailed off with a shrug.

"What?"

"A little different."

"How so?"

"Just . . . different. Even, well, odd."

Bronwyn was about the most nonjudgmental person I'd ever met, and she adored children. For Bronwyn to describe anyone, but especially a child, as "odd" was saying a lot.

"Anything else?"

"Nothing comes to mind."

"Okay, thanks. I'm sure none of this has anything to do with us. Carlos asked me to check it out, so I'll go do that, and then Maya and I are supposed to go look through some clothes at an estate sale. You can watch over the store?"

"No problem. Don't forget to take a jacket!" Bronwyn

said over her shoulder as she returned to her herb stand, where a customer was browsing.

I was again reminded how fortunate I was to have two such energetic and responsible women working with me. Beyond the thrill and comfort of what was for me a new experience—friendship—their regular presence in the store allowed me to run around town chasing down supernatural mysteries. I hadn't lived in San Francisco very long, but already I had come to realize that it played host to more paranormal mayhem than seemed normal.

It sometimes made me wonder whether my arrival in the City by the Bay was entirely coincidental . . . or whether other forces had helped to guide me to the Haight.

The day was sunny and warm, but I took Bronwyn's advice and snagged my cocoa-brown vintage car coat before heading out. The weather in my adopted town was famously unpredictable. When the marine layer—a bank of fog that hovered off the coast—moved in, it cloaked the city in chill and damp. The temperature could plummet fifteen degrees in as many minutes.

I also made sure I was wearing a carved talisman around my neck, carried small jars of salts and brew in my satchel, and my medicine bag was securely fastened to the multicolored belt at my waist. Boy Scout–like, I was ever-prepared. The charms had helped me to face some truly horrifying scenes of demonic mayhem and all-too-human murder.

Not that I was expecting any such thing at El Pajarito. I was simply checking out an out-of-control store with my good buddy Carlos Romero. No big deal.

What could possibly go wrong?

Chapter 3

The Mission District smelled of beans and tortillas and sounded like a disco. But the area known as the Mission was rapidly changing as wealthy entrepreneurs and well-paid, high-tech professionals moved in, remodeling run-down Victorians and outfitting old art lofts with gourmet kitchens and the latest sound systems. Meanwhile, the artists and immigrants who had made this neighborhood so vibrant and distinctive were now finding it too expensive, and many had fled to the East Bay or out of the area altogether.

But several holdouts remained: my friend Hervé Le Mansec's voodoo supply shop on nearby Valencia was one. And El Pajarito, a few blocks away on Mission, was another.

I took a moment to survey the colorful storefront from across the broad boulevard. The windows were decorated with tropical birds and fanciful flowers, the paint flaking off as if created long ago. The store's sign was simple and hand-lettered, black letters on a white background, painted not by a professional but by someone unconcerned with formality.

"I wouldn't get involved with Ursula if I were you," said a pretty woman in her early twenties.

The woman wore a simple white tank top and jeans. Her long, glossy hair had been dyed an unnatural shade of burgundy, and a colorful tattoo of the Virgin of Guadalupe adorned her bare shoulder.

"Do you know her?" I asked.

"I don't trust her. And that shop . . ." She shook her head. "Something bad about that shop. *Mal ojo. Ojo del diablo.*"

Evil eye. Eye of the devil.

"If you need some help," she continued, "why you don't come inside, let my aunt pray for you?" She gestured toward the shop behind us. Much like El Pajarito, this shop's window displayed a jumble of items: small jars of herbs, Catholic saints in various guises, a variety of small animal bones. "My aunt does cleansing, readings, tea leaves, same as Ursula but better. You can trust her."

"Thank you, but I'm not a customer. Actually, the police asked me to stop by."

"Seriously?" She fixed me with a suspicious look. "Why?"

"Apparently something strange is going on in the shop. Have you heard anything? Do you know Selena, the girl who used to be there with Ursula?"

She crossed herself and went into her aunt's shop, slamming the door.

No love lost there, I thought as I crossed the wide avenue.

Carlos was waiting for me outside, speaking on his cell phone. As I approached he paused to tell a passerby, "The shop's closed, indefinitely," before resuming his conversation.

I studied our surroundings while I waited for him to get off the phone. A bright blue bench sat in front of the store; it looked freshly painted and wasn't even chained, which surprised me. In this neighborhood I would think anything not nailed down would disappear, and quickly.

The windows held a wide array of candles, each with a label: WEALTH, HOMEWORK, PASSION, MARRIED LOVE, STRENGTH. There were bundles of herbs hanging from the ceiling, and a huge glass container was filled with thousands of tiny metal charms in the shape of arms, legs, heads . . . whatever part of the body ails you. Laid out in wide arcs were dozens of ceramic and stone figures of pre–Columbian Aztec deities and Navajo fetishes.

And overlooking it all was Santa Muerte, or Saint Death: a skeleton cloaked in a blue hooded robe, a scythe clutched in one bony hand, a cigarette poised between her grinning teeth. At Santa Muerte's feet was a bottle of rum, a sacrifice to keep her happy.

Because the store was not a crime scene there was no yellow tape across the door, and it occurred to me to wonder what the forensics team had hoped to find. Short of a deliberate poisoning, how could a *curandera* be held responsible for a client's death? I could not begin to imagine how the DA would prove such a thing in a court of law; but then, I was no legal scholar. Apart from a few short stints in jail—all charges were dropped—I remained blessedly ignorant of the workings of the legal system.

I started to turn away from the display window when I caught a movement out of the corner of my eye. Looking back, I saw Santa Muerte tilt her head at me and raise her scythe.

A stone mosaic frog suddenly leapt up, striking the glass with such force that it created a starburst crack.

Chapter 4

I jumped.

"This is what I'm talking about," said Carlos from behind me.

I looked over my shoulder. "You saw that?"

"I didn't *see* anything, but I heard it. Like I said, there's a lot of strange stuff going down at this shop."

He used a key to open the metal security grate, pushed it to one side, then unlocked the front door.

"After you," he said with a gentlemanly sweep of his hand.

"Gee, thanks," I said, stroking the medicine bag at my waist. I entered cautiously, hands turned palm-side out, trying to open myself up to vibrations.

Messy shelves were crammed with aerosol cans promising to cleanse homes of bad feelings, or to bestow financial luck. There were dozens of candles and tiny shrines made out of Altoids boxes. A large selection of talismans and amulets featured Catholic and pseudo-Catholic saints; a folksy, brightly painted *Mano Poderoso* was a splayed hand made of tin, meant to ward off evil and fill one's home with peace, happiness, and family bonding. Multiaction protection crosses, lucky fixed horseshoes wrapped in red string, and gold bags adorned with the image of Saint Cajeton promised to help with employment problems.

I picked up a white silk conjure bag, probably stuffed with herbs, seeds, roots, nuts, oils, and bits of bone. Weighing it in my hand, I felt its vibrations: calm, confident, capable. Whoever put these together had a touch.

By the register was a display of matchboxes containing tiny skulls for hexing. A sign offered to cleanse homes for a modest fee. This was no ordinary housekeeping service, but a *limpia*, or a cleansing of evil spirits, lingering sensations, and pestering ghosts. Also for sale were love spells and fertility charms.

Also on the counter was a stack of receipts and several colorful children's drawings of lilies. An open bag of roasted pumpkin seeds and a half-filled coffee cup remained near the register, as though the proprietor had been dragged off in the middle of a snack. On the wall was a framed newspaper article with a photo of two women and a girl posed stiffly behind the register.

"Is this the shop staff?" I asked Carlos.

He nodded and pointed to the older woman. "That's Ursula Moreno, and the girl is Selena. Not sure about the other woman."

The caption read: "Ursula, Lupita, and Selena, of El Pajarito."

A sweater was draped over the back of the chair, a lemon yellow knit with a white rose embroidered on one breast. I picked it up and hugged it to myself. It had a homey aroma: beans and rice, roasting chilies. The vibrations were peaceful, confident, powerful—perhaps overly so. But I didn't feel the frenetic thoughts of someone intent on wickedness: no guilt or wavering resolve. If this was Ursula's sweater, could she possibly be guilty of what the SFPD suspected?

On the other hand, I had been misled before. I cringed to think of how often.

"Can you tell anything from all this"—Carlos gestured at the overstocked shelves—"mess?"

"Not really."

"How about that sweater you're holding?"

I shook my head.

"Take your time."

"I will."

Carlos was silent for all of sixty seconds. "How about now?"

"Could you give me a few minutes, please? Alone?"

"I'm harshing your buzz, huh?"

"It would make it easier for me to concentrate," I said diplomatically.

Carlos hesitated.

"Forensics has already been here, right?" I continued. "And you know I don't have any fingerprints to screw things up. What could it hurt?"

"Sure you'll be okay by yourself?"

"I'll be fine. Don't take this the wrong way, but if there's something magical happening here, you're not likely to be of much help anyway."

He squinted at me, then nodded and stepped out of the shop.

Getting the sense of retail establishments is challenging because of the residual sensations from the people who have passed through. Add to that the fact that this store's owner had been arrested, and it was practically impossible to ferret out the strange vibrations, to parse them from the normal spectrum of human energy.

I closed my eyes and concentrated, gradually picking up a twinge of something . . . *off*.

When I opened my eyes an aerosol can of Bad Luck fell onto its side and started spinning, spraying its contents everywhere. I wasn't alarmed; most of these sprays were nothing more than cheap air freshener in a clever package. Judging by the sickly-sweet floral scent that enveloped me, that was the case here. Besides, as a witch, I had some protection. The medicine bag at my waist included protective dust, stones, and seeds. I might have been a terrible judge of character, but I was very good at sensing danger.

And I was not one to be intimidated by an aerosol can. Land sakes.

The cash register began ringing, the cash drawer opening and slamming shut. A massive reference book on herbal medicine flung itself off a shelf and landed on the floor with a thud, its pages fanning the air. Brightly colored beads jumped out of the woven basket on the front counter and skittered along the floor. From the corner of my eye I spied a lit candle flying toward my head, and ducked in the nick of time.

"Now that's just rude!" I called out, though I'm not sure who or what I thought would be listening. "Behave yourself."

I hurried to extinguish the candle's flame under the sole of my Keds, and concentrated again. I sensed something building, a mounting tension as intangible yet as real as the change in atmospheric pressure ahead of an approaching storm.

Carlos wasn't kidding. This merchandise was seriously deranged.

Could there be a spirit at work? What if—

The merchandise suddenly fell quiet, and I heard raised voices. Carlos was restraining a man at the front door. He was average looking, a little overweight, a bit jowly. Ordinary, with a countenance that would have been pleasant had it not been distorted in pain and anger, his eyes red-rimmed as though from lack of sleep.

"Let me in—I won't hurt anything!"

"Gary, you shouldn't be here," Carlos said, his voice firm but gentle. "Go on home and rest."

"I just . . . I want to see . . . I don't even know what I'm doing here."

The man grew pale and swayed on his feet, and Carlos grabbed him by the upper arms, urging him toward the blue wooden bench on the sidewalk.

"Easy, now," Carlos said. "Here, have a seat for a moment. Catch your breath."

"Why did this happen, Carlos? How? How could she do this to me? And to Emma?"

I went to see if I could help. Carlos crouched in front of the man, speaking to him face-to-face.

"Why don't I call someone to come pick you up?" Carlos asked.

"My brother-in-law is . . . Wait. Is he still my brother-in-law?" He fixed an anguished look upon Carlos. "Now that Nicky is gone?"

"Of course he is," Carlos said. "You want me to call him?"

"No, no, he's right down the street, parking. He brought the kids over for a visit; they're home watching a movie. We're supposed to be picking up tacos for lunch. I . . . I just—" Gary noticed me. "Who's this?"

"Gary Utley, this is Lily Ivory. Lily is a civilian consultant to the department."

"What kind of consultant?"

"She's . . . it's a little hard to explain, but she helps me to interpret unusual developments."

Gary's eyes narrowed. "What are you saying—she's a *witch*?" He spat out the word as if it were an epithet. "*Another* one? Do you have any idea what that witch did to me, to my family, to my *wife*? First she bilks us out of thousands of dollars, and then—"

"I'm so sorry to hear about your loss, Gary," I said. "Please know that not all witchcraft is—"

"I don't want to hear it!" he said, surging off the bench. He shoved his way into the store, seized a jar of spiritual bath salts, and flung it across the room, where it crashed into a shelf of medicinal oils. "Not from the mouth of a damned *witch*!"

"Hey!" Carlos and Gary grappled for a moment, until Carlos pulled some sort of fancy martial arts move and wound up holding Gary from the back, arms looped around his shoulders so he couldn't move. "*Simmer down.* I know you've suffered a great shock but you have to control yourself. *Gary*, Lily is here to help; she's not your enemy."

Gary seemed to deflate.

"I'm sorry," he muttered. "I'm really . . . I'm so sorry."

Carlos restrained him for another moment.

I wanted to say something further, but hung back. I couldn't imagine the pain Gary must be feeling right now. What would it be like to have a spouse commit suicide? To wonder if you should have been there, should have seen the signs, responded earlier, more forcefully?

My friend Max Carmichael had gone through something similar with his wife . . . who was also Carlos's cousin. Why hadn't I put that together? That must be another reason why Carlos was drawn to this case.

As we stood there—an awkward trio, Carlos holding Gary, and me not knowing what to do or say—another man appeared in the store's open door. He wore wire-frame glasses, plaid Bermuda shorts, topsiders, and a pale yellow monogrammed polo shirt. Looking around cautiously, seeming to take in the state of the store and the way Carlos was restraining Gary, he said, "What's going on? Is everything okay?"

"Knox, we were just talking about you," said Gary. His voice was subdued, and Carlos released him.

"Good to see you again, Knox," said Carlos.

"Hello, Inspector. What's going on? Did . . . did Gary do all this damage? I've only been gone a few minutes."

"No, it was like this before. Mostly. Everything's fine," said Carlos. "Emotions are running high, that's all. Knox, this is Lily Ivory, a special consultant to the department in this case."

Gary muttered something under his breath. Carlos quelled him with a warning look and placed himself between Gary and me.

"Pleased to meet you. Your name's . . . Knocks?" I asked.

"K-n-o-x." The man spelled it out with a smile. He pulled a card out of his pocket and handed it to me. "As in the fort, where they keep the gold."

I looked down at what looked like an old-fashioned calling card:

Knox Saletta

Father and Househusband.

"I'm Gary's brother-in-law," he continued.

"Nicky Utley's brother," Carlos said quietly.

"Oh, I see. I'm so sorry for your loss."

"Thank you." Knox turned toward Gary. "Come on, Gary, you shouldn't be here. Let's go pick up the food. I'm sure the passel is starving. And we don't want to leave Emma in charge of those hooligans for long."

Gary hesitated. "I'm . . . I just . . . I don't know. I just wanted to see the shop again. I guess I'm trying to put it all together. There are . . . so many questions." He turned to me. "I'm . . . sorry. I haven't been myself lately."

"Of course," I said.

"C'mon, Gary," said Knox, slipping an arm over the man's shoulder. "Good-bye, Inspector, ma'am."

Silence reigned for a long moment as we watched the men walk down the street. Knox kept his arm around Gary's shoulders, and appeared to be speaking soothingly to him.

"Poor man . . . and poor Knox, too," I said, shaking my head. "I can't imagine losing a sister to suicide. Or a spouse, of course."

"I'm just sorry he took it out on you. He's been through a lot."

"Yes, indeed. Still, you were pretty impressive there, Bruce Lee. What was that move you pulled? Jiujitsu or something?"

"You didn't think I could handle myself?"

"I assumed you could, but I've never actually seen you in action. Besides, you have a gun, so I figured maybe you'd just brandish your weapon."

He gave me the ghost of a smile. "Brandishing one's weapon is frowned upon, especially when it comes to grieving families. Departmental policy."

We stepped back into the disheveled store.

"So," Carlos continued. "Run through this for me. What are the possibilities, as you see them?"

"If Ursula Moreno put these bags together," I said as I weighed one of the embroidered bundles in my hand, "then she definitely has some power, some abilities. I suppose it's possible she charged these items with so much energy, maybe more than even she knew she had, that they're still vibrating. Now that she's not here to control them, they've gotten a little out of hand."

Carlos frowned. "So if the victim bought something from Moreno, it could have harmed her with its . . . what, vibrations? Some kind of occult power?"

"I've never heard of such a thing, but . . ." I trailed off with a shrug. "Have you tracked down any of Moreno's other clients? Has anything happened to them?"

He fixed me with his grim-cop look. "Sorry to say, it has. Nothing very serious, but enough to make me wonder, at least. Like I said, the mayor's on a bit of a rampage against fortune-tellers of all stripes, especially the unlicensed ones. I'm still checking it out."

A can of All-Purpose Incense Powder sailed toward us, and I batted it away. Carlos looked impressed.

"Unlicensed ones?" I asked.

"According to Article 17.1 of the Municipal Code, fortune-tellers and witch doctors must be licensed in San Francisco."

"I don't much care for the term 'witch doctor.' "

"I don't much care for witch doctors, period. But you ought to find this interesting: The city statute covers necromancers as well."

"Necromancers have to be licensed?"

"Indeed. As well as psychics and spellcasters, if they act for gain, benefit, or advantage."

"What about vintage clothes dealers with 'special' talents?"

"I don't even want to think about that."

"So, about this place. Here's what's really odd," I said, looking around at the mess. "Most practitioners I know keep a tight rein on where they expend their power— they don't want to disperse it, send it out into the world willy-nilly."

"I imagine that could cause a lot of damage."

"Yes, but that's not the only reason. Magical strength is hard-won. You have to give up something to get it, and it's always in short supply. You don't just let it fly around on its own; that's the mark of an amateur. But for a professional like Moreno?" I shook my head. "It makes no sense. She wouldn't have a practice for long."

"Maybe she doesn't intend to."

"How do you mean?"

He shrugged. "She's not very popular with her neighbors. I can tell you that much. So maybe she's feeling like taking herself out. Who knows?"

I hadn't thought of that. Could this situation be the result of a spiteful woman trying to take others down with her? Or could she be a powerful practitioner who was herself suicidal?

"Okay," Carlos said with a sigh. "Thanks for trying. It was a long shot, anyway. If you think of anything else, call me."

"What's your next step?"

"We're still tracking down Moreno's other clients—and other potential victims."

"And what about the missing girl, Selena?"

"We're on the lookout."

"So . . . as far as I'm concerned, that's about it, then? Or did you want me to try to exorcise the place, get rid of whatever's causing all this in here?"

"Don't bother. The store is already trashed. I'm only concerned if you thought it was escalating. Let's leave it for now. You should get back to your shop, and I'll follow up on leads. I'll let you know if we figure it out, but this really isn't your problem."

I nodded, still curious but relieved.

But as I gave one last glance to the shambles in Ursula Moreno's shop, I had the distinct impression it wasn't quite that simple.

Chapter 5

I arrived at Aunt Cora's Closet to find Bronwyn's "gentleman friend" Duke helping a male customer try on a fringed leather jacket. Duke was a retired fisherman in his late fifties, and his somewhat grizzled countenance was most welcome at the shop. Not only was he a deterrent to ne'er-do-wells, but his mere presence seemed to encourage other men to enter what could easily seem to be a feminine realm.

"Duke, will you be here for an hour or so?" Given the frequency with which trouble seemed to find me, I didn't like leaving anyone in the store alone. "Maya and I need to check out some clothes."

"My pleasure," he said in a deep, quiet voice. "My magic woman and I have it covered."

He winked at Bronwyn, whose scarf-folding suddenly went haywire, as though she had lost her concentration.

Armed with Hefty bags and cardboard boxes, Maya and I walked around the corner to the driveway I rented by the month and climbed into the purple van with *Aunt Cora's Closet: It's not old. It's Vintage!* emblazoned on the sides.

As she was fastening her seat belt, Maya muttered, "Those two act like a couple of teenagers."

"I know. Isn't it great?"

Maya snorted. "What with you and Bronwyn and your respective gentlemen callers, it's like a romantic movie around here. One of the sugary ones from the 1950s. Like *Sabrina* or *An Affair to Remember*."

"I knew it!" I said, as I fired up the engine and edged my way into the slow-moving traffic on Haight Street. "You're a closet romantic."

"I most certainly am *not*. I'm a realist."

"Romance can be real," I said. "You should try it; you might like it."

Now she laughed out loud. "One of these days, maybe. One of these days . . . Okay, go straight through the light, then turn left at the next intersection."

"So tell me, how did you meet Betty North?"

"Through Bronwyn. Betty used to come in to buy Bronwyn's teas—you may have seen her at some point. But then she got sick and was housebound for the past several months, before she passed."

"And you were interviewing her for your oral history project?"

"Yes, I interviewed her a few months ago. We had lunch a couple of times since then—I'd drop by with some food, just to say hi and check in on her. She had a boyfriend, but he was as old as she was, so I wanted to be sure she was okay."

"What about her family? No children?"

"She didn't really want to talk about it, so I didn't push. I got the sense she did have kids but that they were estranged. It's weird—most of the old folks I interview like nothing better than to tell me all about their kids and grandkids. But Betty didn't volunteer a lot of personal information, talked mostly about fashion and what it was like to own a small business back in the day. Take the next right; her house is about halfway down the block—the yellow one."

We pulled up in front of a stucco two-story bungalow. Like most of its neighbors the home's entrance was on the second level, over the garage. Maya opened the front door, and we stepped into a small foyer. Plush white carpet covered the living room floor from wall to wall, and though crisscrossed with plastic runners, the carpet was stained here and there along the edges.

An upholstered sofa with lacey doilies on the arms and headrest sat in front of the picture window, flanked by two upholstered chairs. Dozens of porcelain figurines decorated the horizontal spaces, and three lamps with grand lampshades crowded one side table. A large collection of shiny silver—everything from silverware to serving dishes—had been laid out on two card tables.

The dining room was also crammed with furniture, including two large walnut curio cabinets loaded with glittering tchotchkes. One corner held a shrinelike display of vintage military paraphernalia, bordered by paintings of sad-faced clowns. Paintings and drawings hung on every wall, an eclectic mixture of African-inspired art, long-necked animals in graphic silhouettes, and big-eyed paintings of Betty herself: Betty as an ingénue, Betty in a sari and bindi, Betty as the Madonna. And most surprisingly, lots of paintings of Betty in the nude.

I paused in front of a portrayal of a topless Betty.

"She was quite the looker back in the day," Maya said. "Maybe more than you wanted to know about her, right?"

I smiled. "It's not bad. Not really my style, but not bad."

"Her boyfriend, Fred, was—*is*, I guess—an artist. I believe he did most of the portraits."

"He's still around?"

She nodded. "It's sad, really—he lived here with her, but moved out when she went to the hospital. Didn't want to stay here without her, I guess.

"Where'd he go?"

"He moved back into his art studio, near China Basin."

"Doesn't he want his paintings?"

"I'm not sure. I can't really get a handle on Fred. I asked to interview him, but he declined, saying it was Betty who had the interesting life. Which isn't true, of course—*everyone's* life is interesting. And he's an artist, which makes him even more intriguing."

The determined expression on Maya's face made me smile. "I take it you haven't given up on him."

"I thought I'd give him a little time, after Betty's passing." She shrugged but returned my smile. "But yeah, I'm not about to let him get away."

"I like this one," I said, studying a portrait of Betty that emphasized her long swan neck and huge, heavy-lidded eyes. Her blond hair was in an updo, one curl tumbling across her forehead, and she gazed at the viewer with an imperious yet sensual air. "She must have been quite something."

"She was. I was lucky to get to know her."

Betty North was by no means a hoarder, but the house was full of keepsakes and traces of a long life: stacks of *National Geographic* and *Art Scene* magazines, small silver spoons from various locales, souvenirs from the Cayman Islands, posh highball glasses, and plastic hula dancers from the early sixties. Most of the items reflected the swanky style that reigned immediately preceding the Summer of Love, right before hippie ideals ushered in the massive shift in culture, attitudes, and fashion of the late sixties.

I felt excitement build at the prospect of the promised clothes from Betty's boutique.

Mixed among the mementoes of a rich life were medical supplies: dozens of orange pill bottles, boxes of facial tissues, a package of adult diapers, canisters of talcum powder, and assorted tubes of creams and ointments. No doubt about it, growing old required courage and character.

"I feel bad about one thing," Maya said softly. "The last time I visited, Betty seemed to know she wasn't long for this world. She didn't fear death, but she told me she wanted to die here, at home. But when she collapsed we called the paramedics, and then she wound up dying at the hospital."

"That's not your fault, Maya. It's always hard to know when the end has come," I said. "You couldn't just leave her—calling for help was the natural response."

She nodded. "I know. I just . . . feel bad."

I laid my hand on her shoulder. I knew for a certainty that there was life beyond the veil, but since I couldn't communicate with those on the other side, I understood what she was feeling. Death seemed so permanent, so irrevocable. But at least Betty North had enjoyed a long, full life. Unlike Nicky Utley, who was far too young to die, and who had left behind a heartbroken husband and daughter.

"Want to check out the clothes?" I asked.

Maya shook herself. "Yeah, let's do that. Follow me— you're going to love this. There's a 'gen-yoo-ine' rumpus room in the basement."

I trailed her down a narrow stairway—the walls hung

with yet more portraits of a luminous Betty—and into a big room that was, in fact, a rumpus room straight out of the early sixties. An orange Naugahyde bench ran along the circumference of the room and wrapped around the large support pillars. The floor was tiled in black-and-white-checked linoleum. In one corner was a padded black bar, studded with brass tacks creating a diamond pattern, with a trio of high barstools lined up in front. A record player sat on the table with a stack of albums next to it. Little gold flecks in the room's popcorn ceiling glittered in the dim light cast by glass wall sconces in the shape of hourglasses.

Shelves behind the bar held every sort of cocktail glass imaginable: martini glasses, of course, but also highball glasses decorated with gold polka dots, shot glasses with hand-painted hula dancers, large gold-rimmed tumblers, and what looked like authentic antique Coca-Cola glasses.

I picked up a paper napkin from the stack on the dusty bar and read aloud. "*Confucius say, 'Man who take girl fishing, sometimes get hooked.'* Wow. Racist *and* sexist. A twofer. Those were the days, huh?"

"Yup. So sad to see the days of easy sexism and racism are behind us." Maya was holding up a mammy doll from *Gone With the Wind*. "Betty loved *Gone With the Wind*. Couldn't stop talking about it. But she apologized to me, personally since I am, in her words, a 'colored person.'"

"She really said that?"

Maya smiled and shrugged. "I interview old people, remember? It's not unusual to hear outdated, politically incorrect stuff. And to tell you the truth, I'd rather hear it directly and honestly from people. Otherwise . . . sometimes I think a lot of people still believe things like that deep down, but they're two-faced about it."

I supposed she was right about that.

"And now," she continued. "For the clothes."

A door at the back of the rumpus room opened onto a narrow single-car garage just big enough for a Model T. I doubted a modern car would fit, but it made one heck of a walk-in closet.

One side door led, I presumed, outside, while the opposite wall had been lined with mirrors, and every inch of floor space was jammed with racks of clothing and piles of accessories, as well as still more tchotchkes and souvenirs. There weren't even pathways through the items—we had to push aside the clothes.

"This reminds me of a mini Aunt Cora's Closet," I said as I maneuvered past a wall of clothing.

"Or what Aunt Cora's Closet will turn into if you keep cramming it full of junk like old trunks and broken-down kitchen gadgets."

Guiltily, I set down the old-fashioned wood-handled egg beaters I had picked up and started flicking through a rack of dresses.

"Here's a good eighties rack," said Maya.

"I was hoping more for sixties stuff—how about that rack behind you, can you see? Hold something up so I can see it."

She held up an ice-blue Jackie O–style shift, with a matching pillbox hat. "Bingo. Stay there, I'll come join you."

I ducked through a tunnel of sparkly tops with padded shoulders popular during the Reagan administration, then pushed past a rack of negligees and housecoats. These last looked less like items from Betty's boutique and more like overflow from her bedroom closet. There were suits with cropped jackets and narrow skirts in fine tweed wools; their bracelet-length sleeves meant to be worn with gloves and oversized bangles. There were animal print scarves and befeathered bubble hats. Next to them there were several gingham dresses with Peter Pan collars and fitted bodices, adorned with little bows. My favorite was a 1950s dress with sky blue stripes made up of tiny polka dots against a white background. It had a boat neckline and eyelet lace trim on the bodice. Finally, I spied a few cotton plaid patch-pocket dresses, with cap sleeves and red rickrack trim on the bodice, with matching piping on the deep pockets—I might have to keep that one for myself. It would be perfect for gathering herbs.

I was turning toward the rack of sixties dresses when Maya spoke.

"Um . . . Lily?"

"What is it?"

"I'm not sure . . ."

There, between an ebony carving and an ivory figurine of monkeys gesturing *hear no evil, see no evil, speak no evil,* lay a doll.

But this was no ordinary doll. It was made of honey-colored wax, and the identity of the model was obvious: Affixed to the doll was a photo of Betty's portrait, the one with big eyes and swan neck. Blond hairs sprouted from the doll's head. And pins protruded from its body.

"Don't touch it."

"Don't worry. I won't," said Maya, pressing against the shirtwaists at her back as she drew as far away from the doll as she could. "What is it?"

"It's . . . not good."

"Does this mean what I think it means?" Her dark eyes turned to me, searching, with a frown of confusion. "A voodoo doll?"

"Maybe."

"Someone was trying to hurt *Betty*?"

I swallowed hard. "It's possible. I mean, that's what it

looks like, but let's not jump to conclusions—not yet." I cast my gaze around until it landed on what I needed. "Hand me that nightgown, the red flannel."

I wrapped the skirt of the nightgown around my hand and picked up the doll, then swiftly bundled the rest of the garment around it. Since Betty had already passed away, I didn't need to worry about inadvertently hurting her by pressing the pins in deeper or twisting a leg . . . but still. I knew enough not to fool around with this sort of thing.

One thing seemed strange, though: Normally when holding something like this, I would feel its vibrations. The thick flannel would muffle the doll's power, but even still I should have sensed *something*. This doll was absent of sensations. It was . . . null.

"It could just be a harmless souvenir," I said, recalling the crowded curio cabinets in the living room.

"Who would want something like *that* as a souvenir?" Maya asked, outraged.

I had to smile at her reaction. Not so long ago Maya would have denied believing in anything magical; she had a rational, scientific mind and stood with her feet planted very firmly on the ground. But she'd seen too much since she'd been hanging around the likes of me. Her mind was definitely opening to the possibilities beyond the realm of "normal."

"Hello?"

Maya and I jumped several inches at the sound of a man's voice calling out upstairs. We heard footsteps walking around overhead, then descending the steps.

"That sounds like Finn," Maya said. "He's in charge of the estate liquidation."

"Don't mention the doll."

"Wasn't planning on it."

I tucked the wrapped bundle in the bottom of a plastic laundry basket and covered it with a couple of pleated plaid skirts circa 1960.

A man appeared in the doorway, clad in dusty jeans and work boots. He was average-looking but had broad shoulders and a huge smile.

"Maya! Thought it must be you down here. How ya doin', kiddo?"

"Hi, Finn. This is my friend Lily I was telling you about."

"The one with the vintage clothing store, eh?"

"The very one," I said. "Nice to meet you, Finn."

"Same here."

"Maya said you handle estate sales?" I said. "I imagine you see some amazing things."

"That's for sure. We should get together and compare notes sometime. I bet we've met some real characters in the line of duty." When Finn smiled, little crinkles appeared around his blue eyes. "So, find some good stuff? Want to pay me a small fortune to haul it all out of here?"

"We've just started, but I won't be able to take all of it. It's not all vintage." My eyes alighted on several threadbare cotton housecoats. "Some of it's just . . . old."

He glanced around the garage, then back at me, eyebrows raised. "How can you tell the difference?"

"Well, now, that's a trade secret."

"If she told you she'd have to kill you," said Maya.

"In that case, I'll live with the mystery." He winked. "No worries, just gather whatever you can use to one side, and then I'll give you a price for the pile."

"What will you do with the rest of it?" asked Maya.

"Either the Salvation Army or the rag pile, I guess," said Finn. "I can sell the furniture and the knickknacks, but people who come to estate sales aren't really looking for clothing, by and large. Besides, everything would have to be laundered and, well, I don't want to work that hard. So take everything you want. All except the fur coats."

"Betty had fur coats?"

"Three of 'em. Those are a whole different ballgame. As for the rest of the stuff, be my guest. If you need me, I'll be upstairs working on the inventory. Holler when you're done. Set aside what you want. I'll go through it and come up with a price. Assuming we're all in agreement, we'll have a deal. I'll photograph everything and bring it by your shop later."

"You plan to photograph the clothes?" I asked.

He held up an iPad. "Company policy. Everything gets photographed and entered into the inventory log. That way the family has a record of everything sold, and it makes the IRS happy." He checked his watch. "Anyway, if you've got this covered, I'm starting in on all the junk—I mean, the *very valuable* items—upstairs. If you need anything, just give a shout."

"Thanks."

"His job must be a hoot," said Maya after he left.

"Almost as much fun as ours."

"I'd agree as far as the vintage clothing goes. The witch stuff, not so much. Speaking of which, Lily . . . do you think that creepy little doll could have had anything to do with Betty's death?"

"I don't think so. It's definitely creepy but it doesn't feel charged with power. Like I was saying, some people see voodoo dolls as toys—it could have been a souvenir she picked up while traveling."

"Really? Who would want something like that?"

I shrugged. "It's considered kitschy. Anyway, I will look into it, I promise you." I was acting confident for Maya's sake. The truth is, poppet magic made me nervous. Fortunately, my friend Hervé was a voodoo guy;

he would be able to tell me more about this kind of magic.

"For now," I continued, scanning the area for anything else suspicious, "let's go with anything that looks seventies or earlier. Especially cocktail dresses, and suits or professional clothes."

"What about nighties?" She held up a pair of long silk pajamas. The rack behind her held a dozen more.

"Um . . . let's take all the frilly ones, and the ones with matching robes. They won't take up much room, right?"

"True." Maya started tucking pajamas and nighties into one of our plastic Hefty bags.

"Those bed jackets are darling, too," I said, pointing to the pastel rainbow of quilted satin jackets. "But does anyone lounge around in bed enough these days to need a bed jacket? Or are they meant to entertain someone in the boudoir?"

"I think they're like smoking jackets," said Maya, running her hands over a silky coat. "A relic of another time, and another way of life. These days men change into sweats or jeans when they come home, not into a more comfortable jacket."

"With the notable exception of—"

"Hugh Hefner," we said in unison, and laughed.

"Ah, the fashion icons of days gone by," I said. "He would have loved the bar with the sexist napkins."

"Heck, I love the bar with the sexist napkins."

"So how do you know Finn?" I said as we worked our way steadily through the clothes.

"I think Betty knew her time was near and she was trying to tie up the loose ends, to make all the arrangements she could ahead of time. So she arranged with his company for the estate sale, and brought in a Realtor, arranged for cremation, all of that. I told you, she wasn't close to her kids so I guess she wanted to take care of it all. I was here when she wrote out a new will . . ."

There was a little catch in her voice as she trailed off.

"You okay?"

She nodded, but I caught a glint of tears in her coffee-colored eyes.

I'm not by nature a hugger but I was trying to get over myself and to be a better friend. Pushing past some polyester disco dresses, I wrapped my arms around her. Maya didn't seem to notice my awkwardness, but rested her head on my shoulder and sniffed.

"It just makes me sad," she said. "I've never . . . I mean, my grandfather died when I was in high school, but I've never seen someone like that . . . and then she died in the hospital when all she wanted was to be here at home."

"Maya, don't think that way. Betty died because she was old, and it was her time. And it's always sad, always hard to deal with. Gabriel García Márquez wrote: 'a person doesn't die when he should but when he can.'"

She nodded and sniffed again, pulling herself together.

"That's from *One Hundred Years of Solitude*, right? I'm the one who gave you that book, remember?"

"I know." I smiled. "I loved it. But *I* read it in *Spanish*."

"Show-off," she said with a chuckle. "Besides, you used a dictionary, I saw you."

"Hey, that's allowed!"

We laughed and returned to our work, but I couldn't help but sneak another glance at the laundry basket where I'd hidden the doll.

Was I right about the ugly little thing? Was it one sou-

venir among many, the kind of thing a tourist might pick
up in New Orleans or Brazil or one of the Caribbean
islands, never realizing just how dangerous it could be?

Except the picture pinned to it looked like the portrait of Betty painted by her missing boyfriend, Fred.
And if that yellow hair was hers . . . charged or not, that
poppet could be dangerous.

Chapter 6

"That thing is *u-g-l-y*, it ain't got no alibi, it's *uglyyyyy*," chanted Oscar that night when he caught sight of the skewered doll. He danced around the kitchen, doing some sort of circular movement with his hands, and swinging his hips.

I thought he was pretty good, but then I'm a little dancing-challenged.

"It's *uglyyyyy*," he continued as he hopped to the beat in his head. "That thing done got whupped with an *ugly* stick."

During the day, downstairs in the shop, Oscar is a run-of-the-mill miniature potbellied pig. But in the privacy of our apartment over the store, he shifts to his normal guise, a kind of a cross between a gargoyle and a goblin. He has oversized hands, taloned feet, and big batlike ears. His eyes gleam like green glass, in stark contrast to his gray-green scaly skin.

"Thanks for the floor show," I said with a sigh, studying the little doll. I had set it out on a black cloth, drawn a circle of salt around it, and surrounded it with a variety of protective stones: carnelian, lapis lazuli, Apache tear, Tiger's Eye, and hematite. "I guess you're right: it really *is* about as ugly as homemade sin."

"Ugly as a mud fence."

I smiled. Oscar had a knack for imitation, and he'd been taking note of my Texas twang and sayings, mimicking me with uncanny accuracy.

"It's so ugly," I said, "it has to sneak up on a glass of water."

"Know what?" Oscar asked with a grimace, which was his way of smiling. He looked pleased at my playing his game; I'd been in a bit of a mood since I'd come back from Betty North's house.

"What?"

"It's *sooooo* ugly it has to slap its feet to make them go to bed with it!"

"True. It's about as ugly as Grandpa's toenails."

"Ugly as ten miles of bad road!"

"Ugly as the back end of bad luck!"

We dissolved in cackles, as befits a witch with her familiar.

Still chuckling, I stood on my tiptoes to retrieve my massive leather-bound Book of Shadows from a high kitchen shelf. I set it on the counter and started to flip through the old parchment pages, so well-thumbed they felt soft as fabric.

"But I don't understand . . . why would you bring that thing in *here*?" he asked, looking at the doll askance.

"It's not charged," I said. "I'm not sure what we're dealing with, though, so I brought it here to keep it safe. I wouldn't want someone to hurt themselves accidentally."

He shook his head. "I'll never understand your fetish for humans."

"As I have explained many times, Oscar, *I'm* human. As is Aidan, and Sailor, and—"

"I mean reg-lar humans. Nonmagicals. *Cowans*."

"Some of my best friends are reg-U-lar." I pronounced the word with exaggerated care.

"I'm just sayin' . . . I don't trust 'em. Not so long ago those cowans would have burned you at the stake."

"Good thing we live in the present-day San Francisco then, right? Besides, you like Bronwyn—"

"Ooooh, the *laaaady*," crooned Oscar. Bronwyn— "the lady"—cradled Oscar to her ample bosom, which he adored.

"—and Maya—"

"Mayaaaa." Maya, at first rather averse to having what she called "livestock" in the store, had gotten in the habit of sneaking Oscar a portion of her lunch every day. The coddling had only intensified since Oscar's recent disappearance, when he had gone missing from Aunt Cora's Closet for nearly a week, driving us all insane with worry and prompting many promises of spoiling him if only he would return. The constantly hungry little guy had been eating nonstop ever since.

"—and Bronwyn and Maya are about as regular as humans get."

For the Bay Area, anyway. In other parts of the country Bronwyn and Maya might both be considered a bit "out there" but in the freewheeling Haight-Ashbury neighborhood they were positively salt-of-the-earth.

I searched my Book of Shadows. Graciela had given me the ancient tome when I was just a girl. *"This is for you, Lilita,"* she had said. *"Only for you. Learn it, trust it, and add to it; it is one of the sources of a witch's power, filled with the knowledge of her ancestors. No lo pierdas. Don't lose it!"*

Even at that young age I had understood the book's importance, and over the years I had added to the ancient spells newer ones of my own. Part recipe book, part scrapbook, it included spells, newspaper clippings, inspirational quotes, and my memories. I was unsure what I was looking for, but sometimes the book helps me out by showing me something I didn't know was there.

Not this time.

After several frustrating minutes, I slammed the book shut and started to pull the ingredients for jambalaya out of the refrigerator. I had stopped eating pork when Oscar came into my life, so I was substituting andouille chicken sausage for the traditional pork sausage called for by the classic Cajun recipe. And because I had also gotten into the habit of spoiling Oscar since his disappearance, I was going to make a side dish of cheesy garlic mashed potatoes. As far as Oscar was concerned, it wasn't dinner unless there were plenty of carbs smothered in cheese.

"You're not gonna keep that doll *here*, are you?" Oscar jumped up to sit on the edge of the counter, his favorite spot in the kitchen. From here he could "help" me cook, which mostly meant being an enthusiastic tastetester. "I mean, if your Book of Shadows doesn't say anything, that's no good at all, is it? It prob'ly means there's something wrong with it. Not our kind of magic."

He reached for the hunk of cheese I had set on the counter, but I gently slapped his hand away. He rolled his eyes.

"Good point," I said, bringing out an old wooden cutting board and the sharp knife to chop onions. "I should probably go talk to Hervé."

Oscar shivered dramatically. "I don't much care for the voodoo folk. You should ask Master Aidan."

"He's not your master anymore, remember?" I'd been giving Aidan a wide berth since our little showdown, during which I freed Oscar from him. I feared one day soon I would have to face the debt I owed that powerful witch, but so far I had been avoiding the subject. And interestingly, he had not yet come after me.

"Besides," I continued. "Hervé's a good guy. He's helped to save my butt more than once. And by extension, *your* butt."

"*Heh!* You said 'butt.'" Oscar cackled and waved his hand, as if to say *stop*.

"Your green, scaly butt," I continued.

Oscar laughed some more, and wiped his eyes. Goblin humor.

I handed him the chunk of cheese, along with a grater and a bowl. "Make yourself useful. And make sure most of that ends up in the bowl, not your stomach."

For the next half-hour, we cooked together companionably, Edith Piaf crooning in the background. Oscar kept joining in; he had been working on his impressions of both Piaf and Billie Holiday, and he wasn't bad, though he kept forgetting the lyrics. The good thing about singing along with Edith Piaf is that as long as you sounded even vaguely French you could get away with it, at least to an American audience. Lady Day's repertoire was tougher.

"Hey," I said a while later when the jambalaya was simmering gently on the stove, filling the apartment with a delicious, homey aroma. We were letting the flavors of the jambalaya mingle—my mother used to say "to marry"—and playing a game of gin rummy while we waited for Sailor.

"Do you know a woman who owns a shop in the Mission called El Pajarito?" I asked. "Her name's Ursula Moreno."

Oscar shrugged and snuck two cards, instead of one, from the top of the pile. Oscar was a terrible card cheat. Somehow this did not come as a surprise.

Sometimes I let him get away with it. Today I was not

in the mood, and fixed Oscar with the stink-eye. He gazed at me, unblinking, the picture of innocence.

"Time for another round of *Let's Make a Deal*," I said. "I'll pretend I didn't see that you just took two cards if you tell me what you know about Ursula Moreno."

Not that Moreno was any of my concern, I reminded myself. Carlos had been clear: Having checked out the store and told him as much as I was able to, my part was done. Period. End of story.

Still . . . Oscar knew an awful lot about an awful lot, and was plugged into the local magical grapevine in a way I never would be. I was finally learning to ask him outright about what he might know or might have heard, since my otherwise garrulous familiar tended to play such cards close to his chest.

"Oscar?" I prompted him.

He twisted his little muzzle, baring his teeth in a display that would have been frightening if I didn't know him. It was his thinking expression.

"Moreno's pretty good. That kid who hangs around her, though, that's her secret weapon."

"You mean Selena?"

"Like I was saying, you really should ask Maaiiister Aidan."

"I'm asking you. So, do you think Moreno is the type to get involved with fraud? Or to put her clients in harm's way?"

"Usually it's more the fortune-teller people than the *curandera* people that do that sort of thing. If I were you, I'd follow up with that doll."

"I intend to. But wait. The doll doesn't have anything to do with Moreno, does it?"

He shrugged and avoided my eyes.

"Oscar?"

He started picking at his talons, a sure sign that he

wasn't planning on talking anymore about the subject at hand. A few seconds later, he pulled another card, grimaced, and yelled, *"Gin!"*

Just then we heard the sound of boots on the stairs, and I was enveloped by the unmistakable fragrance of roses.

It was my very own gentleman caller, come to dinner.

The next morning Sailor looked at me over the plate of scrambled eggs I'd made with goat cheese and fresh herbs from my terrace garden. The kitchen was aromatic with the scents of fresh-brewed coffee—strong, with chicory— and thick slabs of buttered toast, Texas style.

"And why, pray tell, do you want to go harass an old man?"

I hadn't wanted to ruin the evening last night with talk of suspicious suicide, much less voodoo dolls. Better to broach this subject over breakfast.

"He may be an old man, but if he sculpted a voodoo doll of his beloved Betty, he could be dangerous."

"Does Romero know about this?"

I took a sip of my coffee. "Hmm?"

"I'll take that as a 'no.'"

"This isn't a homicide. At least I hope it isn't. All I have is a vague suspicion concerning a voodoo doll; it's hardly enough to bother Carlos over."

"Seems to me I've heard that line of reasoning before."

"Since when did you become such a fan of Carlos Romero?"

"I'm no fan, but the man knows homicide, and you should tell him what's going on."

"I will, if and when we discover there really *is* something going on. Maya gave me Fred's address, but she didn't have a phone number. I just want to talk with him, to be sure he wasn't involved with making that doll. Will you go with me?"

"Do I have a choice?"

"We all have choices," I said in my sweetest voice. "For instance, I have a choice regarding whom I cook for, and spend my time with, and lo— *um*, like."

Sailor fixed me with a long, smoldering look. I jumped up, practically spilling my coffee in my haste. If I didn't go downstairs to open the store right this very moment, chances were good I would get distracted and open late, as I had many times since Sailor came into my life.

I fixed an extra plate of eggs, toast, and fruit and hurried downstairs. Conrad was a friend who slept in nearby Golden Gate Park and spent a good portion of every day on the curb outside Aunt Cora's Closet. He often did small chores for me, like sweeping the sidewalk or helping me carry in heavy bags of clothes, and I tried to make sure he had breakfast at least most days.

"Good morning, Conrad. Hungry?"

"*Duuuude*," was all he said. This wasn't uncommon for Conrad—aka "the Con"— especially first thing in the morning.

I sat on the curb with him for a few minutes, pulling a turquoise polka dot sweater tighter around me against the morning chill.

"Anything new with you?" I asked.

"*Dude*."

And that was the extent of our conversation.

When Conrad had finished, I took the plate into the store and went through my morning ritual: putting cash into the register, making sure the racks were neat and tidy, spritzing the counter with white vinegar and orange oil, and then sprinkling salt water around the shop widdershins and smudging deosil with a sage bundle. Finally, I lit a white candle and chanted a quick charm of protection.

Bronwyn arrived a few minutes later, and agreed to take charge at the store in my absence. Maya would be coming in soon. She had Oscar to keep her company, and Conrad was at his post outside.

Sailor and I set off to harass an old man.

Fred's studio was sandwiched between a tile store and a plumbing supply company in a warehouse that looked like it was built in the 1930s. We weren't far from the water, and these were old working docks that still saw some maritime shipping business. Most of the freight coming in from overseas by container ship went to the massive Port of Oakland across the bay, so now China Basin mostly dealt with vessel repair and the occasional cruise ship. There was a yacht in dry dock, a stack of shipping containers, and several big rigs that needed a lot of space to park.

When Sailor and I got out of the car, we were met with the caws of seagulls, in harmony with the industrial sounds of air brakes and idling diesel engines.

"Did you know the ancient Greeks believed the caws of seagulls were the rootless souls of those lost at sea?" I asked.

"Anyone ever tell you that you are a font of fascinating yet useless information?"

"I believe I may have been accused of that once or twice in my life, yes." I laughed as we approached the office door, which stood ajar. "*Hello?* Anybody home?" I called out after rapping on the door. Each of the warehouse spaces had a regular door that led to a semifinished office, and big overhead doors that opened onto the warehouse floor.

"Maybe he's deaf," said Sailor.

I pushed the door open wider and called out again, louder: *"Hello?"*

"Maybe he's *dead*," Sailor whispered in my ear.

"Thanks so much, Sailor. You're really helping. I'm so glad I asked you along."

He grinned. "I'm just saying, given your track record it wouldn't be entirely out of left field."

"You're mixing your sports metaphors," I said, and poked my head in through the door.

"Trust you to worry about grammar when you're about to stumble upon a body. See anything worrying?"

"I don't know if it's worrying as much as . . . depressing." The "office" area was empty except for a cot in one corner, covered in a tangle of sheets and blankets. I wouldn't lay any bets on the last time those bed linens had been washed.

An open doorway led to the warehouse proper, and though it was dark, enough light streamed through the grimy windows to illuminate several easels and numerous canvases.

"Hello? Fred?" I tried one more time as I stepped into the office, then proceeded toward the warehouse.

Leaning against the wall were dozens of portraits, mostly of Betty, others of famous personages. I recognized Cary Grant and Marilyn Monroe, Jimmy Carter and Oprah Winfrey. All had the big-eyed look that was popular in paintings from the sixties.

"The blond woman is Betty North," I said.

"You're not planning on decorating Aunt Cora's Closet with any of these, are you?" asked Sailor as he crouched and flipped through a stack of unframed canvases. "I mean, I get that you have a whole retro thing going on, but these eyes are a little much. They follow you."

"We're not here to buy paintings," I said. "Just to—"

"That's too bad," said a new voice.

Sailor and I turned to see a frail-looking, elderly man with a pencil-thin mustache. He held a to-go coffee cup in one slightly shaky hand. Dressed in brown slacks, pulled up high, and a yellow-and-brown argyle cardigan, he wore camel-colored suede shoes. *Dapper* was the word that came to mind. It dawned on me that Fred was the kind of man who might well wear a brocade smoking jacket to receive guests.

"Hello," I said, belatedly realizing that we had essentially walked right into this man's home. I could feel the heat in my cheeks. "I'm so sorry. We called out but—"

He waved off my concern. "Don't worry about it. I ran down the street for coffee. I always leave the door open—you never know who might wander in. I'm Frederick Worthington. Call me Fred."

"I'm Lily Ivory, and this is my friend Sailor."

"You sail?"

"No. It's my name, not my avocation."

"I see." He set his coffee cup on a paint-splattered plank sitting atop a pair of sawhorses. "What can I do for you? You say you're not in the market for paintings?"

"No, I'm sorry—though I really do enjoy them. I saw several at the home of Betty North. I was there to buy clothes for my vintage clothing shop."

"Vintage, eh?" He shook his head. "You wait and see what it feels like when all your *normal,* everyday stuff starts being referred to as 'classic' or 'vintage.'"

I smiled.

"So, you're here about Betty, are you? What can I say about Betty . . . ?" He trailed off with a sigh.

I wasn't sure how to respond to that, so, taking a page out of Carlos's playbook, I forced myself to let silence reign.

"I miss her, you know. She was my muse."

"Your wife was a lovely woman," said Sailor, nodding at the portraits.

"We weren't married. We were together for many years, but never married. As I said, Betty was my muse." Fred fixed his watery but perceptive gaze on me. "If you're not here to buy a painting, what is it that I can help you with?"

"I was wondering if you recognized this," I said, carefully bringing the red flannel–wrapped doll out of my satchel. I placed the bundle on the workbench, untied the knot, and laid it open.

"That's . . . I don't know what that is." Fred drew away with a frown. "That's . . . disturbing. Please, I don't like looking at it. Put it away."

I covered the doll with the flannel. "So you've never seen this?"

Fred shook his head.

"Could it have been a souvenir? Maybe something from a cruise?"

"*No*." He shook his head with vehemence. "Betty . . . I remember once when we were in Haiti, she picked up a 'voodoo doll' that she thought was cute. 'Charmingly primitive,' she called it. It disturbed me, frankly, to play around with such things, and I told her so. But Betty didn't believe in that sort of thing."

"So she wasn't a client of Ursula Moreno?"

"I really don't know," he said with a shrug. "Ursula who?"

"She has a shop on Mission."

"I don't know anything about that."

"The picture of Betty that's pinned to the doll . . . it looks like a photo of one of your paintings."

He looked blank, so I unwrapped the poppet again. He glanced at it, his little mustache quivering.

Fred nodded quickly, then looked away. "Yes, that's the portrait I called *Madonna in North Beach*. I painted it after a weekend spent in San Francisco. You missed North Beach back in the late sixties—it was really something."

"I'm sure it was," I said. "And the portrait?"

"As far as I know it's still at the house, hanging in the stairwell. Unless one of her kids has moved it. I hear they're putting the house on the market."

"Her kids?"

"Betty has a son and a daughter. Her daughter came around a little, but Betty was estranged from her son. But I'm sure that won't keep them from buzzing around now. Death has a way of bringing family together, if only to fight over the spoils."

I glanced at Sailor. Sounded like Fred had some stories about the North clan.

"So you have no idea where this doll could have come from?"

"Maybe . . . could it have come from one of the home health aides? A couple of them were from other countries, though not Haiti. But I guess they're not the only ones who fool around with this sort of thing, right?"

"Do you know the names of those aides?" I asked, but Fred was already shaking his head. "Or remember where any of them came from, perhaps?"

"One was Filipina, one was Vietnamese or Cambodian, not sure. Betty's favorite was Lupita. Young woman, probably about your age. Chubby, pretty, lots of curly dark hair. Her fiancé commissioned this portrait of her." Fred walked over to an easel shrouded with a drop cloth and lifted the material to reveal a half-finished portrait of a nude woman.

I had seen her before: It was the woman in the photo at El Pajarito, the one pictured with Ursula and Selena.

"Do you know how to get in touch with Lupita?"

"No, sorry. I didn't even get a chance to finish this painting, as you can see. When Betty went to the hospital. . . .well, it was left undone. Such a pity."

Chapter 7

"He seems more broken up about his paintings than about losing Betty," I said as Sailor and I drove through the industrial streets of China Basin. "Her death apparently deprived him of a muse."

"People grieve differently."

I supposed he was right. I reminded myself not to be judgmental.

"So, here's the thing," I said. "There was a newspaper clipping featuring Ursula Moreno, her granddaughter Selena, and a woman named Lupita in the out-of-control *botanica* in the Mission. I saw it in the shop when I was there with Carlos."

"You think it's the same Lupita?"

I nodded. "The resemblance is pretty spot-on. Big eyes or no, Fred has a knack for portraiture."

"But what does Ursula Moreno's shop have to do with Betty North? I thought those were two unrelated situations."

"Yeah, funny how that happens to me, right? When it

comes to magical goings-on, I seemed to be a magnet for coincidences."

"You think Lupita's the link between them? How?"

"I have no idea, but it seems awfully interesting that Lupita would have a connection to Ursula Moreno *and* Betty North, and we found what looks like a voodoo doll in Betty's place."

"Did Moreno even deal in such things?"

"I don't know, but I saw some little hex boxes. I'll put that down on my list of things to find out."

"Suppose Moreno charged the doll with magical energy, and then Lupita brought it to Betty's house. Why would she do that? To hasten Betty's demise?"

"Maybe."

"I say again: Why? What motive would she have?"

"Money seems the most obvious motive. It might be worth looking at Betty's will, see to whom she bequeathed her earthly possessions."

"Was Betty wealthy?"

"I really don't know. But she owned a house in San Francisco; that's no doubt worth a lot, given the price of real estate in the city these days. And her house is full of stuff that might add up to some real money when it's sold. Who knows what else she might have had in the bank?"

Sailor nodded, looking out the window as though deep in thought.

"Also, Maya mentioned that shortly before her death Betty put her affairs in order and wrote up a will. It isn't unheard of for people to leave all their money to fortune-tellers."

"I thought Moreno was a *curandera*. That's a far cry from a fortune-teller."

I shrugged, unsure what to think. By all appearances Ursula was, indeed, a *curandera* . . . and a powerful one, at that. But I never quite trusted those who charged for their supernatural services. I knew a lot of magical practitioners believed that demanding remuneration for using their special talents was the only responsible thing to do. But to me, exchanging money for magic could lead a person down a very dangerous path. It was only too easy to be tempted to sell out for ever greater power. Just ask my father.

On the other hand, I might well be reading too much into it. On this topic, it was possible I had a few "issues," as they say here in California. And as Oscar once told me: *"Emotional baggage doesn't fit in the overhead compartment. You have to pay extra to check it."* Goblin wisdom.

"Anyway, it doesn't appear that poor old Fred has gained much by Betty's death."

"It's early yet," Sailor pointed out. "Probating a will takes time. No one would have received anything from her estate at this point."

"You think I'm jumping to conclusions?"

He shrugged. "I'm just saying there's still a lot of investigating to be done. And I'm not all that comfortable climbing onto the blame-the-scamming-fortune-teller bandwagon. It hits a little close to home."

Sailor was Rom, and though he kept his distance from the more colorful members of his family, I imagined this was the sort of thing he had dealt with a lot in the course of his life. I changed the subject.

"Did you *feel* anything when we were with Fred?" I asked. "Pick up any vibrations about him, good or bad?"

"Nothing in particular, but then I didn't try. I'm not supposed to be dissipating my powers with casual readings. It's part of my training with Patience."

"So, that's going well, you said?" I asked.

He nodded.

"You're seeing progress?"

"It hasn't been that long," he said.

When I first met Sailor he'd had some sort of unholy pact with Aidan Rhodes. I wasn't privy to the details of their arrangement, but knew it had resulted in enhancing Sailor's innate psychic skills to startling proportions. But once he managed to break free, Sailor's powers had been compromised. Though he had once railed against his psychic abilities, losing them had left Sailor adrift.

So I was happy that he'd found someone to help him hone his psychic skills. Still . . . last night I'd tried to wheedle a few details out of him and his monosyllabic answers—or, more aptly, nonanswers—drove me nuts. But I supposed it was like asking someone how their psychotherapy was progressing: hard to answer and bound to be a bit loaded.

"Fred brought up one good point, though," I said. "How come your name's Sailor?"

"How come *your* name's Lily?"

I shrugged. "My mom likes flowers. It's probably as simple as that. I'm just lucky she didn't name me Hyacinth or Chrysanthemum."

"You'd be a cute Hyacinth. I would call you Hya."

"Not unless you wanted me to turn you into a frog, you wouldn't."

Sailor laughed. "You little fraud, that's a Hollywood witch move. I'll bet you couldn't even pull it off."

"I could *try*."

"Anyway," Sailor continued. "I always assumed Lily was short for Lilith."

"Why would you think that?"

"Lilith was Adam's companion, before Eve. But she refused to be subjugated to the whims of her man and became a queen of demons instead, wreaking havoc on mere humans. Especially men."

"And this reminds you of *me*?"

I braked at a stoplight and looked over to see him grinning.

"Very funny." I gave him a dirty look. "But seriously, why 'Sailor'?"

Now he shrugged and remained mute.

It doesn't matter, I thought. Still, it frustrated me how closemouthed Sailor was, even about the smallest things. I knew almost nothing about his family, for instance. He knew more than he probably wanted to know about *mine*—he had had the misfortune to meet my father not long ago, and had heard a few too many stories about my mother's inability to deal with her magically precocious child, how she had sent me to live with my grandmother Graciela, and then, as a teenager, how my mother had arranged for a horrific snake-filled exorcism in an attempt to scare the witchiness clear out of me. And afterward, how I was basically run out of my hometown on a rail.

But other than meeting his aunt Renna, who disliked me, I knew nothing about Sailor's people. I knew very little about Sailor's personal history, either, other than one fateful car accident, and Sailor's bargain with Aidan to save the life of the wife who would later divorce him.

Sailor and I were enamored of each other, but we were entering an awkward phase in our relationship. I was getting the idea that he might be just as clueless as I was when it came to romance. The two of us could keep the self-help relationship aisle of a book superstore going strong.

If only there were advice books for the supernaturally endowed.

"So what's next?" Sailor asked.

"I'm thinking about going by Hervé's place to ask him about the poppet I found at Betty's house."

"Good idea. Also, I think you should call Romero and let him know about the connection between Betty North and El Pajarito."

"Will do. Want to come with me to Hervé's?"

"I'll come if you think you need me, but I imagine even *you* will be safe enough with Hervé. Besides, I'm supposed to meet Patience at noon."

"Why don't I drop you off, then? Where to?"

I followed his directions to the corner of Folsom and Pine, and pulled up in front of an old Victorian painted a dove gray with creamy trim. A large bay window was shrouded by deep blue curtains studded with gold metallic stars and moons.

A blue-and-yellow neon sign in the window read:

Patience Blix, Palm–Crystal Ball–Tarot Readings.

Love, Money, Health

Learn the Secrets to Happiness!

Speaking of charlatans conning gullible folks out of their money, Patience Blix's lair was straight out of a B movie. No wonder Sailor had been so defensive about fortune-telling scams.

"What?" he demanded, studying my attempted poker face.

"Doesn't this look a little . . . cheesy to you?"

"It's all in your point of view." Leaning over to give me a quick kiss good-bye, he graced me with a smile and gently tugged my ponytail. "To me, it looks like family."

He climbed out of the car and I practically had to sit on my hands to keep from begging him to invite me inside to meet the mysterious Patience Blix.

Sailor mounted the front steps, let himself in without knocking, and disappeared behind a sturdy indigo door.

*   *   *

I headed for Madame Detalier's Voodoo Supply Shop.
Hervé's store was located in the Mission, only a few city
blocks from El Pajarito.

Hervé was a good friend and a talented voodoo practitioner who would probably be able to tell me something about the ugly little doll. Also, I could use his
phone to call Carlos and let him know what I had found
at Betty North's house. Sailor was right to suggest that I
let the homicide inspector know what was going on, and
I don't carry a cell phone because the vibrations weird
me out. It's a witch thing.

I focused on maneuvering the city's congested streets,
trying to ignore the strange feeling in the pit of my stomach that had been there since dropping Sailor off at his
cousin's house. But it wouldn't be denied.

Was this a premonition? A supernatural warning of
some sort? Or was I just hungry?

Jealousy, came the unbidden thought.

What I was feeling wasn't supernatural at all. It was
the entirely ordinary, and not terribly admirable, sensation of jealousy.

But why? I had no reason to worry. Patience Blix was
Sailor's cousin; probably she looked a lot like his aunt
Renna, well-rounded and middle-aged. Besides, she was
training him and helping him to grow. Sailor had been so
unhappy, unable to draw upon the powers he once
wielded. A man adrift. This training was good for him, and
what was good for him was good for our relationship.

I just wished he would tell me more about what he
was thinking, feeling.

Just listen to yourself, Lily. As I waited while the taxi in
front of me disgorged its passengers, I nearly laughed out
loud. I had spent a lifetime keeping my secrets to myself,
hiding my thoughts and my soul from everyone around

me. Apparently I had been soaking up my adopted region's obsession with self-disclosure, California-style.

And besides . . . Sailor was who he was. He seemed to be happier with me than he had been on his own — evidenced by the fact that he actually smiled and even laughed from time to time — but he was still a taciturn, cynical man. Probably always had been, and always would be. Not only was it unreasonable to expect him to become a Sensitive New Age Guy, but would I even truly want him to? If I cared for him, shouldn't I accept him just as he was?

Better, by far, for each of us to remain true to ourselves and to keep our thoughts safely tucked away. It was the time-honored way of magical folk.

I found a parking spot within a few blocks of Madame Detalier's, and made my way through a sidewalk crowded with hipsters with sculpted facial hair, wearing skinny jeans and chic eyewear, coffee drinks and iPods in their hands.

From the outside, Hervé's shop looked like many on Haight Street: The front window displayed an innocuous collection of various statuettes, embroidered runners, and inlaid pipes. But inside, the ceiling was hung with carved gourds and brightly painted wooden animals. There was an extensive collection of molded body parts, skulls and bones, as well as wax-sealed bottles with mysterious contents, and candles in every color of the rainbow.

A horned creature with a human body and a goatlike head had pride of place in one corner, a pentagram carved on his forehead. At its feet were several lit votive candles, along with a jar of flowers, a croissant on a little plate, a cup of still-steaming coffee, and a large bag of dried pinto beans.

It reminded me of the shrine to Santa Muerte in Ursula's shop window.

Behind the counter stood Hervé's wife, Caterina. She was an elegant woman with traditional blue-dot tattooing across her brow, and in spirals on her smooth cheeks. Today she was wearing a brown and cream mud-cloth dashiki, and her long dreadlocks were tied up in a purple and yellow batik scarf.

"Hi, Caterina, how are you?"

"You're looking for Hervé?"

"Yes, thanks," I said with my best version of a friendly smile. "How'd you guess?"

She looked me over with cool disdain. Caterina didn't like me very much. I couldn't imagine she was jealous in any way—Hervé was a devoted husband and father to their twin boys. But *something* about me set her on edge. A while back, some antiwitchcraft folks had mixed up voodoo with my kind of magic and had vandalized the shop. Perhaps she blamed me for it.

Fortunately, I was accustomed to being disliked. As a witch growing up in a small West Texas town, I had learned at a young age that people were much more likely to spurn me than to embrace me. Still . . . although I could understand this reaction from those who didn't know any better, it hurt when it came from other practitioners.

"They've been expecting you," she said. I noticed the glint of a delicate gold cross on a chain around her neck as she ducked through the bead curtain into the back office.

I waited by the register, wondering about the cross she wore. It had always struck me as odd, given her surroundings. Could Caterina be unhappy running a voodoo supply shop? I had always assumed she shared Hervé's beliefs, but perhaps I had been wrong. Really, I knew nothing about her. Maybe, in my effort to stop judging people and make more friends, I should invite her out to lunch one of these days. . . .

Hervé emerged from the back, a huge smile lighting up his face. He was a powerfully built man, with a rugby player's physique.

"Lily! Always such a pleasure. I was so happy to hear you found your pig."

"Thank you. Me, too. Things were a little rocky there for a bit."

"And you? You are well?"

"Fit as a fiddle."

"I'm pleased to hear it. What can I do for you today?"

I pulled the red flannel bundle from my bag and set in on the counter. Hervé slowly folded back the material.

He stared at the ugly little doll for a long moment, then looked at me, eyebrows raised.

"What can you tell me about it?" I asked.

"It's a poppet."

"Yes, thanks. I knew that much. But . . . have you ever seen it before? Would there be, I don't know, some sort of signature of the person who made it? Anything like that?"

"I'm a voodoo priest, Lily, not a DNA expert."

I stared at it, feeling let down. I knew it was a long shot, but I'd been hoping Hervé might be able to tell me something about it.

Finally he splayed his big hands about twelve inches above the doll and held them there. Breathing deeply through his nostrils, he rolled his eyes back in his head, his eyelids fluttering and lips moving in a silent incantation. After almost a full minute he slowly lowered his hands and placed them on the poppet.

After another moment he shook his head and opened his eyes.

"Anything?" I asked.

"It doesn't feel charged." He picked up the doll without using the cloth and turned it over in his hands, studying the worked wax.

"Can you tell if it ever was charged? Would there be a leftover hum, or anything . . . ?" I trailed off lamely.

"It might have been at one time, can't really tell. Now it's just a lump of wax. It means nothing."

"Wax with *pins* in it."

"People always seem to think the pins are menacing. Originally, pins were simply used to fasten a picture or personal items of the target to the doll, to link them. They aren't necessarily sinister."

"You sure?" I asked, skeptical.

"Lily, one of these days you're going to have to get over your inordinate fear of poppets. You can use them in your system just as well as I can in mine."

I shook my head. "They're creepy."

He gestured with the doll in one large hand. "The poppet itself is a vessel, it's not inherently good or bad. It's all about the intent. So-called 'voodoo dolls' are mostly used for curing. The photo is placed on the object to guide the spell; the pins are there to hold the photo in place, not necessarily to inflict harm. They may be no more threatening than a piece of scotch tape."

"You're saying the doll could be a positive object? Not an attempt to harm the target?"

"I really can't say for sure because I don't know what the person who fashioned the poppet intended. But neither do you. Without more information we don't even know if the doll has any significance. It could simply be someone's toy, a souvenir."

"I wondered about that."

"In my system, when the spirits are angry or disgruntled, they appear red-eyed. When the red-eyed spirit accompanies you, things are bad. But I don't feel that with this doll. I don't feel anything at all."

"Okay, thanks for looking at it." I wrapped the doll up and returned it to my bag. "I really appreciate your expertise."

"And here I thought you were going to ask me about what's going on at El Pajarito."

"You've added mind-reading to your services?" I joked. "That was my next question. Do you know Ursula?"

"Of course. The Mission is like a small town; we're all up in each other's business. The news of her arrest spread pretty quickly."

"Do you know anything about what's happening at her shop?"

"What *is* happening at the shop? Was it vandalized? I looked in the windows and saw a huge mess."

"Things are going haywire. It's as if . . . almost like everything's charged and acting of its own accord. It's really odd. I tried to read the vibrations, but they were chaotic, too difficult to get a handle on. Any ideas?"

He shook his head slowly, as though deep in thought.

"Do you know anyone who might want to make Ursula look bad? Did she have any enemies?"

"Plenty," he said with a broad smile. "Does this surprise you? This business can be rather cutthroat, after all."

"I've always stayed away from *curanderas*, except for my own grandmother, of course. I'm not familiar with the politics."

"Well, let's just say Ursula has more than a few rivals who would have been pleased to hear of her arrest."

"Anyone in particular?"

"I'd better write you a list."

"That many?"

He rolled his eyes. "You know how this sort of thing is, Lily. But you might check with Aidan to see if he's sensed a rogue witch."

I played with a small bottle of *van-van* oil from a display on the counter. "Um . . . Aidan and I . . . well, we aren't talking much these days."

"No?"

"We had something of a falling-out over my familiar. Not to mention the whole thing with Sailor."

I read sympathy in his dark eyes. "Relationships are hard."

"Aidan and I don't have a relationship. I mean, not like that."

"I was referring to you and Sailor," he said, looking amused. "Anyway, if you're avoiding Aidan you should run along. He's—"

"Right here," said Aidan as he ducked through the beaded curtain.

Chapter 8

I reared back and grabbed my medicine bag. My heart pounded as my mind cast about; there were a couple of jars of all-purpose protective brew in my satchel, but such magical devices wouldn't go far with someone as powerful as Aidan Rhodes.

Besides, I was more of a brew-alone-in-my-kitchen-type witch, not so great in an unexpected, throw-down situation.

Caterina's words finally registered: "They've been expecting you." *They*. I should have known. Where was my witchy intuition when I needed it? Still, when it came to Aidan my already dubious intuition wasn't worth a plugged nickel anyway. He threw my senses off, put me in a tizzy.

I didn't want even to imagine the consequences of a serious confrontation between the two of us. Indeed, I had been avoiding that line of thought ever since I had defied him and stolen a valuable object from him in order to free Oscar.

"You look pale, Lily. Are you quite all right?" Aidan asked.

Only then did I realize I was cowering beside Hervé. My voodoo buddy was looking down at me with an amused, bewildered look on his face.

"Sure, I'm just peachy," I said as I lifted my chin and stepped away from Hervé. Might as well face the music. "And you?"

"Oh, I'm peachy, as well," Aidan said with a smile. "It's always so lovely to see you. And I do adore that frock."

Today's getup was a shell-top dress from the fifties, with an azure-and-violet-painted floral design. The flowing skirt was meant to be worn over a crinoline, but that seemed a bit much for my personal style, so I simply let it fall and enjoyed the feeling of it wrapping around my legs as I walked. Happily for me—especially given the way my day was going so far—whoever had owned the garment before me had imbued it with positive vibrations.

"I take it you're here in an official capacity?" Aidan asked.

"Sort of." Two could play at this game. If Aidan was going to act as though nothing had happened, I certainly wasn't going to complain. And now that I had a moment to think about it, I realized Aidan would never attack me in front of Hervé. In fact, his revenge would no doubt be much subtler and more destructive than a simple magical match. It would be the kind of thing that would sneak up and bite me when I least expected. "Have you heard anything about what's going on at Ursula Moreno's shop, El Pajarito?"

"I know something's amiss."

"Could you be more specific?"

"What concerns me is twofold: First, the mayor's on

the warpath about fortune-telling scams and the like. It's caused quite the kerfuffle in the community."

"Kerfuffle?" I asked.

"There's a lot of finger-pointing. One might even say there's a bit of a witch-hunt vibe."

"You can't get the mayor to back off?"

"How would you suggest I do that?"

"I thought he was in your back pocket."

"Why, Lily, I am flattered that you imagine me to have so much influence. I assure you, it is not the case."

I didn't believe him. I once had spotted the mayor in Aidan's office. At the time Aidan had insisted it meant nothing, but I suspected there was much more to it than that. Controlling a politician behind the scenes, puppetmasterlike, seemed right up Aidan's alley.

But for now I let it go. "And what's the other thing that's worrying you?"

"This isn't something many people feel entirely comfortable discussing," said Aidan, flashing a look at Hervé. "But it's possible that there are some . . . mental health issues in the magical community."

"Mental health issues? Like what?"

"The same as afflicts the greater society: depression, anxiety, OCD, ADHD."

"There's no shame in that. After all, this isn't the 1950s; there's help available."

"*I* realize that, and *you* realize that, and even our friend *Hervé* here realizes that."

Hervé cupped his hands over his heart. "Gee, I appreciate your confidence," he said with a sarcastic tone.

"But as a group . . ." Aidan trailed off with a shrug. "We're twenty years behind the larger society in this one area."

"By 'we' you mean . . ."

"The magical community, for want of a better word.

As you can imagine, if someone with magical abilities starts losing touch with reality things can get ugly, fast."

I remembered an elderly friend of my grandmother's back in Jarod, a gentle soul whose descent into senility caused her to magically light fires. Mostly little things—a single match, a small notepad, a leaf—but still. If she hadn't been watched over, she could have taken down the town.

"So you're suggesting what's happening in El Pajarito could be the result of a practitioner with mental illness?"

"Hard to say. It's also possible this thing with Ursula is something else entirely, an infection of some sort that is moving through magical businesses."

"That sounds even worse."

"Indeed."

"Couldn't it be the work of another witch? Someone gone rogue who's got it out for Ursula?"

His beautiful features shifted. Aidan fancied himself the godfather of the magical folks in the Bay Area—with the notable exceptions of Hervé and yours truly, neither of whom recognized Aidan's authority—and he didn't like to think one of "his" people might have gone off the reservation.

I tried a different approach. "Do you know a woman named Lupita, who might have been working with Ursula?"

He shook his head. "Not really. But Ursula had relatives helping in the store occasionally; it wasn't unusual."

"Speaking of relatives, what about the girl, Selena? Do you think she could be with Lupita?"

Aidan and Hervé shared a significant look.

"What?" I asked. "Am I missing something?"

"I saw her the other day," Hervé said in a low voice. "Selena came running in and hid under the altar cloth, right over there. Clearly terrified, but she wouldn't tell me why. I tried to find Ursula, of course, but apparently she'd already been arrested; the shop was closed. I felt.... Caterina and I decided to keep her here with us instead of turning her over to Family and Children Services."

"Selena's *here*? Could I speak with her?"

He shook his head. "I'm sorry, but she spent only one night, then ran away the next day without ever saying a word. Caterina feels terrible about it. She's angry with me for not calling the authorities, making sure Selena was safe."

"And why didn't you call them?"

"I was afraid they wouldn't be able to handle her. Selena is . . . different."

"Different in what way?"

"She reminds us a little of you," Aidan said. The gentleness in his voice was disconcerting. I met his eyes, and the apparently sincere concern in those blue depths was even more so. I remembered Oscar saying: *"The girl's the secret weapon."*

Forcing my attention back to the issue at hand, I said, "In that case, the average social worker couldn't have stopped her anyway. I think you were right to assume she wouldn't do well in the system."

Hervé shrugged. "Still, I should have made sure she was secured. I've checked in with everyone I can think of she might have known, or trusted. But as I said, Ursula isn't exactly popular around here. I think I was probably the closest thing she had to a friend in the neighborhood. I assume that's why Selena came here . . . though I wish I knew why she didn't stay."

"If she's powerful, she can probably take care of herself better than the average young teen on the street." At least I hoped so. Unless one was properly trained, having magical powers could cause more problems than they solved. "So, no idea where she might have gone?"

He shook his head. "Caterina and I have been racking our brains."

"Do you remember the last thing you said to her?"

He took a moment, then shook his head slowly. "Nothing, really. I remember telling her Caterina and I were going to be babysitting my niece's daughter. I thought Selena might enjoy meeting the baby."

"And?"

He shrugged. "And that was it. Next thing I knew, she was gone."

"So maybe she doesn't like babies?" I let out a frustrated breath. It wasn't much to go on. It wasn't anything, really. How did a person find one girl in a vast city like this? I turned to Aidan. "You can't get a feel for her, somewhere, somehow?"

"I've tried. I believe she's cloaked. I don't know whether it was her doing or Ursula's, but she's not as easy to track as another might be."

"Dangitall," I said, shaking my head as I glanced at the list of names Hervé had given me. "I guess there's nothing to do now but to speak to some of these folks. They might know something, I suppose. I swear, it's like puttin' socks on a rooster."

Hervé and Aidan shared an amused glance.

"What?"

"Your Texan comes out when you're peeved."

"Well, then, best shine up the Lone Star 'cause I'm feelin' mighty peeved. Thanks, Hervé, for the help. Please tell Caterina good-bye for me. Aidan . . ." I let that last trail off, and just nodded. "I'll let you all know if I learn anything from these folks."

"I'll go with you," said Aidan.

"No need," I said.

"Happy to do it."

"I'd rather go alone."

Our gaze held. He smiled a slow, knowing smile.

"I don't *need* you," I insisted.

"Sure about that?"

Hervé's gaze shifted from me to Aidan and back again, as though watching a tennis match.

"Fine," I said, giving in to the inevitable. "Tag along if you must. But *I'm* doing the questioning."

"You're the boss."

When pigs fly, I thought.

We headed to the first *botanica* on Hervé's list.

Aidan moved along the crowded sidewalks with an elegant glide, gracefully dodging other pedestrians and bestowing a pleasant smile upon all he passed. His golden hair glinted in the bright afternoon sunshine; his eyes were a piercing periwinkle blue. A strong jaw and a hint of manly stubble kept Aidan from looking *too* pretty. He was stunning, was what he was. Most women—and a handful of men—gawked and a few even came to a stand-still to watch as he walked by.

But I knew it was a facade, the result of a glamour Aidan cast to hide his true appearance. Years ago he had been disfigured by fire during a battle with a demon, and now rarely went out in public. I didn't know if he had been this good-looking before his injuries, or if he had embellished a bit, but in any case his appearance was only part of his appeal. Aidan's aura was so glittery that even those who weren't sensitive could feel it.

Love him or hate him, there was no denying that Aidan was extraordinary.

But maintaining the glamour cost him a lot of energy, especially during the day. It was easier at night, when the portals are open wider, allowing magical folk to more easily call on our ancestors for assistance. It was rare to see Aidan walking around in the afternoon sunshine.

Finding Selena must be important.

About half a block down, we entered Botanica Suerte. The shop's interior was similar to El Pajarito: The jammed shelves held rows of candles, cans of various sprays, bags of herbs, packets of tiny charms.

Aidan and I hung back and watched as a tiny gray-haired customer selected two candles, one labeled "health," the other "fortune," and carried them to the front counter. The woman sitting behind the register, her black hair in a thick braid on top of her head, picked up a sharp pencil and drilled deep holes into the soft candle wax. She grabbed a bottle of essential oil and poured a thin stream onto the candle, rotating it in circles while chanting under her breath.

While we waited, we checked out the store's merchandise, feeling for sensations, errant or otherwise. If this thing with Ursula really was some kind of infection moving through magical businesses, we should be able to sense it. In any case, it was important to remain on guard.

In each corner of Botanica Suerte was an altar. Offerings of roses, fruit, and candy surrounded statues of saints. Candles flickered. As we watched, another customer laid two oranges and a full bottle of rum at the feet of St. Sebastian, knelt, and said a prayer.

"People give offerings of fruits, flowers, and honey to sweeten the paths of those who believe in the saints," explained the proprietor when she spotted me. "The flowers are for having a good life path, protection, health, money, love; it represents peace and tranquility among the family. What can I do for you?"

Her eyes widened as Aidan stepped out from behind a display.

"*Señor Rhodes, perdóneme,*" she begged forgiveness in Spanish. "I didn't see you there—I am so nearsighted in my old age. How are you? What honor brings you to my store?"

"This is my friend, Lily Ivory," said Aidan.

She nodded at me, but we did not shake hands. This wasn't unusual. Sometimes physical contact is a bit more than we magical folks can take.

"Lily and I are looking into the situation at El Pajarito," Aidan continued. "What can you tell us?"

She shrugged and eyed a pair of young women absorbed in reading the contents on the packets of herbs. Their heads were bent low, and they were paying so little attention to us I assumed Aidan had cast a cocooning spell to keep our conversation private.

"You know Ursula Moreno, of course," Aidan said.

She nodded.

"Come now, Maria. No need to be coy."

She waved her hand dismissively. "I don't even know what that means."

Aidan fixed her with an intense gaze and cast her a soul-melting grin. Maria seemed to relax.

"Of course I know Ursula. She undercuts me on *limpias*, cleansings, offering to do them ten dollars cheaper, no matter how much I reduce my price." Resentment rang in her words. "Also, she says her readings are better than mine."

"Ursula Moreno did readings?" I asked. This was news.

"Not her, that girl."

"Selena?" I asked.

Maria nodded. "She's a very . . . *special* girl."

"Do you know where I might find her?"

She shook her head.

"What about Lupita?"

Maria's eyes narrowed. "Lupita's not to be trusted. She only came to Ursula when she needed money. That's all she ever wanted, a sweet little pair of shoes, a new car, a nicer place to live. She even dragged a reporter in here one time. I'm sure to make money."

"The reporter paid her?"

"Lupita never did anything unless there was something in it for her, so I bet she got paid somehow."

"Do you remember the name of the reporter?"

She shrugged. "It started with an M."

"Michael? Mark? Matthew?" I suggested.

"Malcolm? Malachi? Maxwell?" Aidan said.

"That is the one!" Maria said.

"Which one?" I asked.

"Mac . . . no, Max. Max something."

A part of me froze. I knew a Max who was a reporter for the *San Francisco Chronicle*.

"Max *Carmichael*?" I asked.

She nodded. "That could be it."

"What did he look like?"

"*Guapo*. Handsome. Tall, dark. Light eyes."

Not long after I'd arrived in San Francisco, Max Carmichael and I had gone out a few times. It was a short affair, but burned brightly in my memory, perhaps because, other than my relationship with Sailor, I didn't have much to compare it to.

But Max had been on my mind since I realized the parallels between the suicide of Nicky Utley and Max's wife, who had killed herself after a psychic told her to go off her meds. Was this yet another coincidence?

"Let's get back to the point," Aidan said. "Have you noticed anything off about your merchandise?"

She shook her head. "No, all is normal."

"And how about the city officials?" I jumped in. I'd made a big deal about being the one to ask the questions, after all. "Has anyone been in to ask you about fortune-telling? Maybe talked to you about practicing medicine without a license, for example?"

"They've been checking everyone's credentials, and warning us. But I don't 'practice medicine,' as you say. A lot of my clients, they go to the regular doctor but the doctor can't help with what ails them. They have to look for help elsewhere, so they come to me."

"And you tend to them."

"With plants, and prayer, and *lo que quien sabe . . .* what one knows, with who knows what."

"And Ursula did the same, as far as you know?"

"Not as well, but yes, about the same."

"You didn't know her to have any sort of . . . special powers? For good or for ill?"

"As I said, she offered services like I did, and tried to give them away cheaper. But when it comes down to it"—she shrugged and seemed to speak grudgingly—"I suppose Ursula should not be in jail any more than I should."

"What do you know about Santeria?" I asked as Aidan and I walked to the next store on the list Hervé had given us.

"It's essentially a mix of Catholicism and the Yoruba religion, brought to the Caribbean by West African slaves. It spread throughout many Latin American countries in the nineteenth century, and is pretty common among Latino communities here in the U.S."

"I've heard of it, of course, and I've seen people leaving offerings and that sort of thing. But I didn't know it was used in curing."

"Like most belief systems," Aidan explained, "it is concerned with the health of the community, both physical and mental."

"That makes sense. So, other than the fact that Ursula was a fierce competitor, did that interview tell us anything?"

"Not that I could tell. What's the next shop on the list?"

"Botanica de Mercedes."

"Sounds like a car dealership."

"Mercedes means 'mercies' in Spanish."

He chuckled. "I know that. I believe I speak better Spanish than you do, my friend. I lived in Bolivia for five years."

"When was this? How did I not know that?"

"Perhaps because you've never really taken the time to get to know me," he said, looking at me with an odd smile on his face.

This was true. Though circumstances frequently brought us together—in fact, Aidan may have saved my life more than once—I didn't really know him. But neither did I trust him. And I knew that, despite his smiles, he was furious with me at the moment. He was such a good actor it would be easy to be lulled into a false sense of security.

Botanica de Mercedes appeared marginally more up- scale than the others. Its sign was professionally lettered, the name repeated in gold gilt on the window. The front display was more organized, the windowpanes freshly washed. A woman stood in the doorway shooing away a pair of tourists who were trying to take a picture of the shop.

"It's bad luck!" she exclaimed. *"Mala suerte."*

They apologized and hurried off.

"Bad luck?" Aidan asked as we approached.

"Of course," she said, her chin raising a notch. "Hello, Aidan. You must know this, it is bad luck to have your picture taken without the proper preparation. I don't like when the tourists or reporters come around here with their cameras. It's foolish to invite bad luck into one's life like that."

Aidan introduced me to Yasmin, and I reluctantly ad- mitted to myself that having him along on this expedi- tion was helpful.

We entered the store, which shared inventory with the others of its ilk. The walls of the shop were lined with rows and rows of prepackaged herbal blends. They were all marked with labels declaring, in a sloppy handwriting, their different purposes: one to attract money, another to keep away meddlesome neighbors, yet another to increase luck in love.

I noticed half a dozen silver spoons hanging from a row of hooks. It looked almost like the old-fashioned spoons people used to bring back from their travels. I remembered seeing such a collection in Betty North's living room.

"Pretty spoons."

"Magic holders. You've heard of dream catchers? It's like that. The silver, you see how shiny it is? As the magic dissipates, the tarnish returns."

"And then you just polish it again, and that brings more magic?"

She laughed. "As though magic were that easy to come by. It must be cleaned by a professional, someone who knows what she's doing."

"And I take it you do?"

"For a small fee."

"Of course."

"But mostly, I deal in herbs. The best in town. Some I grow in my backyard, others I gather at the Presidio or Golden Gate Park where they grow wild. It's hard to find some of the plants I knew from my home, in El Salvador, so I have my sister-in-law ship me things."

"Isn't it illegal to ship plants and seeds into the U.S.?"

She glared at me. Aidan looked amused. A long moment of silence passed.

"Sorry," I said. "What kinds of plants?"

"*Chichipince* is good for problems with your stomach, or your woman parts. It's really good for that, but they don't have it here. Here they have some things, like chamomile and basil and rue. If you have bad energy, I treat you with peppermint and garlic and chamomile and lemon balm. *Epazote* helps people with gassy stomachs."

"I put it in black bean soup," said Aidan. "I thought it was just for flavor, but maybe it works twofold."

"You cook?" Yasmin asked. "A good-looking man like you?"

A smile was his only response.

"I grew up watching my aunt," continued Yasmin. "Someone would come to her with a broken bone, a foot that was *chueco*, or twisted. She would grind her herbs with a mortar and pestle and mix them with an egg, then rub it on their foot and they'd be cured. Now *I* am the curer. I do purification ceremonies to clear plants of negative energy before giving the herbs to clients. I spray them with *agua florida*, made with orange flower, rose, lavender, and other herbs, and cleanse them with a little rum.

"Plants can retain positive or negative energy from humans. They are living things. If you talk to them and show them affection a tiny plant will grow large and healthy. If you forget about them, neglect them, they will shrivel up and die. An herb is energy, it needs part of your energy."

I thought of my friend Calypso, whose relationship to plants was very much like what Yasmin described: giving and intimate, as a parent loves a child.

"Sometimes you go to the doctor and don't feel well and the doctor does all those tests. They use all their technology to stick you, but still they say they can find nothing wrong," Yasmin continued. "But you know better, because you are not right. These are the people I can cure."

"What can you tell us about Ursula Moreno?"

"I told her it was bad luck to talk to a reporter. One should never allow one's photograph to be taken in a magical context. Some jealous practitioner will use the image against you." She raised her chin in my direction. "I'm sure you know this much, no?"

Not long after opening my store, an article about me ran in the Living section of the *San Francisco Chronicle*. Ever since, I had been involved in some pretty gnarly situations. Maybe Yasmin was onto something.

"Anyway," Yasmin continued, "my practice is all about health. A lot of our people, they don't have good medical care, don't have doctors they trust even if they have the money. I'm all about keeping people healthy."

"And Ursula wasn't?" I asked.

"She was . . . but she was about other things, as well. Negative things. And she thinks her spells were better than mine, more powerful. Lupita came over here to brag, said Ursula was great at *limpias*. Did one for the house of an old lady, claimed she was in line for a fortune now."

"What old lady? Do you have a name?"

She shrugged and shook her head.

"What about her granddaughter, Selena? Any idea where she might be?"

"No, and good riddance. She scares me."

Aidan and I exchanged glances, and silently agreed to move on. We thanked Yasmin for her time and left to try a few more of the names on the list. Everyone we talked to told us some variation of the same thing: Ursula Moreno undercut them with clients, her young charge Selena was "special," and no one had any idea where the girl was now. The opinion of Lupita, meanwhile, was uniformly unflattering. Clearly the staff of El Pajarito needed to work a little on their neighborly relations.

"How about a drink?" proposed Aidan after we heard

essentially the same story from yet another disgruntled shopkeeper.

I glanced at my antique Tinkerbell watch. "It's barely four o'clock."

"Then it's well past time in New York."

I wasn't sure I followed his logic, but since I was hot and frustrated, it was good enough for me. I was ready for a break.

"Where did you have in mind?"

"I know just the place. Follow me."

Chapter 9

Somehow I expected a posh wine bar, or maybe a newly trendy Sinatra-era cocktail lounge. Instead, Aidan led me to a side street where we slipped into a dive bar that could have been snatched whole off the streets of Tijuana. Ranchero music blared from an old-fashioned jukebox, and men in boots and cowboy hats played a lazy game of pool, beers in their hands, razzing each other in Spanish.

Aidan ordered chips and salsa and margaritas from an unsmiling woman behind the counter. We took our seats at a small laminate table in a back corner.

"You come here often?" I asked, looking around.

"Trying to pick me up? No need, I'm yours for the asking."

I took a gulp of my margarita, avoiding his eyes and trying to decide how to handle the man in front of me. We had some serious unfinished business, but if he was going to act like nothing had happened, I supposed I should play along. Still, it put me on edge.

"How have you been, Lily?" he asked.

"Oh, fine, thank you."

"You're not feeling any ill effects from your last magical battle?"

"No."

"You're sure."

"Absolutely."

"And all your friends? Is Oscar still with you?"

"Of course he's still with me. By *choice*, not forced obligation."

He just grinned at me. "Hey, *I'm* the one who was trespassed against. You destroyed my marker, took a perfectly good helper out from under my influence. And do you hear me grumbling?"

Okay, maybe we *were* going to talk about this.

"Listen, Aidan, I'm sorry about—"

He held up one hand, palm-out, and shook his head. This was how things work in the magical community: There were no apologies, but favors and trespasses were committed on a strictly *quid pro quo* basis. I had known that when I stole from Aidan, but in the moment I had been so focused on saving Oscar that I hadn't cared.

"I know I owe you," I said quietly.

"You better believe it. But let's put that aside for the moment and focus on the situation at hand. Unfortunately, before the Oscar debacle you also deprived me of a nicely beholden psychic. Speaking of whom, how do you suppose Sailor will feel when he finds out your old boyfriend Mack is back on the scene?"

"Max, not Mack. And Max was never really my boyfriend."

"What do you suppose your current boyfriend will make of that?"

"None of your business."

"So, the arrival of Mark on the scene—"

"*Max*, as you very well know."

"Right, that's what I said."

"And he's hardly arrived on the scene—I haven't seen him in forever."

"Lily, Lily, Lily." Aidan shook his head. "I don't have to be a fortune-teller to predict you're going to look him up soon, given his involvement in this situation."

I shrugged. Aidan already knew more than he should, no need to fill him in on my plans.

"And how is Sailor? I hear he's training with Patience Blix."

I nodded.

"That's a bit of a coup. She's really something."

"So I hear."

"I have to say, I admire your attitude. A lot of women wouldn't be happy about their boyfriends spending time with a woman like Patience."

"What do you mean, 'a woman like Patience'?"

One lifted eyebrow was his only response.

"What?" I demanded.

"I take it you haven't met her?"

I shrugged and quite literally bit my tongue in an effort to appear nonchalant. "Anyway, it doesn't matter. I mean, she's his cousin, after all."

"Of course."

"Right. Let's get this conversation back to what's important here and now. What's the game plan— where do we go from here?"

"I'll try to find out what's up with the mayor, since I have it on good authority that I'm the power behind the municipal throne and all."

I glared at him.

"And I'll put out some more feelers and see if I can get a lead on Selena, but I'm not optimistic on that score. Say, you know who's great at reading the crystal ball?"

"I'm afraid to ask."

"Patience Blix. But she's also a master at cold reading, so keep your wits around her."

I could feel myself doing something funny with my mouth. "Just . . . see if you can find anything. If there's still nothing on Selena by tomorrow, I'll see if Sailor will ask Patience to help. But to take another angle on all this: Do you know anything about the death of Nicky Utley?"

"Only that it seemed to be the catalyst for the arrest of Ursula Moreno, and thus the disappearance of Selena."

"What's so special about Selena? Is it just that she's magically gifted?"

"Very much so."

"Is that how you know about her? You keep track of such things?"

"Yes, of course," he said dryly. "I have an Excel spreadsheet on my laptop that I update daily."

"You know what I mean."

"As you know very well, I try to help organize the magical community."

I did, at that. I just could never quite figure out why. Was Aidan working for good, or for ill? Were his ambitions selfish, or for the greater good? And with a talented child like Selena . . . was he trying to protect her, or to exploit her?

Unfortunately, I didn't know how to broach those questions with Aidan. Not that he was likely to tell me the truth, even if I did. So I asked a different question.

"Do you think Nicky Utley's suicide was significant in some way? I mean, why jump off the Golden Gate Bridge?"

"They say the Golden Gate Bridge is the number one suicide destination in the world."

"'Suicide destination'? That's a thing?"

"Apparently. Three months after opening in 1935, a veteran was the first known jumper, and since then there have been something like 1500 deaths off the bridge. And that's just the ones that get counted."

"Why aren't they all counted?"

"A Coast Guard cutter fishes the bodies out of the water, but the currents are so strong there's no guarantee they find them all. And it happens fast; it only takes about four seconds to fall from the bridge to the water. If no one's around . . ."

"How do you know so much about this?"

He shrugged. "I fancy myself a bit of a local historian. And I'm as fascinated with the Golden Gate Bridge as the next person."

"Doesn't the bridge have cameras or surveillance equipment?"

"Not for most of the span. Most of the suicides occur at the middle of the bridge, which as you can imagine is the most majestic spot. Right there between San Francisco and Marin, between the wild of the Pacific Ocean and the calmness of the bay. It's . . . iconic."

I nodded and took a sip of my drink.

"Anyway, the only time there was a camera recording that spot was in 2004."

"What happened in 2004?"

"A documentary film crew recorded the bridge every day for a year. I guess the parks commission thought it was granting a permit for a film about the history of the bridge, not realizing it would end up being a documentary about suicide. The footage caught images of a number of people jumping. It's . . . chilling."

"I'll bet."

A moment of silence passed.

"Funding was approved not long ago for a more effective barrier, but it will take a while to make the changes."

"But if a suicidal person can't kill themselves on the bridge, won't they just go elsewhere to accomplish it?"

"Apparently it's an attractive nuisance, offering peo-ple a romantic, inspirational place to end their lives."

"Does anyone ever survive?"

"Sure, a few. But the few who do survive the fall *and* remain conscious have at most ten minutes before hypo-thermia sets in. If the Coast Guard reaches them in time, they've got a shot. There's one well-known survivor who's a high school teacher now. He says the moment his hands left the bridge he realized all his problems were solvable—with the notable exception of one: He had just jumped off a bridge. He's now married, with kids. He's very grateful for his second chance, and talks to people quite openly about suicide."

As fascinating as this discussion was, it didn't tell me anything useful about Nicky Utley, who had not been one of the lucky survivors.

"So, I suppose the case against Ursula Moreno must focus on an herb or something else she gave Nicky Utley that supposedly promoted her suicidal tendencies. But how could they prove a case like that?"

Aidan licked some salt off the rim of the margarita glass. "Personally, I don't believe they're going to be able to make the charges of gross negligence stick. I think they're just rattling cages, trying to look good for the mayor. On the other hand, if Utley gave Moreno a lot of money, they might nail her on fraud charges. And frankly, if Ursula has been bilking people, she deserves what she gets. I'm concerned only about the girl."

"What about the crazed merchandise in her store?"

"I'll make inquiries, see if there are any whispers out there about a rogue witch. The thing is, the sensations are not those of a typical practitioner."

"Which is why you're thinking mental illness?"

"As I said"—he smiled as he watched a friendly—but loud—rivalry break out among the men playing pool—"I think it's possible. Either that, or it's a magical system I'm not as familiar with, which is why I wanted to talk to your pal Hervé. But he was as clueless as the rest of us."

"What about a woman named Betty North? Have you heard of her?"

He shook his head.

"I found a poppet in her house. I think it may have come from Ursula's shop."

"As far as I know, Ursula didn't have anywhere near that kind of power. She's decent with anointing candles and simple housekeeping spells and cleansing, but nothing more sophisticated. As I recall, she's primarily powerless with poppets." He smiled, as though pleased with his alliteration.

"You seem rather cheerful about the whole thing. I don't imagine Ursula Moreno is laughing."

"True enough. You should go speak with her."

"She's in jail."

"Yes, I realize that. And unless I'm mistaken, you're the one with friends in the SFPD. As you may know, the boys in blue are not quite as fond of me. Ask your old pal, Carlos Romero, if he can get you in to see her."

"How come you get to have a nice martini lunch with the mayor, and I have to go hang out in a jail?"

His blue eyes sparkled. "We all play to our strengths, Lily."

I returned to Aunt Cora's Closet an hour before closing. The shop was so busy I was almost distracted from my fruitless tour of the Mission, a missing girl, and an out-of-control *botanica*.

Not to mention the as-yet-unnamed payback I owed to one very powerful witch.

But it was the missing girl that most preyed on my mind. It had been several days since Ursula Moreno was arrested, and since Selena had snuck into Hervé's shop. I took comfort in the fact that, if I could believe the consensus of Hervé, Aidan, and the shop owners, Selena had remarkable supernatural abilities. So she was probably more able to take care of herself than the average fourteen-year-old, at least in terms of basic safety.

Mental health was another thing altogether. As Aidan had pointed out, being treated like an aberrant outsider all one's life didn't nurture the most stable of personalities. The only reason I had made it through my own experiences was because I had the love and support of my grandmother, Graciela.

What if Selena's sole support was Ursula, and Ursula was sent to prison?

As I was kneeling at the foot of a customer, pinning up the skirt of a slinky satin 1940s evening dress, I realized I had forgotten to contact Carlos to tell him about the doll in Betty's place, and that Lupita was a connection between Betty North and Ursula Moreno.

"I'll send this to our seamstress, and we should get back to you within ten days," I told the customer as I double-checked her measurements. There was nothing worse than making something too short. Even Maya's mother, Lucille, our talented shop seamstress, couldn't fix a mistake like that.

Bronwyn helped the woman change out of the pin-laden gown while I went up to my apartment to make the phone call in private. I told Carlos about Betty North's place and the ugly little doll, and that Lupita had worked for Betty as one of her home health aides. Carlos told me they hadn't found any new leads on Selena's whereabouts, and still didn't know what was going on in El Pajarito.

We were about to conclude our talk when I slipped in a request to speak with Ursula Moreno.

As usual, there was a long pause. I could hear the hum of the station behind him, someone yelling, a weary voice saying, *"Give it a rest, pal, will ya?"*

"You think she would tell you anything?" Carlos asked.

"It's worth a try. She must have some idea where Selena might be, and if she's concerned maybe she'll confide in me. You know how we witches can be: rather clannish."

"Don't you mean covenish? All right, I'll see what I can do. Let me make a few calls, and I'll get back to you."

"Thanks, Carlos."

I came downstairs just as Finn, the man in charge of Betty North's estate sale, arrived to deliver the bags of clothes Maya and I had selected. Conrad was right behind him, trying to help, but Finn carried three bags in each strong hand.

"Where do you want 'em?" he asked.

"Here, in the back room, if you don't mind."

I opened the curtain and, with a grunt, he set the Hefty bags down in front of the washing machine.

"Clothes are heavy," he said. "Who knew?"

"You should try them when they're wet. I swear, laundry is the bane of every vintage clothes dealer's existence."

Finn grinned, stepped back out onto the shop floor, and looked around. When he spoke, his booming voice filled Aunt Cora's Closet.

"Nice place you got here, kiddo. Real nice."

"Thank you. We like it. Hey, could I ask you a question?"

"Sure thing. Need me to appraise something?"

"No, nothing like that. I was wondering whether you knew if anyone did a *limpia* at Betty's house."

"Excuse me?"

"A *limpia*—it's a spiritual cleansing of a home."

He smiled. "I *do* know what a *limpia* is—don't forget, I spent a lot of time in the houses of dead people. And we're in the Bay Area. But with regards to Betty's place, I don't know, to be honest. I was called in for the estate sale, but I don't know anything about the intricacies of the house prep, anything like that. Besides, wouldn't a *limpia* be done after the place is cleaned out?"

"Normally, yes."

"I guess it wouldn't be beyond reason, though, I gotta say . . ." He glanced around the store. "I think there might be . . . I dunno, a spirit or something in that house."

"A spirit? Did you see something?"

"I don't know, exactly." He shrugged.

I reminded myself to be patient. When it came to ghosts or spirits or really anything beyond our earthly realm, most people aren't like me. Normal people weren't raised to believe in omens, woods creatures, or the transformational effects of a magical brew, much less the presence of spirits from beyond the veil. When nonwitchy humans confronted something unusual, it was only natural to try to explain it away: too much to drink, a trick of the light, a bad dream. Or that they were losing their minds.

"Did you sense anything out of the ordinary?" I suggested when he remained silent. "A cold spot, maybe?"

"Whispers? A breath on the back of your neck?" Bronwyn joined the discussion, a tad overeager. She had recently developed a fascination with ghosts, and was beginning to view herself as a junior ghost-buster.

"No, no, nothing like that," said Finn. "It's not like I think Betty's ghost is hanging around, or anything. It's just that I can tell things kind of . . . move around a bit."

"You see them move?"

"I haven't *seen* anything. But remember how I told you I take photos? I was going through a bunch and realized that things weren't the way I left them. They'd been moved."

He brought out an iPad and scrolled through pictures, showing me a before and after of one of his display tables.

"So the place wasn't tossed," I said, recalling the state of Ursula's store. "But it does look as if things have been rearranged."

"That's why I was thinking maybe it was a ghost. I mean, it's not like that's the first thing that comes to mind, but if someone was after Betty's valuables they would just grab them and run, wouldn't they? I mean, why take the time to rearrange things?"

I thought back to yesterday, when Maya and I were at Betty North's house. I didn't recall any of the usual indications of a ghostly presence: no strange puffs of air rushing past my bare arms, no tingle at the back of my neck, no sensation of my hair being pulled.

I can't communicate with the dead, but restless spirits are drawn to my vibrations and often try to make themselves known when I'm in their vicinity.

Still . . . If Betty was haunting her old home, perhaps seeking justice for a death hastened by someone with a voodoo doll, she might be too new to the spirit realm to know how to reach out to me. And I hadn't thought to open myself up to the possibility because I hadn't been thinking about ghosts. Could I have missed her attempt to communicate?

Maybe I should ask Sailor to visit Betty's house, to see if he could communicate with whatever, or *who*ever, might be there. Assuming, that is, his mentor gave him permission to dissipate his power.

Then again, probably none of this had to do with ghosts. Might Lupita still have a key to the house?

"Who has access to Betty's house, do you know?"

"Well, Maya has the key code to the lockbox. And me," Finn said. "And of course real estate agents would. The house isn't being shown yet, but there are usually inspectors and Realtors going in and out before a house formally goes on the market."

"Betty hired you to sell her things, right?" I asked.

"Yup. She made the arrangements before she passed. Now that she's gone, I ask her son if I need anything. He's the executor of the estate."

"He has access to the house, too, then."

"I guess he must. But I haven't seen hide nor hair of him. He told me to take care of everything. 'Sell it all,' he said. 'I don't want to deal with it.'"

"He doesn't even want any mementos of his mom?" Maya asked. "What about the portraits?"

"I hate to say it," Finn said with a shrug. "But it's not as unusual as you might think. A lot of times family members don't want to keep anything belonging to the one who passed—except, of course, the money. That they *do* want. Shouldn't complain, of course. Estate sales are my bread and butter, and if more folks cared about their families I'd be out of business. But it does make me sad. I guess you see some messed-up things, too, what with buying and selling dead people's clothes."

Finn's deep voice carried across the shop. A young woman dropped the skirt of a cocktail dress she had bunched in her hands, glanced at us, and left. Another put back a hat festooned with ostrich plumes and rubbed her hands on her pants.

"Sorry," Finn said in a lower voice. "Didn't mean to freak anyone out."

"No worries," I said.

Folks were funny about this sort of thing—they liked the idea of vintage clothes but didn't want to think of them as relics of other lives, most of which were now gone.

I bought a lot of "estate sale" items, which was a polite term for something that formerly belonged to someone who had died.

"Could I ask the name of Betty's son?" I asked Finn. "Or is that confidential?"

"I don't see why it would be. He's listed in the legal papers, which are public for the world to see. Don't remember his last name offhand, but he goes by Knox something . . ."

"As in the fort where they keep the gold?"

"Exactly."

He was the man I met outside El Pajarito the other day. He had been with Gary Utley, Nicky's widower. If Knox and Nicky were siblings . . . then that meant Nicky Utley was Betty North's daughter. And Betty was Gary Utley's mother-in-law.

Which also meant Knox had lost his sister and his mother within a few days of each other.

How tragic.

And how coincidental.

I was closing up the shop when Carlos called to say I could speak to Ursula Moreno if I could make it over to the Hall of Justice before seven.

"You mean, right now?"

"You got something better to do?"

"Actually . . . This is sort of embarrassing, but my friends arranged a little celebration for me tonight."

"Is it your birthday?"

"No. I passed the GED. I now have a high school diploma. Sort of."

"I didn't know that. Congratulations, Lily, that's a big deal. It's not easy going back to school."

I could feel myself shrugging.

"No, seriously," Carlos continued when I remained

mute. "That's a real accomplishment. So, what's the celebration involve?"

"We're getting together at Bronwyn's place for pizza and cards. Poker, I think was what was decided on. Is that lame? They wanted to take me out for karaoke, but I wasn't sure my heart could take it— or more precisely, whether their ears could take it."

"I'd take poker over karaoke anyday."

It hadn't occurred to me to invite Carlos to my graduation party. For most of our interactions he was The Inspector and we discussed acts of crime and malice. I liked Carlos but it was hard to know when and if to cross that line from professional acquaintances to true friends. Now, however, the opportunity seemed to present itself.

"Won't you join us? I would love it if you'd come."

"What time's the shindig?"

"8:00 p.m., at Bronwyn's house."

"That'd work. This crazy witch I know wants to interview a suspect in a crime, but after that, my evening's free. Why don't you hop on your broomstick and zoom on over here?"

"On my way."

Chapter 10

I don't much care for visiting jail, and San Francisco's Hall of Justice on Bryant Street was as cold and intimidating as one might imagine. But at least Carlos was there waiting for me. He escorted me into the jail's visiting room, a dreary cinder block chamber with a long bank of cubicles. I followed the directions to one cubicle and took a seat. A woman was already there, sitting on the other side of what I presumed was bulletproof glass.

Ursula Moreno was a plump, kind-looking woman. I guessed she was in her late fifties or early sixties, though she appeared to be one of those people who looked middle-aged for years on end. She wore her black hair tightly permed, her skin was a rich mocha, and she had a broad forehead, strong cheekbones, and a jutting chin. She put me in mind of my grandmother.

I again reminded myself: *You're a bad judge of character.* I couldn't go around trusting people simply because they made me think of someone I knew and loved.

Ursula picked up a phone handset attached to one side of the cubicle, and I followed suit.

"Who are you?" she asked.

"I'm Lily Ivory. I'm, a, uh . . ."

I held her gaze and an understanding passed between us, like an electric current. She nodded, her dark gaze drilling into me.

"I see. My cards told me you would come."

"Did they?"

"A dark-haired, powerful, young woman."

I wasn't feeling all that young lately, but "dark-haired and powerful" could describe me. Along with at least half the witches in the San Francisco Bay Area.

"And you said your name's Lily? Selena's been drawing pictures of lilies for the last week. She said the scent was driving her crazy."

I smelled roses whenever Sailor was in the vicinity. I never entertained the notion someone else might experience something similar about me.

"What do you want?" she demanded in a tone of curious belligerence.

"Inspector Romero asked me to visit your shop, to try to figure out what was going on."

"What do you mean? Did someone break in?"

I tried to read her, to determine if she was being truthful with me. No luck. Not only was I not talented at reading people, but like most practitioners she was guarded.

"Your merchandise is . . . energized."

"What are you talking about?"

"There's some havoc going on at El Pajarito. You don't know anything about it?"

She frowned and shook her head. "Unless . . . She is with you?"

"I'm sorry?"

"Selena. Where is she?"

"I wish I knew. Inspector Romero said the authorities are looking for her."

Panic crept into her eyes. "Lily Ivory, you must listen. You have to find Selena."

"I'm trying. That's one reason I came to talk with—"

"Find her and keep her with you."

"With *me*? Isn't there a family member . . . ?"

"No."

"I'm sure social services will—"

"No! That will not do, not at all. I'll give the police your name, tell them I want you to take care of her, make you her legal guardian until I get out of here."

"I couldn't possibly take on that kind of responsibility," I protested. "I don't even *know* her. Or you, for that matter."

"But we do know each other, you and I," she said with a slow nod that reminded me, once again, of Graciela and a few powerful practitioners I'd met in my travels. She had that intensity, that strange vibration that many of us gave off. No doubt this was what the other children sensed about me when I was young. It made us freaks.

But among freaks, there is a certain kinship.

"Selena can't go into the foster care system. I think you must understand why. Please, promise me, Lily. *Prometeme, por favor, te suplico.*"

"None of this will matter if we can't find her. Where do you think she might be?"

"She hides. But if you can find her, she will smell the lilies and know she can trust you."

"You don't have *any* idea where she could be? I don't know where to even start."

"I thought she would be hiding in the store, but if not . . ."

She shook her head, and I let out a sigh. I could hardly say *no* to a grandmother asking me to take care of a child for a few days while she was in the slammer. But it didn't take supernatural powers to intuit that assuming the care of a complete stranger—and a teenage witch at that—did not bode well.

"I'll look for her. In the meantime, what's going on at your store? The merchandise seems almost . . . possessed."

"I don't know what you're talking about. Perhaps it is one of my enemies."

I recalled Aidan's warning. What if Ursula was suffering from a mental illness? A powerful practitioner without control of her faculties was a danger to others, no doubt about it.

"Do you know a woman named Betty North?"

"No."

"You're sure?"

"Of course I'm sure."

I wasn't certain I believed her. "Tell me about Lupita."

She winced—just the merest flinch, but unmistakable. I reached for my medicine bag at the same time her hand touched her neck, as if by habit. Was she reaching for a necklace, or a charm? It would have been confiscated when she was booked at the jail. I remembered the police taking my medicine bag the time I had been arrested. I understood why that was done, but it seemed a shame that such items should be taken from us when we most needed solace.

"You do know her, right? The name's Lupita," I pushed.

"I know a lot of people named Lupita."

"I saw a newspaper article about El Pajarito, with the photo of you, Selena, and Lupita. Is she your daughter?"

"She's no good, is what she is." Ursula let out a long breath. "My *sobrina*."

"Your niece? Is she Selena's mother?"

She shook her head. "Selena's mother is no longer with us."

"And Lupita worked for Betty North."

"I wouldn't know anything about that. Lupita didn't spend much time with us—she came every once in a while to take Selena out. I didn't like it, didn't trust her. And then one day she showed up, out of the blue, and brought that reporter with her."

"Tell me about him."

She shrugged. "He was okay, but he's a doubter. His article was not very complimentary. You read it?"

I shook my head and made a mental note to look it up.

"I don't know why Lupita brought him to me. He probably paid her. Lupita doesn't do anything without getting paid. When he was there she acted like we were close, as though she, too, knew something, about magical systems. Always she refused to study. She knows nothing." Ursula fairly spat out this last.

"What about with poppets?"

She frowned. "I said, she knows *nothing*. Poppets require a special talent."

"I've never had much skill with them. They scare me a little."

She nodded, and again we seemed to understand each other without words.

"So you don't deal in poppets at El Pajarito?"

"No need. They don't work well in my belief system."

"Really? I noticed some hex boxes at your store."

"A hex box is a long way from a voodoo doll." She shrugged. "Mostly to discourage nosy neighbors, that sort of thing. Nothing serious. I don't deal in serious hexes."

Our gazes locked for a moment, each sizing up the other.

"Okay, so back to Lupita. What more can you tell me about her?"

"Why do you ask these questions?"

"Because they are important to me. If I do as you ask, you must do as I ask."

"Sometimes, she would come by the shop and take Selena out with her. Selena enjoyed it, so I didn't object at first. But then Selena started bringing things home, shiny little knickknacks, and I asked where she had gotten them. Neither would tell me. I don't think Lupita realized Selena's power."

Perhaps. Or maybe Lupita knew only too well what Selena was capable of, and was trying to use those powers for her own gain.

"Where can I find Lupita?"

"I don't know."

"You don't know where your niece lives? Do you have a phone number for her?"

She shook her head. "Like I said, we weren't close. Lupita showed up when she wanted to."

"Is her last name Moreno?"

"No. Rodriguez, after her father."

I was feeling frustrated and wondering just how much Ursula was holding back—and why.

"Why were you arrested for contributing to Nicky Utley's death?"

She shrugged. "This, I don't know. I have a court-appointed attorney, but he doesn't tell me anything. And they still want me to pay for him! What is that about? I have no money. I thought it would be free."

"Um . . ."

"You look into that."

"Could something you sold to Nicky Utley have contributed, in any way, to her death?"

"*No*," Ursula said emphatically. "That is ridiculous. 'Gross negligence,' the judge said. I don't even know what that means. Practicing medicine without a license? That is ridiculous. I help people, that much is true. But I never said I was a doctor. And Nicky wasn't suicidal when she came to me."

"Why did she come to you?"

"She wanted a baby."

"Were you able to help her with that?"

"There are some teas, some herbs that can help women who wish to become pregnant. I gave her some charms to recite, a few simple spells. Nothing serious, nothing that could harm her. A woman's body is a mysterious and miraculous vessel. Many times, after years of believing you are infertile, it becomes a self-fulfilling prophecy. I tried to help her break through that."

"Do the charms and spells work?"

She almost smiled. "It was worth a try."

"Isn't it possible what you gave her harmed her in some way?"

"If the woman insists on throwing herself off the Golden Gate Bridge, that is very sad. But it certainly wasn't *my* fault, much less the fault of my cures. She had her own mind. It wasn't . . . what do you call it, this magic that takes control?"

"Manipulative magic."

"*Eso es.* That's right."

Ursula held my gaze for a long moment, then placed the phone receiver against her chest, over the orange jail-issued blouse. After a few seconds I heard the thumping of her heart. Slow, steady. An informal lie detector test. The typical liar's heart would beat much faster.

At least, that's what I was supposed to think.

But practiced liars can control their emotions. And sociopaths feel no guilt.

"It is one thing to use magic to protect oneself, or to

encourage others to leave you alone. But to reach out to a virtual stranger and control their actions?" Ursula's gaze through the smudged glass was steady and unflinching. "This requires a power much stronger than mine. More like yours, I think."

I didn't know what to say.

"I didn't hurt Nicky Utley," she continued. "I don't hurt my clients. I'm in jail because of professional jealousy. My competitors resent my success and want to steal my clients. They are lying to the police. I am sure of it. Perhaps they are messing with my inventory at the store, too."

"Anyone in particular?"

She let out a humorless laugh. "Take your pick."

"And . . . how are you doing in here?" I asked, to change the subject. "Do you need anything?"

"It's not so bad—they feed me and there are a lot of women in here who need my help. *Tengo fe. La Santa Muerte me cuidará.*" I have faith; Santa Muerte will take care of me. "The only thing I'm worried about now is Selena."

And with that she hung up the phone and rose to leave. A deputy sheriff came to escort her out.

"Ursula, *wait*. We still need to talk!" I called.

"I am done talking for now," she said, the glass partition muffling her words. "Find Selena, *te suplico*. And maybe loan me money for that 'free' lawyer. Then, perhaps, we can talk more."

Interview over—whether or not I agreed—I rejoined Carlos at his desk. It was piled high with papers and folders. I wasn't used to seeing him in his bureaucratic guise; he was such a man of action. But I supposed paperwork was the bane of modern life.

He lifted his eyebrows. "You solve this thing yet?"

"Not quite. In fact, I learned very little, except that she's worried about Selena. Have you had any luck on that score?"

"There's an APB and an Amber Alert out on Selena, and officers have canvassed the neighborhood. Not only has no one seen her, apparently no one's *ever* seen her leave the shop except to go to school."

"What about her school friends?"

"Far as I can tell, she didn't have any. But one of her classmates, Emma, is the daughter of the victim, Nicky Utley. Emma didn't have any information for us, though."

"What school did they go to?"

"Washington Middle School, on Steiner. That may be how Nicky Utley learned about El Pajarito. From what I gather, Selena drummed up business for her grandmother."

His words rang with disapproval.

"Do you actually know that, or are you drawing conclusions?"

"I'm a cop, remember? I catch the bad guys, I don't draw conclusions. That's for the DA."

Our eyes held for a long moment. "So Selena and Emma are friends—"

"I didn't say friends. According to Selena's teacher and the guidance counselor, she's a loner. The other kids find her . . . strange."

As someone who until recently was an outcast not just at school but in *life*, I could relate.

"So none of them has any idea where she might be?"

He shook his head.

"You searched every inch of El Pajarito?"

"Stem to stern. She's not there, Lily. Chances are good she's with family somewhere."

"According to Ursula, Selena has no other family."

"What makes you think she's telling you the truth? You know how the community can be, closemouthed. Anyway, if we find her, I'll let you know."

"So, have you found anything concerning the poppet in Betty's house?"

"The one you think the home health aide might have brought there?"

"Lupita worked for Betty North, and is Ursula's niece, and both were connected to Nicky Utley. I think it would be worth talking to her about it. Not to mention, Selena might be with her."

"Got an address or phone number?"

I shook my head.

"Ursula wouldn't tell you?" he asked.

"She says she doesn't know. They weren't close."

"*Any* way of finding her?"

"If I did, I wouldn't be asking you."

Carlos sighed. "Do you at least have a last name?"

"I do," I said as if bestowing a great present. "Rodriguez."

"Lupita Rodriguez," Carlos repeated as he jotted it down in his notebook. "Okay: Lupita is a nickname for Guadalupe, so we're probably looking for a Guadalupe Rodriguez."

"Well, that's something, isn't it?" I said encouragingly.

"Not really. Rodriguez is a common name, like Smith or Jones. It won't be easy to hunt her down."

"If anybody can do it, you can. You're the Man."

"Yeah, yeah, yeah. I'm the Man."

"Hey, Carlos. Can I ask you something?"

"Fire away."

"If Nicky Utley's death was a homicide instead of a suicide, you'd be looking at the husband first, wouldn't you?"

"I would. And I did. Gary has an alibi for when Nicky died. Also, there were witnesses to the jump. One poor guy tried to save her, with no luck. He was pretty shaken up, as you can imagine. But none of the witnesses reported seeing anyone resembling Gary in the vicinity. He's in the clear."

"You went through something similar with your cousin and Max, didn't you? I am sorry for being so personal but I couldn't help but notice the parallels."

He nodded. "I think you know I'm more open to the paranormal than most of my colleagues," said Carlos. "But it's precisely because of that understanding and respect that I get so angry about people who make a mockery of this sort of thing, who aren't careful."

I felt a wave of pleasure that, at the very least, he apparently believed I was in the "good" camp.

"So," Carlos said, clapping his hands and rubbing them together. "Is it time for poker?"

"It's not like we're playing for money, or anything."

"You have to play for a *little* money, just to make it interesting."

I smiled. "Oh, hey, speaking of money: Ursula can't afford a lawyer but she says the 'free' lawyers aren't free, somehow. Is that true?"

"She's not paying for his services. It's a court fee."

"What's the difference between a court fee and a payment?"

"I don't make the rules, Lily."

"So her legal representation isn't free."

"It's not much of a fee, certainly nothing compared to the cost of hiring a private defense attorney."

"Okay, but still . . ."

He shrugged again.

I blew out an exasperated breath. "How do I pay the fee for her?"

"Ask the court clerk." He smiled. "You know, around here there's a word for someone like you."

"Humanitarian?"

"Sucker," he said with a wink. "Which just happens to be my favorite kind of person with whom to play poker."

Chapter 11

A piece of popcorn sailed across the table and hit me square on the nose.

"Lily Ivory, as I live and breathe," said Bronwyn in a terrible rendition of my Texas twang, "I *do* declare: You're *cheating*."

"I'm *not* cheating, I'm *winning*. That's two different buckets of possums."

Sailor studied the back of his cards with a frown, as though trying to figure out if I could see through them. "And here I thought *I* was the psychic."

I threw the popcorn back at him. He grinned, caught it, and tossed it to Oscar, who was attending tonight in his piggy form. Even though we were among good friends, Oscar only showed his natural self to a very select group of magical folk.

Despite having eaten half a dozen slices of pizza, Oscar was on constant popcorn-patrol under the card table. In his search he kept bumping up against legs, of the human and furniture variety, and occasionally lifted the entire table, sending us lunging after toppling beer bottles. It was a little like playing cards aboard a storm-tossed ship.

"How come every time I win," I demanded, raking in a pile of matchsticks to add to my already substantial mound, "everyone thinks I'm cheating?"

"'Cause you're a witch," mumbled Maya. She perused the cards splayed on the table, her lips moving silently.

"Yes, but *you're* counting cards." I looked to Carlos, the sole representative of law and order at the table. "Isn't that illegal in Vegas?"

"Want me to arrest her?" he asked. "I'm off duty but I could roust her tomorrow."

"And this isn't Vegas," said Bronwyn. "We're playing Bronwyn's house rules: Counting cards is a learned skill, involving math, so I allow it. Witchcraft, on the other hand . . ."

"For *one* thing, witchcraft is a learned skill, too. You think it comes easy?" I demanded. "And for another: I am *not* casting spells over these cards! Land *sakes*!"

The group dissolved into laughter. Conrad started to gather the cards to deal a new hand, and Duke got up to replenish our drinks.

"So, Carlos, you simply have to tell me what's going on over at Señora Moreno's shop," said Bronwyn. "Lily here seems to think it's confidential."

Carlos stuck out his chin, thoughtful. "It's not so much confidential, as we have no idea what's happening. At this point, I'm thinking maybe it's a poltergeist."

"Like the movie? I saw that as a kid," said Maya. "My mom wouldn't let me stay in the same room as the television after that."

"Dude," said Conrad with a sympathetic nod.

"That's not out of the question, actually," I said. "I mean, poltergeists are often associated with adolescent girls. Ursula's granddaughter, Selena, is fourteen."

"So sad you still haven't found her," said Bronwyn as she filled a bowl with potato chips, then "accidentally" dropped the half-full bag on the floor and with her foot nudged it under the card table. "Dear me! I'm so clumsy."

"I saw that," I said. "And even if I had somehow missed your subtle maneuver, Oscar is noisier than a corn-husk mattress with that chip bag."

Oscar appeared from under the table, the chip bag firmly planted over his snout. We all laughed, and Maya snapped a photo with her phone. Several vigorous head shakes send the empty bag flying, and revealed a muzzle encrusted with potato chips. He snorted, then glared at us with his pink piggy eyes as he attempted to capture the crumbs with his inadequate tongue.

"*Aw*, poor piggy. I think he's embarrassed," said Maya.

"C'mere, pig," said Sailor, and brushed the crumbs off Oscar's porcine schnoz. "Give the poor guy a little dignity."

Conrad shuffled the cards and did some sort of fancy thing so they splayed like an accordion in the air before coming back together. He dealt the cards rapidly and with such panache I wondered whether he had ever been a pro, but when I asked he simply replied, "*Dude.* Ante up! Five matchsticks a piece."

As we picked up our cards and assessed our hands, Carlos said, "So, seriously. Could you folks who are knowledgeable about this sort of thing explain poltergeists to me? They're not normal spirits, are they?"

I glanced at Sailor. Eyes still glued to his cards, he said, "Poltergeists aren't 'normal' in the sense that they're not ghosts, or departed human souls. They're believed to be low-level spirits, such as elementals, or even psychokinetic energy let loose upon the world. I'll bet two matchsticks."

"And why are they associated with adolescent girls?"

Carlos asked. "I'll see your two matchsticks, and raise you one."

"The adolescent part is easy," said Bronwyn, tossing a trio of matchsticks into the pot. "After all, adolescence is a time of great energy, but also great strife. Under certain conditions and circumstances, negative energy can be thrust outward. Oh, sorry, Sailor! Didn't mean to butt in."

I heard a loud snort from beneath the table as Oscar reacted to Bronwyn saying "butt."

"No, by all means, go on," said Sailor. "You're absolutely right, and though I've gone up against a couple of poltergeists, I'm certainly no expert."

"Okay," Carlos said. "I guess the adolescent part makes sense. But is it limited to girls?"

"The evidence, such as it is, points to a feminine energy," said Sailor. "It is considered more receptive, less active."

"Is this a theory espoused by men, by any chance?" Maya put in, upping the ante by another two matchsticks.

"I know it sounds sexist, but . . . males and females do tend to emit energy with different wavelengths," Sailor explained. "Not sure what to say about that, much less whether it's a nature- or nurture-type situation. I avoid that theoretical debate, by and large."

"I'll just bet you do," I said, gazing at him across the table.

"I'm more of an action guy," he said softly. His mouth was open slightly, and his tongue wandered to the inside of his cheek. We shared a secret smile.

Bronwyn started humming the *k-i-s-s-i-n-g* song again, and I broke the eye contact with a blush. "Um, sorry. I lost track. How much are we up to, now?"

"It's five to you, dudette," said Conrad.

Having polished off the potato chips, Oscar was now snoring under the table. I kicked off my shoes and rested my feet on his warm backside.

"Anyway, most folks agree that poltergeist activity is a psychokinetic phenomena—the girls' own innate powers organize and focus ambient energies, resulting in . . ."

"Chaos."

"Exactly. Then again, there's a theory that poltergeists are low-level minions who escape when a demon is called without success. And Maya, I would like to point out that such demons are typically called by middle-aged men."

"So, which do you believe?" Carlos asked. "Minions, or psychokinetic energy?"

"All of the above," replied Sailor. "Poltergeist literally means 'noisy ghost.' I think lots of events get lumped into the same category, even when they're caused by different things. As is the case with most unexplained phenomena, people are looking for a single, easily understood cause rather than dealing with the complexity of the situation."

"You're saying poltergeists are easily understood?"

"Within the context of elemental spirits and out-of-control psychic energy," Sailor said with a shrug.

Carlos nodded, thoughtful, and turned his attention back to the game. I was pleased to see Carlos and Sailor engaged in a civilized discussion. Their paths had crossed long before I had met either of them, when a psychic associate of Sailor's gave Carlos's cousin—Max's wife—some misguided advice with devastating consequences. Sailor had not been directly involved, but had been tarred with the same brush. Since then, both men made an effort to be civil around each other, at least in front of me, but were hardly best buddies.

The game proceeded, and when I asked for two cards,

I received two queens to add to the three tens I already had. I tried to stifle my glee: a full house, queens high.

For a moment I considered folding, lest I be accused of witchcraft again. But then I reconsidered. After all, my friends were unlikely to burn me at the stake over a game of cards, and durnitall, I had a *full house*. So I held my head high.

"I'll see your five and raise you . . . ten."

"Oooooo," Bronwyn and Maya said together.

"Them's fightin' words," Duke said, and Carlos nodded.

"You sure you know what you're doing there, missy?" Sailor asked, squinting at me.

"Oooooo," Bronwyn and Maya repeated.

"Dude," Conrad said, sounding shocked.

"You *go*, Sailor," said Carlos and took a swig from his beer bottle. "I like a man who's not afraid to get his ass kicked."

"Too rich for my blood," said Maya and folded her cards. "Bronwyn?"

"Nope. I'm out. How about you, Duke?"

"Well, I'm mighty tempted to see this through to the end, but you know what they say about poker: 'Fold and live to fold again.'" He tossed his cards down on the table.

I looked at Carlos.

"Not me, kid. I didn't become a homicide inspector by underestimating my opponent."

"So it's down to two," Bronwyn said. "Lily and Sailor."

"Two tough, battle-hardened veterans. Each sizing up the opponent in a duel to the death," Carlos said, displaying a whimsical side I had only suspected was there.

"Dude and dudette," Conrad whispered. "May the force be with you."

"Which one?" asked Maya.

"*Dude*."

Sailor studied me for a long moment. He took a pull on the ice-cold beer Duke set in front of him.

"You got this, Sailor," Duke said with the attentiveness of a boxing coach tending to his fighter.

"Yeah, take her down, my man," said Maya.

"Hey!" I exclaimed. "How about a little support from the distaff side?"

"Last I heard, you were trying to get me expelled from this particular casino for counting cards."

I laughed, conceding her point.

"Not that it did me any good," said Maya, getting up to clear a few of our empty glasses. "I can count all night long, but if all I'm dealt are crappy cards, that's all she wrote."

"But you know what they say," chirped Bronwyn, waggling her eyebrows, "unlucky at cards, lucky at love."

"Yes, because I have been so demonstrably lucky at love," said Maya in a sardonic tone. "I blame Conrad for my deplorable showing."

"*Dude*, in my own defense, I'll just say that while I *rock* as a dealer, I have the smallest pile of matchsticks of anyone here at this table. Maybe Oscar should take my place; he'd probably do better."

Upon hearing his name, Oscar snorted awake and got up to look for more food, lifting the table and causing the soda and beer bottles to rock precipitously. We grabbed onto our drinks.

"Let's finish this game, quick," said Sailor, pushing a small mound of matchsticks into the kitty. "I call."

"*Full* house. Queens high," I said proudly, laying my cards on the table.

"Wow. Thought she was bluffing," muttered Duke.

"It's witchcraft, I'm telling you," said Maya.

"Nice try there, Sailor," said Carlos.

Sailor lifted one eyebrow and laid down his cards, faceup, with a dramatic flourish.

"Royal flush."

"You cheated!" I cried. "You saw my cards!"

Sailor smirked, and I picked up a handful of matchsticks and tossed them in the air so they rained down upon the gang.

"*Never* play cards with a psychic," Bronwyn said, shaking her head.

Oscar jumped around in excitement, once again bumping the table but this time sending everything flying. Maya lunged for the pitcher of sangria while the rest of us scrambled to contain the damage. Conrad scooped up soggy potato chips and pizza crusts while Oscar vacuumed the floor of errant peanuts and beer.

Bronwyn just let loose her hearty, warm laugh, waving off our concern for her table and carpet.

"And *always*," Bronwyn added, "bring a pig to a poker game."

"I'm sorry I can't come up," Sailor said after he saw me to my door and gave me a kiss that took my breath away.

"You'd rather go hang out with Precious than come upstairs with little ol' me?"

He smiled. "Her name is *Patience*, not Precious, as you very well know. And I think we both know what I'd *rather* be doing. But we've got something set up for midnight. It's a timing thing."

"Well, I hope all this training is worth it."

"Me, too."

"And I'm glad you got a reprieve for earlier in the evening at least, so you could come to the party. I had a really good time."

"Me, too. I'm proud of you, Lily, you diploma-holder, you. I guess you showed algebra who's boss."

"At long last. Solving for the 'x' nearly did me in."

We shared another delicious kiss, and then I watched him climb onto his motorcycle and roar away.

I carried the remnants of the red velvet cake Bronwyn and Maya had baked for me—decorated with a pointy witch's hat made of frosting—through the shop and upstairs into my apartment. Oscar trotted along behind, morphing into his natural, garrulous self as soon as we were hidden from view of any curious passersby.

"That was some party, I tell ya," he said, his eyes never leaving the cake.

"It was, wasn't it?"

"Hey, I know! You should take that test again, get another party. Take it quick, before you forget everything."

I laughed. "I don't think it works that way. This was a onetime deal."

"Next time you and me play cards, no more gin rummy. We should play poker, for *money*."

"No way. You cheat!"

"Nah. Besides, they all said *you* cheated tonight."

"I did no such thing. I was lucky, is all."

"Lucky at cards, unlucky in love," Oscar reversed Bronwyn's adage from earlier in the evening.

As silly as it was, my stomach clenched a little.

"Hey, did you hear when Bronwyn said 'butt'? *Heh!* And then that one time, when Carlos had two pair and Duke had absolutely nothing, but he was bluffing? And then Maya . . ."

I put away the cake and brushed my teeth while Oscar followed me around recounting virtually every hand we had played tonight. He was quite the multitasker: even while continuing his eternal quest for food, he had been checking out everyone's cards.

I was about to change into my nightgown when I spied my crystal ball sitting, dusty and neglected, on a side table in the living room.

Before Aidan and I had our falling-out, he had been trying to help me develop my scrying skills, or the ability to see visions in the crystal ball. But in this area, at least, I was one sorry excuse for a witch. I hated to admit that I hadn't gotten any better, but the truth was that I hadn't. And it was my own fault. I'd been skating along on my other abilities and hadn't been doing my homework.

Besides, after taking the GED I had flat-out declined to do any more studying for a while. I wanted a break.

In other words, I had no excuse. "Do it or don't. *Hazlo o no*," my grandmother often said. She was like a Latina Yoda with a cauldron.

But now, I felt a sense of urgency egging me on. Selena was just a girl, and though chances were good she was with Lupita, or had sought refuge with someone she trusted . . . what if she hadn't? What if she was all alone, frightened, and convinced no one cared? Besides, Ursula mentioned she had been drawing pictures of lilies. So maybe we had some sort of connection.

I had to try. *Hazlo o no.*

So I dusted off my crystal ball. It really was a work of art: The base was made of filigreed silver and gold and studded with semiprecious stones. The crystal itself was a polished glass sphere with a few random mineral deposits that looked like ethereal clouds trapped within.

I placed it on a clean white linen cloth atop the old steamer trunk that doubled as my coffee table and sat cross-legged on the floor. The key to scrying was to see without seeing, to concentrate without concentrating, which was about as easy as it sounded. I closed my eyes, took several deep breaths, and tried to locate my third eye in the center of my forehead.

I had some serious doubts about my psychic anatomy in this regard, but Aidan had assured me that I did, indeed, possess one.

Slowly, I opened my eyes and gazed into the depths of the crystal.

I saw shadows and whispers, tantalizing tidbits snatched as though from a dream; unconnected threads I was unable to piece together into a meaningful whole. At long last, I thought I caught a glimpse of Selena's thin face, surrounded by flashing lights.

And I tasted something. Was that . . . salt?

It wasn't much, but it was a lot more than I was accustomed to seeing in my crystal ball. Under the circumstances, though, it was of no use that I could see. What I needed was an address, or a sign of some sort. A pin on a map would be nice.

I tried once more, but a little practice seemed to have made me even less able to see.

I leaned back, frustrated.

"Watcha doin'?" came Oscar's distinctive growl.

"Trying to concentrate without concentrating."

"*Ugh*, I hate that kind of thing. Like those pictures where you're supposed to let your eyes go blank and then see a secret picture? I never see nothin'."

"Me neither. I thought you'd gone to bed?"

"I was feeling a mite peckish."

I smiled. When was my familiar *not* peckish?

"How about a grilled cheese sandwich?" At least cooking was something I was good at. A little domestic wizardry would go a long way right about now.

"With a slice of cake after?"

"You already had two slices at Bronwyn's house."

"But three is the best number. Every witch worth her salt knows that."

The next morning I opened the store as usual, smudging widdershins, salting deosil, and then lighting a single white taper candle that I had "dressed" by massaging it with olive oil. As I walked through the steps of my daily ritual, I thought of Ursula Moreno's mornings at El Pajarito: how she must have laid out sacrifices of fruit and bread, beans and tortillas at the foot of Santa Muerte, lighting the figure's cigarette, placing a cup of hot, sweet Nescafé by her side.

I remembered Graciela doing something similar. Every morning, she would mix her instant coffee, put in three heaping teaspoons of sugar, then take the steaming cup out to her garden, where she would meander and talk to her plants. Gathering a stalk of verbena or sprigs of oregano and basil and *epazote*, she would return to the kitchen and crush the herbs with a stone mortar and pestle she claimed had originally belonged to an Aztec shaman before the Spanish conquest of Mexico. Graciela would take the fragrant herbs, mix them with beans, fill a few tortillas, and place them on her altar atop a bureau in a tiny closet. On the altar were pictures of ancestors and photos of those whom Graciela loved, yours truly included; fresh flowers that she replaced every few days; candles; and a stone figure with its hands in the shape of a cup, into which she placed her herbs before starting to pray. There was also a battered Hot Wheels car, an old keychain, a picture of a marmot, quotations and pictures ripped from newspapers and magazines.

I never knew whether she was praying for her loved ones, or for the people who came to her for help. Graciela didn't charge for her services, not exactly, but she did ask for a contribution in the form of a charitable donation. When people understood how powerful she was, they gave what they could: a chicken, fresh farm eggs, a knitted shawl.

When it came down to it, Graciela wasn't all that different from Ursula Moreno. Maybe that was why I felt compelled to help Ursula. Either she was telling the truth about Nicky Utley, her shop, and Selena, or she was losing her mind, as Aidan had implied. Or she was ripping everyone off—perhaps contributing to the deaths of her clients—and needed to be stopped.

So what should my next step be?

Who was this Lupita, and *where* was she? Could she be the one wreaking havoc in the shop? According to Ursula, Lupita didn't have that kind of power, something Aidan had tacitly confirmed. Had she been powerful, he would have made it a point to meet her. But if Lupita had Selena with her, could she be using the girl as a weapon? And if so, why?

After finishing with my morning cleansing ritual, I opened the shop door and said good morning to Conrad.

"Dudette, your paper." He handed me the *San Francisco Chronicle*.

"Thanks. How about a bagel today?"

"Duuude."

That meant yes. The morning was foggy, so I pulled on my wool car coat, hung my Brazilian shopping basket over my arm, left the shop under Conrad's watchful eye, and made my way down the street to Coffee to the People, a café that was a true throwback to the Summer of Love. Unlike many of the stores of the Haight-Ashbury, Coffee to the People wouldn't have to change a thing in order to fit in with the upcoming festival. I suppose they could lose the Wi-Fi connection and a few posters for contemporary political causes, but otherwise the café was the same as it had been when it opened, back in the hippie heyday.

After Conrad and I made short work of breakfast, I went inside to assist a lone customer looking for an outfit for the Summer of Love Festival. Mornings were slow at Aunt Cora's Closet, so she and I had a blast digging through the merchandise to find the perfect peasant skirt, a Grateful Dead T-shirt, and a Mexican serape. We topped it off with soft fringed leather boots, and a wide leather belt with scrollwork.

"I look *exactly* like my mother in 1967," the woman said, looking in the mirror. "I'm . . . adorable."

I laughed. "That you are."

Maya walked in as the woman was leaving, a recycled Aunt Cora's Closet bag clutched in each hand.

"First sale of the day already?" Maya said.

I nodded. "Yep, the entire transaction took less than twenty minutes. She knew what she was after."

"Funny how some people seem to camp out all day, while others are in and out," she said, setting down her chai soy latte as she spread the newspaper open on the counter.

I straightened up the dressing room, hanging up the discarded blouses and skirts. It never ceased to amaze me how the process of trying on clothes resulted in something resembling the aftermath of a hurricane.

"Anything interesting in the paper today?" I asked.

"Depends on what you mean by interesting," Maya said. "A house in Pacific Heights sold for nearly a million dollars *over* the asking price, which, I don't mind telling you, doesn't bode well for my future ability to afford living in my native city."

"Maybe real estate prices will become more reasonable in the future."

"And maybe pigs will fly in the future."

Oscar lifted his head from his purple pillow and snorted.

"Sorry, Oscar," Maya said. "Didn't mean to cast aspersions on your porcine name. Oh, *here's* a fun story: The Bridge Troll is back."

Chapter 12

"There's a *Bridge Troll*?"

I flashed on Nicky Utley, standing in the middle of the Golden Gate Bridge, buffeted by winds, looking down at the churning water. I had tasted salt when I looked in my crystal ball—could it have been the salt off the sea? Was it trying to tell me something? Could there be a supernatural explanation for her death, something that had nothing to do with dangerous herbs or possessed items from El Pajarito?

A *troll*, of all things, scaring people into the frigid waters below?

Because I had abandoned my witchy training before it was completed, there was a lot I still didn't know. I was certain many things cowans thought were myths or fairy tales were real—like the Good People of the woods, for example. And shape-shifting critters like Oscar. But I wasn't sure about unicorns, satyrs, or . . . trolls.

Maya laughed and showed me a photo of a small bronze sculpture.

"This is the little guy. After a section of the Bay Bridge

collapsed during the last big earthquake," she explained, "an artist fashioned a troll out of bronze and attached it to the underside of the bridge to guard the repairs. When the old span was shut down, the troll went missing. Apparently someone has made a new one. He's on the underside of the new bridge, out of the sight of drivers so no one runs off the bridge trying to spot him. But he's cute, isn't he?"

I nodded. *Cute.*

It seemed so very Bay Area that some artist, somewhere, had gone to the trouble of making a bridge troll . . . and that the transportation agency had given the go-ahead to install it. It just went to show that even people who didn't "believe in magic" made symbolic gestures of safekeeping: crossing themselves, knocking on wood, or sculpting bridge trolls.

"And in *other* bridge news," Maya continued, sipping her chai soy latte. "There's been another suicide off the Golden Gate Bridge."

"*Another* one?"

"According to this, there are a couple of dozen a year, so I guess it's not that surprising. So sad. Hmm . . . this is interesting."

"What's that?"

"Apparently the mayor's started a campaign to crack down on fortune-tellers."

"I heard something about that."

"It says here: 'We provide guidance and counsel, and yes, a little magic. Who doesn't need a little magic in their life? And who is to say that I haven't made that magic happen?'"

"Who said that?"

"The spokesperson for the San Francisco Fortune-Tellers Association. Did you know there was a San Francisco Fortune-Tellers Association?"

"News to me," I said, rearranging the belts that hung from small brass hooks. "I can't say I've ever thought about a fortune-teller union. But according to Carlos, they have to be licensed by the city. Who's the spokesperson?"

"Let's see . . . Patience Blix. Great handle."

"*Patience Blix*? Is there a photo?"

Maya folded the paper and held it up.

She didn't look like Sailor's aunt Renna.

Patience Blix was a bombshell. A cascade of raven hair curled around her heart-shaped face. A huge smile showed perfect, white teeth, framed by dark lipstick. Her piercing eyes were lined with kohl. A plunging neckline showed an abundance of cleavage.

She was spectacular.

"Now that's what I call drop-dead gorgeous," Maya said. "Wow. You ever hear of her?"

My lips felt stiff. When I spoke, I mumbled, "She's been training Sailor."

"Wow," Maya repeated, her eyebrows shooting up.

Good thing Patience is Sailor's cousin, I thought, then chided myself for such an unworthy sentiment. But the idea of Sailor spending a lot of one-on-one time with a woman who looked like Patience Blix gave me a sickly sensation in the pit of my stomach.

I glanced down at my own modest chest. My size made it easier to fit into vintage fashions, but at the moment I felt inadequate, downright boyish compared to the luscious woman in the photo.

"Hey, check this out," said Maya. "The article refers to Patience Blix's 'pulchritude.' When's the last time you read that word in the newspaper?"

"I'm not sure I even know what it means."

"It means 'beauty.' Doesn't sound like it though, does it? Sounds like something nasty."

Like the thoughts running through my head at the moment.

"Wait. . . . Could I see that article?"

I checked out the byline: Nigel Thorne. Nigel had been at the *Chronicle* forever and enjoyed showing off his vocabulary. I was familiar with his work because he was the paper's unofficial "woo-woo" reporter, the one who caught all the paranormal stories. He, and to some extent, Max Carmichael.

It occurred to me that I should stop by the *San Francisco Chronicle* and have a little chat with Nigel about the mayor's fortune-telling clean-up campaign. And if Max happened to be in the newsroom I could ask why Lupita had brought him to El Pajarito. Let's see what Sailor had to say about *that*.

Ugh. *Grow up, Lily.* I should talk to Max, yes, but it was ridiculous to be scheming to make Sailor jealous. It was childish and unworthy of a grown woman like me to react this way just because Sailor had a gorgeous cousin. And hadn't mentioned how attractive she was. And wouldn't tell me what they were doing during all those hours they spent together, late at night . . .

A trio of customers came into the shop, and I tried to shake it off.

"Maya, would it be possible for me to read the transcript of the interview you did with Betty North?"

"Sure. I'll call it up."

"You . . . you don't mean call it up on the phone, do you?" I'm an idiot with computers. Now that I was the proud possessor of my GED, I was thinking that I should get over my fear of technology and catch up with the modern world. But for the moment it was easier to rely on Maya, who hardly ever made fun of me even though she had cause.

Maya smiled. "No, I'm going to download the file

from the cloud. Tell you what, I'll send it to the printer, where said device will miraculously spit out paper marked with ink so you can read it the old-fashioned way."

"I appreciate that. And I particularly appreciate your understanding attitude about the whole thing."

She squeezed my arm and headed for the laptop.

The rest of the day I was haunted by the fleeting image of Selena I had glimpsed in my crystal ball.

What, if anything, did it mean? I wished I could talk to Gary, Nicky Utley's widower and father of Emma, Selena's schoolmate. I imagined Carlos was right; the girls were probably not friends. Young witches were often outcasts. Still, I wondered whether Emma could give me a clue as to Selena's whereabouts.

Unfortunately, not only was Gary vehemently anti-witch, but despite what Carlos had said, I kept wondering if he was somehow involved in his wife's death. Haranguing him didn't seem like my best option, especially alone.

So I decided to follow up with the next best thing: Nicky's brother, Knox. He had been friendly enough when we met at El Pajarito, and had even offered me his card. I dug it out of my bag and gave him a call.

Knox told me he'd be home all day with the kids, and I was welcome to stop by. He lived across the bay, in El Cerrito, a residential community north of Berkeley on the BART line to San Francisco. The homes here were small, comfortable but not fancy, built on small lots just after the Second World War.

Knox's house was a compact one-story, with an overgrown yard geared more towards children than landscaping. On the patchy front lawn were several balls, a plastic bat, and two bikes lying on their sides.

Three laughing children were playing a game of hide-

and-go-seek that extended from the front yard to the unfenced back. When they saw me coming up the walk they ran into the back, yelling for their dad.

Knox met me at the door wearing the same tortoise-shell glasses and plaid Bermuda shorts as the other day, but now with a salmon pink polo shirt.

"Hi! Come in, come in. Sorry about the mess. I meant to clean up but somehow I never manage to get anything done, what with the kids running in and out all day."

"It's fine, really. It feels like home."

Knox chuckled as he led the way to the kitchen. "Yep, I guess it is homey. At least there's that."

The house was old-fashioned suburban, simple but comfortable, the fridge covered in children's drawings. A framed poster showed Norman Rockwell's iconic painting of a family sitting down to Thanksgiving dinner.

We settled into a breakfast nook with a view of the backyard, where the kids were now playing on a swing set and monkey bars. Knox poured two glasses of iced tea garnished with lemon.

"I'd like to say the state of the house is unusual, except that, I gotta confess, it's always like this. Four kids. *Four*. I don't know what I was thinking."

I smiled. "I always wanted to be part of a big family."

"Me, too." He shrugged and stared at his children in the yard. "I mean, I had my sister—Nicky and I were fraternal twins—but I always wanted a brother as well."

"I'm so very sorry for your loss."

He nodded. "Thanks. It's been tough. Nicky . . ." He trailed off with a shake of his head. "One part of me can't believe it, but then . . . is it possible to be shocked by something, even when you're not actually surprised?"

"I think so, yes. What was she like?"

"Nicky was . . . well, I guess the best way to say it is we were very different. I always wanted a normal life, a tra-

ditional kind of existence. Which I got, with a twist, of
course: My wife works outside the home, while I'm the
househusband."

"As it says with pride on your card," I said with a smile.
"I noticed the Norman Rockwell print in the hall, too."

"It's always been a favorite. When I was a kid . . . well,
Nicky and I didn't have much of a normal childhood."

"Was it . . . difficult?"

"It was for me. I mean, we weren't beaten or anything,
nothing like that. Our dad was a good guy, strict but loving. But we were military brats, moving around every
couple of months, or every year at most."

"That sounds challenging."

"You learned how to be the new kid in class—that's
for sure. I attended sixteen different schools before grad-
uating high school. And friends were made and then left,
no lasting relationships. My dad worked all the time.
That sort of upbringing can leave a person sort of . . .
disconnected. So Nicky and I were close—we were each
other's only constant in those years."

Silence reigned for a long moment. I imagined we
were both thinking of Nicky—her loss must be felt even
more acutely for her twin, and only childhood friend.

"All those years, all I ever wanted was a nice, normal
home, to go to one school and make friends like everybody else, to be part of a community." Knox gestured to
his messy, lived-in kitchen. "Someplace like this, nothing
fancy. Now, my kids are always asking me about what it
was like to serve and spend time in exotic-sounding
places like Okinawa, so probably they'll want to run off
and join the military. Maybe it skips a generation."

"Do you know," I said, "I've never seen a picture of
your sister?"

He got up and grabbed a couple of framed prints
from a small, paper-strewn desk in the corner. "Here's a

photo of the two of us; I'd say we were about ten when this photo was taken. We were stationed in Germany. And here's a wedding photo, with Gary."

Seeing Nicky's smiling, open countenance—first as a girl in braids, then as a bride in a lacy white gown—made her death less abstract, and thus more heartbreaking.

"She's lovely."

Knox nodded, looked at the photos for a long moment, and then set them aside. "I was the firstborn, apparently—by only a few minutes, of course, but I took my role as older brother seriously. I tried to take care of her . . ." He cleared his throat and shook his head, as though to rid it of the memory.

"Do you know why your sister was going to Ursula at El Pajarito?"

"She wanted a child. She'd tried the usual ways, and nothing worked. So I guess a witch doctor was the final call." His eyes flew to mine. "Oh, I'm sorry. I forgot. You're a . . . ?"

"Just a special consultant to the SFPD," I said with a smile and a shrug. This was not the time and place to launch into a defense of witchcraft. "But wait—I thought Nicky and Gary had a daughter."

"Emma's actually Gary's biological daughter; his first wife passed away. Nicky doted on Emma, but wanted to experience pregnancy and biological motherhood and all it entailed. The physicality of giving birth was very important to her. But she was no kid, and with every year that passed, the likelihood went down. I tried to reason with her—what's the difference between adopting and having a bio-child? It's the *raising* of a child that makes a person a parent, not donating one's genes."

As someone who had been rejected by her bio-parents, I had to agree.

"But," Knox continued, "Nicky told me that was easy

for me to say, since I'm sitting here with four biological kids."

Two of those kids chose that moment to open the sliding glass door and run into the kitchen. They were red-faced and sweaty from their antics on the jungle gym.

"*Dad!* Can we have lemonade?" asked a boy about six.

"You're interrupting, honey," said Knox, his tone kind but firm. "What do you say when adults are talking?"

"'Scuse me?"

Knox smiled. "Yes, you may have some lemonade. Need some help?"

"I can do it," the boy insisted.

"Use a plastic cup, and help your sister."

"'Kay. Come on," he said to his younger sister. "I'll help you."

The boy crossed over to the refrigerator, but the little girl lingered, staring at me. I smiled and winked at her. She flashed me a shy grin before hustling after her brother.

"Sweethearts," I whispered to Knox.

Knox smiled as he watched them, his eyes shining with pride and love.

"They're the reason I tried not to judge Nicky, even though I couldn't support what she was doing. I'd do anything for these little monkeys. Anything."

"And . . . I know this is probably hard to talk about, but what can you tell me about your mother?"

He settled back against the bench. "Ah, yes, Betty." The joy left his eyes. I could smell the turn of his mood: a slightly metallic, chalky scent, like gunpowder.

"How can I describe Betty?" His eyes were still on his children, who were now heading outside, carrying orange plastic cups with exaggerated caution. Halfway to the door the boy stopped to take a large gulp of lemonade, and his little sister mimicked him. Then they passed

through the sliding glass door and closed it after themselves. "Betty was glamorous. Beautiful. Classy, I guess
you would say."

"I saw the portraits of her. She was lovely."

He laughed wryly. "I suppose you mean the topless
pictures? Fred's a trip."

"They're not all topless, though," I said with a smile.
"Fred seems to have a knack for portraiture—there are
some beautiful renderings."

"I suppose," he said with a little sigh, sipping his tea.

"I'm surprised you don't want any of them."

"I just . . . I don't really want Fred's juju hanging on
my walls. It was tough enough dealing with my mother—
now, the *memory* of my mother—without having to
think of her . . . that way."

I have a difficult relationship with my mother as well,
and since I hadn't been around her as an adult, I'd never
really had to deal with the idea of her as a sexual being.
I supposed she and my father had experienced passion;
after all, she had been a beautiful young woman. And
little else besides sheer animal attraction would explain
how two such different personalities as she and my
worldly, ambitious father had managed to get together.
But the very thought of their sex life was enough to send
the likes of me into a tizzy.

"Was Betty in the military also?" I was trying to put
this family portrait together in my mind; somehow the
pieces just didn't fit.

"No, never, not at all. They didn't see eye to eye on
that, or on anything else. In fact, they never even married. The way I heard it, Betty and my dad got together
only long enough to conceive us. As far as I know, that
was about the extent of their interaction as a couple.
When we were very young, hadn't even started school

yet, Dad came and packed our bags; and from then on we were living in military housing. I hardly ever saw Betty after that—maybe once or twice a year, tops."

"I'm sorry."

He shrugged. "I don't think she was the maternal type. As an adult I can understand it: She was chic, sophisticated, a giver of cocktail parties. A couple of snotty, demanding kids didn't really fit her image. She had us relatively late in life for the time—in her late thirties. Maybe she thought she wanted to change her life, but when the reality set in . . ."

I nodded. "Reality can be a pail of cold water."

"That it can. I didn't start having kids until I was a little older, myself, and while it was a good decision to wait, all things considered, I sure could use a little of the energy of youth." He laughed, and I followed his gaze out the window, where the kids were running around and shrieking as they engaged in a pretend sword fight with long reeds from an overgrown water garden.

"Do you know anything about Betty being interested in anything occult?"

He shook his head. "No, nothing beyond tea. She was a fanatic for tea, so she used to get herbal concoctions from all over. But once Nicky said Betty told her not to go to El Pajarito for help, if that's what you're asking."

"Did she say why Betty warned her away?"

"Not in particular—I think she just wanted her to stick to proven medical methods. But once Nicky became obsessed with the whole natural motherhood thing, she was willing to try anything, and seemed to lose interest in anything else. I wish . . . I just wish I had known, that I'd been closer to her when it happened. Maybe I could have intervened, somehow."

I reached across the table and covered his hand with

mine. His vibrations were brittle, humming at a high pitch at odds to his calm countenance. Parents were often like this, I'd found: outwardly serene, but inside on high alert, watching their kids and planning for dinner and worrying about paying the bills, all at the same time. A juggling act. But could there be something else there? Guilt?

He squeezed my hand and smiled, then drew it away.

"You don't know anything about the girl named Selena, do you? She was a classmate of your niece, Emma."

He shook his head. "I've been making a point to spend time with Emma ever since what happened. But they live in the city, so I don't really know her school friends. You'd have to ask Gary about that. Or, better yet, Emma herself."

"Speaking of Gary, what do you think of him?"

"Gary? He's . . . he's a great guy. Really."

I tilted my head. "The way you say it makes me wonder if you really mean it."

Knox laughed, though I heard little humor in it. He kept scratching the back of his hand absentmindedly while he looked out at the yard, watching his little bundles of energy jumping and running through the tall grass.

He opened his mouth but hesitated another moment before speaking. "I knew Gary before he and Nicky married. Heck, I was the one who introduced them. He and I worked at a movie theater in college. He really is a great guy. But . . ." He blew out a long breath, and ran a hand through his hair. "I feel disloyal no matter which side of this I come down on. Here's the truth: Gary had an affair. There's no excuse for it, I know that. And I was furious with him on behalf of my sister. It's just that . . . Nicky really was acting nuts for the last year or so. What can I say? Maybe it's different for men than for women, I don't know. I love my children so much, I can't imagine life without them. If I didn't have them, perhaps I'd be as crazy as Nicky got in the pursuit of motherhood. So this isn't an excuse, but I guess part of me understands why Gary would turn to someone else."

I followed his lead and watched the children play for a few minutes, wondering whether Carlos knew about Gary's affair. The inspector was the one who always told me, after all, that the husband is the first suspect in any suspicious death. It was enough to make even a romantic soul cynical about relationships of the heart.

Gary had an alibi, but alibis were sometimes fabricated.

"If you want to know the truth," Knox continued, "I think Gary's guilt over the affair is part of the reason he's been having such a hard time dealing with Nicky's death. In fact, knowing Gary, I doubt he will ever forgive himself for it."

"Is he still seeing the other woman?" I knew the minute I said it my question was too nosy. But Knox seemed to be in the zone, that mood some people get into when they start talking and don't stop. It might have had to do with me—as a witch I seem able to cast a spell of comfort and trust that encourages people to speak. Or maybe as a househusband he was simply starved for grown-up company.

Knox looked surprised. "*No*, no. It wasn't really even an affair, really, more like something that got out of control. You know how it is: You've been drinking, you're coping with heightened emotions, you're with someone attractive and . . . boom."

I *didn't* know how it was. My relationship with Sailor was my longest romantic attachment, by far. I wondered what it would be like to be married for many years, long enough for the passion to wear off, the initial attraction replaced by a deeper love, with luck. But if that love was tested . . . Under the circumstances, perhaps Knox was right, perhaps anyone would be tempted.

"Did you have any indication Nicky was suicidal?"

"Not at all. She wanted to get pregnant, so I imagine she was distraught when she lost the baby."

"She lost a baby?"

"That's what she told me. A miscarriage, early on."

The sort of thing that can be caused by the wrong dose of the wrong sorts of herbs, I thought to myself. Maybe the police were aware of this and were using it to build their case against Ursula.

I glanced at the clock over the refrigerator, a cheap reproduction of a Parisian bistro clock, with big hands made of metal scrollwork.

"Could I ask you one more thing? Are you the one handling Betty's estate sale? Have you been going over to the house at all?"

He shook his head. "There's a professional estate liquidator taking care of all of that. Frankly, I don't want to deal with it. Like I said, I wasn't close with my mother. Barely knew her, actually. And as you can see, I've got my hands full here."

"So, you didn't arrange to have a *limpia* done on the place?"

"A *limpia*? Is that . . . you don't mean Filipino spring rolls, do you?"

I smiled, "No, that's *lumpia*, I think. A *limpia* is a sort of spiritual cleansing of a house."

He shook his head, a frown of incomprehension on his brow. "Should I have? No offense, but I'm not really into that sort of thing."

"No, I just wondered. Okay, well, thank you for your time and for sharing so much with me, Knox. I should let you get back to your kids, and I'll get back to work."

As we were getting up, we heard someone come in through the front door. A moment later Gary walked into the kitchen with a young teenager.

Chapter 13

"Gary, Emma," Knox said. "We were just talking about you."

Gary did not look pleased to see me. Emma, for her part, looked curious but blank. She was tall and pretty, wearing makeup and a short skirt, her feet shod in platform sandals. She looked awkward in the too-mature getup. I couldn't help but think of a little girl playing dress-up in her mama's closet.

"Hello, Gary," I said. "And, Emma, nice to meet you. My name's Lily."

She mumbled a hello and looked at her pink nails.

"What are you doing here?" demanded Gary.

"She's just . . ." Knox looked at me, a question in his eyes, as though he had only at this moment realized it was odd that I was here, asking about their family.

"I'm trying to find Selena," I said. "No one seems to know where she is; we're worried about her."

"You mean that charlatan's granddaughter? She's an aberration, that one."

"Gary," Knox admonished. "She's a child."

"I'm sorry," he said, one hand reaching up to rub the back of his neck as he blew out a long breath. He glanced at Emma. "I know she's just a girl, but she was the one who told Nicky about El Pajarito in the first place. And that girl seems to know things she shouldn't."

"Like what?"

He shrugged. "She and her sweet little old grandma were geniuses at cold reading. You know what that is? Fortune-tellers use it to scam people, make them think they're reading their minds. I wish . . . I just wish we had never met Ursula *or* Selena."

"Emma, do you have any idea where Selena might be?"

She shook her head. I sensed she had more to say, and wished I could think of an excuse to speak to her alone. But looking into the angry, grief-stricken, and possibly— given what Knox had told me—guilty countenance of her father, I doubted he would permit it.

I studied Gary for a moment. It didn't take a witch to sense the anger that emanated from his well-padded frame. But was there more going on here? Was I picking up on guilt that went beyond that of a man who'd had an affair and whose distraught wife had killed herself?

Knox escorted me to the back door, and I waved good-bye to the kids. They seem overjoyed to see their cousin Emma, whose attempt at teenage nonchalance fell away as she kicked off her heels and ran to join them.

As I was making my way around the side of the house to the street, I heard a burst of clapping and yelling.

I turned around to see the kids egging their father onto a small trampoline.

Gary stood to one side, unsmiling, watching me leave.

As I drove back across the Bay Bridge to San Francisco, I couldn't stop thinking about Selena.

Aidan mentioned Patience Blix was skilled in reading

the crystal ball and might be able to envision Selena's whereabouts. Would she do it? Was it worth a shot?

If only I had something that belonged to the girl. I should have thought to take something when I was in El Pajarito . . . clothes would be best for the likes of me, but for someone like Patience something metal would be better: a necklace, perhaps. Something Selena had worn close to her body. Most intuitives who were skilled in psychometry were able to pick up vibrations from metal jewelry.

I made a mental note to ask Carlos about going back to the store and picking something up.

But in the meantime, I happened to be driving right by Patience Blix's neighborhood. If she was as skilled as Sailor and Aidan kept insisting, what with being the head of the Fortune-Tellers Association and what-all, she should be able to look into her crystal ball and give me something to go on.

Even as I thought this, I knew it wasn't true. Magic didn't work that way. If it were that simple, murderers and ne'er-do-wells wouldn't get away with a darned thing. But still . . . I was right here, and I was burning with curiosity about this particular clairvoyant.

I drove around the block four times, debating whether or not to knock on Patience's door. On the one hand, I should have come prepared. On the other, I might well chicken out if I gave myself too much time to think about it.

What was I afraid of? This was Sailor's cousin, the woman who was training him to become stronger, and better. Surely I wasn't threatened by that, was I? So she was beautiful, what was the big deal?

While these thoughts were crowding my head, a Camry pulled out of the parking spot less than half a block from Patience's fortune-telling sign. I pulled in.

Enough with the indecision, Lily. This isn't about you, and it's not about you and Sailor. It's about Selena, a fourteen-year-old girl who needs help.

I got out of the car and climbed the wooden steps to the front door, painted a deep blue. The sisal doormat was decorated with a huge eye.

Ringing the bell, I gazed directly into the tiny camera in the corner. *Not so much of a psychic that she didn't need a little electronic assistance,* said a snide voice in my head.

An angry buzzing noise spurred me to open the door.

Straight ahead was a flight of carpeted stairs, a velvet cord strung across the first step from which hung a sign marked *"Private."* To the left, through a wooden archway, was the front parlor, a large room almost completely devoid of furniture. A worn Oriental rug lay upon the gleaming hardwood floor, and in the center of the rug was a small round table. It was covered by a heavy blue brocade that matched the floor-to-ceiling drapes and was flanked by two straight-back wooden chairs. An overhead chandelier and wall sconces cast an ambient glow across the room. On the walls were mirrors of all types: round and square, oblong and rectangular, antique and brand-new. One concave mirror radiated gold and silver spikes, like a sun. In the mirror's reflection the room appeared serene but distorted. Double doors at the back of the room separated the rest of the home from the parlor where Patience conducted her business.

I had barely taken it all in when the double doors slid open and a woman appeared.

She was even more beautiful than her photograph. Backlit by the sunny room behind her, Patience Blix was the embodiment of a romance novel heroine: Her hair was abundant and glossy, curling around her face and falling in a tumble down her back. Her mouth was full-lipped and generous, highlighted with red lipstick. Sparkling green eyes were lined in kohl. She was dressed in the best Hollywood Gypsy fashion: a purple peasant skirt, loose white blouse cut low across her ample bosom, a scarf tied jauntily around her waist, and lots of gold jewelry. Ropes of necklaces cascaded into her cleavage, big gold hoops in her pierced ears gleamed against the dark mass of her hair, and bangles adorned her slim arms. Gold anklets circled her slender, sandal-shod feet.

She smiled. At least, I thought it was a smile until she cocked one eyebrow and I realized it was more of a haughty smirk. She was amused, peering down her nose at me even though she was only a few inches taller.

"Lily Ivory, I presume?"

I nodded. Maybe she *was* psychic.

"I've been expecting you."

"Have you?"

"I saw it in my crystal ball."

"Really?"

She laughed, a sound like merry, tinkling bells. "No, of course not. Sailor said you might drop by. Have a seat. May I offer you some tea?"

"Um, no, thank you," I said, feeling off-balance. What did it mean that Sailor had assumed I might drop by? Was he annoyed at the thought? Amused by it? He couldn't read my mind, so did this mean he now knew me well enough to anticipate my movements? And if he could, what did this imply about us and our future together?

I slipped into one of the wooden chairs at the small round table. A stack of well-thumbed tarot cards sat to one side, and a large crystal ball held pride of place in the center.

Patience took the chair across from me.

For a moment we stared at each other.

She let out a husky peal of laughter. "You're not . . . quite what I expected."

"Is that right?"

She shrugged, the mocking smile never leaving her face. "When Sailor said you were a powerful witch, perhaps even more powerful than Aidan Rhodes, I pictured . . . someone else."

"Like who?"

"A woman. Not a little girl."

A small mirror flew off the wall and landed on the table with a clatter.

Patience jumped and I enjoyed a moment of satisfaction at seeing her smile slip. She regrouped and raised an imperious eyebrow.

"No need for parlor tricks," she said in a dry tone. "I'll take your word for it. Yours, and Sailor's."

"Sorry about that," I said, trying to calm myself down. "It wasn't intentional."

She shrugged, a slow, sensuous movement that seemed to promise . . . something. I wondered if she was aware of her effect, and suspected she was.

Great balls of fire, I thought. It was a good thing she and Sailor were cousins, because . . . how could a man resist a woman like Patience?

"What is the nature of the training you are giving Sailor?"

"Why don't you ask him?"

I had, of course, many times. And he remained mute on the subject. Which was totally his right, since it really was none of my danged business. And now what was I doing . . . ? Asking Patience about him, behind his back? *That's low, Lily. Get a grip.*

"Sorry. Never mind. I'm not here about Sailor," I said. "Aidan told me you are skilled at reading the crystal ball.

I'm looking for a girl, a fourteen-year-old who may be in danger. Can you help me find her? For a fee, of course."

"Do you have something of hers? A piece of jewelry, a lock of hair? An article of clothing, maybe?"

"No."

"And you think I can, what? Just conjure out of mid-air?"

"Why not? Everyone keeps telling me you're talented. So show me."

For the first time, she gave me a genuine smile. "Are you going to double-dog dare me next?"

"If I have to."

"You are very . . . droll."

"I try."

She settled back in her seat, tilted her head, and folded her arms across her chest. "You've met this girl?"

I shook my head.

"Been in her space, at least? Do you have some connection to her? This isn't some random name out of the paper, for instance?"

"Of course not. I was in her grandmother's shop, where she spent a great deal of her time. I touched a lot of things she might have touched. And I met her grandmother, though I didn't touch her."

Patience nodded. "All right. Let's see if you're the powerhouse everyone thinks you are."

"How do we do that?"

"I'll use you as a conduit to the girl. We'll hold hands and I'll read you."

"I . . . I don't know about that." I folded my hands in my lap. Like any witch worth her salt, I was habitually guarded, my emotions and sensations protected by the medicine bag around my waist, as well as a lifetime of shielding myself from others.

"Why don't you just look in there"—I nodded at the crystal ball—"and see without seeing? Unless that's beyond your abilities."

She gave me a patronizing look.

"Or . . . I could try to get something from the grandmother's shop," I offered.

"That might help. But let's first try it my way. What are you afraid of?"

You, I thought. *Me. But especially of me and Sailor.* And that was just for starters.

"Let me ask you about something else. How does a 'cold reading' work?"

"It's a technique used by fortune-tellers with no actual psychic powers. It's a very old parlor trick, in fact, which is also used by stage magicians. It involves pretending to know something about the subject, throwing out general statements until you stumble across something that rings true with the client. Then you build upon that. If it's done with enough confidence the client believes you're psychic, and you gain her trust."

"So it's fraud."

"Such a harsh word. I prefer to think of it as acting."

"But it's still a scam. I thought you were a genuine psychic."

In her face I saw a flash of annoyance, but she continued, "Once the client is emotionally involved, the reader tosses out more generalizations, watching the client's reactions to see when they've hit the right buttons. For instance, I might say: 'Lily Ivory, you are searching for love, but you are afraid. Afraid to allow yourself to be vulnerable, to trust. Afraid your boyfriend might not be faithful to you.' "

Two more mirrors fell, this time crashing onto the wood floor and sending glittery shards skittering across the room.

Patience and I both jumped up and twirled three times, counterclockwise. Each of us then pocketed a small piece of the shattered mirror that we would touch to a gravestone in order to avert the seven-year curse. I didn't like to think I had anything in common with this gypsy woman, but clearly we shared some traditions.

"Sorry," I muttered.

She shrugged and made a sweeping gesture, inviting me to return to my seat.

"My fault," she said. "I am not accustomed to dealing with one such as you."

"You sound adept at cold readings," I said.

"The average lawyer knows how to bribe a juror, too, though they may never do so."

"So you're saying your fortune-telling is truthful, not a scam?"

"Most people come to me because they don't have enough faith in themselves. They know what they should do, but lack confidence in their intuition. All I do is confirm what they already know. Yes, they pay me. But if they didn't come to me, they might pay a therapist to achieve the same result. My way gets faster results, and I guarantee you it's more fun for everyone involved."

"You don't have any genuine insights then?"

"I didn't say that. I have insights . . . but most of them I don't share with my clients."

"Why not? Isn't that what they're paying for?"

"You should know as well as I do that great harm can come from telling someone what is in their future. Generalities are one thing, but the very act of knowing one's future *changes* that future. And that would not be a responsible thing for me to do."

We stared at each other for a several beats.

"This is all very interesting," I said. "But I'd like to get back to the important matter: locating the girl."

"All right," said Patience. "What happened when you tried to read your crystal ball?"

"Not much. It's not one of my strengths."

"No? That's rare for one of your talents, isn't it?"

I shrugged.

"Let me read for you, and then we can talk."

With the exception of Graciela and Sailor's aunt Renna, I'd never allowed another practitioner to read for me and I certainly didn't want to start now. But there was something about the challenge in those green eyes. I didn't want to back down in front of this woman.

"Come now, you're not afraid, are you? According to you, a girl's safety is at stake," Patience said.

Who's playing double-dog dare you now?

I blew out a long breath. I needed to find Selena. But was this the only way? Not only was I afraid of allowing Patience, a virtual stranger, to access any part of my psyche, but it could possibly prove dangerous. When Aidan and I had connected, the resulting power surge caused some serious collateral damage. I wasn't at all sure I could control what might happen if Patience and I linked. And what if our energies clashed?

She reached across the table, rested her hand on the cloth for a moment, then slowly turned it palm up. Her fingernails were freshly manicured, her fingers festooned with gold rings. I placed my right hand on the table, inching it toward hers.

I looked into her dazzling, teasing eyes. Just as her fingers were about to wrap around mine I reared back, leaping up so quickly I knocked my chair over. It landed with a thud on the threadbare Oriental carpet.

The fortune-teller's laugh rang in my ears as I ran out the door and down the front steps. I didn't slow until I hit the sidewalk.

Idiot.

What was I truly afraid of? That our energies would

merge and create something out of control? Possibly. But property damage can be repaired. Was it that Patience would be able to read my mind?

Or did my fear stem from worry that Patience would tell me something about Sailor, or my relationship to him, that I didn't want to hear?

I had learned the hard way to be guarded in my life, to make sure when I was going into a potentially hazardous situation that I was armed to the teeth. So that's what I would do: I would brew, cast myself a centering, protective spell, and then come back to deal with Patience.

It would help to know more about her, though. Sailor was no help; Aidan not much more. Where else could I turn?

The newspaper. Nigel Thorne had quoted Patience in his article in the *San Francisco Chronicle* about fortune-telling scams. The article hadn't said anything about Patience being implicated, but that by itself meant nothing. Nigel was far too crafty a journalist to make unsubstantiated claims against anyone.

In person, however, Nigel might be more forthcoming about what he had uncovered about the delectable Patience Blix. Maybe now would be a good time to stop by the offices of the *San Francisco Chronicle*.

Out of the corner of my eye I caught my reflection in the shiny plate-glass window of a real estate office.

Today I was wearing a sundress featuring bright red cherries against a turquoise background. It was one of Lucille's reproductions, not true vintage but patterned on a dress from the early sixties. I wore a little red cardigan over the sleeveless bodice. I had thought the outfit was darling when I tried it on in the store, but in Aunt Cora's Closet I had been surrounded by friends and positive vibrations. Now . . . with my feet clad in scarlet

Keds, and my hair swept up in a ponytail tied with a gauzy turquoise scarf . . . Patience was right. I looked like a girl on her way to an after-school dance. Not like a grown woman.

Not like *her*. Nothing like Patience Blix, sexy, busty, confident, Rom fortune-teller.

Upon returning to my car, I resisted the urge to bang my head against the roof of my car. Goodness knows I'm no stranger to self-doubt, having experienced it often enough in my life. But this felt different. This stemmed from something I couldn't control, couldn't cast against. Being in love meant making myself vulnerable with no guarantee my feelings would be returned, and oh, was *that* a challenge.

What I *wanted* to do was to cast a love spell over Sailor, to ensure his everlasting fidelity and adoration.

But I couldn't. I *wouldn't*.

Graciela had drilled that lesson into me: *You must never use your power for the wrong reasons, m'ijita. That is not what it is for. And selfish reasons are almost always the wrong reasons.*

When I was in the fourth grade that lesson was driven home. I had developed my first crush on a boy, but he didn't return the sentiments, and my days were spent in a tizzy, my nights in painful, agonizing yearning. With the single-mindedness of youth I searched my grandmother's Book of Shadows for a love spell, and set about gathering the ingredients. Graciela found me in a neighbor's henhouse, searching for a spotted egg with a greenish cast. She grabbed me by the arm with impressive force for a woman of her diminutive stature and dragged me, protesting vehemently, back home.

"*No puedes forzar el amor, Lilita*—you can't force love. It will come or not come, it has its own energy in its world. It is a living, breathing entity. If you try to force it, you will corrupt it, and then you will destroy it. Understand? *M'entiendes*?"

And then she made me clean the kitchen *and* the bathroom with a pail of hot, sudsy water and an old toothbrush.

I wished I had the benefit of Graciela's wisdom as I sat behind the wheel of my car. I took a deep breath and tried to locate her. I couldn't do this for anyone else, but recently my grandmother seemed to have carved out a little place for herself inside the core of my being. It felt a little like when I was casting, reaching out through the years to the ancestors, and to the Ashen Witch, my guiding spirit. But this was quieter, more direct, and I immediately felt warm and connected. And calmer.

No, I wouldn't cast a love spell over Sailor. That was wrong, unethical, a violation of my powers.

What I *would* do, I thought as I turned the key in the ignition and pulled out onto Fillmore, was to stop by the offices of the *San Francisco Chronicle* to see what Nigel Thorne had to say about Patience Blix, the mayor's campaign against larcenous purveyors of magic, Nicky Utley's suicide, and El Pajarito.

Chapter 14

I was pleased to see the newspaper office was still abuzz. Journalists were becoming an endangered species as readers turned to the Internet for their news, and advertising revenues fell. The trend worried me, as I considered journalists among the last stalwarts against official corruption and vice. But then, perhaps they were simply finding their way onto the Internet, a medium to which I was a stranger.

I really *did* need to get over myself and join the twenty-first century. Put that on the list. Right after resolving this particular case of suspicious death and magical mayhem.

When I stepped off the elevator, I glanced around the big room full of cubicles. I didn't even know if Max Carmichael was still working regularly at the paper, much less what I would say to him if I saw him. I wanted to ask him about interviewing Lupita and the gang at El Pajarito, but it was awkward speaking with an ex-boyfriend. I hadn't had a lot of experience with this sort of thing.

I let out a sigh of relief when I spotted Nigel Thorne,

who had helped me out with my first paranormal case in San Francisco.

"Well, look who's here," Nigel said, his hawklike eyebrows shooting up. He was slouchy and potbellied, and had what looked like a coffee stain on his yellow oxford shirt. Long yellow hairs from his beloved golden retriever adorned his dark slacks. "Long time no see, Lily. How you doing?"

"I'm well, thank you. How about yourself?"

"Doin' okay. Wife's redoing the bathroom. You want to talk about dust?"

I smiled. "Maybe later. Right now I was hoping to talk about fortune-tellers."

"You saw today's article? Nice one, huh?"

"Well written, as always. And well researched. How did you get the fortune-tellers to talk to you?"

He shrugged. "I've got a way with people."

"Max Carmichael was the one who started the series, wasn't he? I seem to remember he wrote a piece on the *botanicas* in the Mission."

Nigel nodded.

"Do you have any idea why Max was poking around El Pajarito, in particular?"

"I asked him to do it as a favor. I'd set it up as a kick-off to the series, but a crisis at City Hall took precedence and I wasn't able to go. Max filled in for me, but he's got more important things to do these days."

"How is he?"

"Well."

I glanced around the room again. "Is he . . . here today?"

"Nope, he's freelance so you never know when he'll be stopping by. You should give him a call."

"I might just do that. I don't suppose you'd have a copy of that article he wrote about the *botanicas*, do you?"

"Sure, it's in the archives. I'll print it out for you," he said with a grunt as he leaned forward over his keyboard, typed something, and his desktop printer started up. He leaned back in his chair, which squeaked in protest, and fixed me with a look. "But something tells me you didn't come all the way over here just to ask for a reprint of an article. What's up?"

"What can you tell me about Patience Blix?"

"She's a knockout."

"So I've noticed. I was hoping to have a slightly more elevated discussion, perhaps about what she's like as a person."

He grinned. "Well, there's no evidence she's been bilking anyone. From what I can tell, she's taking over for Renna as the informal head of the local fortune-tellers. She appears to be a smart businesswoman, doesn't want any part of *bujo* cons."

"What's a *bujo* con?"

"It originally referred to a way to scam people out of money. *Bujo* means 'bag,' and refers to the bag of money people are told to bring to the con artist so as to remove a curse. The con artist substitutes the bag with the real money for an identical one containing worthless paper. The victim is told not to open the bag until a specified period of time, giving the con artist time to get away. Nowadays *bujo* refers to any kind of scam to wring money out of the wallets of idiots. I mean, to steal from gullible, vulnerable citizens."

"What prompted the mayor to launch his recent crusade?"

"As long as the fortune-tellers didn't get greedy, and the victims were mostly tourists, City Hall didn't care. But recently a few high-profile victims started raising holy hell when they realized they'd been snookered.

Rule number one in running a con: Don't target someone who can fight back."

"They were victimized by *bujo* scams?"

"Those, as well as a number of others, such as conning
the elderly into leaving all their worldly goods to Madame Sees-the-Future. Hey, if the fortune-tellers were
legit, why didn't they predict that their victims were
about to go toes-up?"

"Maybe they did. Maybe that's how they knew whom
to target."

Nigel's eyebrows shot up. "Hadn't thought of that."

"What about the owners of *botanicas,* like those in
the Mission? Why is the mayor targeting them?"

"Same reason. Disgruntled customers with connec-
tions in high places."

"Any specific cases?"

He shrugged and glanced at a glassed-in private office. "We can't talk about a lot of the cases at this point.
But there are one or two . . . Why are you asking?"

"Have you heard of Nicky Utley?"

"Killed herself, right? And now the DA's charged that
woman from El Pajarito. That's why you're interested in
Max's article?"

I nodded. "What can you tell me about that case?"

"Not much. Don't see how the DA will be able to
make the charges stick. Can you imagine trying to explain that to a jury? Dollars to donuts a judge'll toss the
case soon enough. Shame about the dead woman,
though. Her bad luck that the Golden Gate Guardian
didn't spot her in time."

"Is that like the Bridge Troll?"

Nigel laughed. "No, the Golden Gate Guardian's an
actual person. You never heard of him?"

I shook my head. "Who is he?"

"Guy who monitors the bridge. They say he's talked dozens of people out of jumping. True hero, in my book."

I agreed, but since, as Nigel pointed out, he had not been on guard when Nicky jumped, I didn't suppose it was particularly relevant. I asked the next question on my mental list.

"What about the woman at El Pajarito named Lupita? Her photo was included with Max's article. Someone told me she volunteered to bring a reporter to the shop."

"You gonna make me do some work? Hold on." Nigel rummaged through his messy desk, pulled out an old notebook, and started flipping through it. "Let me see here. . . . Yeah, here it is. You know, that was odd. One Lupita Rodriguez came in, proposed the story. That doesn't happen often with people from that community. That's why I jumped at the chance, and pitched the idea to my editor for a series of articles about supernatural issues."

"Do you have an extra copy of the article?"

He passed one over. I skimmed it: Max had interviewed several of the same shop owners Aidan and I had visited, including Ursula Moreno. The article described their shops, the merchandise, and the services offered in a flowing prose that sometimes bordered on the poetic. Max also described the need fulfilled by such shops: that people who were too poor or alienated by "modern" medical services looked to these *curanderas* for culturally relevant solace and hope. His sympathy was obvious, but so was his academic skepticism.

"Did Lupita ask to get paid, do you know?" I asked.

"She did, as a matter of fact," said Nigel. "But we don't pay for stories."

"So what was in it for her?"

"Not sure, to tell you the truth. She seemed pretty

happy with the article though, called to thank me. I remember she said her fiancé got a real kick out of it."

"Do you have a phone number for her, or an address? Any contact information?"

He shook his head. "She always came to me, and when I insisted I needed a number she gave me the one for the store, El Pajarito. But when I tried calling to fact-check something, the woman who answered said Lupita was almost never there, and was surprised she had given me that number."

"So, what's the next article in the series going to focus on?"

"Haunted houses."

"Seriously?"

"Believe it or not. I got the idea from Max's article, the bit about *limpias,* or spiritual housecleaning. I'll be interviewing some folks who claim to be able to see ghosts, but mostly the article will focus on how rumors of hauntings affect real estate values. Because, you know, I'm a *serious journalist.* Did you know in California real estate deals a seller has to disclose any death that occurred at a home, because so many people won't buy a house where a death occurred?"

"Really? I've never heard of such a thing."

"Good. That's what makes it news."

"Well, I should let you get back to work. So," I said, hoping to sound casual. "You don't expect to see Max anytime soon?"

"Matter of fact"—he thumbed through a dog-eared agenda—"looks like he's supposed to come in for a four-thirty meeting. Want to stick around?"

"Oh, no. Thank you, though."

"Want me to tell him you were looking for him?"

"No. No, I . . . actually, yes. Thank you. Here's my card."

"I imagine he remembers the number."

"Maybe. Thanks, Nigel."

"Good to see you, Lily. You take care, now."

"You too. And good luck with the remodel."

He rolled his eyes and snorted. "'His and hers' sinks. You believe that?"

Early that evening, in my apartment, I placed my Book of Shadows on the counter and flipped through it until I found the section on fertility spells.

I had never worked much with these kinds of spells because I didn't feel comfortable with such weighty magic. My grandmother did, though; she was also an experienced *partera*—midwife—as were many traditional *curanderas*.

Fertility spells were among the most difficult magic because they were meant to bring forth life. What could be more profound, more complicated, and more difficult than that?

How easily life can be taken away compared to how difficult it was to bestow, I thought. And that, I realized, was another reason to be suspicious of Ursula: A practitioner should not be so casual with fertility spells. On the other hand, I supposed she was right; perhaps conception sometimes involved emotions and belief as well as straightforward biology.

"Watcha doin'?" asked Oscar.

I was almost certain his question was the preamble to asking when he could expect his dinner. But I chose to take it at face value.

"Studying up on fertility spells."

Oscar's huge green eyes got even larger and more luminous, and he spoke in an awed, fierce whisper. "Mistress is going to have a baby? I *thought* I noticed you putting on weight!"

I stood up straighter and glanced down at my stomach. Was it pooching out? Was I looking *pregnant* now?

"Mistress *is*! Mistress is going to have a baby! Is it Sailor's?"

"Who else's would it be?" I said, momentarily distracted from the ridiculousness of our conversation by the notion that I could be pregnant with another man's baby.

Oscar started hopping around, but I couldn't tell whether it was out of agitation, or excitement, or both. He scampered up to his cubby over the refrigerator and disappeared within.

Belatedly, I realized I had misled him.

"*No*, Oscar. I'm not going to have a baby, not with Sailor or with anyone else. Apparently I need to cut back on the red velvet cake, though. Come down from there—are you hiding?"

He crawled out of his cubby and jumped down to the kitchen floor.

"This isn't about *me*," I continued. "I'm trying to figure out what happened to a woman who went to Ursula Moreno for help with fertility."

"Oh." Oscar looked crestfallen. Then I realized he was hiding something behind his back.

"What are you hiding?"

"Nothin'."

"So what's in your hand?"

"In what hand?"

"The one behind your back."

"Nothin'." He shrugged. "I'll put it back."

I craned my neck to see. It looked like a bit of cloth of some sort, covered in a hodgepodge of lace and ribbons and dried flowers.

"Oscar, what is that?"

He shrugged again and kicked his taloned feet. "It's a Ruerymplegandling cloth."

"A what, now?"

"A Ruerymplegandling cloth."

"A rue . . . ?"

With exaggerated patience, Oscar enunciated slowly: "Rue. Rymple. Gandling. Cloth."

At my blank expression, he gasped. "You tellin' me you've never heard of a Ruerymplegandling cloth?"

"I can't say as I have. What is it? May I see it?"

He hesitated.

"Please?"

Oscar laid the item on the kitchen counter. It was a scrap of cloth, a bit of broadloomed raw silk into which had been woven colored ribbons and feathers, lace, and long-dead flowers. There were even two powdery old butterfly wings attached to one side.

He gazed at it and caressed it gently with one over-sized, scaly hand.

"Oscar, does this belong to you?"

He nodded.

"Did you have it before you met me?"

He nodded again. "For the longest time. You wear it when you're introduced to the faerie court. So's the Good People of the woods don't try to eat you, or whatever."

"Well, that seems useful."

"My mother gave it to me. She brought me to the ceremony right before she had to change back."

Oscar's mother suffered under a curse that turned her into stone. Anytime we came across gargoyles, Oscar searched for her, looking for her face among the carved countenances.

I stared first at the Ruerymplegandling cloth, then back at my familiar. "And you were going to give it to me?"

"To your baby. Not to *you*," he said, laughing so hard he began to snort. "I know you want to be introduced to the woodsfolk, but a Ruerymplegandling cloth is for helpless little babies, not grown-up *witches*!"

He cackled some more at the absurdity of a witch my age appropriating a Ruerymplegandling cloth.

"That's very sweet of you, Oscar. Thank you for thinking of it."

He shrugged. "Weren't nothin'."

"Anyway, I'm sorry to disappoint you, but I was looking at fertility spells because I was trying to understand what happened to Nicky Utley, the woman who jumped off the Golden Gate Bridge."

"Why do you care?"

"Because I think she may not have made that decision of her own free will."

"Well, *duh*. Hey! I have an idea! Let's have mac-and-cheese for dinner!"

"In a minute. What do you mean by 'duh'?"

"She was on the bridge because of the spell, right?"

"How do you mean?"

"Fertility conjures involve tossing the charged charm into a mystical body of water. The Golden Gate Bridge is built over some pretty mystical waters."

The Golden Gate Bridge was not only a gorgeous example of classic Art Deco architecture; it had also been constructed in an enchanted spot. The bridge spanned the site where the ferocious Pacific Ocean met the serene San Francisco Bay, and connected urban San Francisco to the wilds of the Marin Headlands. I had tossed charged charms from the bridge on more than once occasion, myself.

"Why didn't I think of that? Oscar, you're a genius."

"Aw, go on," he said and ducked his head. "You would have come up with mac-and-cheese eventually."

"I meant about the bridge, not dinner. So maybe Nicky Utley went to the middle of the bridge to toss a fertility charm over the railing into the water below," I thought aloud. "And then what? She became so overwhelmed by emotion that she threw herself over as well?"

"But why would you go through the trouble of casting a fertility spell if you're just gonna kill yourself?" Oscar pointed out.

"That's true. Maybe—"

The phone rang. Few people have my home number, and since I had a form of witchy caller ID I knew it was Sailor before I even picked up.

I wasn't surprised, either, when he told me he was canceling our date for dinner, citing more training with Patience.

I blew out an exasperated breath.

"Everything okay?" Sailor asked.

"Not really, no." I wasn't in the best frame of mind, having spent all day running around speaking with Knox, and Patience, and Nigel. What was worse, I *still* didn't feel any closer to finding Selena, or Lupita, much less figuring out what was going on in Ursula's shop or how it fit in with the death of Nicky Utley.

"What's wrong?" asked Sailor. "Do you need me?"

"No, it's just that . . . I have something I want to ask you."

"Shoot."

"It's . . . I mean, it's probably silly. I just, I don't even know . . . oh, never mind."

He chuckled. "Is this a question better asked in person?"

"Probably." I tried to stop there, but for some reason kept talking. "It's just . . . you and Patience."

"Yes?"

"She's . . . I mean, I saw the article about her today in the paper. And . . . she's gorgeous."

Silence.

"I mean . . ." Having started this, I might as well finish. "What do you two do, all that time together?"

"We're training, Lily. You know that."

"What kind of training?"

"Tell me what's really going on."

"I stopped by to see her today."

"May I ask why?"

"I was hoping she could find the missing girl, Selena."

"Find her how?"

"Aidan said she's pretty skilled with the crystal ball."

"You saw *Aidan*? When was this?"

"He was at Hervé's shop when I went by."

"Did he try anything? Are you okay?"

"I'm fine. He acted like nothing had happened, more or less."

"Huh. I hate to say it, but that's worrying. Aidan's not the type to let something like this go."

"I know. He made it clear that I owe him, but for the moment I think we're working together. He's trying to find Selena, too."

"I'll just bet he is."

"What does that mean?"

"You told me everyone thinks this girl is powerful, right? Aidan likes to keep powerful people right where he wants them."

"Maybe, but he seems genuinely worried about her welfare."

There was silence on the other end of the line. After a long pause, Sailor said, "That might be. But if and when you find the girl, keep her out of Aidan's clutches. If you can."

"You think he's really that bad?"

"You're seriously asking *me* that?"

"I . . . Listen, I'd like to ask Patience to look for Selena again, and maybe speak with her more about fortune-telling scams."

"Why?"

"I think it may be relevant."

"Is that really why?"

I bit my lip and didn't reply.

"Tell you what, I should be done about midnight. Meet me at my place," Sailor suggested. "We'll talk more about Patience in person, if that's what you'd like."

My heart lifted. "Okay. See you then."

"Good. Can't wait."

I hung up with a smile. And then made a decision. If Sailor wasn't coming over, I could spend the evening checking something out. I bustled around the kitchen gathering items to place in my satchel: a small Mason jar of all-purpose shielding brew, a bag of salts, another of mixed herbs. My medicine bag was tied around my waist, as usual, but under the circumstances I thought it wise to take some extra protection.

Oscar watched me, concern in his big green eyes. "Does this mean no mac-and-cheese?"

"'Fraid so. But there are plenty of leftovers in the fridge. Why don't you make yourself a nice dinner? With cake *after*, not before."

"Can't I come with you?"

"I'm going to the Golden Gate Bridge, and I doubt pigs are allowed. I've never even seen a dog on the bridge."

"I'm no *dog*," Oscar said, annoyed. He was a proud little guy. By and large, Oscar was pleased with his piggy guise, but he hated being compared to a dog. I had tried to explain to him that I was a dog person, that they were a human's best friend, examples of loyalty and devotion and all that. He remained unimpressed.

But then I thought about the Ruerymplegandling cloth Oscar had planned to share with my supposed baby. I relented.

"All right, come along if you want. But I'm sorry to say, dog or no, you'll have to wear a leash."

Chapter 15

The sign clearly read: *No Dogs Allowed.*

I looked down at Oscar. He returned my gaze, pink piggy eyes imploring.

My familiar wasn't a *dog.* So strictly speaking we weren't breaking the rules. But probably the forbidding of livestock was implied.

I glanced around, searching our surroundings. There were no guards, no security of any sort that I could see. Probably someone was sitting in a guardhouse watching the entrances to the bridge on a closed-circuit TV. But even if so, it would take a while before someone could get here.

Graciela always said: *It's easier to ask for forgiveness than for permission.* A handy motto, especially if you happened to be a witch who occasionally needed to color outside the lines.

"Hurry," I said. "When breaking the rules it's best to be quick about it."

Oscar trotted at my side as we walked along the pedestrian walkway, heading for the center of the span.

Several passersby paused to laugh when they saw Oscar, some patting him as we hurried along. But most were too occupied to notice us; they were taking pictures, soaking up the beauty of the sunset, and appreciating the majesty of their surroundings.

The tourists were easily distinguished from the locals by their lack of warm clothing, having underestimated how chilly San Francisco could be in the summer. Though it was cold and windy, I had lived in San Francisco long enough to realize that "summer" wasn't the warm season here. So I had come prepared, and was snug in my vintage wool coat and scarf. The setting sun cast a glorious orange light on the Tuscan red paint of the bridge. Streaks of clouds hovered over the horizon, and a fogbank slowly rolled in from the ocean.

Oscar and I passed dozens of people snapping photos that would never manage to capture the glorious light of the here and now. A little boy cried when his red helium balloon was caught by a strong gust of wind; his father comforted him as the balloon danced in the breeze over the bay. A young couple attached a padlock to the metal railing, then tossed the keys into the gray water below, laughing and kissing.

The Golden Gate Bridge was a wondrous place. I found myself understanding, with some chagrin, why it would be a glorious place to end it all.

Amid the throng of the living I felt whispers of ghosts. Could one of them be Nicky Utley? Or was I sensing the remnants of the hundreds of souls who had thrown themselves off the span into the churning waters below?

At the halfway point, I stopped and leaned over the four-foot-high rail, noting the lack of any other form of restraint or safety net. No cables, no fence, no obstructions of any kind that I could see to prevent someone from resisting the temptation to climb up and over.

"Don't jump," came a voice from behind.

"*Aidan,*" I said, surprised, and more than a little trepidatious. "What in the world are you doing here?"

Oscar snorted and hopped about, his typical response to Aidan, but then hid behind my legs. I wasn't sure if he had seen Aidan since I freed Oscar from his obligation to his former master.

"You stole my line," said Aidan. "What are *you* doing here?"

"Enjoying a sunset stroll with my familiar, of course."

"Of course. Anything more to it than that?"

"I've been trying to figure out what happened with Nicky Utley. I wanted to feel . . ." I shook my head and looked out at the gray nothingness. The wind whipped my hair, and I could taste ocean salt. "There is something very seductive about the ocean here. Somehow it makes sense that folks kill themselves jumping off this bridge."

Aidan frowned. "Do you want to tell me about it?"

"Tell you about what?"

"About whatever it is that has prompted you to consider, even for a moment, jumping."

"No. No, of course not. I was trying to put myself in Nicky Utley's position, hoping to learn something about what happened that night, that's all. Really, Aidan."

He smiled. "Sorry. Must be the influence of such a magical spot."

"So why *are* you here? Did you learn anything new about Selena?"

"No, sorry to say, I haven't. But I walk out here often," he said. Like me, Aidan couldn't seem to keep his eyes off the slate-gray water below.

"Really? Why?"

He shrugged, and avoided my eyes.

Just then a police officer walked past us, nodded politely to me, and greeted Aidan by name. His eyes flickered down to Oscar, who was still unsuccessfully attempting to hide his girth behind my skirts.

Aidan gave the officer a beautiful smile. "Nothing to worry about," he said reassuringly.

"Evening, Mr. Rhodes. Ma'am." The officer continued walking.

"You know him?" I asked a moment later.

"In passing."

"I thought you weren't a fan of the police."

He grinned. "I have no problem with the police, though they occasionally have a problem with me."

"How did he know your name?"

"I told you, I come here often."

Hold on. "You're not . . . I mean, you couldn't be the . . . Golden Gate Guardian?"

"No, of course not." He would not look at me, but embarrassment rolled off him in waves.

"You are! Aidan *Rhodes* is the Golden Gate *Guardian*?"

"Keep it down, would you please?" Aidan said in an urgent whisper. He looked around and said quietly, "*No*, I'm not. The real Guardian is Sergeant Kevin Briggs of the California Highway Patrol. Over the years, he's credited with saving more than two hundred souls. But he can't be everywhere at once. So others pitch in from time to time."

"When did you . . . how did you start doing this?"

"A few months ago I saw a man climb over the railing. He just stood there, looking down at the water, for the longest time. I introduced myself, and we started talking. It turned out his wife was in the hospital, he didn't know how he was going to pay the medical bills, he had lost his job, and his father had died recently. I guess everything had come crashing down on him all at once."

Aidan paused and turned to watch the sun setting.

The fading light bathed the stunning planes of his face in an otherworldly, golden glow.

"Did you cast a spell over him?" I asked.

"I tried, but he was so wrapped up in his misery, he didn't respond to my magic. I figured the longer I could keep him talking, the less likely he was to jump. Frankly, I kept expecting some help to arrive, someone with a net or something," he said, chuckling. "I almost panicked when I realized it was just him and me. So I asked what his wife would do without him, and he said if he died she would be able to collect his life insurance. Which wasn't true, of course; very few life insurance policies pay in cases of suicide. I didn't tell him that, though; figured that might depress him even more. So I just kept talking."

"What made him change his mind?"

"I asked him how his wife would feel the moment she realized he was gone, that he wouldn't be there to help her when she left the hospital. . . . A very long hour and a half later, he accepted my offer of help."

"That's amazing, Aidan," I said. "What a wonderful thing to have done."

"You needn't sound so astonished. Is it so hard to imagine me doing a good deed?"

"It's not that. Really. I just . . ." I trailed off with a shrug.

"It's just that you are more likely to think of me manipulating the mayor from my office, then out in the world helping people."

"Or stealing Oscar's wings and holding them hostage, that sort of thing, yes."

He shrugged. "I do what I have to do."

I decided I'd circle back to that line of thought later. "So, after talking the first man off the bridge, you kept going? Now it's a regular gig?"

"After speaking with the officers who have witnessed

more of their fair share of suicides off this bridge, I realized that I just got lucky connecting with a man like that. So I got some training, and now I walk out here at night whenever I have the chance."

"That's really . . . something . . ." I trailed off, feeling as though my response was painfully inadequate. Aidan Rhodes, patient, understanding, suicide counselor? This was a whole new side to him, one that I'd only suspected lurked somewhere beneath that too perfect exterior. It was difficult to reconcile this with his selfish, brutal side, to which I'd also had ample exposure.

Nor was I forgetting the troubled history between him and Sailor, and him and Oscar . . . but the truth was, it was so much easier for me to dislike Aidan when he wasn't nearby. In person, there was some undeniable connection between us—perhaps it was just the recognition of kind, the inkling of kinship between powerful witches.

I worried about myself sometimes. When I started spellcasting I tapped into a deep, murky part of my core that sometimes scared me. I became oblivious to all, and hell-bent on succeeding in whatever I willed, even if others fell by the wayside. That tendency toward single-mindedness seemed to be increasing with time and experience—in direct proportion to my growing power—rather than diminishing.

I suspected that not only did Aidan know this about me, he understood—even *admired*—it. Sometimes I appreciated that, but usually it worried me.

"I feel almost like spirits are trying to speak with me when I stand here," I said. "But as usual, I can't understand them. Do you think it's possible Nicky's trying to make contact?"

"You mean, if her death was the result of murder rather than suicide? That her restless spirit is seeking you out? Possibly. But a suicidal woman might also leave behind a restless spirit as well."

"True enough. I don't really know why I came here. I just thought maybe I could feel something, or I would see something that gave me some insight. Maybe I should see if Sailor can make contact with anyone, or sense anything." *If Patience would allow him to*, I thought.

"You and I could try," said Aidan. After a rather pregnant pause he added: "Together."

"That doesn't go well. Remember what happened that time we linked our powers?"

"I wasn't prepared last time. I believe I'm more in control now, as are you."

"But . . . San Francisco is my adopted city. I would feel pretty rotten if we managed to melt the Golden Gate Bridge."

Aidan laughed. "You're right. Something like that would tar the reputation of the magical community for many years to come. But, as I said, I'm prepared this time. And you're much more polished than you once were. I think we could risk it."

Tourists pushed past us. The sun had gone down, leaving only an orangey night sky and the light of the overhead lamps reflecting off the breezy wisps of fog.

The bridge would be closing soon. It was now or never.

Aidan's blue gaze met mine, and I had a sudden visceral memory of what it felt like to kiss him. For months now, being with Sailor had been so overwhelming that I hadn't even *thought* of another man. And I wasn't thinking of being with Aidan in that way, either . . . but there was no denying the memory. The strong, deep, frightening connection I had felt when our lips met.

Aidan held out his hand.

"Don't be afraid. I'll be with you."

"That's what I'm afraid of."

He ignored this. "Check that your guard is up against me, and then cast a summoning spell using my power as conduit."

"You think?"

"Seriously, Lily. You are much more powerful than you think you are. If anything, *I'm* the one who should worry that you'll siphon off part of my energy. Do you want insight into what happened with Nicky Utley, or not? Maybe it will tell you something to help locate Selena."

He was right.

I'm not a necromancer and have never been able to communicate directly with those who have passed on to other dimensions, but sometimes they were able to send me visions or sensations.

I closed my eyes, stroked my medicine bag, and centered myself. It was crucial to feel safe when casting; I was cautious of Aidan, but when I connected with my ancestors and tapped into the power of my guardian spirit, the Ashen Witch, serenity and calmness washed over me.

I started chanting a simple charm that helped me open to the energy of the spirit world:

You are welcome here, you are invited.
Come to me, reach out to me, allow me to see.
Take my hand. Help me to understand.
Until moon and sea are reunited.
I call to thee; so mote it be.

I reached out and clasped Aidan's hands in mine. The moment our palms met, I felt a current rush and throb between us. Then he leaned down slightly and we touched our foreheads together.

There it was.

The energy sang between us. Every atom, every molecule in my body zinged to attention, became encircled by vibrating rings of energy. My hair lifted from my scalp, and for a brief moment I wondered if this was what it felt like to be electrocuted. But there was no pain—on the contrary I felt allied and connected to a great energy source beyond anything I had ever imagined. It was similar to when I was spellcasting, and the portals between me and my ancestors opened . . . but multiplied a thousandfold.

I held my breath, but the metal of the bridge didn't start fluxing, so that was something. And then . . . flashes. Glittery, shiny bits of light engulfing me. Silvery flickers of brilliance. Was that sunlight glinting on the water? But that couldn't be; the fog was rolling in, and the sun had set.

Leaning far over the railing, gazing at the water below, I felt strong hands at my back.

And then the terror of weightlessness as I fell, the water rushing up to meet me.

Chapter 16

I was yanked away a split second before hitting the water.

"Lily," I heard a stern voice calling. "Lily, come back. *Come back!"*

It was like waking from a nightmare, in the nick of time. I came out of the trance to find Aidan's arms wrapped around me. Just as before, we were still standing in the middle of the bridge, by the railing. Aidan was reassuring passersby that he had me, that I was fine.

"What happened?" I asked, my voice muffled by the damp fabric of his overcoat.

"You seemed to want to jump." He pulled away slightly to study my face. "You sure there's nothing you want to share with me?"

I managed a rueful smile. "My troubles might make me hopping mad, but they don't prompt me to jump off a bridge. Believe me."

"Did you see anything? Feel anything?"

"A lot of shiny lights, and then . . . I think I was envisioning Nicky headed over the rail, toward the water."

"That's it?"

I nodded. "Except . . . there were hands at my back. I mean, her back."

"Tell me exactly what you felt."

"I was leaning over the rail, looking at the water. I had no idea of jumping—my attention was captured by the light flickering off the water. And then I felt hands at my back."

"Were the hands trying to save you or trying to push you over the rail?"

"I guess that's the $10,000 question."

Aidan held my gaze for a long moment, then shook his head.

"The $10,000 question," he said, "is this: Whose hands were they?"

"Didja see *that*?"

The whole way home Oscar nattered on about seeing Aidan, excited but nervous. To calm him down when we got home, I encouraged him to sing a little Billie Holiday karaoke—*Stormy Weather*—while I made three-cheese mac-and-cheese. He finished off a huge wedge of cake before crawling into his cubby over the refrigerator.

I filled my old claw-foot bathtub, adding bath salts from the Dead Sea, infused with lavender and rose petals. Sitting back in the hot, fragrant water, I breathed deeply and reflected upon what I knew. Rolling it over in my mind.

If Nicky Utley had not committed suicide—and my vision raised that possibility—who *had* killed her? If she had walked out to the center of the Golden Gate Bridge to cast her spell charm into the churning waters below, might she have leaned out so far that someone could have pushed her without being seen?

According to Carlos, there were witnesses to Nicky's

death; if someone had pushed Nicky, surely someone would have mentioned it. I tried to imagine Carlos's reaction if I were to ask for a list of the witnesses so I could go interview them.

On the other hand . . . could we be dealing with someone who was able to push her from afar? Even someone skilled in poppet magic would have had to have known when Nicky Utley was on the bridge, and when she was leaning over the rail . . . there was no way to see something like that from afar, was there? Unless, of course, one had the gift of sight, like a certain fortune-teller I knew.

Could I somehow pin this on Patience?

I chided myself. *That's the jealousy talking, Lily.* Why in the world would Patience go after Nicky Utley?

Maybe I needed to take a different tack.

Who might want Nicky Utley dead? Was her husband, Gary, so sick of her quest to become pregnant, or perhaps so enamored of a girlfriend, that he would kill her? Or did he have a financial motive? As Aidan pointed out, suicide voids most life insurance policies, but perhaps Nicky had money of her own that Gary would inherit if she died.

Who else stood to benefit from Nicky's death? Nicky Utley was Betty North's daughter, and Betty had recently died. Which reminded me, I still hadn't found out who benefitted from Betty's will.

Nosy-witch fail.

Maybe Maya knew. After all, she had witnessed the signing of the revised will. I would ask her tomorrow. If the heir was Ursula Moreno, then I guessed she would be up on those fraud charges. This was exactly the sort of thing the mayor's campaign against fortune-tellers was targeting.

But then . . . Knox told me Betty had warned Nicky

away from El Pajarito. So surely Betty wouldn't have left her estate to Ursula Moreno. But then, unless Betty had specified that someone else inherit her estate, Knox was now the sole surviving family member. He had four kids. That must be expensive, especially in the Bay Area.

Who else? There was Fred, Betty's boyfriend. Could he have wanted to inherit Betty's house so badly that he was willing—and able—to kill Nicky Utley? Maybe to keep her from reuniting with her mother? But that would still leave Betty's son, Knox, to inherit, and taking out both of Betty's children would surely arouse suspicion.

Finally, what about Selena and Lupita? They were missing, which seemed mighty suspicious. Unless, of course, they had simply run off to Mexico or somewhere where life was less complicated than with Ursula and her possessed herbal store.

Then I remembered: Maya had printed out the transcript of her talk with Betty.

I got out of the bath and pulled on a Victorian-style robe made of soft lawn, then crept down the stairs to the store. I found the transcript near the register in a manila folder neatly labeled: *Betty Marie North.*

I started flipping through the pages as I climbed the steps, pausing to read when I found a relevant section.

Betty: *I'm sorry to say I haven't got a maternal bone in my body. I love my children, of course I do, but . . . they're better off with their father. They call themselves military brats, can you imagine? They seem quite proud of their father, and I think the strict lifestyle has been good for them.*

Maya: *Do you ever see them?*

Betty: *Rarely, I . . . I'm sorry. It's not something I like to talk about. But do you know, recently I've been doing a little babysitting. Me! Can you believe that? For the first time*

I understand why people might like children. Does that sound terrible? Of course it does. But then, this is not a typical little girl. She's very special.

I froze.

Ursula mentioned Lupita sometimes took Selena with her on outings. Could one of those outings been to Betty North's house? Hervé said Selena left right after he and Caterina spoke about babysitting—maybe it gave her an idea, jogged her to think about Betty. If Selena was fourteen she was too old to need a babysitter *per se,* but she might well have spent time with Betty. Finally, Finn had mentioned that things had been moved around in Betty's house.

Maybe it wasn't a ghost at all. Maybe it was a little lost girl.

It was worth a try.

I pulled on the same dress I'd worn that day, pondering logistics. Maya didn't answer her phone; she typically went to bed early. I considered calling Finn or Knox to get the combination for the lockbox at Betty's house, but it was almost ten at night, which was late for a lot of working people. And even if it wasn't, what possible legitimate reason could I offer for wanting access to Betty's house?

I called Sailor and left a message that I wouldn't be coming over tonight, after all. It was on the tip of my tongue to tell him why, or to ask him to meet me at Betty's house. But he was busy with Patience.

Besides, if I was right, and Selena was hiding in Betty's house . . . it would be best to deal with her myself, just the two of us "oddballs."

Finally, I rifled through the steamer trunk that doubled as a coffee table in my small living room. In it I kept tucked away, out of sight, many of my most precious magical items. I pushed aside small crates of stones and crystals, packages of rare feathers, and bags of specialty dust from cemeteries and dust storms, until I unearthed a leather-bound box. Setting it on the couch, I opened it to reveal a Hand of Glory, which I had long ago recovered from a supernatural crime scene. It was a gruesome artifact, but came in handy in cases such as these.

A genuine Hand of Glory is the preserved left hand of a hanged man, in whose palm is placed a candle. The one who holds this macabre item can open locks and see in the dark as though it were bright as day. As much as I didn't relish touching the grisly thing, it was one of my most useful possessions.

"Where we going?" asked a sleepy-sounding Oscar from behind me. He was wearing an old-fashioned nightcap, the kind pictured in old books of fairy tales.

"What's with the nightcap?"

"What, you want a drink? Okay, I'm game. What'll it be? Scotch? Bourbon? Brandy?"

"No, not that kind of nightcap—the actual nightcap. The one on your head."

He shrugged. "I found it in the shop. Don't you think it looks good on me?"

"It looks great on you," I said with a smile.

"So, where we going?"

"You're not going anywhere, you're staying here."

His shoulders slumped and he kicked at the ground. "I'll wear the stupid leash."

"No, sorry, little guy, not this time. I . . . well, it's hard to explain. But tonight I'm better on my own."

"Is it dangerous?"

"No." At least, I didn't think so. How dangerous could a teenage witch be? *Don't answer that.*

"I should go with you. You might need your Oscar backup. You know how you are."

"Listen . . . I really don't think it's dangerous this time.
I'll bring my protective amulets and a jar of brew. And if
I sense anything worrisome, I'll call for you, okay? Go on
back to your cubby."

He grumbled, but disappeared into his bed over the
refrigerator.

Twenty minutes later I pulled up to Betty's yellow
stucco house, switched off the engine, and sat for a moment, studying the building from the safety of the car. It
seemed vaguely sinister now, a dark facade against the
city-bright night sky. When I was here with Maya—was
it only two days ago?—it had seemed cheery enough, full
of souvenirs of a good life. Now I couldn't help but think
about that ugly voodoo doll, Betty's estrangement from
her children, Nicky Utley's suspicious death, and the
havoc being wreaked at Ursula's shop. How did it all
come together?

I couldn't figure it out.

With no further insight, I climbed the front stairs and
extracted my macabre charm. The Hand of Glory did its
job and unlocked the front door with ease, then filled the
house with light.

Finn had been hard at work. The cabinets had been
cleared of their curios, which were now laid out in neat
groupings on long tables covered in white cloths. The
furniture had all been priced, each tagged with a 3 x 5
card holding a description: "*Antique walnut highboy with
cherry and oak inlay, circa 1920 with original hardware*"
and "*Cherry dining room set, 1950s, with two leaves to
seat ten.*"

The descriptions revealed a salesman's skilled ability
to make lemonade out of lemons: an ugly, plaid-covered
couch became a "*Midcentury classic streamlined sofa.*" I
smiled. Every once in a while I acquired some truly
wretched items for Aunt Cora's Closet, but lo and be-

hold, if they were presented with sufficient aplomb, someone would go home with that shiny Lycra jumpsuit they'd always wanted.

I stood for a moment in the living room, breathing deeply, trying to feel.

But I sensed no errant vibrations. Nothing more than the creepiness of trespassing in a stranger's house, uninvited, in the middle of the night. Witchy sensitivity or no, that was just plain eerie.

I checked the bedrooms and found more of the same: white-cloth-covered tables holding everything from ceramic dogs to silk flowers, and items of furniture tagged with prices and descriptions. The many prescription bottles had been discarded, as well as all prosaic, everyday objects such as toothpaste and toothbrushes. As the little items of daily life were culled, the traces of Betty North disappeared.

The house was no longer a home, but one huge display case.

It made me feel sad for Betty. Was she mourned by anyone besides Maya, and perhaps Fred? Did her children grieve for her? One of those children had supposedly committed suicide, I reminded myself, not long after her mother's passing.

Had death connected Betty with her daughter in a way that life had not?

In the kitchen the cupboard doors stood open, displaying sets of china alongside more utilitarian dishes. A stack of vintage cookbooks sat on the counter, and I squelched the impulse to thumb through their pages . . . but I made a mental note to ask Finn about them. I was trying to resist buying vintage kitchen accessories, but surely cookbooks were another matter altogether.

The door to the stairs leading to the rumpus room was ajar. Thick carpeting muffled my footsteps as I descended.

Finn had been at work here as well. There were tables lining the walls, and two in the center, all covered in white cloths with shining silver items neatly laid out: several tea services, platters, charger plates, pitchers, vases, cutlery. They gleamed brightly, even in the dim light of the sconces, but in their formality they looked out of place against the bright orange Naugahyde of the rumpus room.

Halfway down the stairs I paused, midstep.

An apparition stood at one of the tables, polishing silver.

Chapter 17

She was dressed from another time: a ruffled pink-and-purple ensemble that looked like an old-fashioned grandmother's idea of a child's wardrobe, not that of a modern American teenager. Her hair was pulled back tightly and hung in two long, tight braids down her back, both tied with pink ribbons. She appeared painfully thin, with gangly arms and legs. Two sparkly brooches, so large and garish they looked absurd on her small frame, were pinned to her lavender sweater. And her hands were covered with prim white cotton gloves.

She was laying things out, humming absentmindedly, off-key.

"Selena?"

She looked up, and I almost wished she hadn't. Her eyes bulged in her thin, pinched face, and were so dark they looked black. But it was the emptiness that worried me. She didn't seem surprised; indeed, she hardly seemed to register my presence.

"Selena, I'm Lily. Lily Ivory. Your grandmother Ursula asked me to find you and take care of you until she can come home."

Carlos said Selena was fourteen, but this girl looked younger than that, just on the verge of adolescence. Much less mature than her schoolmate Emma Utley, for instance. But then, I'm no expert when it comes to kids.

Still . . . I couldn't shake the sense that something was wrong. I knew it. I felt it. *She doesn't fit in. She's weird. A misfit.*

"Hablas ingles?" I asked her if she spoke English, hoping the answer was yes; my Spanish is a strange mélange of English, Spanish, and Nahuatl, the language of the Aztecs that my grandmother grew up speaking. The only Spanish I speak fluently is the version I used for spellcasting and ordering herbs and specialty items, like Dragon's Blood resin and freeze-dried bats.

"I knew you were here. I smelled lilies," Selena finally said, wrinkling her nose and turning back to rearranging the silver serving spoons. "Betty didn't like the silver to be mixed up. She said they went in this order. It's important to place them in order."

I watched her for a long moment as she laid out the place settings, complete with dessert spoons and salad forks in addition to the basic spoon, knife, and fork.

It was like looking in a mirror at my adolescent self: gawky, fearful . . . *magical.* I was picking up her powerful vibrations from across the room.

Great. A troubled teenage witch.

Selena seemed to study the layout for another long moment before finally nodding and giving the silver a final pat.

"Betty says always to wear white gloves when handling silver. Not rubber gloves. Rubber tarnishes."

"My grandmother told me the same thing," I said,

walking toward her slowly. "Though we didn't have nearly this much silver, just a serving bowl or two."

"I used to help her clean it. We washed off the tarnish. Betty says no matter how bad the tarnish, it can be removed with ketchup. Not the toxic stuff."

"Ketchup?" I gave a soft laugh.

"What's funny?"

"I've never heard of using ketchup to wash tarnish off silver."

"What do *you* use?"

"To tell you the truth, I mostly ignore it."

Selena shook her head, looking down at the silver arrayed before her. "You shouldn't do that. That's not right. Silver is meant to be shiny."

She started humming again, picking items up and cleaning them.

"Selena," I began in as gentle a voice as I could manage. "I'd like you to come home with me."

She gazed at me, an empty, unblinking stare.

Selena gestured to the brooches on her chest. "I didn't steal these. She gave them to me. She said I could have anything I wanted in the house. *Anything.*"

I nodded. "Okay. I'm sure you can keep the brooches. It's not a problem. Hey, Selena . . ." I felt compelled to get her out of this house, bring her home and feed her. It was late and it occurred to me Betty's spirit might be lurking, perhaps kept here by Selena's energy. I wanted to get Selena on my turf, surrounded by my magical resources, so I could control things . . . and try to figure things out. Though controlling Selena was going to be a challenge, I could feel it.

"Do you like pigs?" I asked.

That got her attention.

"I've got a miniature one," I continued. "Though with pigs, even miniature is pretty hefty. But he'll like you, no worries. As long as you pet him occasionally, and maybe sneak him a snack now and then."

She shrugged, and started pulling off her gloves. Her fingernails were chewed to the quick, red and raw looking. *Poor thing*. My heart hurt on her behalf. And yet . . . part of me wanted nothing to do with her, didn't want to be reminded of my own past, of who I used to be. It was like ripping the Band-Aid off the scab of my youth.

But fortunately for me, my grandmother Graciela had been there to guide me, to give me love and mentoring at that fragile time in my life.

"I'll stay here," said Selena with a shake of her head.

"Selena, you can't stay here by yourself."

"I *can*. I *have*."

"Do you know where Lupita is? Has she been around? She shook her head.

"It's important that I speak with her."

"I haven't seen her, but that's okay. I don't really like people."

"Selena, you can't stay here. There's going to be an estate sale here in the house. It'll be full of people."

"I don't like people coming in here."

"I understand. But it's not really Betty's house anymore—"

"It *is*."

"Still, there will be people coming through here. First for the estate sale, and then when the house is for sale."

"I can hide. I'm very good at hiding."

"Maybe so. But . . . you need someone to look after you."

"I *don't*."

"You must be hungry. There's no food here, sugar pie," I said, the endearment a relic from my own childhood. I remembered my mother saying it to me, when I was young and she still looked upon me fondly. "I'm an awfully good cook, if I do say so myself. You like enchiladas? Tacos?"

This got her attention. Her thin lips parted, a tiny pink tongue darted out to wet them. "I like cheeseburgers better."

"Well, it just so happens I make a mighty mean cheeseburger. Best you've ever tasted. Just ask my pig."

"Pigs'll eat anything."

I smiled. "I suppose that's true . . . but I really do make a good burger."

"All right, then. Want me to drive? I can drive."

"No, thank you, I'll drive."

She shrugged, tucked the gloves in the oversized pockets of her skirt, and swept regally past me up the stairs.

As I trailed along behind, I tried to quell the sense of foreboding. My instincts were shrieking at me to put some distance between me and the girl. But I couldn't. She was a child, and I had promised to help her.

And I had no doubt that if this odd girl—this strange young woman—was shunted into the foster care system, someone was going to get hurt.

"Where's the pig?" Selena asked as soon as we walked into Aunt Cora's Closet. We had stopped at an all-night grocery store for hamburger, buns, and ice cream. I had everything else I needed in my well-stocked kitchen.

"He might be upstairs." Now that I had freed Oscar from Aidan's service, he disappeared even more frequently than he used to. "But if not, he'll be back soon enough."

"What is this place?" She walked around the store, her hands out at her side, palms forward, feeling for vibrations.

"It's my shop. I sell vintage clothes."

She glared at me, her eyes narrow slits. "*Dead* people's clothes."

"Sometimes, yes," I said, clamping down on my exasperation. First Finn, now her. "I prefer to think of them as reclaimed, or antique. Passed down."

Suddenly she ran across the shop and flung open the brocade curtain that led to the workroom where Finn had set the bags of clothing I'd purchased from Betty's estate.

Selena fell to her knees in front of one pile, and brought an emerald green shirtwaist dress up to her nose.

She inhaled deeply. "These are Betty's clothes."

"Yes. I bought them from Finn, the man who's organizing the estate sale."

"I know. But . . . but *why* did you take Betty's clothes? What right do you ha-ave?" Her voice cracked on the last word.

I went to her side and reached out slowly, very slowly, and placed my hand on her head. She was like a wild animal; I didn't know which way she would jump, or if she would run away. Or bite.

The palm of my hand tingled before I even made contact. The girl's energy was frenetic, unfocused, zinging every which way. I remained absolutely still for a moment, afraid to spook her. Then I began to stroke her head, slowly and gently. Her hair was bound in tight braids on either side of her head, but a few soft wisps around her temples had escaped.

After a very long time she looked up, her eyes dark and impenetrable, and said: "Do you ever wish you could cry?"

I finally coaxed her away from Betty's clothes, but Selena showed little interest in anything else as we went upstairs to my apartment. She didn't seem to notice my

good luck and protective charms: the urn of stinging net-
tles at the front door of my apartment over the shop, or
the mirrors, or the botanical nosegays that hung from
black ribbons.

"Can I watch something?"

"Pardon?"

"On TV."

"I don't have cable—but there are a bunch of DVDs
on the table there."

"Oh. Weird." She plopped down on the couch. "I'm
hungry."

"I'll start the hamburgers. Want to help me?"

She didn't answer, already absorbed in hunting through
the stacks of DVDs. I had been collecting these for Oscar
in an attempt to keep him busy and out of trouble. As I
headed to the kitchen, I reflected upon the benefits of an
electronic babysitter.

Speaking of my gobgoyle, I kept expecting Oscar's
face to appear out of his nest of blankets over the refrigerator. I respected his privacy so I never peeked into his
cubby. But when he didn't come out at the smell of cooking hamburger, I knew he had gone out for the evening.
Too bad; I would have liked to have heard his take on
the young witch.

I called Selena to the kitchen table and set a cheeseburger, fresh melon and strawberries, and a tall glass of
milk in front of her. She dove in, shoveling the food in
her mouth like a starving child.

I hesitated to ask her too many questions, but I
needed some answers.

"Did you know Nicky Utley, Betty's daughter?"

"Betty's daughter ran away with the military," she
mumbled around a mouth of cheeseburger. "Her son
did, too. But it was okay because they were with their

dad and Betty was a free spirit." Selena licked a dab of ketchup from the side of her mouth.

"And did you know the grown-up Nicky?"

She shrugged. "A little. But Lupita said Nicky only pretended to like her mother to get Betty's stuff."

"What stuff in particular?"

"The house and everything."

"I sure would like to talk to Lupita, sugar pie. Do you have a phone number for her?"

She shook her head and gulped her milk.

"No idea at all where Lupita might be?"

She shrugged. "She got engaged, or married or something. I haven't really seen her since then. But . . . she's like that."

There was sadness in her words. I had the distinct sense that Selena had been shunted around from one person to the next. Ursula was in jail, her friend Betty had died, and Lupita had disappeared.

"I spoke with Ursula the other day," I said. "She's doing just fine, and she asked about you."

Selena stopped chewing, midbite. Her eyes were wary.

"Would you like to go visit her?"

She didn't respond but resumed eating.

I reached out and stroked her head, then gently tugged one of her braids, and smiled. "There's plenty more if you want another burger."

"Ursula's with the police?"

"For now, yes."

"The police . . . they were mean when they took Ursula away. Lupita always told me never talk to police."

Great. That sort of attitude was not going to be helpful.

She polished off the last of the sesame-seed bun in silence, then started in on the fruit. She was so small I didn't know where she was putting it all.

Plate clean, Selena followed me into the living room, where we made a bed for her on the couch. I tucked her in and she resumed watching the DVD she had chosen earlier, one that I liked but was far too tame for Oscar's taste: *Charlotte's Web*.

Before I had finished cleaning up the kitchen, she was fast asleep.

I stood over her for a moment, watching the slumbering child and feeling the weight of guardianship settling upon my shoulders. What would I do if Ursula was convicted and sent to prison? That probably wouldn't happen—but what if it did? Was I really willing—was I even *able*—to take on this teenage witch?

I went downstairs to use the phone in the store, so I wouldn't be overheard, and called the only person I knew with experience raising a miserable, out of control, annoying, adolescent witch.

My grandmother Graciela.

"I'm not convinced she knows what she's doing," I said after giving Graciela the lowdown on Selena's situation. "Certainly she has power, but . . ."

She laughed and muttered something in Spanish that translated loosely into: "What goes around comes around."

"What should I do?"

"Your best. That is all any of us can do."

"Do you think I should take Selena on if Ursula is sent to prison?"

"I don't know. I will tell you this, though, *m'ijita*: Beware the poltergeists. Remember the time in gym class?"

I winced. I could have gone the rest of my life without remembering that particular incident—but how could I forget? Basketballs flying through the air, then popping with ear-shattering *booms*. Kids running every which way, screaming, a few laughing hysterically, contorted faces looking at me, fingers pointing.

Nothing quite like adding wild supernatural energy to the trials of being a kid coping with acne and pubescence.

Selena was strong enough to cause the havoc in Ursula's store. Might she also have accidentally—or even on purpose— harmed the customers of El Pajarito?

"Any advice?" I asked.

"You remember the *Gutta Cavat Lapidem* charm? It requires a teardrop talisman. I think . . . I think it's in your Book of Shadows, page 176, between the lavender sleeping charms and the one about growing pains. Carve a talisman, imbue it with the charm. That will help."

"Okay, thanks. Oh, one more thing before I let you go: How's my mom? She's been on my mind lately. Have you seen her?" I sent my mother a check every month, but never heard from her. I was flat-out too chicken to call her since it was pretty obvious she didn't want any contact with me.

"I see her at the Piggly Wiggly sometimes. But she hides behind the toilet paper display, doesn't want to talk to me," she laughed.

"Next time you see her, tell her, um . . ." I couldn't bring myself to say *Tell her I love her*. So I concluded lamely, ". . tell her I'm thinking of her."

Graciela sighed. "I will if you wish me to, but she may see that as a threat, *mi querida*."

True. This was a sad state of affairs.

"In that case . . . just tell her I wish her the best."

After hanging up, I dialed Carlos. He didn't answer, so I left a message on his voice mail.

"Two things: first, I found Selena. I know you're probably duty-bound to turn her over to the care of Family and Children Services, but I guarantee you, Carlos, she's better off here with me. She's . . . a handful. A magical handful, if you know what I mean. Second, I think she might be responsible for the situation in Ursula's store. It might well be poltergeist activity connected to Selena's energy. So if you could give me a few days with her, maybe I can reverse, or at least stop, the damage."

I tried to think of what else to say, but it was hard to know how to end a message like that.

"All righty, then . . . I guess that's about it."

I hung up but lingered behind the counter, looking around the peaceful shop floor, dimly lit by the streetlamps on Haight Street. Not all that long ago, I had been very much like Selena. But now . . . I had a group of steady, loyal friends, and my power had grown stronger— not just more controlled, but more robust. I could feel it. I was proud of Aunt Cora's Closet, and had grown to adore my adopted city and state. For the first time in my life, I could truthfully say I was happy. Surely, I was meant to help Selena find her path, as Graciela helped me to find mine.

I jumped when the phone rang.

It was Carlos, calling to say he would be right over.

This time, he accepted my offer of a cup of tea. We sat with our steaming mugs at the linoleum table in the back room of the shop.

Carlos took notes as I recounted everything Selena had said. He told me he'd had no luck hunting down Lupita. He'd gotten in touch with a dozen Guadalupe Rodriguezes, but none was the woman we were looking for.

"So Selena can stay here with me for a while?" I asked.

Carlos nodded. "If I can trust your take on the situation—and I think I can—then I have to agree that putting the girl in foster care isn't a good idea. So I'll keep her current whereabouts to myself for the time being. But Lily—I'm goin' out on a limb here. If anything happens to that child and the brass learn I knew she was with you, I can kiss my career good-bye."

"Understood. I appreciate your confidence in me," I said.

"And I'll need to talk to her, sooner rather than later."

"I figured as much. But again, I'd like you to trust me when I say I think it's best to give her a little time. She's pretty freaked out, and I don't think it would help her to open up if she felt like she was being questioned by the cops. No offense, but whoever picked up Ursula left a pretty vivid impression."

He frowned. "Okay, I'll leave it for a few days. But I'll need to talk to her eventually."

"I know. Just let me get her settled, and we'll work up to it. So, what about Betty North's will? Who did she leave her estate to?"

"That's a complicated question. She had a will, but recently wrote a new one. Problem is, the new one's being contested, as it appears not to have been properly executed."

"And who were the heirs in the wills?"

He hesitated. "I'm sorry. I can't discuss that with you at this juncture."

It was on the tip of my tongue to tell him that I couldn't help figure out this possible homicide without all the pertinent information, but then I remembered that Carlos didn't want me figuring it out. That was *his* job. I was in charge of quelling the chaos in Ursula's store, and in taking care of Selena, at least for the meantime; nothing more.

Still and all, it was mighty frustrating.

"But . . . you've considered inheritance as a motive, I imagine?"

He nodded but said nothing.

"I know you knew Gary and Nicky from church," I began. "But I'm wondering . . . You did check him out, didn't you?"

"You already asked me that. Of course I checked him out. Why don't you stop beating around the bush and tell me what's on your mind?"

I felt scummy repeating what Knox had said—it felt as if I were betraying a trust. Still, Knox hadn't asked me not to tell anyone, so I plunged ahead.

"Gary Utley had an affair."

"I know. He told me. Cried like a baby."

"Oh."

"Is that it?"

"Yeah, I guess it is. I just assumed you didn't know. Doesn't it make him seem suspicious?"

"It's a red flag, of course it is. But I gotta tell you, Lily, a lot of people have affairs. Maybe even most people. But that doesn't mean they kill their spouses. Anything else?"

"You mentioned there were witnesses to Nicky Utley's jump off the Golden Gate Bridge?"

"Yeah, one guy reported it, and three others hung around to give statements."

"And they didn't see anything . . . out of the ordinary?"

"All they saw was Nicky jumping. Believe me, this was one of the first things we checked out."

"Could you give me their names? Maybe I could talk to them?"

"They were all tourists, from out of the country. But like I just said, I questioned them all carefully. They didn't see any magical hoo-haw, nothing like that."

"Magical hoo-haw?"

"It's a technical term. Homicide cop lingo."

I smiled. "All right. Thanks for stopping by, Carlos. I hope I didn't get you out of bed?"

He shook his head. "I was right down the street. Thank *you* for finding Selena. I'll rest more easily knowing she's not out on the streets somewhere. But Lily . . ." He hesitated, as though searching for the words. "Don't make me sorry that I went against policy and let her stay here."

"I won't."

"And . . . be careful. Don't go snooping around."

"Who, me?"

"I'm serious, Lily. This whole case feels hinky. The fact that we can't locate Lupita Rodriguez might mean she's involved, but it also might mean she's been disposed of, just like Nicky Utley and maybe even Betty North. There are too many bodies that seem to be connected somehow. Do you understand what I'm saying?"

I nodded. "Yes, Inspector. Hinky means not good. Got it."

He gave a final nod, and left.

As I passed by the kitchen I noticed my Book of Shadows, still splayed on the counter. It was opened to a quote from Anaïs Nin:

And the day came when the risk to remain tight in
     a bud
was more painful than the risk it took to bloom.

The first time I read those words I was torn between embracing my powers and wishing I could reject them. Was Selena my most recent challenge, as

Graciela had said? Was it time to reexperience my childhood trauma, but from the perspective of an adult?

As I flipped through the book to see what else it might reveal, I alighted upon a photograph of me with Graciela, when I was in middle school. It had been taken not long after the gym class debacle, if I remembered correctly. There weren't many pictures of us—like Yasmin at the *botanica*, Graciela was superstitious about photos, and wary of those who took them. Although a photograph—mere paper and chemicals—wasn't anywhere near as powerful as a lock of hair or fingernail clippings, it could be used by a talented spellcaster to focus intent. It simply wasn't smart to have one's countenance shared with anyone other than a trusted family member.

In the photo I was unsmiling, dour, skinny, standing on the stoop of the humble little house I shared with Graciela. My grandmother smiled slightly for the camera, chin jutting out in her stubborn way. The image captured well the gentle strength in her dark eyes.

At the time I was already several inches taller than she, though I hadn't realized it. She loomed large in my life, as in my memory. My medicine bag was strapped to the waist of my younger self, and I held another charm bag in one hand. Looking closely, I spied a teardrop talisman like the one Graciela recommended I carve for Selena.

"What's good for the goose is good for the gander," I said under my breath, as I flipped the book open to page 178—my grandmother was off by only two pages; how did she *do* it?—and then stayed up carving and casting over a special talisman for Selena. The teardrop shape centered energies, and the *Gutta Cavat Lapidem* charm calmed them, rather than allowing them to flail about in a crazed, ADD-sort of way.

I chanted as I placed the tear-shaped talisman around the sleeping girl's neck.

"With this talisman I do glean, calm and serene the spirits who clean. *Les suplico, ma tzitzimitl, ma timocuit-lahui.* Grant this child rest, just as is best. So mote it be."

I repeated these words, faster and faster, until they all ran together and I could feel them swirling and cohering, forming a cone of protection over Selena's sleeping form.

She roused for a moment, stared at me with blank, uncomprehending eyes, and then rolled over and went back to sleep.

The next morning I rose early and brewed coffee. A sleepy Selena joined me in the kitchen, taking a seat at the table but remaining silent.

"Good morning, sugar pie. How are you? Did you sleep all right?"

She shrugged. I made her a mug of hot chocolate with cinnamon, then brought out a dozen eggs, corn tortillas, and fruit and started making breakfast.

At the smell of food cooking Oscar bounded down from his cubby over the refrigerator. His big, bottle glass green eyes were a little bleary, making me wonder what he'd been up to last night, and how late he'd gotten in.

It took me a moment to realize—Oscar hadn't transformed into his piggy form. He remained in his natural state even as he pulled out a chair and joined Selena at the table.

He stared at her. She stared at him. His eyes narrowed, and so did hers.

Oscar turned to me. "First you bring home a *cat*, then a *toddler*, and now a . . . uh . . . ? What do you call *it*?"

"She's a girl, Oscar. A . . . almost a young woman, aren't you, Selena? Also, she's right here with us so we can speak to her directly."

Selena started mumbling, chanting a curse.

Chapter 18

Oscar's chair screeched as he reared back, snorted, and made some sort of sign with his long fingers, as though staving off a hex.

"Mistress!" Oscar shouted. "Make it stop! It's *hexing* me! I'll hex you right back, you little—"

"Hey! *Knock it off*, both of you! Selena, Oscar, there'll be none of that in my kitchen. *No hexing allowed.* Am I clear?"

Selena rolled her eyes and Oscar looked disgruntled, but both fell silent. I hurried to put plates of food in front of them, and in this, at least, they had something in common: They both dug in with abandon.

I sat and I sipped my coffee, watching while they finished their meals.

"Selena, would you like to take a shower?" I asked in my most diplomatic tone, as it was clear she hadn't had access to clean clothes in a while.

"No."

"Would you rather help me with the dishes?"

She didn't reply, so I sweetened the deal. "I hung a

pretty bathrobe I think you'll like in the bathroom. And after your shower, we'll go downstairs and you can choose a new outfit from the store."

That got her attention.

"Anything I want?" she asked.

"Yes."

"From the whole store?"

I nodded.

She seemed to mull it over. "I want to wear my brooches."

"That's fine, you can pin your brooches on your new dress, or whatever outfit you choose."

"All right."

While Selena was showering, Oscar sat on the counter and glowered as I prepared a breakfast burrito for Conrad. Then I went through Selena's discarded clothes, but the sensations were the same as last night: scattered, unfocused energy, and plenty of it. I hoped the talisman would help address that.

Oscar followed me around the whole time, scowling and muttering, and emitting an occasional *harrumph*.

"I don't want to hear it, Oscar," I said firmly. "Selena's a young girl who needs our help. End of story."

"I doubt it's the end of the story, Mistress. She's trouble, is what she is."

"She is trou*bled*, that much is true. Which is why she needs friends, now more than ever. Her grandmother's in jail."

"Prob'ly runs in the family," he snorted.

"Oscar, I would really appreciate your help with her."

"Mistress! I know just the thing. Have you heard of the Lomax-Rhody hex?"

"That is not what I meant. She needs us, Oscar."

"*I* don't need *her*."

"Oscar, seriously, I would really appreciate your help

on this one. I can't be around to watch her all the time. Would you stick with her, make sure she doesn't take off, or do something that could hurt someone?"

He grumbled.

"I'd consider it a favor."

He didn't look convinced.

"Never mind," I said. "I'll understand if you aren't up to the challenge. After all, she's pretty strong."

He perked up immediately, inflating his green scaly chest. "She's not stronger than the likes of yours truly."

"No? You're sure? She could be a real challenge."

He blew out a dismissive breath. *"Please."*

"Then you'll help me? I'd really appreciate it. I made her a *Gutta Cavat Lapidem* talisman, which should help focus her energies."

Oscar leaped off the counter and stomped into the living room, grumbling something about not needing ". . . no stinkin' teardrop talisman to keep the likes of her in line."

Selena emerged from the steam-filled bathroom freshly scrubbed and clad in an embroidered cotton bathrobe, her long dark hair hanging wet down her back. We headed downstairs to Aunt Cora's Closet, which didn't open for another half hour. Oscar followed us down, transformed into his pig guise halfway down the stairs, and curled up on his purple silk pillow for his after-breakfast nap.

"What suits your fancy?" I asked Selena.

"I want to wear something of Betty's."

"Hmm. That might not work out. Not only do the clothes need to be laundered first, but I don't think they'll fit you. Betty was a grown woman."

"I don't care."

"Tell you what: Why don't you pick out something else for the time being, and I'll see what I can do about finding something of Betty's that might suit you? I'll get it laundered, and if need be Lucille, the seamstress, can take it in. Deal?"

She nodded begrudgingly.

Selena wandered around the store aisles at first half-heartedly, then with growing interest. Twenty minutes later she chose an early-sixties sundress that reminded me of the style I liked for myself. It had deep pockets on a wide skirt, handy for carrying pouches and bits of herbs and plants. Even though it was tailored for the petite dimensions of a former generation, it was still too big for her, so I put a pink thin belt around her waist to cinch it in.

"That's just lovely on you," I said. "Come over here and take a look."

Selena stood back and admired herself in the three-way mirror. The reflection caught the pair of us: both wearing vintage sundresses, with long dark hair and a slightly haunted look in our eyes.

"Now don't you look pretty," I said, and felt a wave of something new from Selena—something like hope. "Hey, check us out—we could be sisters."

She stared at our reflection, her face blank.

"Would you like me to braid your hair for you? Or would you rather leave it down?"

Our eyes met in the mirror. Her gaze shifted to my hair.

"Ponytail, like yours."

"Sure. Then we'll *really* look like sisters," I said with a smile. I retrieved a brush and an elastic hair band from behind the counter and pulled her still-damp hair into a high ponytail.

Selena took a seat on the stool behind the counter and, without saying a word, watched closely as I performed my morning ritual of cleansing and smudging and lighting a protective candle.

I was bringing Conrad his breakfast and trying to introduce him to the sullen, silent Selena, when Bronwyn showed up for work. I was so relieved to see her I gave her an enthusiastic hug.

"*My goddess*, what's got into you this morning?" she said with some concern, patting my back. Bronwyn knew I wasn't much of a hugger. "Is everything all right?"

"Yes, very much so." I gave her a significant look. "Look who's here!"

"Well, hello there!" said Bronwyn. Purple gauzy coat fluttering behind her, I caught whiffs of cinnamon and cloves as she hurried over to Selena. "Selena, I'm Bronwyn. Do you remember me from El Pajarito? I used to buy herbs from your grandmother."

Selena nodded solemnly. "*Epazote* and juniper berries. Turmeric root. Sometimes rose hips when you didn't have enough from your garden."

"Just so," said Bronwyn with a warm smile. "What a memory!"

"Selena's going to be staying with me and Oscar for a little while."

"Isn't that wonderful! Selena, my granddaughter's out of town, but when she gets back, perhaps you'd like to meet her. She's younger than you, but quite mature for her age."

Selena, now studying the jewelry inside the glass display case, didn't answer.

"Speaking of which," Bronwyn continued, "Lily, Beowulf's staying with me for a few days while they're on vacation, but I hate to leave her home alone. Would it be all right if I brought her in? I know you worry about fur on the merchandise . . ."

"By all means, bring her in," I said. *Bronwyn—you're a genius*, I thought.

When Bronwyn returned a few minutes later with

Beowulf—Oscar had named her this, despite the fact
that she was female—the usually standoffish feline made
a beeline for Selena.

A smile broke out across the girl's thin face. She
scooped the cat up and cradled her, crooning off-key.

Bronwyn and I exchanged glances, then both got back
to work: I started tagging new inventory, while she filled
unbleached cheesecloth teabags with her special mix-
tures of dried herbs and roots.

The bell over the door chimed as shoppers began to
stop by, many of whom were looking to put together out-
fits for the Summer of Love Festival. The phone rang,
and I could hear Bronwyn answering with her typical
singsong: "Aunt Cora's closet, it's not old, it's vintage!
How may I help you?"

Selena watched silently, still cuddling Beowulf, while
I found a peasant blouse and Indian-print skirt for a customer, pairing the skirt with a wide leather belt that had
a big brass O for a buckle. A few love beads, a pair of
brown suede boots, and a headband to hold back her
curly hair, and she was good to go.

One of the great things about costume-based festivals
was that they brought a whole new clientele into Aunt
Cora's Closet. Once we nailed down her costume, the
customer wondered whether there might be any vintage
dresses that would fit her. I found two sundresses in her
size, sixteen, which was quite a coup because most vintage clothing was not sized for today's women. This was
why Maya's mother, Lucille, our talented shop seamstress,
had started creating reproductions of vintage clothing
sized to fit our clientele and made of fabrics that were
machine-washable.

As I rang up the woman's purchase, I realized Bronwyn was still on the phone.

"Well, it has been *such* a joy to hear from you, Max. Don't be a stranger!" she said. "Here she is now, I'll hand you to her."

Bronwyn covered the speaker and whispered loudly: "It's *Max*."

"Thanks," I said, reaching for the phone.

"Max *Carmichael,*" Bronwyn added. As though I might be confused.

"Thank you, Bronwyn," I repeated. I could feel my face burning.

"Um, hi," was the best I could come up with.

"Lily." At the sound of Max's voice I was instantly brought back to the time we were together. Max Carmichael was an attractive man, but it was his voice that slayed me. I swear, the man should be a radio announcer. I'd happily listen to him narrate my entire Book of Shadows.

There was a long pause. I wondered if Max felt as awkward as I did.

"Nigel said you stopped by the *Chronicle,* and wanted to talk to me," he said.

"Yes, thank you for returning my call." *This was good,* I thought. It was all business.

"Is this something we can discuss over the phone, or would you prefer to meet?"

"Actually, if you have the time I would love to talk face-to-face."

He chuckled. "I suspected as much. I remember your aversion to the telephone."

As a witch, I rely on vibrations and body language to provide insight into others. The telephone masks these extrasensory sensations, at least for me. Or maybe it was the humming of the electronic wires that threw me off. Either way, I avoided telephones whenever possible.

"How about I take you to lunch?" I asked.

Juliet Blackwell

"I'd love that. I have to be in North Beach for an interview this afternoon. We could meet at Mona Lisa's, how about noon?"

"Perfect. I'll see you then."

I hung up but rested my hand on the receiver for a few seconds, pondering. After a moment I could feel Bronwyn's interested gaze.

"What?" I demanded.

"How's Max?"

"You would know better than I. You spoke to him much longer."

Bronwyn started humming, and returned to her tea blends.

"I asked him to meet me for lunch," I explained. "I need to talk to him about an article he wrote for the paper."

Bronwyn's eyebrows rose. "Well, now, doesn't that sound like fun?"

"Maybe I shouldn't go," I said quietly, glancing at Selena, who had finally released Beowulf but remained focused on the jewelry in the cabinet.

"Nonsense," said Bronwyn. "You scoot. Selena and I will be fine. She can help me put together my tea bags, right, Selena?"

Selena started *tsking* and shaking her head. "These silver pieces are very tarnished. Can I go upstairs for some ketchup?"

"Sure," I said.

She ducked through the brocade curtain. Oscar let out a long-suffering porcine sigh as he hoisted himself up off his pillow and followed her.

"Ketchup?" Bronwyn asked.

"She says it takes the tarnish off."

"Does it work?"

"I have no idea. But as long as it keeps her busy, I say

let her at it. What could it hurt? Bronwyn, are you *sure* you can handle things until I get back? I need to pick up a few supplies in Chinatown while I'm in the neighborhood."

"We'll be just fine. Duke will be coming by later, Conrad is right outside, and after all, Selena is just one girl."

One very special girl, I thought.

North Beach is surrounded by Chinatown, the financial district, Jackson Square, and Cannery Row. Originally settled by Italian immigrants, the neighborhood's ethnic flavor is reflected in its many restaurants, shops, and cafés, as well as the beautiful Saints Peter and Paul Catholic church that crowns Washington Square. Tourists swarm to North Beach, but it's also a favorite of locals in search of a good meal, an espresso, or Italian pastries. At night the vicinity is full of music and nightlife, and is the destination for folks seeking strip shows and the like.

It's a hopping place, even on a Tuesday in the middle of the day. I found a parking space within walking distance of Chinatown, and after stopping at my favorite Chinese apothecary for herbs and roots to replenish my supplies, I walked the several city blocks to Mona Lisa Ristorante.

Max was seated at an outdoor table, his long legs stretched out in front of him, studying the menu. With his dark hair and complexion, he could have been a local lounging at a café in Florence.

As I approached, he looked up. Max had startling, light gray eyes, like pinpoints of light. They were sad eyes, and once upon a time I had hoped to bring them joy.

I reached for my medicine bag to steel myself against old yearnings. What I was feeling towards Max wasn't romantic; Sailor was so much better for me than Max ever was, or could be. But even though I *knew* that, a part of me longed for a different life, the sort I had once thought was possible with someone like Max. A normal life, the kind that had always been denied me.

I recalled what Knox said about yearning for a "regular" home while he trailed his military father around the globe. Maybe it wasn't just witches who yearned for such things. But when it came right down to it, was anyone's upbringing "normal"?

"Lily," Max said as he rose to greet me. "Good to see you."

He leaned in to give me a hug but I stepped back.

"Sorry," said Max.

"*No*, no. *I'm* the sorry one. In more ways than one," I said with a smile. "It's just . . . I don't . . . I'm just . . ."

"It's fine, Lily," Max said, his light gaze sweeping over me. "It really is. I understand. It's just good to see you. You look wonderful, by the way. I take it life is treating you well?"

"As they say in Texas, I could complain, but then so could the devil."

He chuckled. "And what does that mean exactly?"

"I really have no idea," I said, joining him in a laugh. "Sometimes I think these sayings serve to fill a gap in the conversation when you don't know what else to say."

"That sounds like a good enough reason to me. Please." He gestured to the seat across from him at the small iron café table.

The waiter took my order for an iced tea and Max and I perused our menus, a move inspired, on my part, more by the desire to do something than from interest. We exchanged a few polite remarks, me commenting on a pasta dish, Max pointing out the tiramisu.

Our drinks arrived, accompanied by a basket of warm sourdough bread and a dish of olive oil sporting a few flakes of chili and sea salt. After our waiter left with our meal orders, Max asked me what I had wanted to talk to him about.

"Ursula Moreno owns a shop called El Pajarito that you included in a story on the *botanicas* in the Mission. Do you remember your interview with her?"

He nodded. "That was a while ago. But yes, I remember."

"Is there anything you can tell me about that interview? Anything unusual that didn't wind up in the article?"

He pushed his chin out slightly, as though trying to remember. "I don't recall anything out of the ordinary, other than the fact that some local witch doctors are using so-called magic to try to cure cancer, or some such nonsense."

I felt myself tightening up. *This was good*, I thought. This was the disdainful side of Max, the cynical skeptic who couldn't deal with my powers. It was useful to be reminded.

"Did Ursula claim to be able to cure cancer with magic?" I asked.

"To tell you the truth, I don't remember exactly who said what. I interviewed a number of shop owners for that story. But I gave all my research to Nigel—it was his series, I just stepped in when he couldn't do those first interviews. He wrote a recent article following up on some of those types of scams."

"Yes, thanks. I read that one, as well as yours. But I noticed the photo in the article that you wrote. It was a picture of Ursula Moreno, a girl named Selena, and another woman named Lupita Rodriguez. Was Lupita your initial contact?"

Max sat back in his seat and nodded. "Yes, she was."

"How did you meet her?"

"She approached Nigel, said she could introduce him to some people."

"So she just came to the newspaper offices out of the blue?"

"If I recall correctly, she was hoping for compensation."

"Nigel told me y'all don't pay for stories at the *Chronicle*."

"We don't. She probably thought the publicity would bring more business into the shop."

According to Ursula, Lupita wasn't involved in the running of the shop. So how would she have benefited from more customers? On the other hand, maybe Ursula had lied, or misled me for some reason.

"Do you remember a young teenager there, a girl named Selena?"

"I do."

"What were your impressions of her?"

"She was quiet. Seemed intelligent. A little we—" He cut himself off.

"Weird? You can say it."

"She was different. Clearly something was going on there, though whether she was somehow disturbed, or simply far too intelligent for her age, I wasn't sure. Our interaction wasn't that extensive. Why do you ask?"

"I think she's a lot like me. Or the way I was when I was her age."

Just then the waiter appeared with our meals. Pasta carbonara for Max, eggplant parmesan for me. My mouth watered at the sight of the generous mound of eggplant slathered in melted cheese and a fragrant tomato sauce, and I belatedly remembered Oscar's comment about my putting on weight. Maybe I should have ordered a salad. Still, as the delectable aromas wafted up from my plate I was glad I hadn't, and nodded when the waiter offered to sprinkle more parmesan on top of my meal.

I'll have yogurt for dinner, I promised myself, and dug in.

I was on my second mouthful when I realized Max wasn't eating. When I met his eyes, he asked, "What do you mean, she's a lot like you were when you were her age?"

"A freak of nature."

"Is that how you see yourself?"

"Yes, frankly, I do." I sat back with a smile. "But the *good* news is that I'm coming to terms with it. Maybe nature needs a few freaks to balance out all the normal folks. In any case, in the words of the immortal Popeye, 'I yam what I yam.'"

"You're an incredible woman, Lily," Max said softly. "And much, *much* more attractive than Popeye."

"Um, thank you." We shared a smile. "Is there anything else you can tell me about your time spent with Lupita, or in the store, or with Ursula? Anything odd, at all—besides Selena?"

He considered this. "I remember Lupita spoke a lot about her upcoming wedding, but Ursula didn't seem impressed. Lupita told Selena she could be a bridesmaid, but again, Ursula seemed to downplay the idea, as if she was afraid to raise Selena's hopes. It struck me because the family tension was pretty overt."

"Did anyone mention the fiancé's name, or anything else about him?"

"Sorry," he said with a shake of his head. "I didn't meet him, and it wasn't pertinent to my story so I didn't follow up."

"Did Lupita or Ursula say anything about working with a woman named Betty North? Maybe doing a cleansing for an old woman?"

"I don't remember in particular."

"How about Nicky Utley?"

"They didn't mention any names. In fact, that's something I recall: that Ursula made a big deal out of the confidentiality of her clients."

"Rats," I said as I sat back, frustrated. "Confidentiality doesn't do me any good, in this instance, I fear."

He smiled. "Sorry about that. I don't feel like I've been very helpful, but to tell you the truth most of the interesting stuff made it into the article. And like I said, it was a while ago."

"I appreciate you trying. So," I said, changing the subject, "how's your brother?"

"He's doing great. He's getting married."

"Really? That's wonderful news! Do you like his fiancée?"

"Very much. She's very steady and seems to help him stay the course. Takes the pressure off of me to make sure he's okay."

"You are *such* an older brother," I said, and again flashed back on my conversation with Knox. He hadn't been able to take care of his sister, in the end. Was he beating himself up over it . . . or could he have had something to gain from Nicky's death? I tried to shake off the thought. *This was the problem with hanging around a homicide detective,* I thought. You started to see everyone as a suspect.

"And how are you doing?" I continued. "Are you getting married anytime soon?"

He shook his head and sipped his beer, holding my gaze. "How about you?"

"I don't think I'm the marrying kind," I said with a nervous chuckle.

"I don't know about that," he said. "I think any man would be lucky to have you."

I opened my mouth to respond, but had no idea what to say. Instead, I just sat for a moment and enjoyed the peculiar but undeniable intimacy of two people who had once shared something important, but realized they weren't right for each other.

We ordered espressos, and Max insisted upon sharing a dessert of my choosing. "The crème brulée is excellent here, as is the tiramisu."

"In my book," I said, "it's not dessert unless it's chocolate."

"I've said it before and I'll say it again, Lily Ivory: You are a woman after my own heart."

I ordered a double chocolate flourless cake, à la mode, and we shared bites. Dessert finished, we argued over who should pay—I insisted; lunch was my suggestion—and with the bill paid I rose to leave.

"It was great to see you, Max," I said, holding my hand out.

He took my hand in his, and placed his other over it. "Great see you, too. I've missed you, Lily."

He didn't let go of my hand, and his gaze lingered. I looked away nervously, and blurted out, "I'm actually seeing someone."

Max laughed, and let his hands drop. "As a matter of fact, so am I. It's for the best, isn't it?"

"It is."

"I trust he treats you well?"

"Yes, yes, he does. And is she good to you?"

"So far, we've managed to do well by each other."

"I'm really glad for you, Max. I . . . I hope we can be friends."

"I would like that."

I didn't tell Max who the new man in my life was. There was bad blood between Max and Sailor, stemming from the tragedy with Max's wife. Besides, as nice as it had been to see Max again, I doubted we would be barbecuing together or going out on double dates.

As I walked back to my car I heard a familiar roar and looked up to see a motorcyclist turning the corner. Was that Sailor? Probably not—I was forever thinking it was him when a motorcycle went by. Still, he lived not far from here, in Chinatown. It could have been him.

Not that it would matter. Unless . . . If he saw me having lunch with Max, he might jump to the wrong conclusion. As I had recently discovered, jealousy was no respecter of logic.

I decided to take a detour and drop by Sailor's apartment, which was on the second floor of a building on Hang Ah Alley. His motorcycle wasn't out front, but I climbed the stairs anyway. On the landing outside his door lingered the ghost of a man killed in a gambling fight more than a century ago. Sailor claimed it didn't bother him and that this was why the rent was so cheap, but the ghostly presence always made me feel mournful.

I knocked, but there was no response. I tore a page out of a small notebook I kept in my satchel and wrote a note: *Was in the neighborhood. Sorry about last night—I found Selena. Miss you.*

My pen hovered over the paper. At last I wrote simply, *Lily.*

Chapter 19

I used a rare pay phone to call Aunt Cora's Closet and check in with Bronwyn. She told me all was well, so I bought a few items at my favorite Chinatown bakery and set out to make one more stop before returning.

When Sailor and I visited Fred after finding the poppet at Betty's house, I had known very little about Betty and her family. Perhaps it was time for another chat with the elderly artist.

Fred's place in China Basin looked exactly as it had the first time I was here, with the door standing slightly ajar. Once again there was no response to either my knock or my "*Hello*?" But in the warehouse area, I spotted Fred sitting on a stool in front of a canvas, apparently so absorbed in his painting that he hadn't heard me.

I watched in silence as he dredged his long-handled brush through the creamy paints on his palette, then dabbed bits of color on the canvas. It was fascinating to witness the flicks of his wrist, his skill and concentration as he brought the painting to life.

Not so long ago, while helping to solve a homicide at

the San Francisco School of Fine Arts, I had felt something of a kinship with the artists. Artists were often outsiders, the "weirdos" of society—a little bit like witches. Sadly, I hadn't had much chance to pal around with the artists at the school, because in addition to a murderer there had been a vicious demon running around, so I'd been a little busy.

"Hello, Fred?" I ventured again.

"Oh! So sorry. I didn't hear you come in." The elderly man removed earbuds and gestured at an iPod. "My granddaughter bought me this. She loaded it up with all the greats: Frank Sinatra, Tony Bennett. Can't get enough of 'em."

"You're more technologically advanced than I am," I said with a smile. "I'm still fond of LPs."

He chuckled. "I remember you from the other day, don't I? Sorry. My memory's not what it used to be. I can't remember names for the life of me . . . but you came to ask about that ugly doll you found at Betty's house."

"That's right. I had a couple of other questions, if you don't mind." I held up the pink plastic bag. "I brought treats from Chinatown. *Char siu bau,* almond cookies, and sesame balls."

"Thank you, that's very kind, but unnecessary. I'm happy to have a visitor. What did you want to ask me?"

"Did you ever meet Betty's children?"

He nodded, wiping his brush on a white rag. "In the last year or so her daughter, Nicky, had started coming around, visiting fairly regularly. It was a pretty big deal because they hadn't been close previously. It made Betty very happy."

"What was Nicky like?"

"Nice gal. Pretty, like her mama. I wanted to paint her, but she wouldn't sit for me."

"What did she and Betty talk about when they got together?" I knew I sounded pushy, but I needed to know.

"I don't really remember," Fred said with a shake of his head. "Just the usual mother-daughter stuff, I guess. I know she was trying to have a baby. Seemed real important to her. Mostly, though, I think she just wanted to have a relationship with her mother, and it's a good thing too, since it turns out Betty was nearing the end. Some people thought Nicky was after Betty's house, but I didn't believe that."

"Who thought that?"

"Actually . . . I guess Betty mentioned it to me herself, asked me if I thought it could be true."

"Do you think it was?"

"Who knows what motivates people?" he said with a shrug. He crossed over to a paint-spattered utility sink and scrubbed his hands. "But I didn't think so. I didn't know Nicky well, but she didn't strike me as that type. If you ask me, it was that Mexican gal who put the idea in Betty's head. "

"You mean Lupita?"

"Right! That's her right there." He gestured toward the easel that held Lupita's portrait last time I was here, but it was empty. He shook his head. "Thought it was there . . . must have misplaced it. Her fiancé commissioned it."

"Who is her fiancé, do you know?"

"I don't remember his name. Sorry. I met him just the one time, at Betty's. Guess I should have asked for the money for the painting up front, huh? Live and learn." He pulled a paper plate from under a counter and took his time arranging the pastries, then set them atop a worktable. "Mmm, I love Chinese pork buns."

"Could you tell me what he looked like?"

"Just a regular guy. White guy. I can't say as I remember—didn't really pay attention. I'm a little more observant when it comes to women," he said with a wink.

"How was it any of Lupita's business who Betty left her house to?"

Fred waved his paintbrush in the air. "You wait and see what it feels like to grow old. Sometimes the nurses who take care of you every day feel closer to you than family."

"What about Knox?"

"Who?"

"Betty's son."

"Maybe I met him, I don't recall. But I wasn't at Betty's all the time; I've always kept my studio, and slept here often."

"What did Betty say about her kids?"

"Not a lot. When I first met her, she said they'd run off with the military. I thought she was joking."

He resumed painting, bringing to life a fanciful scene of dancers in North Beach.

I thought back on our conversation: Had I learned anything helpful? Not particularly. But . . . I just couldn't imagine the old man in front of me offing Nicky and Betty.

Would Fred even have been strong enough to walk to the middle of the Golden Gate Bridge and push a woman over the rail? On the other hand . . . paintings could be used for something akin to poppet magic. Could this fellow be a secretly powerful practitioner? Hard to believe.

I watched for another long moment, wondering whether he had family. He said his granddaughter had given him the iPod, which I hoped meant he was in contact with relatives.

It occurred to me to call Max's brother, who taught at

the San Francisco School of Fine Arts; could there be a place for Fred there? I didn't much care for his style, but it certainly was distinctive. And he'd been around the art world a long time. I imagined he could teach young artists a thing or two.

"Well, I should leave you to your painting," I said, then paused. "By the way, do you want the portraits you left at Betty's house? The estate sale's this weekend. If you don't claim them, they might be sold."

He waved me off. "That's probably for the best. It'd be nice if someone wanted them enough to buy them. Maybe they'd appreciate them."

"I think they're a lovely tribute to Betty."

He shrugged and placed thick swaths of blue paint on the canvas to create a background for the dancers dressed in the white, green, and red of the Italian flag.

Before I had a chance to say good-bye, he put the earbuds back in, and seemed to lose himself in his painting.

Back at Aunt Cora's Closet, things were mellow. Maya had arrived and was thumbing through today's newspaper, Bronwyn was cleaning the herb jars that lined her shelves, and Selena was sitting on the floor, diligently cleaning a small silver locket under the watchful eyes of a pig and a cat.

"Our Selena seems to have quite a knack for cleaning and repairing old jewelry," said Bronwyn. "She also has a way with animals; neither Beowulf nor Oscar have let her out of their sight all day."

"That's for sure," said Maya. "Hey, look. The ad for Betty North's estate sale is in the paper."

Selena's head popped up at the sound of Betty's name.

"That's good," I said, speaking as much to Selena as to Maya. "That way her things will go to good homes, to be appreciated and taken care of. What's the ad say?"

"Let's see . . . 'This is a nonsmoking, no-pets home chock-full of rare collectibles. Items include an antique Chinese eight-panel screen; Karen Scholav seventeenth-century screen; Sally Kimp sculpture; bronze wall sculpture by Elis Gudmann; Waterford crystal stemware; vintage Nicholas Ungar full mink jacket; grandfather clock from Bavaria circa 1935; large antique silver-plated trays, vases, and cutlery; Hoover empower wide path vacuum; Lladros sculptures; enameled jewelry boxes; jade, ivory, and stone carvings; assorted quality costume jewelry; Swarovski crystal chandelier; Waterford, Royal Albert old country rose china; Royal Doulton character mugs; wood carved ducks; circus ephemera; Christmas decorations; free style portable oxygen concentrator Airsep.'"

Maya paused to take a deep breath.

"And the list goes on. Wow. There's a bunch of furniture listed, too." Maya set the newspaper on the counter with a rattle. "I knew Betty had a lot of stuff, but when you see it all listed like that, it's kind of overwhelming."

"I guess it could really add up," I said, looking over her shoulder at the list. "From what I saw at the house, they aren't pricing things cheap."

Unlike items at a yard or garage sale, merchandise at estate sales was usually prime. A professional liquidator like Finn would winnow out the junk prior to the sale, selling most of it to dealers like me, donating what was left over to a thrift store, and throwing the rest away. What remained were the quality items which, while a bargain compared to new, would bring in a fair chunk of cash. And considering what houses in San Francisco sold for these days, regardless of condition, Betty's heir stood to inherit a lot of money.

"I'm sure Finn's being fair, though. Canadians are always fair."

I laughed. "Seriously?"

"He *is*, he told me," put in Selena.

"You know Finn?" Maya asked her.

Selena nodded and put her head back down.

I hadn't told my friends the exact circumstances of how I had found Selena or why she was staying with me, much less that she had been hanging out at Betty's house, before and after Betty's death. Given what we'd been through together, they were good about not asking me a lot of detailed questions.

"So," I said as I hung up a couple of dresses that had been left outside the dressing room, "you're suggesting that because of his nationality he must be fair?"

"They're also funny. A lot of comedians are Canadian."

Maya nodded. "Comedians and news anchors."

"Yep," said Bronwyn as she spritzed her counter with an organic blend of white vinegar mixed with rosemary essential oil. "Good people, the Canadians. If it weren't for the weather . . ." Bronwyn trailed off with a wistful sigh.

"That's their ace in the hole," Maya said. "If the weather were nicer, the whole country would have been overrun long ago, and they wouldn't be so polite anymore."

"Or funny," said Bronwyn.

"Or well-informed," I added with a laugh. "I get it. You win."

"You know, Finn's sort of cute," Bronwyn said, wiggling her eyebrows in Maya's direction. "Might he be single, by any chance?"

Ever since Bronwyn had found happiness with Duke, she seemed determined to fix up everyone around her. I wouldn't be surprised if she put up a sign on her herbal stand offering matchmaking services, not unlike the sign for *limpias* at Ursula's store.

"He mentioned a wife," said Maya in her signature dry tone. But . . . was it my imagination, or did I detect a wistful note? Bronwyn cast me a significant glance, and I knew she was thinking the same thing.

Maya's love life would have to wait, however. At the moment I had bigger fish to fry: I needed to ask Maya about a few things. But not in front of Selena.

"Bronwyn, okay with you if Maya and I go in the back room for a few minutes?"

"Of course. Selena and I can handle the ravening hordes," she said, gesturing around the empty store.

"Thanks," I said. "Maya, a moment?"

Maya followed me through the curtain into the work room.

"Lily, please tell me this isn't a be-open-to-romance pep talk. Because as much as I love Bronwyn, she's about to send me round the bend, as you would say, with her motherly advice on how to land me a boyfriend."

"She just wants you to be happy."

"I know," she said with a smile, grabbing an apple from the fruit bowl and taking a seat at the table. "Maybe someday I'll walk in here with an engagement ring, make you both swoon with happiness for me. So, what's up?"

"I was wondering about the day Betty North went to the hospital. Could you tell me what happened, exactly?"

"It was right after lunch. I went to use the bathroom, and when I came out she was on the ground. This . . . it wasn't that unusual for her to feel dizzy or need to go to bed. She wasn't in good health."

"Were you alone? Just the two of you?"

"Just us for lunch, but one of the home health aides was at the house."

"Which one?"

"I don't remember her name, sorry."

"Do you remember anything about her? Maybe her nationality, where she was from?"

"She was Latina, but from here. No accent."

"Could it have been Lupita Rodriguez?"

"It could have been . . . but I really don't remember."

"You were a witness when Betty signed her will, weren't you? Do you remember who she left her estate to?"

"No, sorry." She shook her head. "I didn't look at it in detail. It was a preprinted form, the kind of thing you buy at a stationery store or off the Internet, and fill in the blanks. There was a notary public there; all I did was witness Betty's signature."

Nigel Thorne had mentioned that houses lost value if someone died on the premises. Was it possible that Lupita did something that day to make sure Betty died in the hospital so as not to depress the home's sale price?

That seemed a little complicated. Not to mention Maya would have called the paramedics to take Betty to the hospital whether Lupita was there or not; anyone would have.

Besides, I had no proof Lupita had brought the voodoo doll into the house, or that she had any stake in Betty's estate. But then why would she disappear? Unless she'd already gotten what she wanted . . . Ursula had sworn Lupita didn't have power, but what if she and Lupita were working some sort of elaborate *bujo* scam to wring Betty dry? Perhaps Lupita had already absconded with a bunch of cash and other valuables, and Ursula was planning to join her as soon as she was free, leaving the unwanted Selena in my care.

Well, *that* was a depressing line of thought.

I heard a commotion on the other side of the curtain. "Sounds like customers. We should go help Bronwyn."

And then there was a terrible sound, like someone stifling a scream.

Chapter 20

Selena's hands were clapped over her mouth, and she was making muffled grunting noises, like a small animal.

"Selena, what is it? Are you okay?" I demanded.

"That's *wrong*."

"*What's* wrong?"

She pointed to an ugly wax doll lying on the floor. It looked like the poppet Maya and I had found at Betty's house, but this time there was no photo attached.

"Where did you find that?" I asked.

"In . . . the . . . pocket," she said. Her voice quavered as she held up a quilted pink housecoat, one of several we had bought from Betty's estate.

"Where did you find this?" I asked.

"My fault," Maya said. "I brought a bag of Betty's clothes from the workroom to the counter to sort through when things got quiet. The housecoat must have been in that bag."

Just then, a trio of teenage girls entered the store, laughing and chatting.

Selena whirled around in surprise. Two hats flew off a

nearby shelf, a vase of sunflowers crashed to the floor, and an umbrella hopped out of a metal holder.

Oscar careened across the shop toward the teenagers. Excited to see a pet pig, the girls giggled and squealed and fussed over him, oblivious to the unfolding mayhem in the store.

My piggy familiar was a first-rate decoy.

I used the pink housecoat to pick up the doll, grabbed Selena by the wrist, and pulled her through the back room and upstairs to my apartment, locking the door behind us.

"*Calm down*," I said. "You have to get hold of yourself."

"But . . . that's from Ursula's shop."

"I thought your grandmother didn't deal in dolls like this." I placed the ugly thing on the steamer trunk, and surrounded it with protective stones as I'd done for its twin.

"Not the doll, the *wax*. It's not the right wax, can't you feel it?"

"So someone used the wrong wax? But the wax is from Ursula's store?"

"It isn't meant for dolls. Never for dolls, Ursula says. Can't you feel it? It's not right."

Confused, I took a calming breath, centered myself, and studied the doll. It was crudely molded, but without a photo attached it didn't feel as sinister as the first one we had found. On the other hand . . . I held my hand over it. Was it humming? Maybe Selena was right; maybe it was "wrong" somehow. Perhaps the doll was charged. The beige wax might well hold hair or fingernails or something else belonging to the target—something much stronger than a photograph of a painting.

The sound of hooves on the landing told me Oscar

had arrived. I got up to let him in. Before I'd even closed the door he transformed to his natural form.

"I'm tellin' ya, she's—"

I put my finger to my lips, cutting him off.

"So, Selena, are you saying this doll made Betty sick?"

No answer. She just stared at me with that strange lack of affect.

"Selena, I want you to tell me about Lupita. She used to take you to Betty's house, right?"

"She was nice."

"Did she . . . could she have brought the doll there?"

Selena shook her head vehemently.

"Did she do any other sort of magic at Betty's?"

Another head shake.

I reached out and stroked her head. She didn't pull away.

"Sugar pie, did you ever do magic there?"

"What kind of magic?"

"Any kind?"

"Not really. Lupita said I shouldn't waste my powers. She said they were too important."

"Don't you have any idea where Lupita is now? Do you know where she lives? Or how about her fiancé? It's very important that I speak with her."

She shook her head, and her lower lip trembled, and it dawned on me that in the past few weeks, Selena had been torn away from everything and everyone that was familiar to her: Ursula, Lupita, Betty.

I remembered her asking: *"Do you ever wish you could cry?"*

In a shoebox I kept a lump of red wax that I used to make conjure balls. I divided it in half and handed one chunk to Selena, then started playing with mine. The wax became pliable under the warmth of my hands, and the sensation of rolling it between my palms was calming, centering.

Selena soon followed suit and began to knead her wax.

Finally, after several minutes of silence, Selena ventured, "Lupita said Nicky was only hanging around because she wanted Betty's money. Is that true?"

What could I say? I honestly didn't know.

"I don't think so, sugar. I think Nicky didn't grow up with her mom, but once she was an adult, and a mother herself, she wanted to change that, to get to know her mother."

As I spoke the words stabbed at my heart. Would I ever know my *own* mother?

"Is it true that Emma's dad killed Nicky?"

My heart skipped a beat. "Why would you think that?"

"I heard you talking to that man last night. The policeman."

I hesitated, not sure what to say. As gently as I could, I said, "We don't know what happened with Emma's mom."

"I don't think she killed herself."

"You don't? What makes you think that?"

"Emma's mom came to Ursula looking for magic. She wanted to have a baby. Ursula said she was doing well. Why would she quit?"

Good question.

"I was thinking, if Emma's dad hurt her mom, he'll go to jail, right?" Selena said. "Then Emma won't have a mother *or* a father to take care of her. She'll be like me."

Her sensitivity surprised me. I searched her face but she still seemed impassive, playing with the wax, molding and grooming it, rolling it into little balls, then mushing them together and starting over.

"That's true," I said.

"But Emma's lucky, she has an uncle, and maybe other people, too, to take care of her."

"Your grandmother should be coming home soon, Selena. And if not, for whatever reason, you can stay here with me."

Her hands stopped their incessant movement. Still tightened her grip so hard her knuckles turned white and the wax squeezed out between her fingers.

"Selena?"

Her gaze met mine for an instant before returning to the worktable in front of her.

"I can stay here?" she asked in a small voice.

"Yes."

"With Beowulf?"

"Actually, Beowulf lives with Bronwyn's daughter's family most of the time. And I'm sorry to say I'm allergic to cats, so I won't be adopting one. But, I was thinking . . . Maya has gotten to know some of the people over at the Humane Society. What if we looked into a volunteer job over there for you?"

She shrugged.

"They need people to help with some basics, like washing and brushing the animals. And even more importantly, to socialize them so they're more adoptable. To take them for walks, and play with them, and pet them."

"To love them."

I had to clear my throat. "Yes, exactly."

She started kneading the wax again, stacking up little balls and figures she had molded. After a moment, she nodded.

"I want to do that. Work at the Humane Society."

"Let's ask Maya to help us arrange it."

"And if Ursula doesn't get out of jail, I'll stay here with you."

"With me and Oscar," I corrected. "This is his home, too. But yes, you'll have a home."

"Okay."

Oscar dropped his head in his big hands and groaned.

Way too early the next morning, I was awakened from a deep sleep by a puff of pizza breath. Oscar was perched on my brass headboard, leaning so far over that I opened my eyes to the disconcerting sight of an upside-down gobgoyle face mere inches from mine.

"What's up?" I croaked, glancing at the clock: 4:27 a.m.

"You'd better come see."

I followed him downstairs and through the workroom. He halted at the brocade curtains that separated the area from the shop floor.

Cautiously, I nudged the drapes open.

Chaos.

A parasol skittered down one aisle. Several pairs of gloves, attached at the wrists, fluttered in the air like white cotton butterflies. An Hermès scarf—a real find—wrapped and unwrapped itself around a mannequin's head. Racks of frothy dresses had been knocked over and the sparkly contents of the junk jewelry trunk lay scattered across the floor.

I caught a pink satin cocktail dress in midair.

"What did I tell ya?" Oscar looked at me with reproach. "This is what happens when you let strangers sleep on your couch."

"Is it a . . . ?"

"*Poltergeist,*" Oscar said in a sinister whisper.

I held up my hand, palm-out, releasing an orangey red light. I walked the perimeter of the store, tripping over crumpled dresses and stumbling through piles of accessories, but my words did not falter. In a loud, command-ing voice, I repeated: *"What is dark be filled with light, remove these spirits from my sight. Powers of protection, powers that clear, remove all those who don't belong here. I call on my energies from history deep; we are entitled to sweet sleep."*

By the time I walked around the store twice, things settled. The gloves lay lifeless on their shelf, nothing flung itself at us. I looked around the mess and sighed.

"That should do it for now," I mumbled. "But I don't understand. That talisman should have kept Selena from accidentally calling a poltergeist."

"Maybe that's why they're here in the shop, and not bothering *her*. She's upstairs, sleeping like a baby. Like I should be."

"I suppose you're right. Maybe it's displaced energy. Still, it seems strange."

"Or maybe your magic is compromised."

"Excuse me?"

"What?" said Oscar.

"What did you just say?"

"Um . . . that your magic is compromised?"

"Why would my magic be compromised?"

"On account of you're jealous."

"What are you talking about? What do I have to be jealous of?"

Oscar had a deer-in-the-headlights look.

"Oscar, do you know something you're not telling me?"

He shook his head, slowly.

Oscar had an infuriating way of keeping his mouth shut just when he had something useful to say. Unfortu-nately, I knew he would not speak until he was ready. Oscar supplied information strictly on a need-to-know basis as defined by some obscure goblin code of ethics.

I let out a sigh. "Let's go try to calm things down with Selena, make sure she's safe. We'll deal with this mess in the morning."

"It's already morning," Oscar pointed out.

"True, but . . . I can't deal without coffee. Let's have some breakfast, and then will you help me clean up before Bronwyn gets here?"

"Cheesy eggs and home fries?"

"Sure," I said with a smile. If a person has to wake up to a poltergeist, it was nice to have a gobgoyle by her side. Cheesy eggs and home fries seemed a small price to pay for such loyalty.

Upstairs, Selena was indeed sleeping like a baby. She didn't stir at the clatter of cooking or the smell of food, so Oscar and I ate, and then went back downstairs to clean up the mess.

"So," I said, hanging up yet another prom dress, "you think I'm jealous, do you? Why would I be jealous?"

Oscar shrugged. He was sweeping up scattered herbs. "'Cause of Patience being a real looker."

"I'm not *jealous*, Oscar. I trust Sailor. He would never do anything like that to me." I paused but couldn't seem to let this subject drop. "And besides, they're cousins."

"Yeah, cousins, *heh*," Oscar said. He moved aside a rack of negligees to sweep under it. "Cute."

"What's cute?"

"You are."

"Meaning?"

"The Rom call *everybody* cousin," said Oscar.

That brought me up short. "What?"

"*What*, what?"

"The Rom call everybody cousin?"

"Well, maybe not all the Rom. I don't know 'em all. There are lots of different groups: the Irish Travelers, the

Cygarie in Poland and the Zingerie in Italy. But Sailor's Rom all call each other cousin."

I stared at him.

"Like in Spanish, right?" Oscar continued, suddenly an expert on kinship systems. "You call older friends *tio* and *tia*, even though they're not really your aunt and uncle. And people your age are *primo*, like 'cousin,' more a term of affection than blood relation per se."

"Wait, wait, *wait*. Sailor and Patience aren't actually *cousins*?"

Chapter 21

Oscar's huge eyes widened as he realized he'd said the wrong thing.

My heart pounded and my cheeks blazed. A mason jar of dried peppermint fell from the shelf, and a honey-jar spell imploded, its golden contents oozing across the counter.

"Um . . ." Oscar said, clearly debating his next move, "Mistress?"

The broom yanked out of his hands and rocketed like a missile across the shop floor.

"Let me fix you a cup of tea. Or maybe a shot of tequila?" Oscar offered, heading for the cupboard in the back room. This was a big deal for my familiar; he wasn't great with the nurturing.

I fell, more than sat, in a chair at the workroom table and tried to rein in my emotions. *Jealousy*, I thought. Fangs sunk deep into my gut and twisted. I'd never truly experienced it before, not like this. Not this ghastly, deep-down, nauseating sensation of rage and fear and self-doubt.

I put my head down on the table.

Oscar placed a cup of tea at my side. It must have been half booze; I could smell the alcohol wafting into the air.

Oscar transformed into his piggy guise when Bronwyn came into the shop.

"Tough morning?" she asked, picking up the tea cup and wrinkling her nose. Then she took in the state of the shop and asked, "Did you do this?"

"No, not most of it. We had a poltergeist last night," I said with a long sigh, lifting my head. "But it's a little bit me. I'm sorry. Are things a mess out on the floor?"

"The rack of prom dresses fell over. Easily fixed." She took a seat across from me. "What's wrong?"

"I just found out that Patience and Sailor aren't really cousins."

"They aren't? How do you know?"

"I . . . actually, I guess I don't know for sure. But apparently in Sailor's family everybody's called cousin, whether they're a blood relative or not."

"And?"

"Have you *seen* her?" I grabbed the day-old newspaper off the stack of recyclables and slammed it on the table.

Bronwyn glanced at the photo of Patience and smiled. "You're lovely, too, Lily."

"Thanks. But you're my friend so you have to think that. We both know I don't hold a candle to her. She's . . . gorgeous."

"And you assume Sailor will be swayed by her physical attributes, even though he's in love with you?"

I shrugged, still concentrating on reining in my emotions lest I accidentally lay waste to my store. "He's a man. And he has eyes."

"You know, just to play devil's advocate here, you

spend time with some pretty good-looking men, as well. Carlos has a very attractive way about him. And Aidan has stopped many a woman in her tracks."

"Those . . . relationships, or whatever you want to call it, aren't romantic."

"I know that, and you know that, but from the outside it could be looked at another way. And didn't you have lunch with Max, just yesterday? Sailor understood, didn't he?"

"I . . . might not have mentioned it. But anyway, it wasn't like that. I would never go behind Sailor's back."

Bronwyn nodded, sympathy shining in her soft brown eyes. "And you don't think Sailor's capable of the same kind of consideration?"

I gave her a grudging nod. "I guess you're right. But I'm just saying, if Duke was spending his days—and some *nights*—with the delectable Patience Blix, you might be singing a different tune."

"Jealousy isn't about another person, Lily. It's about yourself."

"Which means?"

She chuckled. "It's normal to worry about losing something you value. But you should talk to Sailor about what you're feeling, not make assumptions. Besides, you know nothing about this Patience woman—for all you know, she could be married and madly in love with her husband. Or her romantic interests may lie in an entirely different direction. You never know."

"I guess you're right."

"Of course I'm right. Now, why don't we get this place straightened up and ready for customers, and then you can go talk to Sailor?"

"Oh, I don't think—"

"Nonsense. These kinds of feelings tend to fester, and

no good ever came of that. The sooner you get it out in the open, the better. I'll keep an eye on Selena."

"Fine," I said, wishing she weren't right.

A faint floral fragrance hung over Hang Ah Alley, a lingering scent from a long-ago German perfume maker who used to have a factory here. The scent mixed with other spices used not only in the food, but also in the healing arts of Chinatown, lending the alley a distinctive aroma.

I climbed the stairs to Sailor's apartment and tried to ignore the ghostly sensation on the landing outside his door. I knocked softly, half hoping he wasn't home.

My heart fluttered when I heard noises from within.

But the moment Sailor opened the door, I was happy to see him. As always. The top button of his Levi's was undone, and his shirt hung open. Sailor's broad chest was lean but muscled, and its black hair invited my touch. Just the sight of him made me feel warm and shivery and calm and excited, all at the same time.

"I was just thinking about you," Sailor said, taking me into his arms and kissing me.

After a long moment, I pulled back. "We need to talk."

"This is more fun," he said, leaning in for another kiss.

"I agree. But we really do need to talk."

At this last, his mood shifted and he released me. "All right," he said as we stepped into the apartment and he closed the door. "What's up?"

Sailor's apartment smelled even more strongly of pleasant spices. I knew he didn't cook, so I wasn't sure where the scent came from—perhaps it was Sailor himself. I couldn't get enough of his scent.

The apartment was small: a galley kitchen, a living

room just big enough for a table and an upholstered armchair under a reading light, a stack of books sitting on the floor beside it. There were piles of papers and books everywhere, but no bookshelves. The bedroom consisted of a bed—also strewn with books and papers—and a closet, with a tiny bathroom attached. That was about it.

I took a seat at the table, and he sat backwards on the chair opposite me, his arms crossed over the back. It was a posture simultaneously defensive and aggressive.

He searched my face, unsmiling. I felt tendrils of energy reaching out, trying to worm their way into my thoughts.

"Are you trying to read my mind?" I demanded, stroking my medicine bag and slamming shut the gates to my thoughts.

He shrugged. "Thought it might help."

I didn't know how to be in a romantic relationship in the first place, much less one wherein my partner knew my every thought. Everyone has secrets, private corners of their soul and their mind that they don't allow anyone to access. But among magical folks, secrecy is almost a religion.

Sailor had never been able to read my mind, which was a great relief to me. Had his training with Patience made him so much stronger that he could now push past my defenses? Was that even possible? And if so, did I need to protect myself against *Sailor*?

This did not bode well for our relationship.

"Unfortunately," said Sailor, "I can't read a damned thing. So you'll have to tell me. What's going on?"

"Why didn't you tell me about Patience?" I blurted out.

He cocked his head as though trying to understand what I was saying. "What *about* Patience?"

"She's . . . gorgeous. And she's not your cousin."

He leaned back, crossing his arms over his chest. "She *is* my cousin."

"I'm not going to argue the definition of cousin with you."

"Glad to hear that."

"You know what I'm saying."

"Almost never. But speaking of relationships, you and Max have a nice time yesterday?"

"I *thought* I saw you ride by."

He just waited.

"I had to talk to him about an article he wrote about El Pajarito and Ursula Moreno."

"Uh huh," he grunted, sounding unconvinced. "You could've asked me to come along. I like having lunch in North Beach bistros."

"No, you don't."

"I do if you're having lunch in a North Beach bistro with another man."

"It wasn't like that, Sailor. You know that."

"Do I? It seems to me you and Max were pretty hot and heavy there for a while. The way he looks at you . . . No, I *don't* know what it's like between you two."

"You have nothing to worry about, Sailor. I promise."

"And neither do you."

"And . . . there's something else. Selena is going to be a challenge, I can tell. Taking on a teenager would be a lot to ask of a boyfriend, but a teenager with special needs is even tougher. You didn't sign up for something like that."

He stared at me with his beautiful, unreadable eyes.

"And you *did*?"

"No, not exactly, but . . . Well, yes, I guess I did. I did when I told Ursula I would look after her, and then I told Selena if Ursula didn't get out, she could stay with me."

"And you think I wouldn't be willing to do the same?"

"I'm . . . I don't mean to put words in your mouth, Sailor. But I can never tell what you're thinking. If Graciela hadn't stepped in to help me back in the day, when I was just a little younger than Selena, I'd be . . . I don't know what I'd be. Toast, probably. So I feel an obligation to pass it on, as they say."

"Let me get this straight: You are committing to help raise this little witch, Selena, and you're letting me go?"

Tears stung the back of my eyes. As a witch, I can't cry. But as a woman, I often felt the desire to do so.

"You don't think very much of me, do you?" he asked.

"I think a great deal of you, Sailor. And maybe now, with Patience—"

"Enough about Patience!" He threw up his hands in exasperation. "I don't *want* her, Lily."

"She's just so freaking gorgeous."

"Yes, she is. But she's not my type."

"Gorgeous, sexy Rom women aren't your type?"

"Not at all."

"Why not? Aren't you human?"

He rose from the chair and came around the table; I stood to face him. He stopped in front of me, so close I felt the warmth of his body, only inches from mine.

"I guess I prefer nosy, stubborn, Southern women."

"Really?"

"Really."

"But . . . what about Selena?"

"If I can handle a grown-up witch like you, I'm certainly not going to be frightened off by a teenage version. In case you hadn't noticed, I'm made of pretty stern stuff."

I took a deep breath, remembering what Bronwyn had counseled me. I willed myself to believe that he was telling me the truth about Patience. And that he was enough of a man to take on not only me, but possibly my guardianship of Selena, and all that might entail.

"So, you really prefer nosy, stubborn Southern witches to unencumbered gypsy sexpots?"

He nodded, moved closer to me, and gave me a slow smile.

"Well, now," I said with an exaggerated Texas twang, tilting my head and batting my eyelashes. "Y'all got yourself one of them li'l fillies right here."

"Don't I just? Now, can we get back to the kissing?"

Selena was sitting on the floor near the register at Aunt Cora's Closet, wearing a pair of white cotton gloves. She appeared intent on repairing and cleaning every piece of jewelry in the shop. Her single-minded industriousness made me feel a little like I was running a sweatshop, but I was glad to see her occupied.

"Did you know," asked Bronwyn, "Selena has a knack for memorizing every herbal blend I can come up with? She can repeat complicated orders from yesterday morning without blinking an eye. Watch: Selena, what did I mix for Susan Rogers?"

Without looking up from her task, Selena recited: "Two parts echinacea, one part black-eyed Susan, mix with ground rose hips, shredded ginger root, add turmeric for color and anti-inflammatory properties. Combine with dried orange peel and bergamot to taste. Only sunflower honey for sweetening."

"You see? She's like an herbal recipe tape recorder."

"That's amazing." With a memory like that, why hadn't she told me every nuanced detail of what she had done at Betty's house? Was she afraid to tell me? Or could loyalty to someone be keeping her mute?

Why, oh why, couldn't mind-reading *be one of my skills*? I wondered if Sailor might be able to read her.

Would it be ethical to ask him to try without Selena's knowledge and consent? Would the all-powerful Patience allow him to "dissipate his powers" in the attempt?

Or . . . now that I knew what I did about some of Ursula's "wrong" wax being made into poppets and placed in Betty's house, and about Lupita, I wanted another peek at El Pajarito. Preferably without an impatient homicide inspector looking over my shoulder.

I glanced at the human tape recorder sitting quietly and cleaning jewelry. Should I bring Selena along? She might be able to tell me something about what was happening in the shop, and maybe even make the connection to what had happened to Nicky. It was her home, after all. Or at least it *had* been. Would it be too sad for her, or might it be good for her to go back?

I decided to just come out and ask her. She was so small that it was easy to think of her as a child, but she was fourteen years old. At that age, I had known my own mind.

"Selena, would you like to go with me to El Pajarito?"

She jumped up and grabbed her sweater.

"I'll take that as a yes," I murmured, then turned to Bronwyn. "Can you handle things here?"

"Of course, Sunday afternoons are slow. But"—she dropped her voice to a whisper—"are you allowed to go back there? I thought it was a crime scene?"

"No, not at all," I stretched the truth. "There's not even crime scene tape across the door. It's just a mess, is all. No worries."

Besides, I could protect myself and Selena easily enough; we would wear our talismans, and there wouldn't be scary people there, just out-of-control store supplies.

That Bad Luck spray had no chance against yours truly. Not to toot my own horn, but I wasn't that easily cowed.

And I had the distinct impression that neither was
Selena.

Selena and I peered through the metal security grates
that covered the front of El Pajarito.

Santa Muerte's cigarette dangled from her bony mouth
at a rakish angle, and her skeletal visage appeared to
smile. But Selena only had eyes for the bedlam beyond
the display window.

"Wow," said Selena. "That's a real mess."

"You can say that again." If and when Ursula was released, she was going to have one heck of a time getting
things back to normal.

I was pleased to see that although Selena was shocked
by the mess, she did not appear to be traumatized.

"Shall we go in?" I asked my partner in crime.

"How? It's locked, and I don't have a key."

"Good point," I said. I had been so intent on making
sure Selena and I had protective talismans, I had forgotten to bring my Hand of Glory. "What about around the
back? Is there a window, or something?"

Selena's eyes were wide and serious. "We're going to
break in?"

Adhering to the code of normal people had never
worked all that well for me, so recently I had embraced
the "witches' code": *An it harm none do what ye will.* In
my grandmother's words, *"haz lo que necesitas,"* or "do
what you need to do." The "do no harm" was implied.

All of which is to say I wasn't above breaking into
Ursula's store to look for evidence of a doll similar to
the poppet found in Betty North's house.

"We're hardly breaking in, now, are we? After all, it's
your grandmother's store, right?"

Her eyes narrowed. "Is that why you invited me

along? So you wouldn't get in trouble for breaking and entering?"

"No, of course not. I invited you along because I thought you could help me figure out what might be going on here. I also thought you would enjoy being back."

"Hmmm," she said, giving me a speculative look, as if I were a juvenile delinquent and she the schoolmarm.

"C'mon," I said.

"Where we going?"

"Around back."

"Can't. The gate to the alley behind the store is locked."

"Let's try next door."

The neighboring business sported a huge sign advertising: "Money Orders, Send Money Back Home!" Through the front window I spied a ray of afternoon sun shining through a small window in the door at the back of the store.

"Follow my lead," I said, and we went in.

A long line of people waited patiently for their turn at one of the tellers, who sat behind thick slabs of bulletproof glass.

I marched briskly past them toward the rear of the store, Selena close on my heels. We pushed through the door at the rear, and into the alley. The door swung shut and locked behind us.

"Why didn't anyone stop us?" Selena asked.

"Never underestimate the power of a self-confident woman in a vintage dress."

The narrow alley was lined with trash cans and recycling containers. One end was closed off by a brick wall, the other by a chained gate topped with barbed wire. By virtue of the locked gate, the alley was populated by no one but the two of us and, I was certain, vermin.

A little blue bench sat next to the back door of El

Pajarito, the twin of the bench out front. Cigarette butts littered the concrete in a semicircle around it. Apparently Santa Muerte wasn't the only one with a nicotine habit.

As I had hoped, the alley access to Ursula's store wasn't as secure as the street entry. There was a door and an unbarred window, and the door appeared to be secured with a simple doorknob lock. I pulled a credit card from my satchel and slipped it between the doorframe and the knob as I had seen done in movies. I wasn't at all sure this would work, but figured it was worth a try. My backup plan was to break the window, which I hoped wouldn't be necessary. Sure enough, after working the credit card a few minutes, the lock mechanism released.

"You can open locks?" Selena said, more awed by this simple trick than any of my magic she had witnessed.

"Watch and learn, young grasshopper," I said, feeling smug. Unfortunately, the door opened only a few inches before being caught by a chain.

Selena snickered.

I smiled at her, pleased to hear her laugh. If I couldn't break into the store, at least I could amuse my ward.

I pulled a chopstick from my bag, and shut the door as far as I could while still allowing enough room to maneuver. I closed my eyes and concentrated on envisioning the chain sliding. After another few moments—and a couple of swear words—it fell away.

"You're amazing," said Selena.

"Thanks. Hey, before we go in, this is what I'd like you to do: Feel for anything out of place, anything odd."

"The whole place is 'out of place.' It's a mess."

"I mean at a deeper level. See if you feel anything 'wrong,' the same way you did with the wax doll you found in Betty's clothes."

"Okay."

We entered El Pajarito.

Unlike the shop floor, the back of the store was neat as a pin, the air scented with bleach and a sweet-smelling detergent I always associated with Mexico. Boxes were labeled in a neat, tight handwriting: *Holy water, Lourdes; Holy water, Guadalupe; Holy water, Jerusalem. Candles: success, love, family, scholarship, car accidents.*

A desk held a neat stack of papers, and wire baskets labeled "In" and "Out" for bills and invoices. I flipped through the bills in the "Out" basket: business taxes, what looked like a greeting card, a credit card bill. All stamped and ready to go; I picked them up and put them in my satchel to drop in the mail for Ursula. It was the least I could do.

There were a couple of paintings on the wall that reminded me of a Rorschach test: black ink on a red-brown background. To my mind they looked like twin demons; if I looked long enough I saw open mouths complete with fangs.

"You see what you want to see," the experts would say. I remembered meeting with a middle school psychologist after the incident with the exploding basketballs. She showed me a series of images, and even though I saw demons then, too, I told her I saw butterflies and kittens playing with a ball of yarn. I may have been young, but I wasn't stupid.

"What are these pictures of?" I asked Selena.

"Nothing," she said, hands splayed at her side as she attempted to sense something. "They're abstract."

Apparently she wasn't stupid, either.

Time to face the mayhem in Ursula's shop.

I paused in the short hallway that led to the shop floor, taking a moment to steel myself. What I had said to Carlos the other day wasn't a joke; this was highly unusual behavior in merchandise. I'd witnessed the occasional rogue activity, but only under a specific set of circumstances: when I was under the influence of strong emotions and physical connection—like lovemaking. *Other* people worried about accidental pregnancies or STDs. *I* caused dresses to dance or rose petals to appear.

Could the same principle apply under different circumstances? Maybe the merchandise in Ursula's store was responding to the strong emotions Ursula had felt upon being arrested and hauled off to jail.

Or . . . maybe it was Selena's influence. At her age I had wreaked havoc without meaning to, calling without intent but with the energy and neediness of youth. In addition to the basketball episode there had been an unfortunate incident during chemistry lab that had required a HazMat response team. The memory still made me cringe.

But if Selena were the source of the commotion at the store, could she be causing it from afar? Was the merchandise reaching out to harm anyone using it? That suggested intention, which would be beyond a poltergeist's ability.

Selena stood behind me as I paused to take in the shop floor. It looked about the same as when I'd been here with Carlos: candles and figurines and bags of herbs scattered around the floor, the shelves half-empty. The food left at the foot of Santa Muerte was turning; flies settled on the rotting fruit and dried-out tortilla.

Suddenly I realized: We weren't alone.

Chapter 22

I pushed Selena back into the hallway with one hand and held up the other, wheeling around to my right and letting out a blast of power. A large stack of tarot cards fanned out through the air, landing willy-nilly, and yet another shelf fell off the wall, its contents shattering on the floor.

Patience Blix held her hands over her head, ducked, and spat out something in a language I didn't understand.

"*Stop it!*" she yelled.

"*You* stop it!"

"*I'm* not doing anything," Patience said. "*You're* the one taking the place apart."

"You scared the *bejeezus* out of me."

"What in the world are you *doing* here?"

"I think you stole that line from me," I said. "What are *you* doing here?"

"I'm trying to figure out what's going on," Patience said with a grim set of her mouth. She raised her chin slightly and looked past me. "Hi, Selena."

"Hi," Selena said quietly.

"I thought you said you didn't know Selena," I said to Patience. "*Or* Ursula Moreno."

"I never said that," Patience said, raising one arched brow. "You assumed it."

"I guess I shouldn't be surprised. Lying by omission is probably a skill mastered along with cold reading and *bujo* drops."

"*Bujo* drops? The witch has been doing her homework."

"I keep my ears open," I said with a shrug. "What are you doing here, Patience? And how did you get in?"

"I have my ways, just like you. Listen, I'm glad you found Selena, but now we need to find Lupita and figure this thing out. This campaign against fortune-tellers is about to put me out of business."

"I thought you were aboveboard. Beyond reproach."

She smiled. "Of course I am. That doesn't mean I want cops coming by every other day, scaring off my clientele. I need calm vibrations to work. And they seem no closer to resolving this, so I thought I'd see if I could feel something."

Could I believe her? I didn't want to. I really, *really* didn't want to. But it actually made sense. And, I reminded myself, Sailor trusted Patience. Aidan admired her. I should stop allowing my emotions to color my reaction to her.

"And . . . any clues?" I asked.

"Not really. I was hoping to find something to help me track Lupita down. But . . ." She looked around the jumble and heaved a deep sigh. "Considering the state this place is in, I don't know what I might find. Selena, I take it you don't know where we could find her?"

Selena shook her head, looking around the shop with wide eyes. "Look at these silver charms. They're so *tar-*

nished. Lily, can I take them back to the shop and polish them?"

"Sure." While she gathered the pieces, I asked Patience, "If Selena finds something that belonged to Lupita, could you read it, maybe intuit her location?"

"Want to take my hand, and try something together, you and me?" Patience suggested, in the same taunting tone she'd used when I went to her lair to ask for help finding Selena.

"All right."

She looked surprised. "Really?"

"If you think it can help us find Lupita, I'll do it. Sailor trusts you."

"And you trust him. Is that it?"

"Implicitly."

A broad smile broke out over her pretty face. She gestured to Selena. "Your guardian, she is very trusting, is she not? So, is there something here that belonged to Lupita? Maybe a ring, something personal?"

"She wasn't here that much," said Selena.

"How did Ursula get in touch with her?" asked Patience.

"Voice mail."

"*What* voice mail?" I asked.

"If Ursula needed to talk to Lupita, she called a voice mail number and said she had some money for her."

"What's the number?" I asked, irked that Selena hadn't mentioned this little factoid earlier.

"I'll dial it if you want," she said, picking up the handset of the phone behind the counter. Then she handed it to Patience.

Patience smiled like the cat that ate the canary.

I tamped down my annoyance. I was vying with the fortune-teller for *Selena's* affection now? *Get over yourself, Lily.*

Patience left a message that Lupita had an inheritance coming to her, and included her phone number. I had to hand it to her— she sounded very convincing. Much more so than I would have.

"Well, I guess that about does it for now," said Patience. "We wait and see if she calls."

"And you'll let me know when she does?"

"Of course."

I didn't exactly believe her, but what could I say?

It dawned on me that the entire time we'd been in the shop, Ursula's merchandise had been quiet. Either that was a good sign, suggesting the source of the disturbance had dissipated; or it was a very bad sign, indicating a calm before the storm. I couldn't shake the feeling that trouble was imminent.

"Let's get out of here," I said.

We turned to go.

A man stood in the hallway.

"Leaving so soon?" asked Carlos Romero. *Inspector* Carlos Romero.

From the expression on his face, I wasn't sure the friendship we had shared at the pizza-and-poker party was going to get me very far.

Half an hour later, Selena and I limped back to Aunt Cora's Closet in disgrace. Actually, *I* seemed to be the only one of our trio who was concerned about my reputation. My teenage ward appeared no worse for wear, her attention focused on her silver charms. And Patience had withstood Carlos's scathing interrogation with an air of boredom. In fact, she had made a wisecrack about being the bad kids to Carlos's middle school teacher, which had made me laugh despite myself.

But as I drove across the city I wondered if Carlos would trust me again. I hated to disappoint him . . . especially since this expedition to El Pajarito hadn't revealed anything new. If only Selena had informed me of Lupita's voice mail number the night I'd picked her up, this could all be over by now.

Why hadn't she mentioned it before?

Aunt Cora's Closet was closed on Mondays, which was a good thing. The combined appetites of Selena and Oscar had laid waste to my kitchen cupboards. Time to restock.

Like most people I patronized a local chain grocery store for basic household items, but whenever possible I preferred to shop at one of the many farmers' markets held throughout the city. On Mondays there was one at the United Nations Plaza, which was the fancy name for an open area not far from City Hall. Most days the plaza was full of homeless folks passing the time and panhandling. But on market day it was a bustling bazaar of farmers, artisans, and food trucks hawking their produce and goods.

Sailor had a rare day off from his training and offered to accompany us. Bronwyn and Maya seemed to sense I could use their support in dealing with Selena, so even though it was their day off, too, they insisted they wanted to come along.

Oscar, for his part, would not be denied.

"You'll have to wear a leash," I said as Selena and I gathered shopping bags and baskets.

He glared and crossed his arms over his skinny chest.

It seemed doubly humiliating for Oscar to be leashed in front of Selena, who didn't make things easier when she surprised us both by laughing out loud. We had never heard her laugh before; it was a sweet, melodic sound.

Unfortunately, the fact that she was giggling at Oscar on his leash gave the sweetness a mean-spirited edge.

It was a gorgeous day to stroll through the stands of

produce and handmade goods at the market. In addition to fresh fruits and vegetables, a person could buy locally produced honey, olive oil, responsibly fished seafood, antibiotic-free chicken, prepared foods, fresh-cut flowers, all sorts of jewelry, knitted items, ceramics, and artwork.

At one end of the farmers' market was an inflatable jumpy house, which moved and bounced with the energy of the laughing, screaming children inside.

Selena stopped in her tracks. She gazed at the kids, then at the parents waiting outside the jumpy house. I read yearning in her eyes; did she long for a "normal" life as desperately as I had when I was her age?

Bronwyn seemed to notice as well, and came to lay an arm across her thin shoulders.

"Don't they have fun?" Bronwyn asked Selena. "Do you want to go in?"

Selena shook her head and turned away, and we moseyed along an aisle of vendors who sold stone fruits and verdant leafy greens. It was slow going, as we had to step carefully around strollers, and make time for all who wished to admire Oscar. I felt myself begin to relax. Holding Sailor's hand, accompanied by good friends, I took delight in the warm sunshine and the milling, good-natured crowd.

I stocked up on some kitchen staples and purchased the ingredients for gumbo, cornmeal crust pizza, spaghetti, and a few other dishes to feed the two hungry creatures living with me.

"Could I try one?" Selena asked, pointing to a kiosk selling Greek gyros.

"Sure, why not?"

Sailor found us a table near a man playing folk tunes on a violin, and our group dispersed to buy lunch before returning to the table and settling in. Maya decided on a burrito, Bronwyn opted for Thai salad rolls, and Sailor and I split a plate of Afghani food.

I bought Oscar a gyro, too, and he made short work of it, then watched the progress of every bite of Selena's gyro. She ate slowly but steadily, and no sooner had she finished the gyro than she asked for dim sum. After that, she tried falafel, then Thai chicken satay, and finally a slice of cherry pie. Sailor had to buy Oscar his own slice of pie so he'd stop whimpering and snorting.

Then Selena asked for a piece of chocolate cake.

"Don't you think you've had enough, sugar pie? I wouldn't want you to get sick."

Her eyes narrowed at me. "I never get sick."

"Okay . . . but I think you've had enough for now."

"At Betty's house you said if I came with you I could eat."

"That's true, and you've eaten well, haven't you?" I said.

Selena opened her mouth to respond, but Sailor cut her off.

"She said no," said Sailor, gathering our things to toss in the nearby trash and recycling containers.

Selena shrugged, and we resumed our shopping. Sailor and Bronwyn stopped at one booth to sample olive oils while Maya and I paused to check out some handmade batik scarves. I looked up from a particularly beautiful emerald green scarf to notice Selena making a beeline for a display of crafts created from old cutlery.

An artisan had created funny faces and dancing figures from forks, knives, and spoons. Mobiles made of antique silverware hung from an overhead bar. As the pieces moved in the wind, they clacked and chimed pleasantly.

Selena lifted her face to the mobiles, and I realized they danced more each time she looked at them. Was she calling the breeze, somehow? The sun glinted off the shiny metal, casting little bubbles of light on the ground and on the passersby. When the reflected light moved over Selena's pinched features, it was as though it was caressing her. More lights gathered, so many that her features were bathed in light. A look of pure, reverential joy passed over her face.

Maya came to stand next to me. "She seems enamored."

I nodded. "Well, at least we know there's one thing that makes her happy. Two, if you count making fun of Oscar."

"When did she make fun of Oscar?"

One of the challenges of having normal nonmagical friends was remembering when to keep my mouth shut. As close as we were, Bronwyn and Maya did not know about Oscar's true form as a gobgoyle, much less that he could speak and interact like a human.

"Oh, she just thought he looked funny on his leash," I improvised.

"Well, I gotta say, a pig on a leash *is* pretty funny-looking."

I had to smile. "I suppose that's true."

I couldn't take my eyes off Selena, who didn't take her eyes off the mobiles. Finally I said to Maya, "I know you and Bronwyn wanted to buy supplies. Why don't we meet up with y'all later? Would you mind taking Oscar with you? If we don't run into you again let's all meet back at the car."

"Sounds like a plan," said Maya. "See you later. C'mon, pig."

I joined Selena at the kiosk.

"Would you like one of the mobiles, Selena?" I offered.

She looked startled. "You mean, like, a present?"

"Exactly like a present." I checked one of the price tags. *Ouch.* But it was handmade by an artist using antique silverware. Besides, at this point I was willing to pay a pretty penny to make Selena smile.

"People don't give me presents," she said.

"What, never?"

She shook her head.

"Well, then, it's about time to change that, don't you think? Let this be the first of what I'm sure will be many gifts."

She started shaking her head, narrowing her eyes. A basket of mismatched antique spoons fell from a card table to the grass below.

"Calm down, Selena. It's fine, we won't buy anything now, and we'll talk about this later, okay?"

"'Kay," she said with a sullen shrug.

What was she angry about? I trailed her into the stream of people, giving her a little distance.

Sailor fell in step beside me. "Have you ever heard of silver magic catchers?"

"Um . . . one of the women at a *botanica* mentioned it to me when I was there with Aidan. Why? You think those mobiles are examples of magic catchers?"

"No. But they were responding to Selena. Surely you noticed."

"I did. They were reflecting light onto her. She seemed to enjoy it."

"She more than enjoyed it. I think she has a relationship to metal, probably more profound than she realizes. Think back when you were a kid—everything seemed normal, right? It's only when we get older that we start to realize that not everyone had those same experiences, that not everyone is like us."

"You're right." I nodded. "Looks like I have a little homework to do, researching metal magic. If I want to help her with it I'll have to figure out what it's all about."

I took Sailor's hand as we followed Selena. This simple

act—holding his hand in public, in what Oscar would scathingly refer to as "PDA" or public display of affection—made me feel almost giddy. My breath caught in my throat when I thought about what it really meant to have a man in my life . . . to have *this* man in my life. He was astute and sensitive and kind, despite his sometimes gruff exterior.

Up ahead, Selena was checking out antique pocket watches. I glanced at a display of beautiful late-season nectarines, great pyramids of the peachy fruit. I picked one up to smell its heavenly perfume, then held it to Sailor's nose.

When I looked back at the antique-watch display, Selena was gone.

Chapter 23

"Where is Selena?" I asked Sailor, putting the nectarine back atop the fruit pyramid. "Where did she go? Did you see?"

Sailor shook his head. "I was looking at you. But she can't have gone far. Must be at one of the neighboring stands, probably looking at more jewelry."

We hurried through the crowd to the spot where we had last seen her.

The watch display was empty, but the elderly seller said he had seen a girl walk off with a man she seemed to know.

"Can you describe him?" I asked.

"Good-lookin' fellow, if I do say so myself. Blond hair, blue eyes . . . I mean, I don't much notice good-lookin' men, but this fellow was something else."

Aidan Rhodes.

We found them at a table near the food kiosks.

Actually, *Sailor* found them. Not by looking, but by intuiting.

They sat on opposite sides of the table, talking, while Selena finished off a wedge of chocolate cake. Aidan's golden hair gleamed in the sunshine, and even at a distance I could see the periwinkle blue of his eyes.

As we approached, Sailor cautioned me. "Be careful."

"I will."

"I mean it, Lily. Take a moment to center yourself."

He was right. Thinking I'd lost Selena had scared me, and when I was scared my power surged, sometimes with disastrous results.

I closed my eyes and breathed deeply, thinking of my guardian spirit, my grandmother Graciela, the long line of powerful women who had gone before me.

And then I went to yell at Aidan and Selena.

"What in the *Sam Hill*?" I said. "You scared the *stuffing* out of me, Selena. I thought something had happened to you."

She looked at me, impassive, apparently unmoved.

"And *you*," I said, turning on Aidan. "You're a grown man. You should know better than to whisk a child away from her people. What were you *thinking*?"

"Hello, Lily, what a pleasure. Do have a seat," Aidan suggested, no more impressed by my wrath than Selena.

With no other options open to me, I sat down heavily in a chair between the two. Sailor remained standing, arms crossed over his chest, his eyes hidden behind dark sunglasses, like a badass bodyguard. Aidan didn't even spare him a glance.

"Selena and I were talking about her future. Would you like to join the discussion?"

"I . . . of course."

"Selena will be under my protection," Aidan said.

"She's already under *my* protection," I said.

Our eyes met and held, a silent challenge.

"Selena," Aidan said after a moment. "Why don't you and Sailor go look for some perfect tomatillos? We'll catch up with you in a few minutes."

Selena looked from Aidan to me, as though sensing the tension.

"We should all stay together," said Sailor, stepping toward our little group.

"Lily will join you in a moment," Aidan said, his gaze not moving from my face. "No need to worry, Sailor. We're right out here in public. What could happen?"

Selena got up and meandered toward the fruit stands.

"Sailor, please stay with her," I said. "I'll be fine. This won't take long. Please."

With obvious reluctance, Sailor went to join Selena.

"Was that for Sailor's benefit?" I asked. "You wanted to pull rank on him, put him in his place?"

"You have no idea how little Sailor matters to me. This is about Selena."

"You can't have her, Aidan. She's only a child; she's not capable of looking out for her own interests."

"You make it sound as if my motives are suspect. Surely you've noticed how powerful she is. If she's not under my protection, someone else might well step in."

"Someone already has: me. I'm taking care of her."

The knowledge that I'd just lost track of her in a public place hung, unspoken, in the air between us.

"Also, Oscar's on the job," I added. "Most of the time." *When he wasn't on a leash and taken elsewhere.*

"Oscar's a good bodyguard. But . . . listen, Lily. Selena's not the only one I'm concerned about right now. When you and I connected, the other night on the bridge, I felt a change in your power."

"What kind of change?"

He hesitated, as though choosing his words with care.

And that made me nervous. Aidan almost never hesitated.

"I have a proposal for you. I'd like you to come work with me."

"You want *me* to work for *you*?"

He gave me a half-smile. "Not *for*, but *with*. I'm suggesting a partnership."

"With you," I tried to wrap my mind around the idea. "Lily Ivory in partnership with Aidan Rhodes? That sounds . . . complicated."

"Complicated, but interesting. Like most worthwhile things in life."

"What's going on, Aidan?"

"Things have been ratcheting up in our fair city. Even officialdom has started to notice—witness the mayor's clean-up campaign. And I'm . . ." Again with the hesitation, and the reaching for words. His blue eyes cast about, taking in the marketgoers and picnickers. Finally he seemed to come to a decision, and met my gaze once again. "I'm not as powerful as I used to be. As I *need* to be. I have limitations that need to be addressed."

"What kinds of limitations?"

"I don't think this is the place or the time to get into details. Suffice it to say that if you and I combine our powers, I believe we'll be strong enough to keep things under control. We can look after Selena together, give her guidance and make sure she's safe, and then if things go well, she will become a powerful witch in her own right and will be able to step in to help."

"I'm, uh . . . I mean, we can work together from time to time, of course."

"I'm not talking about that—that's what we've been doing so far. But now we need to come together, a united front. Publicly."

"What about Sailor?" I asked.

"What about him?"

"He's not going to be thrilled about me working for you."

"It doesn't matter. Your relationship's not long for this world, anyway."

"I'm *sorry*?"

"Listen: I know what you think of me. You suspect I have other motives. But I released Sailor in the first place because I could sense the feelings you had for each other. Love makes people vulnerable, which for normal people is part of its beauty. But you aren't normal, Lily. Given your abilities, being vulnerable makes you dangerous."

"You're saying magical people can't experience love?"

"Not the kind of love you're thinking of. Not true, selfless love."

"I don't believe that," I scoffed. "You're making this up as you go along. You're jealous of what Sailor and I have."

"I wish it were that simple. Tell me: How many powerful people do you know who are in a loving relationship?"

I thought of Graciela and her witchy friends; my father; Aidan. Finally, one occurred to me: "Hervé!"

Aidan shook his head. "Different system entirely. Hervé's relationship is an integral part of his belief system; the dyad is an important source of his power. But that is not the case for you. Your relationship to Sailor, your desire for love and connection, makes you vulnerable."

"So you tried to send Sailor away because you're a nice guy?"

"Is it so hard to believe I would do something for altruistic reasons?"

"I think you rarely do anything that isn't in your interest, one way or the other."

"Think what you will about my character, Lily, but

deep down you know I'm right about this. We're much more alike than you've ever wanted to admit."

I felt a subtle shift in the atmosphere and looked up to see Sailor and Selena approaching the table, a little brown paper bag of tomatillos in hand.

"Time's up," said Sailor, glaring at Aidan.

Aidan rose. "Monopolized your woman for too long, have I? No worries, I'm late for an appointment, anyway. Selena, remember what I said. I'll see you soon. And, Lily? Always a pleasure."

Sailor waited until we got back to Aunt Cora's Closet, Bronwyn and Maya went home, and Selena was upstairs with Oscar before grilling me about my conversation with Aidan.

But I didn't know what to make of what Aidan told me; I needed time to process it, think it through. So I equivocated.

"I think . . . he was saying that things might be ratcheting up in San Francisco lately."

"Ratcheting up, how?"

"Just mayhem-wise. He wasn't specific. But you have to admit there's been a lot going on, supernaturally speaking, since I arrived."

He smiled and tugged my ponytail. "You *do* seem to be something of a lightning rod for trouble. I'll grant you that."

"And at my last showdown, at the oak tree . . . it seemed like my foe was defeated a little too easily."

"It wasn't all that easy. And you had help. From your grandmother's coven, and the woodsfolk, and Oscar. Not to mention your guardian spirit."

"I know. But still. It's just a little worrying."

"Good thing I'm getting stronger, too, then, right? As are you, if I'm not mistaken."

"I am getting more powerful but . . . Anyway, I think I may have to work with Aidan."

He tilted his head slightly in question. "Work with him how?"

"We need to partner, combine forces, make sure we've got control."

"I thought you told me you and Aidan 'combined forces' once and you melted metal?"

"That was a while ago. We were unprepared, but we're both more in control now, and he's got a better handle on me. We linked the other night and didn't have a problem. In fact, it allowed me to experience a vision."

"When was this?"

"The other night I went to the Golden Gate Bridge to try to figure out what happened with Nicky Utley."

"And you met Aidan there?"

"Yes, he was there, but that's not my point—"

"Why didn't you tell me?"

"I . . . I don't know. Everything's been so crazy lately, and we haven't had a lot of time to talk. I wasn't deliberately not telling you. My point is that things are different now between Aidan and me."

"Could this have anything to do with Aidan wanting influence over Selena?"

"He and I need to work together to keep her safe."

"Or so he says." Sailor shrugged. "Ever occur to you we need to keep *her* safe from *him*?"

"The thing is . . . I believe him, Sailor. I think he wanted to make sure she was okay, that I could protect her, that's all."

Sailor pushed a strand of hair out of my eyes, and stroked my cheek with one finger. When he spoke, his voice was very quiet.

"You are a trusting soul for one who has seen so much."

I didn't know what to say. This was the second time

today I'd been called "trusting"—by psychics, no less—which was the opposite of how I felt.

"I'd like to arrange a discussion with all three of us: you, me, and Aidan," Sailor continued. "Just so we're all on the same page. In the meantime, do me a favor: Promise me you won't let him in here when I'm not around."

Only then did I realize he still had his jacket on.

"You're not staying?"

"I have to go—"

"— work with Patience," I said with a nod, peeved. "Fine."

He raised one eyebrow. "It worries me when a woman says *'fine.'* "

I gave him an insincere smile. "Whatever could you mean?"

"I have to do this, Lily. You know that. And after seeing Patience, I'm going to have dinner with my aunt Renna and see what she thinks about my progress. This encounter with Aidan is further proof that I need all the strength I can gather. If you need to have someone at your back, I intend to be that man. I trust Aidan about as far as I can throw him."

I blew out an exasperated breath.

"I'm sorry, Lily. You're going to have to be patient a little longer."

"Patience isn't my strong suit." Pun intended.

He gave me a crooked grin, and kissed me. "Don't I know it."

First Aidan, now Patience. *Grrr.*

I didn't have the mental space to deal with both of them at the moment. But I could do something about my feelings toward Patience, at least. Sailor's devotion to that sexy fortune-teller was driving me round the bend. *Enough.*

I took a cedar box down from the high shelf it shared with my red leather-bound Book of Shadows. Taking a bundle of dried sage, I lit the ends and then smudged the inside of the cedar box with the smoke, using a feather to direct it into each corner, then laying the bundle in a large scallop shell in the middle of the box.

While the sage smoldered and purified the box, I brought the newspaper article featuring Patience and a pair of scissors over to the kitchen table.

Oscar crouched atop the table, eyes huge.

"Whatcha doin'?" he growled.

"Nothing. Oscar, I've asked you not to stand on the table." I started to cut out the photo of Patience out of the newspaper.

Eyes never leaving my hands, Oscar crawled off to stand on a chair. His gravelly voice dropped to an awed, excited whisper. "Mistress is doing *voodoo* on Patience Blix?"

"No, of course not."

"Then whatcha doin'?"

"And I'm not your mistress anymore, remember?"

He shrugged.

I turned the cutout picture over and inscribed her name in careful block letters in red ink.

"You *are*!" cried Oscar. "You're doing a *hex* on Patience Blix!"

Chapter 24

"You're *hexing* Patience?" Selena gasped as she joined us in the kitchen. "No way! I'm gonna tell."

"No, of *course* I'm not hexing anyone. I would never do such a thing. I never . . . um, *almost* never, hex."

Selena and Oscar stood on either side of the table, watching me, wide-eyed. I let out an exasperated breath.

"If you *must* know," I said as I gathered three garlic cloves, a hunk of burdock root, and basil leaves that I had soaked in water and left in the light of the last full moon, "I'm making a vexation box."

"What's that?"

"It helps a person cope with something—or someone—that's annoying her no end."

With a sharp intake of breath, Oscar whispered, "You're going to *kill* Patience?"

Selena gasped.

"Really, Oscar? After all this time you think I'd use my powers to kill someone?"

He shrugged one scaly shoulder. "If she was going after Sailor."

Selena snorted.

"I would not *kill* someone for going after Sailor," I said as I brought the ingredients over to the box, where the smudge bundle had stopped smoking. "Tear her hair out, maybe," I added, muttering. "Wipe that smug smile off her face . . ."

Oscar snickered.

I removed the sage bundle, and placed the garlic cloves, burdock root, and five basil leaves in the box.

"Cedar is a protective wood," I explained to my rapt audience. "Sage purifies, and basil is also protective—especially when it has been infused with the light from a full moon. Burdock root helps to expel negative ideas. And garlic is protective and repels bad thoughts."

"So you're trying to protect Patience?"

"Not hardly. It's a vexation box. This *woman*"—I held up her smiling picture and concentrated on it—"is vexing *me* greatly."

I placed the photo in the box, under the garlic, and shut the lid. I picked up the box and gave it a couple of hard shakes, noting with satisfaction the burdock root and garlic knocking against the sides.

Then I started to yell.

Oscar ran away to hide in his cubby over the fridge, and Selena scooted over to the living room couch and pretended to read one of Oscar's Agatha Christie novels.

I yelled a little more, shook the box a few more times, and started feeling better. Finally I placed it back on the high shelf.

"Who wants hot chocolate?" I asked.

Oscar stuck his snout out from under his blankets. I could see one glass-green eye peeking out.

"Is it safe?" Selena called from the living room.

"Much safer now, I'll tell you that much. A vexation

box captures anger and annoyance. That way I don't lose my temper."

"I'll bet that would be bad," said Selena as she came into the kitchen.

"You should *see* it!" said Oscar with a loud cackle. "Things flying every which way—or every *witch* way, get it? Like a poltergeist! It's *awesome*! Mistress, could I have double marshmallows in my hot chocolate?"

Later that evening I brushed Selena's long hair while she played with a ball of red wax. With every stroke, I remembered the comforting feelings from childhood, when Graciela would sit behind me and do the same, working through tangles with patience and tenderness. A simple, intimate act repeated endlessly through the generations.

Though her hands worked ceaselessly with the wax, her energy felt calm, tranquil. Maybe time for another attempt at getting information from my closemouthed ward.

"Selena? What did you do at Betty's?"

She shrugged.

"I mean magic. What sort of *magic* did you do at Betty's?"

"Not much. Lupita said I shouldn't dissipate my powers."

There was a lot of that advice going around.

"So what *did* you do?"

"Mostly polished the silver. I like to make things shiny."

The first time I had seen Selena at Betty's house, cleaning the silver, she was wearing white gloves. The gloves kept fingerprints from the metal, but could Lupita have suggested the gloves for another reason entirely? I thought about what Sailor had said at the farmers' market, that Selena might be unaware of her strange relationship to metal. When Selena cleaned the tarnish from the silver, did she imbue the metal with some of her power?

Could the silver have been trapping her magic?

"Can you tell me anything about Lupita's fiancé?" I asked as I started to plait her hair into two long braids.

She shrugged. "He was nice. He had a hard childhood like me 'cause he was different too. A lot of people are. I'm not a freak."

"No, you're not. You're special, in a good way. So, what's the name of this fiancé?"

She shrugged. "I . . . forget. I'm bored."

"Selena, are you afraid to tell me who Lupita's fiancé is? Is it someone I know?"

"I forget, that's all. I can't remember *everything*. I'm hungry."

"You're safe with me, you know. Selena, you can tell me things, even scary or hard things."

"I know," she said with another shrug, throwing the lump of red wax onto the kitchen table where it landed with a dull thud. "Whatever. Can I go?"

"Tell you what," I said, giving up and looking pointedly at my familiar. "As a special treat why don't you and Oscar choose a movie while I make us up dinner trays?"

With obvious reluctance, Oscar ambled over to the DVDs and starting thumbing through the stack. After considerable negotiating the two settled on a selection: *Speed*. Oscar was a rabid Sandra Bullock fan, and Selena announced that Keanu Reeves was "way cute."

I made sandwiches and fruit salad, and the three of us settled down for an early dinner on the couch. A little witch family.

A half hour later a bunch of desperate people on a

bus were trying not to get blown up, and I was wishing we were watching *Charlotte's Web*. The phone rang. I knew it was trouble before I picked up.

"Hello?"

"It's Patience."

Yep, I thought. *Trouble.* I glanced at Selena and Oscar, who were engrossed in the movie, and moved into the bedroom to speak in private. "What a lovely surprise."

She chuckled. "Oh, yes, I'm sure."

"How did you get this number?"

"I told you, I have my ways. Listen, Lupita Rodriguez just called me."

"Seriously? Where is she? What did she say?"

"She said she had a message for you."

"What is it?"

"She wouldn't say. All she said was she already knew she was getting an inheritance, and then she said to tell you to meet her at the Sutro Baths."

"When?"

"Now."

"Okay." I snatched a hand-knitted wool sweater off my bed.

"*Bonne chance.* Try not to get yourself killed."

I hesitated. Probably meeting Lupita alone wasn't the smartest move. On the other hand, I was a witch. A powerful one. And the Sutro Baths were a public place. Nearby Ocean Beach, Seal Rock, and the famous Cliff House restaurant drew plenty of visitors. And on the other side of the Sutro Baths was a popular hiking spot named Land's End, so there were always people milling about in the parking lot.

Still . . .

"Is Sailor with you?" I asked.

"He was, but he had a family event to go to with his aunt Renna."

"Oh, that's right. Okay then, want me to pick you up, or should I meet you there?"

"*Whoa*, Nellie. I never said I'd go with you."

"We need Lupita to tell us what's going on. You said yourself, this is important."

"So is my beauty sleep."

"It's only half past six. I need backup. And besides, Sailor would never forgive you if you sent me off to get killed all by myself."

"Better we should get killed together?"

"Much better."

The remnants of a massive turn-of-the-century bathhouse and entertainment structure, the Sutro Baths were now a warren of crumbling cement foundation and walls, standing pools of water, blocked stairways and passages, and tunnels perpetually damp from the nearby Pacific Ocean. The ruins hugged a gentle slope that led down to the sea, with a view of massive Seal Rock which, as its name implied, was a favorite resting spot for dozens of barking seals and sea lions.

It was a dramatic locale. Former mayor and entrepreneur Adolph Sutro opened the huge complex in 1896. It had accommodated hundreds of people in its pools, some of which were fed by the ocean at high tide. The ferries and Cliff House Railroad were constructed to carry visitors here from the then-faraway heart of the city of San Francisco.

I had clambered around these ruins once with Max Carmichael, following a champagne brunch at the Cliff House restaurant. It seemed a lifetime ago.

I parked in the lot on the uphill side of the ruins. There was only one other couple nearby, arranging things in the trunk of the car. I scanned the horizon: the street on one side, the forest on the other, the ruins below. No Lupita, no Patience. While I waited I gathered my things: a backpack full of brews and salts, just in case, an extra scarf, and a pair of gloves. It got cold here by the ocean.

Five minutes later, a silver Toyota Prius pulled into the lot.

"I'm impressed," I said as Patience climbed out of her car. "Looking out for the environment?"

She gave me a scathing look. It dawned on me that Hervé also drove a Prius. Apparently it was the automobile of choice among local practitioners of magic. I glanced at my comparatively gas-guzzling Mustang. Not that I drove a lot, but still. Once again, I was out of step not only with cowans, but with the magical community.

"So, what's the plan?" Patience raised one eyebrow, looking out over the ruins, the Pacific Ocean stretching out beyond in gray nothingness.

"Lupita didn't say where to meet her? Nothing more specific than the Sutro Baths?"

"Nope. Told you this was a bad idea."

"Well, we're here now. Either we wait here, or we go looking for her."

Patience had pulled out her smartphone and was scrolling through messages.

"Shall we?" I asked. "Or do you need time to check social media?"

"How about I wait for her here while you scope out the ruins?"

"Buddy system," I said, handing her a flashlight. "Besides, she specified the ruins, right? Not the parking lot."

"Why do I need a flashlight? It's still light out."

"Just in case. C'mon, let's go. She's probably waiting for us down below."

"Just out of curiosity, do you have a plan of some sort?"

"Sure."

"And what might that be?"

"Find Lupita and see what she says."

"That's it? That's all you've got?" Her sardonic tone reminded me of her "cousin," Sailor.

"I didn't say it was a *complicated* plan. Let's go while there's still daylight."

Patience pressed her lips together, but took the flashlight and marched off toward the ruins. I trotted along behind, trying to keep up with her long strides.

The stones and half-toppled walls were gray and slick with moisture from the fog and ocean spray. We had barely begun climbing over the concrete half-walls when I heard an electronic tune: Patience's phone.

I waited while she chatted, laughing and charming the person on the other end of the line. When she hung up I gave her a look.

"What?" she asked.

"Do you suppose you could refrain from using your phone for, oh, say, ten minutes?"

She rolled her eyes. Just then her foot slipped on a slick chunk of foundation and, as she fell forward, the phone flew from her hands, crashing on the rocks below.

She cried out, then glared at me. "Look what you made me do!"

"Oh, what a shame," I said.

"Did you do that? Make me fall?"

"No, of course not. Even if I'd wanted to, I don't have that kind of power."

"That's not the way I hear it," she mumbled as she retrieved her broken phone, swore a mean streak, and slipped the device into her pocket.

"What do you mean by that?"

"Aidan says you're going to be running things around here, eventually."

"*Aidan* says that? Aidan Rhodes?"

She shrugged.

"What else did he say?"

"Ask him yourself, why don't you?"

We continued slowly down the hillside. The ruins were dank, and composed of tiny roofless rooms. Here and there were signs of human visitors: candle stubs, a few dead flowers, a potato chip bag. Lots of cigarette butts, a discarded lighter. I imagined kids came here to smoke and drink and get away from their parents. But I had heard rumors of a ghost or two inhabiting these chilly ruins. Which wouldn't be surprising; I had crawled over ancient ruins in Europe and Asia and Africa, and every single one was haunted. The Sutro Baths were young by comparison, but a century was plenty of time to have attracted resident spirits.

Ahead of me Patience climbed onto the top of a low cement wall and cast the beam of her flashlight into the hollows below.

"Lupita?" I yelled. The wind blew off the ocean, muting my words.

"Any sign of her?" Patience asked.

"No. This is ridiculous . . . she's got to be here somewhere. She asked us to meet her."

"She asked *you* to meet her. And since she probably wants to kill you, why would she show herself? She'll just pop up and knife you, or something."

"You're a real ray of sunshine, you know that?"

"Well, this has certainly been a bust. Face it, she's not here. I'm going home."

"You can't just 'go home.' This is important."

"So is being home."

"Afraid you'll miss reruns of *Desperate Housewives*? Or is there a show called *Desperate Psychics*?"

"Oh, that is so very clever. Ha ha, I am laughing at the clever little wi—"

I put a hand on her arm to cut her off as a woman appeared at the top of a nearby precipice.

"Lupita?" I called out.

The woman was backlit by the setting sun, and I couldn't make out her face.

"Are you the one who took in Selena?" she asked, yelling to be heard over the nearby surf.

"Yes, I'm Lily. Lily Ivory. I—"

"I have to warn you," she cut me off, her tone urgent. "He'll—"

Her words ended in a gurgle, and she tumbled off the wall, falling away from us.

"Lupita!" I cried out.

Patience and I gawked at each other for a moment, then scrambled over to her, slipping on the slick rocks as the daylight began to fade.

Lupita Rodriguez lay on the rough, rocky ground, writhing, her hands at her throat. Her eyes were wide-open, terrified.

I knelt by her side.

"What is it?" I demanded. "Lupita, can you speak?"

Lupita's voice was a croaking whisper. "The painting. He has . . . painting—he's using it to—"

Her words cut off in another gurgle. Above the roar of the ocean, I heard air whistling in her throat as she struggled to breathe. She looked at us, panic in her eyes.

"What is it? What's wrong with her?" Patience asked.

"Someone's casting against her . . ." I shone my flashlight into the nearby crevices, trying to spot a poppet. "Call 911!"

"My phone's broken, remember? *You* call."

Dangitall. "I don't have a cell phone."

"What do you mean, *you don't have a cell phone*? How can you not have a *cell phone*?"

"Why is that hard to understand?" I spat the words,

fear making me frantic. "We have to help her. Do you see anything? A doll, or . . . a painting? Someone is using something to cast against her from afar. Or else—go find a phone. Try the restaurant."

Patience stood atop a wall and started shouting: *"Help! Call 911, we need help!"* She had an impressive set of pipes, but I feared the wind and the waves would drown out her words.

"You'll have to go to the restaurant," I said.

She yelled some more.

"*Breathe*, Lupita," I said gently to the woman in my arms.

Adrenaline coursed through me, my heart was pounding, but it was essential that Lupita remain calm. The more she panicked the worse it would be. This was a classic witch's trick, to make a victim complicit in her own demise.

"Try to relax," I urged. "Just concentrate on breathing."

But Lupita continued to struggle, not heeding my words.

And then a gunshot rang out.

Patience fell.

Chapter 25

She disappeared on the far side of the wall.

"Patience!" I scrambled over to her. She was on the ground, flat on her back. "Are you okay? Were you hit?"

She sat up, unhurt but spitting mad. "No, I'm *not* 'okay'! Someone just took a *shot* at me!"

"You're fine," I said, sagging in relief against the damp concrete wall, softened by moss. Frantically, I tried to think what to do.

Another shot rang out, striking the crumbling wall above our heads and raining dirt and pebbles down on us.

"We have to get out of here," I said, ducking. "Someone will hear those gunshots, surely they'll call the cops. But . . . I don't think we should wait here."

As if to underscore my words, another volley missed Patience by only a few inches. We both screamed. My ears rang with the blasts as car alarms wailed from the direction of the parking lot.

I wondered how Lupita was doing—was she shot?— but couldn't risk checking on her on the other side of the wall.

"Why don't you carry a *cell phone*?" Patience said. "What's *wrong* with you?"

"Drop the phone thing already, will you? I'm sure someone's called 911 by now, but for all we know the shooter's on his way over here to finish us off. We have to get out of here."

"Can we squeeze through that tunnel?"

Tunnel was a nice word for what was really a gap between slabs of fallen concrete. I shone the light into it; it seemed to be only a few feet long, and at the other end appeared to be a large open space.

"I think so . . . follow me," I said. I was smaller than Patience and crawled in first, happy now for my less voluptuous figure. I took my medicine bag off and held it in front of me so it didn't become dislodged as I was squeezing through—this also made it handy to concentrate on keeping myself calm. The rocks scraped and bruised me as I forced myself along the tunnel. It opened onto a chamber littered with beer cans.

"You can make it!" I called back to Patience. "Give me your hand, and I'll pull you through."

"I can't!"

Another gunshot, another squeal of fear.

Panic flooded my veins.

"Patience?" I yelled. "Were you hit?"

"No. But I . . . I don't think I can make it."

"Yes, you can. You *have* to." I reached back through the tunnel. "Take my hand. You can do it."

With my other hand I stroked my medicine bag, and then I started chanting, rallying my concentration, focusing the energy of my emotions, letting my fear fuel my anger.

I pulled so hard my shoulders strained. Patience grunted and complained. I gave one final, mighty tug and she popped through, sending us tumbling on the sandy ground.

She looked around, then turned appalled eyes to me.

"This is *worse*! Now we're trapped!"

"No we're not," I said, gesturing to a yawning square of black on the rear wall. "This way."

I hunched over and started through the gap.

"Wait! I lost my flashlight."

"Keep a hand on my shoulder, and follow me."

We stumbled along, hoping against hope for a way out, but saw no sign of an exit. We appeared to be in a room used as a shrine of some sort. There were candle stubs and the remains of food set on a piece of driftwood arranged to form a makeshift table.

"What is this place?" Patience whispered.

"Probably just somewhere kids like to hang out."

"I don't like it," said Patience.

"Neither do I. I was hoping for a way out. We have to get back to Lupita."

"Screw Lupita," Patience said.

"Patience, really."

"Sorry if that sounds harsh," Patience said. "I promise to mourn for her, but in the meantime I'm planning on getting the hell out of here. Priorities."

I pointed the flashlight at her. The kohl that had outlined her beautiful eyes was running down her cheeks, and I hadn't realized until that moment how frightened she was—how frightened we both were.

It dawned on me with sudden dread that I had left my backpack next to Lupita. If the person choking her went to see if she was dead and discovered it . . . I could be in trouble. Serious trouble. Someone with the power to cast from afar would find more than enough material in the backpack to make me vulnerable. Yet another reason to go back.

Once again, I willed myself to transform my fear into power. Closing my eyes, I started to chant.

"This is no time for your meditation crap," said Patience.

"I'm not meditating," I said. "I'm chanting. Or I was until you interrupted. I suppose it's too much to hope that you have skills that would be useful in this situation? Something beyond profit-making scams?"

"Oh, sure, I'll just pull up one of these boulders and use it as a crystal ball, shall I?"

"I'd appreciate that, yes. Thanks."

"No need: I can already see the future. Three women found dead in the Sutro Baths ruins."

"Way to look on the bright side, Patience. That's exactly what we need right now."

"Like you're doing anything useful."

"Let's focus, shall we? We have to get out of here."

"And just how do you suggest we do that?"

I scanned the stone and cement walls, casting the light here and there, hoping against hope for a crevice or small opening that I had somehow missed. But the only way out was the way we had come in.

Patience seemed to be reading my thoughts. "What if he's waiting on the other end, with his gun?"

"We can't stay here forever."

A rat darted across the damp floor.

Patience screamed and lifted up one foot, then the other, as though dancing the tarantella. "Ew, ew, *ew*! I *hate* rats!"

I wasn't particularly fond of them, myself. But as I watched the rat disappear behind a chunk of broken concrete, it gave me an idea.

"Help me move this," I said. "I think there might be an opening behind it.

We pushed and grunted, finally budging the concrete boulder. Sure enough, there was an opening. It was hard to see beyond it, even with the flashlight, but I could smell the salt of the ocean.

Unfortunately, the crevice was even smaller than the one we went through to get here. There was no way Patience would make it through.

I met her eyes.

"Don't you dare leave me here," she said.

"I'll come back for you, I promise."

"I was just kidding about the witch's mark." She started to cry. "I have a weird sense of humor, I know. I'm sorry."

I reached out and hugged her, then leaned back, holding her hand, and looked into her beautiful eyes, now smudged with kohl.

"I promise: *I will come back for you.* Do you believe me?"

She nodded and sniffed.

"I'll leave the flashlight with you. But you might want to save the battery. Just sit and stay calm, maybe meditate or something."

"Meditate, just me and the rats?" She gave a humorless chuckle, and I joined her.

Pretty soon we were both laughing so hard we snorted. Our laughter had a hysterical edge to it.

"Okay, my grandmother used to say I was double-backboned. So I guess that's good."

"Sounds like it would make it even harder to fit through that hole."

I laughed again. "No, it's an expression. It means having a lot of guts. Or being so stupid that you'll do anything."

"Your own grandmother called you stupid?"

"Not in so many words. Maybe . . . she insinuated a certain lack of caution."

"Lily, I . . ." She shook her head. "Be careful."

"You worried about me now?"

She smiled. "Of course, I am. I don't know if I can make it out of here without you."

"I'll be back. I think I need you to help me push through."

Before heading into the hole, I took a moment to chant, and stroked my medicine bag. My magic could not move these mountains, but all I needed was an inch or two.

Handing my flashlight to Patience, I gave her one last hug.

Then I knelt and, holding my medicine bag out in front of me in one hand, started wriggling through the tight passage. Until I got stuck.

"Push," I said.

I could feel Patience's hands shoving unceremoniously on my butt. I had to fight the panic that bubbled up, and wondered whether I would be found like this, dead from a gunshot, or exposure, or asphyxiation.

But I kept chanting, concentrating on slipping through the rock crevice, using the panic to fuel my concentration, my focus.

Finally, I was spurred on by a puff of fresh air on my face. I felt bruised and scraped, but I managed to squeeze both shoulders past the opening of rock and concrete. After that, the rest was easy. Relatively.

"I made it!" I yelled back through the crevice.

"Where are you?" Patience's voice was muffled.

"I—"

A man loomed in front of me. I screamed.

I held my hand up and let out a blast of power just as Sailor said, "*Lily!* It's me!"

He fell back, striking his head on a jagged piece of concrete.

"Sailor!" I cried, running to his side. "Sailor, I'm so sorry. Are you hurt?"

"I was just hurled against a concrete wall. Yes, I'm hurt."

"I'm so sorry. I didn't realize . . . But, if you're complaining at least I didn't knock you out."

"What's going on?" Sailor asked as he sat up, cradling his forehead in one palm. When he brought his hand away, it looked black in the moonlight. Blood.

"Sailor—"

He batted my hand away. "I'm all right. Just a flesh wound. Are *you* all right? What's going on?"

His question brought me back to the gravity of the situation. I looked around but the sun was setting, and I didn't want to use Sailor's flashlight for fear of being spotted by the shooter.

"Someone was shooting at us. We went through a tunnel to escape, but got stuck. We were afraid to go out the way we came for fear he was waiting for us."

"Who's 'we'? Is Selena here?"

"No, Patience. She's still inside, I barely made it out."

"*Patience?* Why is—never mind. We'll straighten all that out later."

"How did you know to come here?"

"I saw something. In my wine, believe it or not. I was at Renna's for dinner, and I felt a wave of anxiety. I was about to take a sip of wine when I had a vision of the Sutro Baths." He reached out and cupped my head. "Typical, plaguing me on a nice evening with my family. You sure you're all right?"

I nodded. "A few scrapes and bruises, that's all."

Despite his fear for our safety, Sailor seemed pleased

to have been able to sense that I—or *we*— were in danger. His abilities were growing under Patience's tutelage.

"Who was shooting at you?"

I shook my head. "We didn't see who, but Lupita mentioned a 'he.' Sailor, I have to get back to her."

"Lupita's here? In the tunnel with Patience?"

"No, she's over there . . . Someone was casting over her to prevent her from telling me something important."

"Did she say anything at all?"

"Something about him having her painting."

"So you think it's the old artist, Fred?"

"I have no idea. But I have to get to Lupita, *now*. I don't know how much longer she has. Would you call 911?"

"No need. The cops are already here." He gestured toward the parking lot, where emergency lights flashed red and blue. When I stood and peered over the concrete bunker I saw uniformed officers with flashlights searching the ruins.

Surely the shooter wouldn't still be lurking, would he? Would he be willing to take that chance, or so arrogant he thought he wouldn't get caught?

"They're going to want to talk to us," said Sailor.

I nodded. "I have to see if they found Lupita and were able to help her."

We made our way across the crumbling mounds of slippery concrete and twisted rebar until finally reaching the chamber next to where we had seen Lupita. Sailor and I sat with our backs against the wall for a moment, catching our breath. Sailor motioned to me and cautiously peeked over the top of the wall.

He sat back down.

"Anything?" I asked.

"She's gone.

"As in . . . dead?"

"As in, not there."

"Maybe the police got to her, took her to the hospital."

"Maybe. But I doubt it."

I stood and peeked over the edge.

Lupita was gone. But someone had left a note under my backpack.

We extricated Patience from our hidey-hole and then gave our statements to the police, a process that, I can say from experience, takes far longer than one would expect.

By the time we left the Sutro Baths, it was late. Sailor insisted we go to my place to talk everything through, Patience included.

Once Patience got over her teary gratitude at being rescued, she regained her haughty mien. Still, she elected to leave her car in the parking lot for the night. The police had found bullet casings on the ground nearby, and were treating it like a crime scene.

Sailor followed closely behind the Mustang, on his motorcycle.

"*Stop* it," I said to Patience as she yanked the rearview mirror toward her, for the second time, to fix her makeup. "I need the mirror to drive."

"What's with this old jalopy? A *normal* car would have a vanity mirror."

"You ever think about the literal meaning of 'vanity mirror'?" I asked in my most innocent tone.

She didn't deign to answer. Still, I was impressed that despite everything, she not only had hidden an eyeliner pencil somewhere on her person, but had managed not to lose it at the bath ruins.

I, on the other hand, had been lucky to hold on to my medicine bag. I seemed to have lost an earring, and though I had recovered my backpack, the extra scarf I had brought was gone.

Probably taken by whoever left the note.

That thought chilled me to the core. I had worn that scarf, so it carried a trace of my energy with it. Not much, but enough for a skilled practitioner to focus intent upon me, to cast against me.

"I don't see why I have to be here," whined Patience when I refused to take her home, insisting we follow Sailor's suggestion and reconnect at my apartment. I wasn't wild about letting Patience into my personal domain, but under the circumstances. . . .

"I think Sailor's right; we need to work together to figure this out."

"I don't have to do any such thing. I agreed to meet you at the Sutro Baths, which just goes to show no good deed goes unpunished. I'm too nice, that's my problem. It gets me into trouble."

I glared at her, but she was too intent on her reflection in the rearview mirror to notice.

We arrived at my apartment to find Oscar and Selena bickering over a game of poker. From what I was able to tell, Oscar was trying to teach Selena Five Card Stud, but she turned out to be a much better cheat than he was.

I asked Selena whether the Sutro Baths meant anything special to her or Lupita. She shook her head. I didn't want to scare her by letting her know what had happened there and instead put in a DVD of *The Jungle Book* and tucked a blanket around her. She and Oscar, in his piggy form, sat on the couch and watched our trio with wide, cautious eyes.

I poured three shots of tequila and Sailor, Patience, and I settled in at the kitchen table.

Sailor unfolded the note. On some kind of strange parchment was a message written in code:

X i,
   J I f tpn h pg st. Zpv l j dbo u zpv.
   Hj m, p f.

                                        —b g e

"What kind of an extortionist writes in code?" asked Patience, in a scathing tone. "The fool's criminal career is doomed to be short-lived, I say."

"Can you read it?" I asked her.

"Of course not. It's gibberish."

"I mean 'read' it. With your third eye, or whatever."

She sighed and picked up the note, closing her eyes, releasing a long breath through her nose. After a moment she opened her eyes and shook her head. "Cloaked. You're dealing with someone who has some knowledge."

"It looks like . . ." I held the note up to the overhead light. "Yes! I think it's invisible ink. Probably lemon juice, or vinegar."

"Or urine," said Patience.

"That's disgusting," I said.

"*What*? It works the same way as lemon juice. Everybody knows this."

"Why invisible ink?" Sailor interrupted. "Are we dealing with a ten-year-old?"

"Good question," I said.

I lit a candle and carefully held the note over the flame, not so close it would catch fire but near enough to heat the ink.

Sure enough, more letters emerged. Still, they made no sense.

Xjudi,

   J ibwf tpnfuijoh pg zpvst. Zpv lopx j dbo vtf ju
bhbjotu zpv.

   Hjwf nf uif mkffq, ps fmtf.

                                          —b gsjfoe

"*Xjudi?* Could it be . . . the Basque language, or Na-vajo, maybe? Something obscure like that?"

"I don't think so," said Sailor. "There aren't enough vowels. Every language uses vowels when it's written in our alphabet, right?"

Patience shrugged and poured herself another shot of tequila.

"Wheel within a wheel," said Selena. Apparently overcome with curiosity, she had left the couch and was now hovering near the table, looking at the note over our shoulders.

"Wheel within a wheel?" I asked.

"It's a simple Caesar shift," she said.

"I'm sorry?"

"A Caesar shift. It's a cipher. Rot one."

"You can decipher this?" I asked. "Is that what you're saying?"

She nodded. "You just shift the letters over. In this case you would rotate the wheel one letter. That's why it's called Rot one."

"It's that simple?" Sailor asked.

"A is b, b is c. Like that."

I grabbed a pencil and replaced each letter with the one next to it in the alphabet. Translated, the note read:

Witch,

   I have something of yours. You know I can use it against you.

Give me the ljeep, or else.

—a friend

"Told you," Selena said, and returned to watch the movie with Oscar.

"Well, there you go," said Patience, reaching for the tequila again. "Just give him the *ljeep*, and everything's fine."

Sailor moved the bottle out of her reach. "Don't you think you've had enough? We need to keep our wits about us."

"*You're* not the one who got shot at tonight, fell off a wall, and shoved into a black hole. You wanna see my bruises?"

Sailor poured her a half-shot.

"So, the question now is: what does he mean by *ljeep*?" I asked.

"Maybe he made a mistake," said Patience. "He meant to write 'Jeep', by which he means your precious Mustang. Vanity mirror or no."

"That's ridiculous," I said.

"You have a better idea?" Patience said tartly.

Sailor was looking up *ljeep* on his smartphone.

"Anything?" I asked.

"There's a big sale on Jeep Wranglers at the dealer on Van Ness." He scrolled through the rest of the search results. "That's about it. That can't be his meaning. Maybe he got it wrong."

"I want to go home," Patience whined.

Sailor and I exchanged a glance. I nodded. "I don't think there's anything more to be done right now. I'll cast a protection spell, but I doubt I'll be threatened again tonight. Apparently I have an *ljeep* this person wants, so I should be safe in the meantime."

"Then why was he shooting at you at the ruins?" Sailor asked.

"That was related to Lupita. I think he was trying to keep her from telling us something."

"Probably something about the *ljeep*," Patience muttered. "Funny word. What rhymes with Jeep? Peep, cheap, leap, creep, weep. . . ."

"I'd better get her home," said Sailor. "You sure you're all right?"

"Oscar's here, and my apartment's the safest place I know of. It's like Fort Knox around here."

He smiled. "A magical Fort Knox."

He gave me a hug, a kiss, stroked my head, and looked into my eyes. "Take care of you, hear me?"

I nodded. "Thank you for coming to my rescue. You're my hero."

"Not that I did much . . . but, I'll take it," he said with a warm smile. One more kiss, and then he got my motorcycle helmet out of the closet and tossed it to a sour-looking Patience.

"Let's go, cousin," said Sailor. "I'll take you home."

"On the *motorcycle*?"

"Limo's in the shop."

"Why can't we use the witch's Mustang?"

"Take it if you want," I told Sailor.

"Nah. Then I'd have to come back and change vehicles again. C'mon, Patience. I can see into the future: You're going to be one heck of a motorcycle mama."

"For the record, at this moment I hate you both." Patience took another swig of tequila, slammed her glass on the table, and swept regally past Sailor, snatching the helmet from him.

"Good night, Patience," I said. I doubted we would ever be best buddies, but we'd shared something tonight.

I grabbed a small jar from a kitchen shelf. "This is mug-wort salve—it will help the scrapes and bruises. And . . . thanks for meeting me at the Sutro Baths. It was inter-esting."

"Oh, yeah, sure, it was a hoot. Do me a favor? Lose my number."

I didn't point out that *she* was the one who had called *me*. I got her meaning.

Chapter 26

I fixed Oscar and Selena a snack of cheese and crackers and fruit, and left them to finish the movie.

While they were occupied, I slipped into my bedroom, closed the door, and dialed Graciela.

Tonight I had been shot, chased into a dark hole, left a mysterious note to decipher, and still had a crime—or several—to figure out. But what was really weighing on my mind, what was eating away at me, was what Aidan had said: that I was not destined for love.

So when Graciela answered, I recounted what Aidan had told me. I prayed she would tell me what I wanted to hear: that Aidan was messing with my mind, probably as part of some Machiavellian plan.

"I think he's right," she said without hesitation.

"About my needing to work with him, or . . . that I shouldn't have a relationship with Sailor."

"Both."

"What you mean by *that*?" I could hear her eating something, and felt a deep stab of annoyance.

"I heard some rumors. I think something is building

in San Francisco. Think about it, *m'ija,* you have seen a lot of supernatural situations since you arrived in that city—a lot of trouble, even for the likes of you. And it was a parrot who told you to go, no? You know how birds are. *Listo.* Very smart."

"It was just a fluke—he was repeating something he had heard, probably."

"It was a sign, and you knew it. It is no accident that you were drawn to the city by the bay."

"Okay, well, be that as it may, what about the other thing? The . . . love thing?"

"You have always had difficulty understanding that the path of power requires sacrifice."

"So you're saying powerful people can't experience love? My friend Hervé is married and adores his wife."

"His path is not yours."

I heard crunching sounds, and some rustling around. I lost my temper.

"What in the world are you *doing*?"

"Eating chips, and making *chiles rellenos.* They used to be your favorite."

"It's the middle of the night in Texas."

"*Como se dice?* What is it you kids say? I'm a 'party animal.'"

"This is serious, Graciela. I have to know: What will happen? Will I hurt Sailor if I stay with him?"

Even though my witchy intuition was compromised by telephone lines, I could sense that I finally had her full attention. When she spoke, she sounded irked.

"*M'ijita*, I am just an old woman. I am not an Oracle. You have to find your own path. There *are* no easy solutions. Yes, you can try to walk away from the truth, from the hard path, just as you did when you were a girl. But you are no longer a child: You are a woman. So deal with it. My dinner's ready."

*   *   *

I tucked Selena into her bed on the couch, kissed her on the forehead, and wished her good night.

"Is everything going to be all right?" she asked, her serious eyes searching my face.

"Of course it is," I said, trying to convince myself as much as her.

She seemed doubtful, so I tried again. "You'll be okay, Selena. I promise you that I'll do everything in my power to make sure of that. And I don't mean to brag or anything . . . but I'm a pretty kick-ass witch."

She didn't return my smile but rolled over and closed her eyes.

I went into the kitchen to reconnect with my familiar.

"Oscar, do you have any idea what this is all about?" I whispered.

"Sorry, Mistress. I got nothin'. And you've got me on loony girl guard"—he gestured toward Selena,—"so I haven't even had time to work on my karaoke, much less go out and scout or anything."

"Okay, thanks. I want you to know I really appreciate your being here. It puts my mind at ease to know you're on the job."

"Aw, shucks." He waved off my thanks and puffed out his chest. "She's just a slip of a girl, no match for the likes of me."

"I guess we should all get some rest. No doubt this will be here waiting for us in the morning."

Oscar crawled into his cubby over the refrigerator, and I sat and gazed at the strange note for a while. *Ljeep*? Could it be a typo, a mistake?

And Patience was right: What kind of extortionist writes an unintelligible note?

I sat back as a wave of weariness washed over me. And dread. If Aidan and Graciela were right, and something was revving up in San Francisco . . . what did that mean for me, and mine?

It meant I had to be strong. And powerful. As kick-ass a witch as I had just boasted to Selena.

But did it really mean I had to give up Sailor?

Other people drink or meditate or pray when they feel they are at a crossroads. I brew.

I filled my cauldron with river water and put it on the stove to boil. Then I gathered some herbs and roots from my terrace garden and started grinding them with my stone mortar and pestle. Little by little I dropped them, along with a small lock of my hair, into the brew.

I chanted as I did so, stirring the pot doesil until the contents began to swirl on their own. Then I closed my eyes, thrust my face in the steam, breathed deeply, and called to the Ashen Witch.

Finally I used my *athame*—a ceremonial knife—to cut a tiny X in my palm, and held it over the cauldron. As soon as the droplet of blood hit the brew a great burst of steam rose and coalesced overhead: the amorphous face of the Ashen Witch, looking down at me.

I had hoped she might actually speak, or write with smoke in the air like the witch in the *Wizard of Oz*, or otherwise give me a clear message. But instead, all I felt was a growing sense of clarity.

No. I refused to give up Sailor. I would *not.*

My whole life people had been telling me I was a freak, not like everyone else. First, I was an outcast among my neighbors in Jarod, Texas; later I was weird even among magical folk. I never finished my formal training and I was always getting the rules wrong, bumbling around because I was unaware of how things were "done." So now I would use it to my advantage. Aidan said magical folks weren't able to open themselves up to love because it made them vulnerable; but what if I embraced the vulnerability, and used it the way I did my anger: to make me, braver, stronger?

"Tell me how! Tell me anything!" I begged my guardian spirit, but she was already gone, lost amid the steam that hung just under the ceiling, as mysterious and hard to pin down as the fog hovering over the Bay.

I looked back to see Selena standing at the kitchen table, wide-eyed and frightened.

"It's all right, sugar. Let's go to sleep. Want to sleep with me tonight?"

"No. I'll stay on the couch. Did you figure this out?" she held up the parchment note.

"Not yet. We're working on it. Do you have any other ideas?"

She shook her head, and let me lead her back to the couch and tuck her in.

I awoke to a thumping sound.

Something was wrong.

A frisson swept up my spine as though an alarm had been tripped. I stopped to listen, then cautiously got out of bed and passed into the living room.

Selena wasn't on the couch.

I heard a muffled yelling and thumping coming from the kitchen.

A piece of plywood had been wedged over the opening to Oscar's cubby. I recognized the wood from an old packing crate in the backroom of Aunt Cora's Closet. But it was covered in symbols that functioned as a magical padlock.

"I'm coming, Oscar!" I yelled. I used a piece of chalk to negate Selena's childish—but effective—scribbles and then was able to dislodge the wood.

An outraged gobgoyle is not a pretty sight.

"She *hexed* me! That little witch *hexed* me! She caught

me unawares, while I was sleeping! Of all the low-down, dirty . . ."

I was relieved to see that while he was embarrassed at having been tricked, my familiar wasn't hurt.

"Well, don't feel too bad," I said. "I didn't wake up, either."

"Yeah, but you never wake up. It's always *me* that wakes you up."

"You got me there. Where could she have gone? To El Pajarito, do you think?"

"Good riddance, is what I say. I'll show her, I'll—"

"Oscar, listen. She was wrong to do what she did, of course she was. But I have to find her. I *have* to."

"I don't know where she went! I was asleep, and then . . . I think she sprinkled pixie dust on me or something. I was having the wildest dream, and by the time I woke up she had trapped me! A piece of wood's no match for the likes of me, but she *hexed* it. That little . . ."

"She didn't say *any*thing?"

He mumbled something.

"What was that?"

His eyes narrowed. "She said 'rot too.' She should rot, is what."

"Rot too?" That made no sense. Unless . . . I cast my mind back: Selena had said it was a Caesar something-or-other, wheel within a wheel . . . if Rot One meant to shift the alphabet over one letter, then Rot Two would mean two letters. Maybe whoever wrote the note just threw in an extra complication . . . but why?

The sheet of parchment was still on the kitchen table. I sat down and moved the letters in *ljeep* over one more place.

It spelled *kiddo*.
Give me the kiddo, or else.

Chapter 27

I grabbed a fistful of the silver charms Selena had polished, set my crystal ball on the steamer trunk, and settled in before it.

I centered myself and drew upon my anger to blast away my anxiety. Cradling the charms in one hand, I thought of Selena and gazed into the depths of the crystal.

At first, there was nothing. Just a few wispy clouds, as always. I tried to exert my focus, while not focusing.

And I saw something, clear as day.

Selena was standing at one of the display tables at Betty's house, as I'd first seen her. She was wearing white gloves and that ridiculous pink and purple ensemble, polishing a silver tea set.

And then I saw the inner door, the one I had noticed at the back of the garage-turned-closet, when Maya and I were sorting through Betty's clothes. It was ajar, and beckoning. I had assumed that door led outside, but perhaps it was something else altogether.

I lingered a few more precious moments, to see if I

could pick out anything else from the clouds in the crystal. There was nothing more.

I grabbed the car keys, stuck the Hand of Glory in my satchel, and found the one item I knew this killer had touched: the poppet Maya had found in Betty's clothes.

Normally, a practitioner's poppet couldn't be used against him, but this fellow, though clearly talented, was just as clearly not well trained. Since he had attempted to imbue the doll with his own intentions but didn't know how to sustain them, I might be able to make the wax work against him. It was the best I could do, under the circumstances.

As Oscar and I ran to the Mustang, I realized the Aunt Cora's Closet van was missing. We found it parked a block away from Betty North's house, at an awkward angle to the curb. I pulled up behind it and told Oscar to stay in the car.

"I want to go with you, Mistress."

"Oscar, I need you to stay here in case Selena comes back to the van. I don't know what I'm up against in that house, or even if I'm right. I'll call you if I need you, but right now I want to face him myself."

Oscar grumbled but did as I asked.

I went around the side of the dark house and used the Hand of Glory to let myself in the back door. I moved silently through the house, but didn't see or hear anyone . . . not even Betty North's ghost. I snuck down the carpeted stairs to the rumpus room, hoping to spot my errant charge playing with the silver.

Selena wasn't there. I went into the garage, now emptied of clothes and knickknacks.

And I spotted the door in the back, the one I'd seen in the crystal ball.

It was locked, but opened quickly under the influence of the Hand of Glory.

A dark passage led to a basement with a dirt floor, lit by a single lightbulb hanging from a string. It had been set up as a workshop, and was filled with the tools of a magical trade: jars of herbs and powders, feathers and bones, oils and honey. But they were all a jumble. When it comes to ingredients for a spell, a smart witch keeps everything separate and labeled because it is essential that elements not be combined by accident. A good witch maintained control over her spells.

The portrait of Lupita I had seen in Fred's studio was pinned to one unfinished wall. Lupita's image had been scraped and stabbed, the canvas slashed across her throat.

And lying on the worktable was a wax doll with long brown strings approximating hair. It looked vaguely like me, and was wrapped in my missing scarf.

I immediately went to work, using the poppet I had brought with me. Molding and forming, warming the wax with the warmth of my hands, and chanting under my breath, I began to cast my spell. As I mumbled, I called upon my ancestors, and in particular to the Ashen Witch. My intent concentrated and focused as the energy flowed through my heart and hands before streaming into the wax.

I formed the soft wax to look as much as I could like the Lily doll.

I heard someone coming down the stairs to the rumpus room. Unwrapping the scarf as quickly as I could, I sprinkled it with the brew I had brought in a wide-mouth Mason jar, and dressed the new doll in it, so that it looked like the original Lily doll poppet. I laid it back on the workbench.

I buried the other doll in the earthen floor and pressed the dirt smooth with my foot. I was wiping my hands just as the door opened.

"Lily Ivory," Finn said. He seemed surprised to see me, but not overly so. "Fancy meeting you here."

"I thought I'd look around for some more clothes for the shop."

His smile broadened, and he glanced around the basement. "Where's the kiddo?"

Thank the goddess, I thought to myself. *He doesn't have Selena.* I would worry about where she was later, but at least Finn wasn't holding her captive.

"Asleep at home," I lied. "Safe and sound."

"Guess I'll have to roust her out of there, then."

"You won't get past the front door. Not while I'm alive."

He laughed, then nodded and shrugged. "I guess you're right. I'll just have to kill you."

"Good luck with that."

"So, did *you* figure out the message, then? I thought Selena would get it; she always struck me as a bit of a martyr. I figured she'd be able to decipher my message and come to me of her own accord. We used to play together, writing each other messages by mixing up Rot One, Rot Two. . . ."

"You played together, or you used her?"

"She and I are good friends. She's my little helper."

"You had her clean the silver, didn't you? She didn't realize she was imbuing the metal with power, which you then appropriated. The silver would tarnish as you depleted the power, and she'd clean it again."

"She's handy to have around, that one."

"She's protected now. You won't be using her anymore."

"On the contrary, I'll do anything I want." He grabbed the scarf-wrapped doll from the workbench and held it up. "Do you know what this is?"

"I'm a witch, remember?"

"Not a very good one, as far as I can tell. I tested you with those photos I showed you—you had no idea what was going on! None at all! Didn't catch on to the silver magic, or Selena's being here, or anything. And Lupita said you were supposed to be really something."

"Where is Lupita now? Is she okay?"

He kept talking, ignoring my question. "I only started training a few months ago and I'm already better than you. Imagine what I could have done, if my useless parents had only recognized my talents. Instead, they just beat me every time I did something they thought was weird. Well, there'll be plenty of time later to settle old scores."

As he spoke, he handled the doll. If he had been as good a practitioner as he thought he was, he would have felt that the poppet's vibrations were off. But as I had hoped, he was focused on me.

"That's terrible, Finn. My mother rejected me, too."

"Oh, right, we're going to swap childhood sob stories? *Boo hoo.* I don't think so."

"That's not what I meant. I'm simply saying that I know how hard it is to be a magical child."

"Yeah. Yeah, it was. Until I discovered Satanism."

"Satan has no place in the magical world."

"Whatever," he said with a shrug. "I called on a few demons, but they never answered. But then I went by El Pajarito for supplies one day, and met Lupita. Overheard her trying to talk Ursula into pulling a scam over on Betty. Ursula chased her out of the store, I asked her out for a drink, and the rest, as they say, is history."

"And then you approached Betty about handling the estate sale?"

He nodded. He appeared pleased to share with me how it had all come together. "Lupita introduced me to Betty, and we went to work on the old lady so she'd leave us the place. Didn't take much—Betty didn't really have anyone. I see a lot of that in my business; it's really sad." He let out a sigh. "But it was when I met Selena that a whole new world opened up. She fell asleep and stuff started . . . happening. I finally figured out it had to do with the shiny things she loved so much."

"Selena's a magical child. She needs guidance."

"She's a freak."

"She's special, like you and me. She's lucky, though. She has Ursula."

He laughed. "Ursula is going down. After a very long engagement, Lupita and I were recently married. That makes me Selena's uncle. Now that I'm a widower, I'm the closest relative Selena has. She'll come live with me now. I promised Lupita that I would always take care of Selena."

"So you found a way to capture her magic? Is that how it worked?" I asked. "Was Lupita in on it from the start?"

"Lupita's the one who told me how to make a voodoo doll. She got me supplies from Ursula's shop. But she didn't have any power. That was all me. It's amazing what a person can learn on the Internet these days. I did my homework."

It was true that a person could learn witchcraft from books or the Internet; but to practice it responsibly, one had to learn far more important and difficult skills: how to control the power and use it responsibly, how to rein in one's own ambition and selfish desires. Not to mention how to maintain a spell over time. The "null" poppet Finn had created revealed that his magic dissipated quickly.

"Did you try to summon a demon to watch over Ursula's store, by any chance?"

For the first time, Finn looked uncomfortable. "Yeah,

not sure what happened there. I sort of . . . let things fly, I guess. Then I couldn't figure out how to walk it back. Whatever, I don't need the stupid store, anyway. When Lupita and I got together I thought that place was going to be a cash cow—I even encouraged her to get more exposure for the store with that newspaper article. I'm good at things like that, good at marketing, making business plans. But . . . I dunno, it's such a dump now and I don't feel like cleaning it up."

"But you're planning on inheriting this house?"

"Sure. Betty left the place to Lupita until that interloper, Nicky, started sniffing around. I followed her to the Golden Gate Bridge and when she leaned over the rail to drop something in the water, I saw my chance. Boom, a little shove and bye-bye, Nicky. Didn't even need to use the poppet I made. I told the police I tried to grab her, even worked up a few tears." He grinned. "They thought I was a poor traumatized tourist from Canada!"

I felt queasy, and tried to use the sensation to fuel my focus.

"Anyway, Knox thinks he's inheriting this place, but he's got another thing coming when they validate the new will. As Lupita's husband, *I'm* next in line to inherit Betty's property, and heck, my workshop's already set up here. I'll sell off the rest of Betty's crap, pocket the money, and that'll be that. Oh—except I'll keep the silver, I guess. Let Selena earn her keep."

He looked at the doll in his hands, the one wrapped in my scarf.

When he met my gaze, his eyes were cold and empty.

"Do you know what this is?"

"I think so."

He laughed again and shook his head. "I don't think you do. If you did, you'd be shaking in your boots, kiddo. This is a special doll. A *Lily* poppet."

I kept my face blank.

"Right now," he continued, "I hold your fate quite literally in my hands."

"Do you, now?"

Holding it in his left hand, he picked up a screwdriver from the workbench, held it over the doll's midsection, and smiled.

"Don't," I said.

"So sorry, Lily."

"I'm serious, Finn, *don't*. Think about who you are, about all the people you have hurt. Is that what you want your life to be about? To leave a trail of pain behind you?"

"Why not? *My* life has been full of pain."

Raising his arm, he stabbed the doll with the screwdriver, and immediately doubled over. He looked at me in surprise, shock and confusion on his flushed face.

"What did you do?" he asked. "How did you *do* that?"

"Stop, Finn," I pleaded. "Put the doll down, I'm begging you."

He had dropped the screwdriver, but now held the doll in both hands, and gave it a vicious twist.

He cried out and fell to the ground, screaming and moaning, writhing in pain. The doll lay on the dirt beside him, not far from where I had buried the wax figure Finn thought he was using to hurt me.

Seems I had a gift for poppet magic, after all.

It is a terrible thing to witness someone in agony, on the brink of death. I tried to summon compassion for Finn, but felt my heart harden. He had tried to harm Betty, and had pushed Nicky Utley into the cold gray waters of the San Francisco Bay, just so he could inherit a house. He had murdered his wife, Lupita, and would have used Selena for his own gain. Who knows what he would have done to her when she was no longer of any use to him?

Finn reached one hand toward me and whispered, "Help me!"

Selena burst into the room and threw a handful of shiny silver cutlery in the air with white-gloved hands.

The spoons twirled, catching the light of the bare bulb in their depths and reflecting circles of light. As I watched, the dots played across Selena's face, then began to gather. They spun together and created a cone of light over Finn.

He collapsed and lay twitching on the ground.

"Did I kill him?" Selena asked in a voice so small I could barely make out her words.

"No . . . he hurt himself," I said quietly.

"I *wanted* to kill him," Selena said, her eyes narrowed. "He killed Emma's mommy. He . . . he acted nice to me. But he was *using* me."

"Listen to me, Selena: It is a terrible feeling to be lied to and taken advantage of. I know. But Finn can't hurt you anymore."

Oscar ran in through the door. He stopped short, looking down at Finn.

"*Dang*. You killed him?"

"He's not quite dead. And I didn't touch him, and neither did Selena. He hurt himself, thinking he was hurting me. Finn became the object of his own destruction."

"Good witch trick," Oscar said with a nod. He yanked one thumb in my direction. "Hey, Selena, this one has plenty of secrets up her sleeve. She'll teach you well."

Chapter 28

That Saturday was the Haight Street Summer of Love Festival. We dressed in our sixties garb, like a rather unconventional hippie family: me and Sailor, Selena and Oscar, Maya and Bronwyn and Duke. We strolled around, looking at arts and crafts and eating corn on the cob while listening to classic rock inspired by famous former Haight-Ashbury residents like Janis Joplin, Jefferson Airplane, and Ike and Tina Turner.

After the festival, Sailor and I took Selena to the Golden Gate Bridge where we met up with Carlos Romero. Waiting for us at the center of the bridge were Gary and Emma, and Knox and his wife and their four kids. They had brought flowers to throw off the bridge in Nicky's memory.

Afterward, Carlos would take Selena home to El Pajarito. The charges against Ursula Moreno had been dropped when the DA conceded he couldn't make a case against her. I had already spoken to Ursula, who hadn't realized the extent of her granddaughter's power, about the necessity of training Selena properly.

Among so many other things, Selena needed to learn whom she could trust, and how to open up. Fortunately for her, there were good people in the world, and an entire magical community waiting to embrace her. She would be all right. Ursula and Sailor and Aidan and I would make sure of it.

Sailor and I hung back as the group said their last good-byes to Nicky Utley.

I felt Aidan's approach long before I saw him.

Sailor moved to stand between us, bodyguard-style. "What do *you* want?"

Aidan smiled, but met my eyes rather than Sailor's. "Lily and I have some unfinished business. You understand."

"Not really, no," replied Sailor.

"Listen, guys, this isn't the time or the place," I said in a low voice. "There's a memorial service happening. How about we go to the Buena Vista and try their famous Irish coffees? It's on me."

I forced myself to refrain from rolling my eyes as Aidan and Sailor had a macho staring contest, not blinking for a full minute.

Finally, Aidan gave an almost imperceptible nod. "I love Irish coffee."

"Who doesn't?" said Sailor.

"Great!" I said, feeling more cheerleader than witch. "What with training Selena and saving San Francisco and all, we have a lot to talk about. Let's go."

A flash of light drew my gaze. From the midpoint of the Golden Gate Bridge, Selena had thrown a silver spoon over the railing. Its shiny surface caught the sunlight as it twirled through the air, finally splashing into the churning gray waters below.

She smiled before turning away from the bridge.

Keep reading for a preview of Juliet Blackwell's
newest mystery in the bestselling
Haunted Home Renovation series,

GIVE UP THE GHOST

Coming from Obsidian in December!

It's hard to ruin a Pacific Heights mansion. After all, it's
Pacific Heights.

One of San Francisco's nicest neighborhoods, Pacific
Heights sits atop a crest with world-class views of the
Golden Gate Bridge, the Bay, the Palace of Fine Arts, and
Sausalito. In the late 1800s, following the gold rush and the
acquisition of California, when robber barons were ex-
ploiting workers and stealing land to amass their fortunes,
this is where many of them chose to spend their ill-gotten
gains: on the mansions studding this hill, one after the
other, like a lineup of enormous ten-bedroom, five-bath,
turreted, multistory, wooden-and-stucco beauty queens—
historic testaments to taste, craftsmanship, wealth, and
ruthlessness.

But I had to hand it to Andrew Stirling, the fiftyish,
plump, rather pallid man standing with me in the foyer.
The mansion called Crosswinds now gleamed with the
plastic-feeling newness of a really expensive, really modern, really wretched remodel.

And, apparently, it was beset by ghosts.

"Cost me millions to bring this place into the twenty-
first century," Stirling was saying while I tried to rein in
my distaste. That was a challenge, as I don't have much of
a poker face. "Wasn't easy to bring it up to snuff. Used to
be nothing but dark wood paneling in here. And see that

fireplace surround? Gorgeous Brazilian granite. Sleek, simple. Real class, something like that. Used to be carved marble, with *cupids*." He shook his balding head. "So kitschy."

"*Mmm*," I grunted. This was my go-to response when I was too busy biting my tongue in order not to alienate the überwealthy potential client in front of me to formulate words.

My eyes cast around, searching for signs of history. Gone were the subtle dents and nicks, the soft edges and refined imperfections seen in historic moldings. Victorian-era parlors and chambers once divided by paneled pocket doors had been opened up and merged into one massive "great room" with no regard for the original floor plan. The windows no longer opened, since the house was now "smart" and climate controlled, the air filtered and recirculated as in a modern hotel. Can lighting in smooth, flat ceilings had no doubt replaced the engraved plaster medallions and crystal chandeliers common to buildings from the late 1800s.

"Not to mention that I paid twelve million for it in the first place." Stirling let out a rueful sigh. "Twelve million for a fixer-upper, basically. But what can I say? I'm a visionary."

"And your Realtor said you were asking thirty-nine million?" I asked. Even for San Francisco, that was a lot of money.

"Most expensive property on the market. Historic, really." He nodded, his pale eyes surveying the open white-on-white decorating scheme of the first floor. "Well worth it, for the right buyer. This location is priceless, of course, and have you checked out the views? Not enough money in the world for something like that. And then the remodel on top of it, everything totally updated, with all the latest technical advancements—what's not to love?"

"Yet you haven't been able to sell it," I pointed out.

"No. Obviously." There was a little tic over his right cheekbone. "That's where you come in."

I'm a general contractor, head of Turner Construction. We specialize in renovating historic buildings. But not like this. Never like this.

Besides, there was nothing left to redo. Unless I missed my guess, this place had been gutted, taken back to the studs, and rebuilt with all new materials. They had kept the classic exterior shell and built themselves a brand-new *Sopranos*-style home within.

Still, Crosswinds had been whispering to me since I stood outside at the base of the limestone stairs, looking up at its rococo Victorian facade, complete with turrets, carved garlands, and gold-gilt shields.

It needed someone to save it. And if the past few haunted-home renovations I had done were any indication, *I* was that someone. Whether I wanted the title or not. Just call me Mel Turner, historic home renovator and up-and-coming Ghost Negotiator.

"And you want me to do what, exactly?" I asked.

"Karla tells me you have experience with this sort of thing," Stirling hedged.

Karla Buhner was the no-doubt frustrated Realtor trying to off-load Crosswinds to some poor sucker for the equivalent of a small country's gross national product.

"What sort of thing would that be?" I asked, all innocence.

People like Andrew Stirling wanted underlings to read their minds, to offer to help so they wouldn't have to be explicit. It was a strangely childish habit that annoyed the heck out of me, and prompted me to respond in an equally childish manner. I wanted to force him to say what he needed.

"It's . . . All right, dammit, it's *haunted*," Andrew said, the visible tic speeding up. He rubbed his cheekbone with a hand sporting two gold rings, which glinted in the sunshine streaming in through spotless plate-glass windows.

"*Really?* Haunted?"

"The ghosts, or whatever it is, appear to be running people off. Every time we have an interested buyer in the house, things . . . act up. Karla says you're the person to deal with this sort of thing. She said you've dealt with things like this before. We need you to fix it."

Just then I heard a squeaking noise overhead. My eyes were drawn up toward the ceiling. "What's that?" I asked.

"This is what I'm telling you about. That's the sound

of the old weathervane. It was the first thing to come down in this house, but you can still hear it when the wind blows. What's *that* about?"

"And there's no other explanation? Is there anyone else in the house?"

"Only Egypt."

"Egypt? I'm going to assume we're not talking about a country?"

"No. A person. Egypt's the caretaker, lives up in one of the attic rooms. You know, when I bought Crosswinds, my kids were still young, but it took so long to do the remodel, they're grown and living on their own. We don't need this huge house anymore. The wife and I are in Sausalito now, great place: it's a Bollinger."

"A Bollinger?"

"Incredible young designer from Germany. Very exclusive. Right on the golf course."

"Ah."

"So, anyway, I don't really believe in this stuff, but things got so bad, my wife, Stephanie, called in a psychic Karla recommended, Chantelle—you heard of her? Goes by just the one name, like Cher or Madonna. Very famous. Hard to get an appointment with her, much less get her to make a house call. Very expensive."

"Uh-huh. And what did Chantelle make of Crosswinds?"

Again with the tic. He massaged his cheekbone. "She says the ghosts of the family that lived here years ago are angry about us doing the remodel. She says the only way to appease them is to track down some of the original architectural stuff and put it back in."

He glared at me. As though I had been egging on his house spirits in some sort of supernatural bid to increase my client base.

"I . . . uh . . . Do you *have* the original fixtures?" I asked. "Did you keep them?"

"Nah. Who wants all this old stuff?" He threw his hands in the air. "I am so sick of this whole place, I can't even tell you. Here's what I need: you get ahold of whatever old crap you can to reinstall—maybe starting with that damn weathervane. If you can't find the original, surely there's some reproduction that will do. And then maybe the ghosts will be quiet long enough to dump it. Then it's someone else's problem."

A thirty-nine-million-dollar dump. Wow.

But Andrew Stirling had deep pockets. And he was desperate. Not to put too fine a point on it, but those were highly desirable qualities in a client. As a general contractor, I was obligated to make a hefty payroll each and every month.

So yes, I was interested in taking on the challenge of Crosswinds and whatever resident ghosts it might contain. I looked over at the anxious Andrew Stirling, who was jangling his car keys—Lexus, of course—as though he could barely contain his agitation.

Number one rule for dealing with overprivileged clients? Imply that you're too busy. Drives them crazy.

I sucked air in between my teeth and shook my head slowly. "I don't know, Andrew. Turner Construction's pretty busy right now. We're working on a place in Cow Hollow, and I've still got a crew over on the retreat in Marin—"

"I'll pay you whatever you want. Seriously, I'll pay double whatever your usual rate is just to take care of this. Track down some of those old fixtures, hold a séance, or whatever it is you need to do, and *get these ghosts off my back*."

"Double my usual rate?" In neighborhoods like Pacific Heights, the higher the rates, the more people respected you. It was sort of like wine: exact same bottle could be said to cost twelve bucks or twelve hundred—guess which one tasted better to someone like Andrew Stirling.

Exclusivity was delicious.

I took a moment, looked around, then nodded slowly. "All right. In that case, I think I can help you out. I have to warn you, though, it's going to make a mess."

"I'm used to it. This place has been a mess since I bought it."

"And it's going to take a while."

Just then I saw something out of the corner of my eye.

A woman creeping down the stairs. She had dark eyes, olive skin, and an exotic flair—or maybe that was due to her white dress and the colorful batik scarf wrapped around her hair, as though she had just stepped off a Caribbean island.

My immediate thought was that I was meeting my first specter at the house. Was this the ghost of some long-dead servant, bound to toil in the Crosswinds mansion through eternity?

"Egypt Davis," said Andrew, "let me introduce Mel Turner. She'll be working on this place. You'll give her whatever she needs. Mel, Egypt lives upstairs. Caretaker for the interim."

Not a ghost, then. Good thing I hadn't said anything embarrassing. Lately, since I had started seeing the spiritual remnants of those not-quite-passed, it had gotten increasingly difficult to tell reality from . . . *my* reality.

Egypt shook my hand, and we exchanged pleasantries; I gave her my business card.

"Please let me know if I can help with anything," said Egypt, casting a rather wary look at Stirling. "You'll be . . . working here, then? Does this have to do with Chantelle's advice?"

"Precisely. Turner here will be spending plenty of time at Crosswinds, so you'll have a chance to catch up. In the meantime, could you gather the list of items Skip removed from the house? Turner will need to know what she's restoring."

"Of course." Egypt's phone beeped, and she checked the screen. "I really have to run. Nice to meet you, Mel. Give me a call if you need anything."

Another wary glance in Andrew's direction, and she left through the front door—a beautiful paneled door with stained glass, no doubt part of the historical facade that Stirling had been forced to keep in order to retain the home's character for the sake of the neighborhood. I imagined if he'd had his way, it would have been some sort of steel-and-glass concoction.

"Do you have time for a quick walk-through of the house?" I asked my new client.

He checked his expensive-looking watch again, sighed audibly, and then gave me a curt nod.

The tour took a while. The rest of the massive four-story house was more of the same, by and large. Happily the floor plan hadn't changed upstairs like it had on the main floor, but all of the original molding and what I'm sure had been built-in cabinets and bookcases had been torn out, replaced by clean lines, polished finishes, and vinyl windows.

We were walking down a sleek white corridor on the third floor when I thought I heard music. Classical music— a Strauss waltz.

"Nice," I said. "Is Egypt a classic music fan?

He gave me a sour look.

"What did I say?"

"Ghost music."

"Ghost music?"

Andrew nodded. "Incessant. It's one of those things potential buyers ask about. I try to act like it's being piped in, but it goes on and off all the time, randomly throughout the day. Drives me crazy."

"At least it's nice music."

"I'm a Grateful Dead fan, myself."

I laughed.

"You have something against the Grateful Dead?" Andrew demanded.

"Not at all," I said, wondering what Jerry Garcia would make of Andrew Stirling. "It just struck me as funny. Sorry."

Once or twice I thought I heard—or felt—some whispering, but though I searched my peripheral vision, no one appeared. Still, I felt sure Chantelle was right about one thing: there were spirits in this house. Unhappy spirits. Perhaps they would try to communicate with me when Andrew Stirling wasn't by my side. A lot of times it happened that way.

"How soon can you start?" Andrew asked as we headed out. "Every day it sits on the market, the worse things get. I'll pay you to drop your other projects and focus on this one."

"I don't leave projects half done, Andrew; but I understand your sense of urgency. I'll get on it as soon as

humanly possible, I promise. I'll have my guy Stan fax a
contract to your office. And in the meantime, I'd like to
speak with Chantelle and to the remodeler who worked
on Crosswinds. Who was that?"

"Skip Buhner."

"Buhner? Any relation to Karla Buhner, your Realtor?"

"Her husband."

"Ah."

I hadn't heard of Skip Buhner. Not that I knew all the
people in this industry, but in the past couple of years,
ever since I had taken over Turner Construction "tempo-
rarily" from my father, I had become familiar with the
major players—our competition—for the high-end historic-
homes business. But then, Skip Buhner didn't appear to
harbor much affection for historic homes. He was more
the *rip it out, buy something new down at the big-box-store*
type of contractor. I imagined he would have lasted about
five minutes, tops, trying to make a crooked original doorframe function before replacing it with a new fiberglass set
that was square.

"He's moved on to a new construction, an office building down on Sansome," Stirling said. "You want to talk
about headaches? Every time they dig, they find evidence of some old ship—did you know that whole area's
landfill is from back in the Barbary Coast days? And then
they have to halt construction and deal with it, file envi-
ronmental reports, and get the bleeding-heart academics
out there to excavate and document it. Like anyone
gives a damn."

"Not much of a history buff, I take it."

"Never have been. The past is gone, irrelevant. It's the
future I'm interested in."

Unless, of course, that past was quite literally haunting
you and keeping you from selling your obscenely priced
home so you could golf in peace and retire to cocktails in
your Bollinger.

I felt a little surge of triumph that Andrew and I hadn't
tripped over any bodies while making our tour through
the Crosswinds mansion.

I know, I know. I'm getting stranger by the day. And certainly there are some houses I work on where my biggest problem is a plumbing backflow issue or dry rot or earthquake bracing. But by and large, when I'm introduced to a haunted house, I tend to trip over bodies. Perhaps with Crosswinds, I would be able to deal with renovation issues and ancient ghosts, rather than getting involved in any contemporary murders. Fingers crossed.

I sat in my Scion outside Crosswinds, looking up at the beautiful Victorian exterior while I placed a few calls. First, I dialed a certain one-named psychic. Chantelle answered with an appealing, husky voice. She laughed when I mentioned Andrew Stirling and Crosswinds.

"He hasn't been able to sell it, has he? I told him so. One thousand dollars."

"Excuse me?"

"I charge one thousand dollars for a drop-in. You're lucky. I just had a cancellation at three."

"But . . . I'm not seeking a reading or anything like that," I clarified. "I just wanted to talk to you about what you saw—and felt—at Crosswinds."

"I understand that, sweetheart. One K, that's my rate. Charge it to Stirling. He'll pay. The man has more money than sense."

Luckily for me, clients with more money than sense were my specialty.

Chantelle's apartment was in a disappointingly 1970s condo building at the corner of Jones and Clay. The doorman, Gabe, had been told to expect me, and he buzzed me right in. He wore a surprisingly formal monkey suit but didn't look the part otherwise. He was young and tattooed, his eyes were bleary, and he had a serious five-o'clock shadow. He had appeared asleep when I walked in.

"How're you doing?" I asked.

He shrugged. "You know how it is. Late night. Chantelle's on the ninth floor."

I let myself into the elevator and wooshed up to the ninth floor.

Down the hall, the door to 916 was ajar, and a woman

stood just outside, in the corridor. She seemed ethereal, beautiful eyes. *Wow.* If this was Chantelle, it was no wonder people spent a thousand bucks for a meeting. Even from a distance, she seemed . . . special. Perhaps she really could tell me something.

"Chantelle?" I asked. "I'm Mel. Mel Turner."

She nodded, and without a word turned and went into the apartment. I followed her.

And found her on the floor, blood pooling.